The POOL HOUSE

Someone lied.

Someone died.

Tasmina Perry is the *Sunday Times* Top Ten bestselling author of twelve novels. She left a career in law to enter the world of magazine publishing, and went on to become an award-winning writer and contributor to titles such as *Elle*, *Glamour* and *Marie Claire*. In 2004 she launched her own travel and fashion magazine, *Jaunt*, and was editing *InStyle* magazine when she left the industry to write books full time. Her novels have been published in seventeen countries. Tasmina lives with her husband and son in London, where she is at work on her next novel.

By Tasmina Perry

Daddy's Girls
Gold Diggers
Guilty Pleasures
Original Sin
Kiss Heaven Goodbye
Private Lives
Perfect Strangers
Deep Blue Sea
The Proposal
The Last Kiss Goodbye
The House on Sunset Lake
The Pool House

Tasmina Perry

The POOL HOUSE

REVIEW

First published in 2017 by HEADLINE REVIEW
An imprint of HEADLINE PUBLISHING GROUP

First published in paperback in 2018 by HEADLINE REVIEW
An imprint of HEADLINE PUBLISHING GROUP

2

Cataloguing in Publication Data is available from the British Library

ISBN 978 1 4722 0852 1

Typeset in Sabon by Avon DataSet Ltd, Bidford-on-Avon, Warwickshire

Printed and bound in Great Britain by Clays Ltd, Elcograf S.p.A.

HEADLINE PUBLISHING GROUP
An Hachette UK Company
Carmelite House
50 Victoria Embankment
London EC4Y 0DZ

www.headline.co.uk
www.hachette.co.uk

For Steph, who liked to read

Prologue

The sand under her feet was still warm, but Alice didn't feel it as she ran. She swiped at the tears as she crossed the beach, leaving the lights of the party behind, glad of the darkness as it swallowed her. When she felt sure she was out of sight, she sank to her knees and sobbed, hugging herself, listening to the drips as they hit the sand.

Crying in the Hamptons, she thought. This is all I ever wanted. Shouldn't I be happy?

But then why had she ever thought she could find happiness here, of all places? *The Hamptons*. Ever since she was a little girl, that name had resonated with her, a byword for wealth, privilege and a charmed life. In her mind, the big houses on Long Island would be an adult Disneyland where movie stars danced with billionaires and where a little girl from Indiana might meet a handsome prince who would change her life.

She'd been half right, she thought, wiping her face and brushing herself down. She had paid a small fortune for this dress; she hated the idea of getting sand all over it.

Heels in one hand, she walked slowly along the beach towards the house. Even though Midsummer's Eve had passed, the sun had fallen completely beneath the horizon and the sky overhead was speckled with stars. She caught the sweet-harsh whiff of woodsmoke; some kids were dancing and laughing around a bonfire down by the water's edge, its flames glinting on the ink-blue water. Oh to be that young and carefree, she thought. Instead here she was, standing in the dark, her fifty-dollar mascara running down her face. She stifled a moan, leaning against the rail of the weather-beaten boardwalk leading to the house. *Their* house.

Alice knew that she had got married too early. The truth was, she probably shouldn't have married at all. She had no reason to believe in happy-ever-after, not after her upbringing. Her mom . . . Christ, was it any real surprise that Alice kept screwing up after having her as a role model? The endless procession of men, the revolving-door stepdads, the days and days when Momma was too hung-over or too badly beaten to get out of bed. 'I can't help loving all the wrong men,' her mom had once said. And Alice, still believing in Disneyland, had told her that she would find the one. But Alice had been wrong. Momma never did find a prince. Who ever did?

Steadying herself, she unlatched the gate and walked through the bushes into the garden. There was no denying that the house looked magical, strings of lights swaying over the deck and two glowing upstairs windows making the weathered clapboard building look like a particularly benevolent pumpkin.

How could anything in such a fairy-tale castle be wrong? she thought for a split second, before the nausea collecting at the base of her throat reminded her how very wrong things were.

Shifting her shoes to one hand, she let herself in through the French windows. The doors were unlocked, as they often left them, lazy days at the beach blurring their sense of caution, but still, there was the possibility that someone was home.

'Hello?' she called, listening, her voice echoing around the room. No, nothing but the soft hum of the air con. There was no one here. David would still be at the party; they all would, drinking champagne, laughing at each other's jokes, smiling politely at boasts about schools and business deals, gasping at the latest gossip.

She went to the fridge and took out a bottle of vodka. Alice was in the mood for spirits, not the weak fizz they had served at the party. Champagne made her giddy, giggly, but right now she wanted to lose herself completely.

She dropped ice into a glass and poured a large measure, hissing through her teeth as it burnt down her throat. Maybe she had been too harsh on David. He was a good husband; not perfect and not what she needed, but a decent man. He'd never hit her or lied to her or even asked very much of her as a wife. As for herself, Alice had responded in kind, giving him as little of the real her as she could manage.

She picked up the tumbler, pressed it against her forehead, taking comfort from the cold, trying to still the noise in her head.

What had people seen back at the party? she wondered. What had they heard? Was she the one they were all talking about back there, the whispers going from one person to the next, the shame spreading outward like ripples.

Yeah? Well let them talk.

She stepped outside; it was too hot in the house, despite the climate-controlled fans, and far too claustrophobic. She wanted to feel the breeze on her skin and look out over the endless sea. She still had that, at least. Maybe she could just jump in a boat and sail away.

Like you'd ever get in a boat. She could barely stand to be around the pool, never even dangled her feet into the water, not even on the hottest days.

3

The noise from the beach was getting louder and a crowd had gathered on the sand beyond the perimeter of the grounds.

Alice shook her head. She didn't need that, not tonight; the sights and sounds of young people having fun. Instead she walked to the right-hand side of the house, taking slow, steady sips of her vodka as she went.

She didn't come to this part of the property much; it made her shiver. She had successfully avoided the pool all summer, made her excuses when everyone else went swimming, and no one had ever asked why.

It was enclosed in a walled garden, with tall hedges that shielded it from the rest of the property. She pushed the white picket gate and went inside, shuddering as she stared at the sheet of turquoise water shimmering in front of her. She forced herself to look at it; she wasn't sure she could feel any more pain tonight, even if the sight of the pool dislodged unwelcome memories. She carefully skirted around the edge of the water, sipping the vodka as she went. It would be so easy just to end it right now, she thought, her eyes focusing on the intense blue. Just one step and a non-swimmer who'd had too much to drink would be gone. That would teach him, she thought bitterly.

The hedges had muffled the sounds from the beach but she could still pick out the rhythmic beat of drums from the bonfire party, the tempo steadily quickening to a frantic climax that reminded Alice of that day, that crazy afternoon in the rain, the wet cotton sticking to her skin, his hands on her . . . She tipped back the rest of her vodka, closed her eyes and let her hips sway.

If only all days could be like that, if only she could have the life she had imagined. If only . . .

Her eyes snapped open when she heard the scrape of the latch, the creak as the gate swung open behind her. Her

4

heart jumped as she turned to face the figure, dark against the inky sky.

'Hello, Alice. I knew I'd find you here. I think it's time we had a talk.'

This summer

Chapter 1

'Skinny macchiato for Jim!' shouted the barista, holding a white cup aloft.

Jem Chapman pushed her way through a sea of skinny gym-kit girls and claimed her coffee. They always got her name wrong, even though she came here every day.

Balancing the drink and a paper sack of groceries, she struggled back towards the door. Although the Blackberry Café was about to close, it was still packed and the only seats were on the sidewalk outside. Brooklyn was buzzing, even this late in the day.

She put her grocery bag on the last empty table and sat down, glad to finally take the weight off her feet. She'd been yomping around New York all day: a trip to the Metropolitan Museum of Art, then window-shopping on Fifth Avenue before another cancelled lunch date with her husband Nat. *Sorry, babe, work thing x* was all the explanation she'd got. So she'd meandered back to Brooklyn via Trader Joe's, swinging by Blackberry on Park Slope's 6th Avenue in what was coming to be a late-afternoon ritual.

She watched a puff of steam rise from the top of her cup. The March air had a cold crispness and it was beginning to get dark. When she and Nat had moved to Brooklyn three months ago, she'd been staggered at the vast array of cafés, juice bars and gourmet kitchens catering to the most fashionable tastes of the day. She had decided to try every single one of them. So why did she keep coming back here?

She turned at a sharp cry. A young mum with a pixie haircut was at the next table, struggling to get her toddler into a stroller without spilling her coffee.

'Do you need a hand?' asked Jem, reaching out to steady the stroller, which was threatening to overbalance.

'No,' snapped the woman, pulling the buggy out of Jem's reach. 'I got this.'

'Sure, okay,' said Jem, sitting back. What, did the woman think she was going to snatch her baby? Maybe she did; this was New York after all. London had its share of weirdos, but over here they seemed to make a profession of it.

The woman turned her back, but her little girl peered around her mother and grinned at Jem, who gave a careful wave. For a moment she wondered why she felt so upset by the woman's reaction, and then it came to her: this was why she kept coming here. Deep down, she was hoping to make friends. Nat worked in the city and the nature of his job as associate editor on *Form*, the men's fashion magazine based in Manhattan, meant he had to stay late at parties and events. The truth was, Jem was straight-up lonely.

The irony was that it was babies just like this one that had persuaded her to come to New York.

'Just think of it, Jem,' Nat had said. 'Two years in Manhattan while everyone else is changing nappies in Kensal Rise.'

And it was true: over the past eighteen months, their friends had all started having children, and those boozy girls' nights out she'd so loved had been replaced by NCT meetings and antenatal reunions to which Jem was not invited. So why not move to glamorous New York? A *Sex and the City* whirlwind of cocktails, chic apartments and yellow cabs, where turning every corner would be like stepping onto the set of all her favourite movies: *Annie Hall, Desperately Seeking Susan, An Affair to Remember*. It was exactly what she and Nat needed. Or at least that was what she had told herself.

A buzzing in her pocket pulled her from her thoughts. She pulled out her phone: an incoming email.

We are sorry to inform you that your application for the job as sous-chef at Buckley-Clinton School has been unsuccessful on this occasion. We will keep your résumé on file and contact you if anything suitable arises in future.

Best wishes,

Julia Cowen, Catering Manager

She looked down at the phone, her stomach churning. Damn. The little girl on the next table dropped her brownie on the floor and started crying.

I know exactly how you feel, thought Jem, shoving the phone back into her pocket and picking up her groceries.

'Are you leaving?' asked one of the skinny yoga girls hopefully, placing her coffee cup on the table to stake her claim.

'Sadly not,' said Jem.

Rain began to fall from the blanket of heavy clouds above. She gripped the paper sack tighter and strode briskly towards their apartment, a five-minute walk from the café. Somewhere a siren pierced the background roar of traffic, and a yellow flash of taxi reminded her that this city moved so fast, it certainly put a spring in your step.

She ran up the five flights of stairs to the top floor, glad to be out of the cold. Their apartment was four hundred square feet under the eaves of an elegant brownstone. It was a beautiful building – straight off a Brooklyn movie set – but Jem had preferred the flat they had seen in the less fashionable area of Crown Heights, close to the Botanic Gardens. Yet Nat had pushed for fashionable Park Slope, arguing that New Yorkers didn't spend much time in their apartments. Easy for him to say, when he spent all day in a huge shiny office and most evenings at glittering parties.

She dumped the groceries on the tiny kitchen work surface and yanked open the door to the solitary storage cupboard, already overflowing with things she had brought with them from England: Marmite, marmalade, Oxo cubes. She stopped as the sight of a box of PG Tips made her feel almost dizzy with homesickness.

Here she was in the greatest city in the world, with her smart and handsome husband, and yet she felt as if she was floating in space without a tether. 'Who'd have thought it?' she whispered, closing the cupboard door and leaning her head against the cool surface.

In Cornwall, where she'd grown up, people spoke of 'that London' with suspicion, dismissing the capital as too fast, too impersonal, too selfish. But Jem had loved it from the first. She loved the wide-open spaces of the parks, the grandeur of the stuccoed buildings, the red phone boxes, the black cabs, and the blue plaques reminding her how many great people had once lived there.

Most of all, she loved their home, a two-bedroom terrace in Kensal Rise with a glass extension that made it feel light and airy. Cornwall would always be home, but that cottage was *their* home, a place crammed with things that made up their history: skis, hiking boots, books, photo albums, furniture they'd bought together from flea markets on the Portobello Road. And then there was all the *stuff*. Their friends always laughed that Nat was an arch-blagger, an expert at using his charm and status as a style columnist to acquire free clothes, shoes and products. The juicer and the coffee machine jostling for space in the kitchen were freebies, and the spare bedroom was an Aladdin's cave of things he had brought home like a hunter back from the kill. Jem knew that he was proud of the designer names printed on the boxes and bags; she knew he wanted to show her how far they had come. But she was beginning to think it had been a step too far.

Emotion swelled in her throat and a single tear trickled down her cheek.

There was a rattle behind her and she turned, wiping her face with her sleeve.

'Hey, babe,' smiled Nat, flinging his arms wide. Nat didn't just enter a room; it was as if he had walked on set. 'Guess who managed to sneak off early tonight? I had a meeting in Williamsburg and it wasn't worth going back into the office.'

He threw his arms around her, kissing the top of her head.

'I'm sorry about lunch. Editor pulled a last-minute meeting on us. Some advertiser wasn't happy and wants more editorial. Thought we could go for dinner instead . . .'

Finally he looked down at her.

'Hey, what's the matter?'

Jem shook her head and looked away. 'It's nothing.'

'It's something,' he said, tilting her face towards his with a finger under her chin.

Jem felt a stab of desire, despite herself. Nat was handsome, with high cheekbones, wide grey eyes and a mop of dark bad-boy hair. She had never quite been able to believe that he'd be interested in her, let alone want to marry her – and consequently she had never really been able to say no to him. She pulled away from him and walked over to the window. It was the one advantage of five flights: there was a great view over the trees down the avenue. On a good day, you could even see the twinkle of the river.

'I got turned down for another job,' she said with a sigh, glad to be able to discuss it with her husband. 'Sous-chef job at the Buckley-Clinton School. You know, the private school on the Upper East Side?'

Nat put his hands on her shoulders and turned her around. 'Well, maybe it's a blessing in disguise,' he said gently. 'I know you want to get back to work, but surely you don't want to go back to working in kitchens?'

Jem looked up at him and frowned.

'It's what I'm qualified to do,' she said defensively, thinking about her years working in the restaurant industry, jobs that had led to her setting up a catering business, Sparkling Jems, two years earlier.

'Jem, you're a businesswoman, not a bloody dinner lady, and it's probably why you didn't get the job; you're way too qualified to spend all day making chicken nuggets.'

'Goujons,' she said, with a rueful smile. He was being as supportive as he could be, she knew that, and New York was a big opportunity for him; she didn't want to look ungrateful. But it didn't change the way she felt.

'I'm good at what I do, Nat,' she said, looking back at him. 'The catering company was doing well before we left, people loved my food, so now it's tough feeling redundant and unwanted.'

'You're not unwanted,' he said, touching her cheek. 'You are a brilliant cook. Sparkling Jems single-handedly improved the calibre of west London dinner parties one canapé at a time,' he grinned. 'And as soon as word gets out over here about how good you are, you're going to be run off your feet with opportunities. Good opportunities.

But for now, just try and enjoy the fact that you've got a bit of time off, and that your husband is making twice as much dosh as he was back in London.'

He pulled her into an embrace and she let herself relax on his shoulder. Nat had so much natural confidence, Jem felt anything was possible when she was with him. After all, it was how he had persuaded her to come to New York in the first place. For all the appeal of the city, it had still been difficult giving up her friends and her business.

'Let's go and rule the world and have the time of our lives,' he'd said, taking her hand as they'd boarded the flight to JFK, and she had been light-headed with excitement at the possibilities that lay ahead.

Thing was, Jem didn't want to rule the world. She just wanted to have a few people to talk to during the day, and a job, something to occupy herself, that she enjoyed.

'I'm lonely, Nat,' she said, knowing it was the right moment to speak up. 'And I'm bored.'

Her husband looked genuinely confused.

'How can you be bored in New York City?'

'No job, no prospect of a job, no friends,' she said, ticking the points off on her fingers. 'I shuffle around Manhattan and back again all day, every day, shopping, killing time in museums – which is costing us a fortune, by the way. You really appreciate the amazing free places in London when it's twenty bucks a throw over here.' She hesitated. 'It's all so . . .'

'So what?'

She shook her head. Pointless. Empty. Draining. That was what she wanted to say.

If someone had offered her a plane ticket to London right then, she would have grabbed it with both hands.

'I'm sick of waiting around for a job that doesn't seem to be out there,' she said quietly. 'I've called every catering firm, contacted every restaurant and there's nothing out there, not unless you want me at Wendy's for minimum wage.'

She expected Nat to get angry, to raise his voice, tell her she was being ungrateful or selfish. Instead he looked at her and smiled. A smile that said 'I've got a solution'. It was one of the things she loved most about her husband: his can-do attitude. In Nat's mind there was never a problem that couldn't be solved. He believed in himself, and although Jem sometimes had doubts, he believed in her too.

'I got a call from Angela Carter today,' he said.

Jem frowned. For a second she didn't recognise the name.

'Todd Carter's wife?' he said. 'Art director, you remember.'

Jem nodded. She had met Todd at one of the few parties Nat had got her invited to. He wasn't a suit kind of guy; he had a mop of dark hair and trendy horn-rimmed glasses, but even in his sweatshirt and jeans he still had that polished, preppy look about him. He had at least been friendly to Jem, chatting to her about Cornwall and growing up near the sea.

'Todd and Angela rent a beach house in the Hamptons every summer. It's an amazing place, ocean-front, great location, and they usually share it with three other couples, split the rental costs.'

Jem nodded, wondering where this was going.

'Well, a vacancy has come up,' he said with a grin.

'Vacancy?'

'From Memorial Day through to the first weekend in September. Imagine it, Jem: our own beach house for the whole summer. I know how much you miss living near the sea. Well, now you can go swimming every day!'

Jem knew she should feel excited, but she only felt a rising anxiety.

'In the Hamptons,' she said slowly. 'Isn't that going to be really expensive?'

Nat made a dismissive gesture.

'It's a bargain. The house belongs to Angela's godfather and he hasn't put the rent up in a decade.'

'But there are going to be other people there?'

He reached out to stroke her face.

'Nice people. Angela and Todd, Joel and Erica, Paul and Rebecca, us. It's going to be fun. And no more lonely Jem.'

Jem hadn't met any of them apart from Todd, and she had to admit she was intimidated by these high-flying society people. Nat seemed to sense her hesitation.

'Listen, Angela suggested we meet everyone for dinner this weekend, and you can see whether you like them. But you will.'

'And what if they don't like us? I mean, they're obviously checking us out.'

Nat laughed. Confident, reassuring.

'Babe, it's a formality. We're in. When I told them you were a brilliant cook, they couldn't invite us fast enough.'

Jem laughed. 'The cooking? You didn't mention my sparkling personality?'

He pulled her into a tight hug.

'And that, of course.'

He held her for a moment, then stood back and looked into her eyes.

'Look, I know this move hasn't been easy for you. The flat's small and you're feeling isolated and – yes – I'm not here as much as either of us would like. But I'm just getting bedded in at the magazine, showing them how good I am, and I'll be able to take my foot off the gas soon.'

He turned her towards the window. 'And look at the lights, Jem! We're in New York, summer is around the corner and we've got a house at the beach. It's all looking good, right?'

Jem smiled, carried along by his enthusiasm. And why not? Why couldn't it be a good thing? That was what they'd come for, wasn't it?

She saw their reflections in the dark window. A young couple, arm in arm, in love. Nothing could go wrong.

'This is going to be the summer of a lifetime,' said Nat. 'Believe me.'

Jem laughed. 'Maybe it is,' she said. And at that moment, she believed it could be.

Chapter 2

Her legs didn't want to work. They were stiff as she climbed out of the cab and shaking as they walked towards Santiago's, SoHo's latest fashionable eaterie.

'I'm nervous,' she whispered, squeezing Nat's hand. 'Why am I so nervous?'

'Because it's an audition,' said Nat.

'I thought you said we were in. Isn't this a formality?'

Her husband shrugged. Even he looked a little edgy.

'Yes, well that's what I thought. But I saw Todd at the gym and he kept mentioning this other couple they've been seeing. I don't know if he was trying to tell me something.'

Jem looked at him in disbelief, wanting to grab him by the lapels and yell, '*Now* you tell me?' But they were here, walking into the cosy glow of velvet and gold of Santiago's. It was too late to back out now.

Jem took a deep breath and forced a smile as the attendant took her coat. She caught her reflection in a mirror and had to admit she didn't look too bad. She had never been a glamorous or girlie girl; would choose jeans and a top over a sparkly dress any time, but tonight, her chestnut hair pulled back into a high ponytail and some gloss on her full lips had given her an outdoorsy prettiness. It wasn't exactly the standard Manhattan look – sometimes she felt as if every woman in New York looked as if they were going straight from the blow-dry bar to a cocktail party – but at least it didn't make her feel a complete outsider.

'Well, maybe it won't be so bad if we don't make the cut,' she whispered more playfully.

Nat frowned. 'What do you mean? This is an amazing opportunity, Jem.'

Jem glanced around to make sure they weren't overheard.

'Twenty thousand dollars, Nat,' she said, almost laughing out loud at the astronomical sum. 'Twenty *thousand* bucks. It's such a lot of money. I mean, it's all our savings – for a handful of weekends at the beach.'

Jem had been incredulous when Nat had told her the price for their share of the summer rental – even if they *did* get through the audition. He had told her it was a bargain, and by the look on his face now, he hadn't changed his opinion.

'You do know some of these houses cost a quarter of a million bucks to rent for the season,' he said, keeping his voice low.

'Maybe, but that doesn't stop it being absolutely mental that people are prepared to pay it.'

The maître d' was beckoning to them, but Nat held up a finger to him, turning to Jem.

'I thought you wanted this too. You've been so excited.'

Jem nodded cautiously. It was true. Ever since he'd mentioned the possibility of the Hamptons house share, she'd spent hours on the internet researching the Long Island towns like Southampton, North Sea and Water Mill, places that looked so chic and stylish, yet sounded so familiar. The sound of gulls wheeling overhead, the smell of salt in the air; she had forgotten how much she missed it. And a summer in the Hamptons would come with all the glamour of Americana that had made her want to come to New York in the first place. But the cost! That one glorious summer could doom them to a tiny top-floor flat forever.

'You know I was reading about the Adirondacks the other day,' she said. 'You can get a house on the lake with a dock and a boat for a fraction of the cost.'

Nat shook his head. 'The Lakes are a four-hour drive away, Jem. We could never get there and back in a weekend. And besides, what goes on in the Adirondacks?'

She nodded. What he meant was 'Who goes to the Adirondacks?' Nat's reasons for going to the Hamptons were very different to hers; and if she was honest, Jem had to admit they were more practical. It could be a way out of that top-floor flat for them.

'Look, I have a job where it's vital to know people,' he said. 'Everyone who's anyone goes to the beach over the summer, you know that. The best parties are there, the best networking opportunities. This could be a way to move up the career ladder much more quickly.'

'I know,' she said, aware how much his work meant to him. It wasn't the safe option; it was a risk, it could bankrupt them. But then if they wanted a normal safe life, why come to Manhattan in the first place? 'I just don't want us to be disappointed, you know, if they decide to go with someone else.'

Nat gave her a flash of that smile.

'No way are they going to choose someone else,' he said, taking her hand. 'Come on, let's show them what they'd be missing.'

They threaded their way through the restaurant. Although it was just past seven o'clock, the place was pumping, the bar clogged with scantily dressed twenty-somethings sipping cocktails and picking at green olives the size of ping-pong balls.

'Hey, Nat, over here!'

Todd raised a hand as the maître d' showed them to a corner booth that appeared to be slightly raised above the rest of the diners. A confident-looking brunette with red lips and big dark eyes stood up and embraced Nat. Nat air-kissed her, then turned back to Jem, giving her an encouraging smile. It was broad and white, but Jem saw a flicker there, a tiny flare of insecurity. No one else could have seen it; no one else knew Nat that well. Her husband was not from a wealthy background; he was a scholarship boy at a public school who'd kept up his work ethic and found himself at Cambridge. He had grown a Teflon coating that eased him through any situation, ingratiated him with every social class, but even Teflon could develop the odd ding and nick. He'd admitted to her once that he'd been taunted at school for being on financial assistance, and how much it had hurt him, and sometimes Jem wondered if everything he did was to prove that he was every bit as good as those from more blue-blooded backgrounds, because their approval still mattered.

'Everyone,' he said, 'this is my wife Jem. And Jem, this is everyone.'

He pulled a chair out for her with a flourish of chivalry.

'Sit down, sit down, both of you,' said the brunette, turning to Jem. 'I'm Angela, Todd's wife. I guess we're going to have to be really cheesy and introduce ourselves. Like we're speed-dating.'

Angela's warmth put Jem at ease immediately, and to her immense relief, she felt included – welcomed even.

'You know Todd, of course,' said Angela. Jem nodded and waved at the man with dark hair and black-rimmed glasses. Todd was friendly and was something of a mentor to Nat. They had met the previous summer on a two-week secondment to the magazine's New York office and bonded over *Doctor Who*; not that Jem had ever known her husband to have any great interest in the Time Lord, but that was Nat all over: never one to miss an opportunity.

'Joel, you go next,' said Angela, pointing to a man with cropped hair and a thick neck.

'I'm Joel,' he said, raising his bottle of beer. 'I went to college with Todd, and to school with Rebecca. Wall Street,' he added, as if that explained everything Jem needed to know.

'My name's Erica,' said a redhead with a sing-song voice. 'I'm married to Joel and I work at *Elite* magazine.'

'The beauty department,' said Angela in a stage whisper behind her hand. 'If you ask her really nicely, she'll get you nail polish and UTI test strips.'

They all laughed and Jem found herself laughing along. An elegant, languid woman with a short blonde bob and a sharper dark suit introduced herself as Rebecca, then turned to her husband. 'And this is Paul.'

Jem raised her eyebrows. Paul was telling her he was an architect but not to hold that against him, but she wasn't really listening; she was noting his Hollywood good looks. Even Nat looked a little shabby next to him.

'Well, that's everyone,' said Angela. 'Now's the time to run while you can.'

'We did ask the cab driver to keep the engine ticking over,' said Nat, but Jem could tell they had passed the first round of the test.

They ordered food and cocktails named after baseball terms – the slider, the loaded base – triggering a rash of good-natured jokes at the expense of the dumb Brits. Nat gossiped indiscreetly about various celebrities he had met since the move, while Angela took Jem under her wing, giving her views on the latest world events; as a producer with one of the afternoon news shows, she had fascinating insights. Even Rebecca, who seemed the most aloof, was interested in Jem's talk of home in Cornwall, declaring herself 'the biggest du Maurier fan'. Just as Jem was beginning to relax, Angela switched to business mode.

'So Nat has explained the arrangement to you?' she said.

'Yes, it sounds great,' said Jem, trying not to sound too eager. 'Tell me more about the house.'

'It's a five-bed, six-bath place in Wainscott, a five-minute drive from Bridgehampton Main Street, not absolute beachfront, but we have private access. It's not as fancy as some, but the room sizes are good, the shower pressure is great . . .'

'And the company second to none,' said Todd, leaning across with a wink.

'So why doesn't your godfather use it in the summer?' asked Jem with interest. 'If it were mine, I think I'd be there all the time.'

'He lives in France.' Angela shrugged. 'Bought it years ago, before the Hamptons was quite so fashionable. He cares enough about the house – or should I say about how much it's worth – to not sell it, but not enough to visit or spend any money on it, which I guess would limit the rental. Anyway, as we're sort-of family, he trusts that we'll treat it like our own place and will paint the fence at the end of summer. And for that we get a really good deal.'

'And what's the kitchen like? I'm imagining Diane Keaton's kitchen in *Something's Gotta Give*.'

Angela smiled. 'I heard you were a really great cook.'

'Well, that's kind of what I used to do in London.'

'Jem had her own catering firm,' said Nat. 'They used to do a lot of media events, society weddings, that sort of thing.'

Jem nodded, although she barely recognised his description. She had been a one-woman operation most of the time and the majority of bookings had been supplying summer parties with tasty buffet food.

'I'm no Martha Stewart,' she said, trying not to blush. 'And I'm still trying to work out what cilantro is. Do you know, I bought a persimmon in Trader Joe's thinking it was a fancy tomato.'

Laughter rang around the table and it was only then that Jem realised how much she wanted this to work. Not just for the beachfront house with the fantasy kitchen, but for the camaraderie and the banter; she felt welcomed and accepted for the first time since they had been in New York. She knew she had been in denial about just how much she had missed having friends, even friends who wanted to talk about breastfeeding. God knows she had tried, joining Pilates classes and hanging around the juice bars of Brooklyn. At the Blackberry Café they still didn't remember her name, but here, at this table, she felt as if she suddenly belonged.

Angela put her hand over her husband's and looked at Nat and Jem directly.

'Listen, I think – I hope – I speak for all of the group when I say that if you like the sound of the house, we'd love you to join us this summer.'

Jem watched them all nodding and felt herself swell with happiness, all thoughts of the twenty grand forgotten. Nat grabbed her hand under the table and squeezed it. She knew he felt it too.

'We'd love to come,' she said, not waiting for Nat to speak.

'Excellent,' said Todd, raising his glass. 'That's settled then. Any last questions before we ask you to sign your souls away?'

Jem frowned. 'Well there is one,' she said. 'Why would anyone possibly need more baths than they've got beds?'

And everyone started to laugh.

Chapter 3

'You. Are. Kidding me!' gasped Jem. 'That's amazing!'

They had stopped the car at the gate of the beach house and Jem was getting her first view of their home for the summer.

'Nat, it's beautiful!'

Looking over the white fence down the long drive, she could see a wide shingle house with dark blue shutters and clouds of white flowers – honeysuckle or possibly jasmine – curling around the porch.

'I told you so,' said Nat with a self-satisfied smile. Jem hooted with laughter and threw her arms around his neck.

'It's so . . .'

'I know,' laughed Nat, reaching across to key in the security code that triggered the automatic gate. 'It's pretty good.'

Jem had to admit she was shell-shocked. She'd never been to the Hamptons before, and the hours – days – she had spent on the internet had prepared her for something beautiful: beautiful people, beautiful beaches and beautiful homes. But she hadn't quite grasped how manicured and pristine everything looked out here. Every bush seemed sculpted, every lawn spray-painted the perfect shade of green. Even the few parts that looked worn and peeling looked as if they'd been artfully distressed by Hollywood set designers. She had read about the area's origins as a community of whaling towns and its historical links to New England and Rhode Island, but from its more recent reputation as the playground of the very, very rich she had been expecting something a bit flashy. Instead, the Hamptons just looked, well, perfect.

Nat parked up in front of the house and they stepped out for a first look at the huge hydrangea bushes and the wide beds of foxgloves and delphiniums. Everything here seemed in bloom, with barely a petal out of place.

'I can't believe we have wangled this,' said Jem, still stunned by the beauty of the property. 'I'm amazed all of Todd and Angela's friends weren't fighting over our room.'

Nat didn't answer; instead he pulled their bags from the boot and nodded towards the house.

'Shall we have a look inside?'

Jem was almost too nervous. It was so lovely from the outside, she didn't want anything to break the spell.

'Apparently Paul is going to be here. He better had be, because we haven't got a key . . .' Nat walked up to the front door and knocked. There was no answer.

Jem stayed on the path, inhaling as deeply as she could, filling her lungs with salt and floral-scented air. The air in New York had been so muggy lately, so stale and lifeless even by the river, but here the light breeze that came off the ocean felt warm and freshly laundered.

'Hey, the door's on the latch,' said Nat, pushing inside. 'Come on.'

Jem crossed her fingers behind her back and followed. Angela had warned them that the beach house was not luxurious. Her godfather had done no maintenance in years beyond a retouch of the shutters in the spring, she had said, so Jem had feared the worst.

Wow. As she stepped into the huge hallway, the first thing that struck her was the light that flooded in from a skylight overhead. Long before the celebrities and the bankers had migrated to the Hamptons, it had been a community for artists, and Jem could see why: the peachy light reminded her of St Ives in Cornwall, where the sun sank low and late, flooding the town with a warm glow. She immediately felt at home and she grinned at Nat, who had dropped the bags to turn and give her a thumbs-up.

'Pretty good,' he said.

'Pretty good,' she agreed.

The floorboards were stripped and the walls, perhaps once white, now faded to cream, were lined with framed old maps of the local area. Jem went to inspect one of them, her finger tracing over names like Canoe Place and Indian Settlement, reminders of an even older time before the painters and the whalers.

'Let's look out the back,' said Nat, crossing the hall to a set of French windows. It led to a wooden deck and beyond it a long garden framed by bushes – and beyond that, the sea. Jem felt her heart jump as she saw the sparkling white and blue.

'Hey, guys, good to see you!'

Jem turned to see Paul crossing the lawn, wiping his hands on the hem of his white T-shirt. She tried not to look at the tan underneath or the bare legs beneath his paint-spattered shorts. He looked as if he was in a Calvin Klein photo shoot. He ran up the steps to greet them.

'Summer starts here, my friends,' he said, winking at Jem. 'How was the journey?'

'Too hot, too long. I think we'll skip the hire car next time and take the Jitney.' She nodded at the paint on his hands. 'You're painting the fence already? I thought you only had to do that at the end of summer.'

Paul smiled. 'Getting a head start. Because I'm an architect, the others think I'm the only one who knows how to use a brush, and it takes longer than you'd think to go all the way around the house.'

'Well, we can grab a couple of brushes and help,' offered Jem.

'No, no. You guys settle in. You're in the blue room,' he said. 'Give me a minute to wash up and I'll show you around.'

He led them inside to the kitchen, which made Jem almost want to cry. White tile floors, scrubbed oak worktops, gleaming copper pans hanging over a range that looked like the bridge of a steam-punk Starship *Enterprise*.

'You like?' said Paul with amusement at her reaction.

'It's like I've died and gone to heaven.'

'That's good, because I think the most I've ever made here is microwave popcorn.'

He pointed out the pool area, set off to the side of the house surrounded by a hedge; the garage where shiny road bikes were kept; and the all-important wine cellar. Upstairs he opened a door and pointed inside.

'And this is your room.'

Jem had to stifle another gasp. It was larger than their entire apartment in Brooklyn, with French windows that opened onto a Juliet balcony. Not much furniture – just a double bed with a chintzy cover, a wing-backed chair and an armoire – but the eye skated over the details, always being pulled back to the view.

'Now that was definitely worth the drive,' said Nat, hands on hips, looking out of the open windows. Beyond the garden was a stretch of pale sand, then the grey ocean edged with breaking white foam.

'Is that really the Atlantic?' asked Jem. It barely seemed possible that this was the same moody, heaving ocean she had looked out on as a child.

'It's perfect now,' said Paul. 'But it can get pretty fresh out there in winter. That's why the sand is so good; it's a real ocean beach. A thousand miles south to the Caribbean, three thousand miles east to Europe. There's a whole lot of nothing out there.'

'But what nothing,' said Jem, looking out towards the fluff of clean white clouds on the far horizon.

Paul nodded, following her gaze. 'Yep, I love this place too. Every year I tell myself I'll try and work out a schedule to only do three days in the office in summer so I can come out here on Thursday night and not go back until Monday, but it never works out.' He turned to Jem. 'Of course, you might be able to go one better.'

'Me?'

'Well, it sounds like you're pretty flexible about where you work, so if you're not tied to the city, you could stay all week. We do have the house all summer and I always think it's such a shame that no one uses it except at weekends.'

Nat flashed Paul a look and put a hand on Jem's shoulder. 'Don't give her ideas. I don't see her enough as it is.'

Jem had unpacked and settled in by the time the others began to arrive. Wanting to make a good impression, she had come armed with the ingredients for iced tea and open sandwiches: loaves of rye bread, ripe avocados and Alaskan smoked salmon. She had guessed right: they all arrived parched and starving after a hot, dusty journey from the city.

Jem positioned herself on the deck and let it all flow around her. She had never been to boarding school, never set foot in one, but this was a little as she imagined it would be: the clatter of multiple feet running up and down the stairs, the noise of running water from different bathrooms, the excitable babble of new arrivals. A long Memorial Day weekend, the start of term.

The rest of their new housemates also made themselves busy. Todd fired up the charcoal pit, Nat and Joel went to the supermarket for meat, Paul and Rebecca mixed cocktails that seemed to go very heavy on the vodka, and slowly the light disappeared from the sky, fading to a cool dark twilight that settled in purple streaks over the ocean. Jem could barely believe she had hesitated over coming here.

When everyone had eaten their fill, the group settled into the blue Adirondack chairs set around the fire pit, Brazilian jazz floating down to them from the house.

'I think it's about time for the first s'mores of the season, don't you?' said Todd, producing a cooler bag and a fistful of toasting forks. He speared the first of the pink marshmallows and settled it over the flames.

'Jem, grab the Graham crackers and we can start the production line,' he said.

Jem had never tasted a s'more before and had to admit that they were terrible for the teeth but delicious all the same. She tucked her feet under her and picked at the marshmallow sandwich contentedly.

'So who was it that had our room last year, or was it just the six of you?' she asked casually. A hush descended around the fire pit and Jem looked up, frowning. 'I only ask because I can't believe anyone would want to give all this up.'

She looked around the firelit faces, but no one seemed to be meeting her gaze.

'Another couple joined us,' said Angela finally.

'So what happened? Did they move away from New York? Start a family?'

'David didn't want to summer in the Hamptons this year,' replied Todd, putting down his toasting fork. 'His wife, Alice . . . she passed away.'

'Oh, I'm so sorry,' said Jem, her face flushing.

'I thought . . . we thought you knew,' said Todd. Jem looked across at Nat, but he just gave a small shrug. Clearly everyone *else* had known.

'I didn't know the details,' said Jem, feelingly horribly awkward.

'Alice drowned,' said Todd gently, grasping the situation and glaring at Nat.

'Drowned? Gosh, that's horrible,' said Jem. 'Where? Not at the beach?'

'She was found here in the pool,' said Angela quietly.

No one spoke, the tension of the moment somehow made all the worse by the incongruous jollity of the jazz coming from the speakers on the deck. Jem was glad her back was to the pool area, otherwise she was sure she wouldn't have been able to stop herself from staring.

'We almost didn't come back this year,' said Todd. 'That's why it was all a bit last-minute, filling the house.'

For a moment Jem watched the six faces of her housemates, once confident, now crumpled in embarrassment. She had been to look at the pool when they had arrived, of course. It was set away from the house in a section walled by thick privet hedges. She had even trailed her hand in the water and she remembered how cold it had been, as if no one had been in there for a very long time. Now she knew why.

'It was an accident, though?'

Jem looked around. No one seemed eager to speak up.

'Alice was troubled,' said Angela finally. 'We all knew that, but I don't think anyone knew how much. She drank a lot. Last summer . . . well, we tried to help her.'

'I told her about a great AA programme in East Hampton,' said Paul.

'Was she drinking by the pool?' said Jem. She knew she

should drop it, that clearly it was horrible for everyone, but for some reason she had to know everything.

'There was a big party a few hundred yards along the beach,' Angela said. 'The owners, the Dobermans, always invite the neighbours, so we'd all gone down. For some reason Alice came back to the house on her own. The next thing we know . . .' Angela's voice started to break up. She puffed out her cheeks. 'Sorry, I thought it would be easier to talk about . . .'

Todd leant across and patted his wife's knee. 'David, her husband, came back to look for her and found her in the pool,' he said.

Jem didn't need to ask if she had been found dead. The group's sombre expressions told her how the story had ended.

'Most likely she fell in. She couldn't swim and was three times over the legal limit. It's not a combination that ends well.'

Erica sat forward, angrily poking a fork into the dying embers of the fire.

'Can we not talk about this any more?'

'I think Jem should know,' said Angela, looking up. 'We asked David, Alice's husband, if we should come back this summer, of course. He agreed it was what Alice would have wanted. This was always a house of so much fun and happiness. For all her problems, Alice loved it here. She wouldn't have wanted it to become the house where *that* happened.'

'I didn't really know Alice. But I agree,' said Nat, finally speaking up, glancing around the group for reassurance.

For a few moments no one said anything. The crashing of the waves seemed louder than they had done even just a few minutes earlier, and a sudden cold gust of wind made Jem shudder.

'Not quite warm enough for al fresco drinks,' said Erica, getting to her feet and wrapping her cardigan around her slender body.

'Yes, let's go in,' agreed Rebecca, draining the remaining wine in her glass. 'We should probably unpack.'

Jem found herself nodding. Suddenly she didn't feel too sociable.

Jem went upstairs to her room, taking her glass of wine with her. She shut the French windows and perched on the end of the bed. Nat followed a few moments later and shut the door behind him. He kicked off his shoes and began unbuttoning his shirt.

'You look at home here,' he said. 'Want me to bring a bottle of wine upstairs?'

Jem didn't move or turn her head to look at him.

'Why didn't you tell me about Alice?' She was trying to control herself; their housemates were on the other side of the wall and would hear a row, and she was so furious she didn't trust herself not to start screaming. She was angry at him for not having told her, but also hugely let down because what had begun so well seemed to have gone so badly wrong this evening.

'You can see why I didn't,' he said.

'Actually, I can't,' she said feeling more and more angry. 'Aside from making me feel stupid out there, and making everyone else wonder why the hell we can't communicate properly with one another, I feel a bit uncomfortable with it all, if I'm honest.'

'Uncomfortable with what?'

She looked at him incredulously. 'With *what*? With this. The house share. Someone *died* in the swimming pool just out there. This was her room.'

'Which is exactly why I didn't tell you,' he said, a little

annoyance creeping into his voice. 'I knew it would give you the willies, make you not want to join the rental.'

'Exactly!' she snapped, then lowered her voice. 'It would have been nice to have been able to make a bloody choice.'

'Listen, I realise it's a shock,' he said, sitting down next to her, 'but you heard what Angela said. There's no point in abandoning the place. Alice loved it and a lot of people have happy memories here. Yes, it's a tragedy, but you have to move on. It's still a great house, whatever happened.'

'It's a great house for *you*, that's what you really mean,' said Jem, surprised at how fierce she sounded. 'It's great for you to be around these people, so screw anyone else.'

'Thanks for making us all sound such heartless bastards,' he said, sitting back.

Jem rubbed her eyes. She couldn't believe he hadn't told her. No, the truth was she *could* believe it; in fact, she wasn't at all surprised. It was Nat all over – business before anything. They sat in silence.

'So you knew her?' said Jem finally.

'Who?'

'Alice, of course. You said "I didn't really know her". But you had met her.'

'Once,' said Nat. 'When I came to New York last summer. I went to some party with Todd and met her there.'

Jem watched his face, trying to picture him at the party, talking to the dead woman, but she couldn't. That was the problem: so much of Nat's life was a mystery to her. She knew it was how his world operated, one party after another, Nat charming his way into the good graces of everyone he met, but she still didn't feel comfortable with it, though she couldn't say why exactly. Perhaps it was Nat's blasé attitude to this tragedy. He might have met this woman, but if he was sensitive about lying in her bed – *this* bed she was sitting on, she thought with a shiver – he had a funny way of showing it.

'Tell me about her,' she said.

Nat gave a small sigh. 'She was a bit younger than us, a yoga teacher or something like that. David Holliday, her husband, was a lecturer at Columbia. It was their first, their only, summer at the beach house.' He shrugged. 'That's all I know.'

Jem paused, trying to picture them, David and Alice, on their first night at the house. She imagined them sitting by the fire, just as she and Nat had done that evening, chatting, laughing and dreaming about their plans for the summer, and felt an enormous wave of sadness.

'Does it really not bother you?' she asked. 'Being here? Sleeping in her bed?'

Nat looked down at his hands before glancing back.

'I probably won't be hanging out around the pool any longer than I have to. But think what it must be like for Angela and the others. Of course it's easier for me, I wasn't here, but they were. Can you imagine?'

She closed her eyes, exhaustion taking over. She didn't want to think about it. Not now and probably not ever. Perhaps that was the only way to deal with it: put it out of your mind. Nat was right: it must be tough for Alice's friends to be back here. And if they could stand it, she should be able to as well.

'I'm going to take a bath,' she said, walking into the en suite and splashing water onto her face. In the mirror, she could see Nat still sitting on the bed, his expression sad, wistful, his gaze fixed on something outside the window. Maybe she was doing him a disservice; maybe he was as freaked out by this as everyone else.

She closed the door, turned on the taps and sat on the edge of the bath, listening to it slowly fill. As the water rose, she touched it with her fingers. Hot, just hot enough to stand. She slipped off her clothes, feeling the cool breeze from an open window brush against her bare skin. This was usually her favourite part of the day, slipping into the water and feeling her whole body relax, but tonight she could hear the boom of the ocean, the twenty-million-dollar soundtrack that came with the house. For a second she wondered how many people would love to be in her place right now, at the start of summer, in the Hamptons, in one of the most chic houses on Ocean Road. It was amazing. The house was amazing. Her life was amazing.

But as she slipped down into the water, letting it rise up to her chin, all she could think about was the swimming pool outside, a plate of glimmering water in the night sky, and Alice Holliday's body floating lifelessly in the middle.

Chapter 4

Alice wasn't mentioned for the rest of the weekend. The group went swimming in the ocean and played Frisbee on the beach, and, keen to impress her new housemates, especially after the awkwardness of the first night, Jem cooked. A chicken salad with feta and mint and a yellow watermelon she had found at a roadside farm stall; fudge brownies topped with salted caramel and pecans; sticky ribs glazed in honey that fell right off the bone. She'd made the ribs and brownies many times before – they were a favourite with clients back in London – but the reception from her housemates was even more enthusiastic. Todd was already talking about next year, which made Nat's face light up like a lantern, whilst Angela suggested that Jem start a blog documenting her cooking at the house.

'You could call it "The Beach Kitchen",' she enthused, already talking about brand expansion and long-term merchandising. Jem was glowing; she felt the faux pas by the fire pit had been completely forgotten.

Monday was Memorial Day and everyone had the day off work, even workaholic Joel, who kept muttering that he should make an appearance at the bank but was persuaded to stay by Rebecca. In the evening they'd gone for clam chowder and steamers at Bostwick, a roadside restaurant outside Amagansett, which was humming with new arrivals, the Hamptons' summer congregation. By the time they got back to the house it was past ten o'clock and drinks on the deck were passed over in favour of an early night. Jem sensed this was a routine the housemates were used to: the last night of the weekend, mentally preparing – anticipating or dreading – for the crack-of-dawn start and the long commute back to the city.

She herself was exhausted and had fallen asleep quickly – she'd often rolled her eyes when Nat muttered that socialising was draining, but the moment she'd slid between the crisp sheets she was out, only stirring when she reached over to find Nat's side of the bed empty. The bedroom was dark, just a crack of light coming from the en suite, where she could make out Nat's outline in front of the mirror.

'Wassatime?' she mumbled, her voice thick with sleep.

'Five fifteen,' whispered her husband, sitting on the edge of the bed. 'I've got to take the hire car back and I've got a nine-thirty breakfast with a PR I'm guessing hasn't got a beach rental this summer.'

Jem groaned. 'When do we need to leave?'

'Twenty minutes, latest,' he said, patting her hip.

'Can you roll me out in my pyjamas and carry me to the car?' she said with a sleepy smile. Nat chuckled.

'Look, it won't be this bad every weekend. Next time we'll get the Jitney. Todd says the six thirty gets you into the city in plenty of time.'

Jem yawned as there was a gentle knock at the door. Angela peeped in, already immaculately groomed and camera-ready.

'Morning, sleepyheads. We're ready to go when you are,' she whispered.

'I offered them a lift,' said Nat, turning to Jem. 'That okay? Angela has to be at work early too.'

'Sure,' said Jem, stretching and sitting up.

'Hey, why don't you stay?' suggested Angela, taking a step into the room. 'It's so early. If you don't need to be back, I'd enjoy a quiet day at the beach.'

Jem had to admit that the idea sounded appealing, especially from this position in a warm bed.

'Good idea. You can start your blog,' said Nat, picking up his overnight bag.

Angela waved to Jem and stepped out.

'I think I will stay,' said Jem, yawning again. With all the excitement of the weekend, she hadn't realised how dog-tired she felt. For months she had spent most of her days alone, and being part of a noisy social knot where you always had to be switched on had been a shock to the system.

'Are you sure?' said Nat. 'We can wait for you if you'd rather.'

'No, you go. I can try out the Jitney this afternoon. I'll report back.'

He leant over and brushed his lips against hers. He felt warm and soft and for a moment Jem wished that he would climb back into bed.

'I've got the Ralph Lauren dinner tonight, remember.'

'Is it going to be a late one?'

'I think so,' he grimaced. 'Sorry.'

'Don't pretend you don't love it,' she smiled.

'You get some more sleep,' he whispered.

When she woke again, the house was in silence. All she could hear was the sound of her own breathing and the roar of the waves on the shore. She put her dressing gown on and went downstairs. The house seemed cavernous with no one in it, her footsteps echoing from wooden floor to high ceiling as she padded into the kitchen. She went straight to the kettle; still English among all this Americana.

Out on the deck, it was already beginning to warm up. The Yanks would have dialled up the air con, she thought, but she preferred the feel of fresh salty air blowing into the house and opened the folding door.

Feeling creative, she rifled around the fruit bowl, pulling out a mango and a blood orange, which she sliced up and mixed into some Greek yoghurt from the fridge. She found a jam jar in the cupboard and poured the yoghurt into it, topping it off with some pistachio nuts and a drizzle of artisan honey she'd found at a farm stand along the Montauk highway.

There was something about cooking that had always made Jem feel happy. She'd fallen into a career in catering, but really her love affair with food had started many years before. Her family hadn't had much money when she was growing up, but her mum had always made her house-keeping stretch far enough to put delicious food on the table each night. Jem remembered hearty sausage casseroles, and mopping up the peppery sauce with thick chunks of home-baked bread; sweet fruit crumbles laced with cinnamon and walnuts and made from overripe fruit sold off cheaply at the local greengrocer's.

She smiled, wondering what her thrifty mother would think of the $10 bunches of heritage tomatoes, and the kale ice cream stashed away in the freezer. She could hear her mutter of disapproval even across the ocean.

'Eat your heart out, Jamie Oliver,' she said to herself as she wiped a smear of yoghurt from the edge of the jar. 'The Beach Kitchen is open for business.'

She pulled her phone out of her dressing-gown pocket and took a photo of her creation. She had to admit it looked pretty good; the clear Hamptons light that flooded through the windows made the image look as if it was straight out of a cookery book.

After she'd finished eating, she cupped her hands around her tea and wandered outside. The rumble of the sea was somehow subdued during the day, but it was still wonderful to see it smiling there beyond the low line of hedgerow. She took a moment to soak in the view, then turned back to face the house.

It was impossible not to see the walled garden that winked at her from the corner of her eye, the line of tall hedges that framed the east side of the property. Apparently whoever had owned the place before Angela's godfather had been inspired by the great English country houses – and for a second, Jem was grateful that this design conceit kept the place of Alice's death out of sight.

She'd tried hard to forget what she'd been told by her housemates about what had happened the previous summer, but she could not. With everyone studiously avoiding the subject since it was first discussed around the fire pit, her imagination had filled the gaps, picturing Alice as a lonely figure. She had no idea if that was correct and she suspected it carried with it more than a little projection of herself onto a blank canvas. After all, the only facts she had were that Alice had left the party down the beach and walked back to the house alone.

Had she had an argument with her husband David? Or perhaps the sheer boredom of being at a fancy event where people looked over your shoulder for someone more connected to talk to had made her want to leave. Jem knew exactly what it was like to feel disconnected at big extravagant parties. The rare times Nat invited her to a luxury launch or a premiere she almost always felt like a spare part; an anonymous invitee no one cared to talk to or even acknowledge, save in reference to her charming husband.

So into the void she created her version of Alice, picturing her sloping off back to the empty beach house, imagining her pouring a drink to settle her anxiety or annoyance. Was she relieved? Angry? Upset? Or had she simply drunk too much? Jem had been there too; it was all too easy to fill the awkward silences with another drink.

Morbid curiosity stirred inside her. Gripping her mug a little tighter, she started to walk towards the pool garden, her heart beating faster as she approached it, dew on the grass numbing her bare feet.

She opened the picket gate and stepped inside. Remove the tragic story and the pool was actually lovely, a quiet and tranquil spot with a small white clapboard pool house strung with fairy lights, giving it the air of an undiscovered enchanted grotto. But it was impossible to remove the story, wasn't it? Impossible to look at the glassy surface and imagine . . .

Jem bowed her head instinctively. She hadn't specifically come to pay her respects to Alice Holliday, but now she was here it seemed like the natural thing to do.

'What happened, Alice?' she whispered.

The group had said that their housemate was troubled and hinted that her death might not have been entirely accidental, but Jem could only imagine her coming out here to find peace, not to do something so terrible and decisive. At what point did the night turn sour? What had drawn Alice to the edge of the pool? What had made her slip?

'*Was* it a slip, Alice?' she wondered. 'Or did you step in?'

She shivered, feeling suddenly mawkish talking to a dead woman. *And a little disrespectful too*, her mind added.

She wrapped her dressing gown tighter around her body and hurried back to the house to dress. She wanted to get away from the house. 'I'd enjoy a quiet day at the beach,' Angela had said, but Jem was suddenly claustrophobic. She wanted to get out and fill her lungs with air, so she put on her trainers and went to find the bicycles Paul had mentioned.

She threw her phone and purse into a backpack, locked up the house and set off down Ocean Road, past the rows of smart houses, long driveways and expansive gardens that, now the weekend was over, were dotted here and there by staff busy with clippers and rakes. It didn't happen by magic after all.

She and Nat often joked about the different ways they liked to spend their vacations. To relax from his hectic day-to-day – attending expensive lunches and swish parties, she thought with a wry smile – Nat liked nothing better than to laze by a pool or on the beach. Jem hated doing nothing, preferring to potter around a coastal town or a hillside village. She loved searching out local artisan products; even though she did not have a particularly sweet tooth she had amassed quite a collection of jams and honeys from her travels.

The sky was a clear blue and a soft breeze took the edge off the heat. She pedalled hard, trying to distract herself from her earlier morbid thoughts. But it was hard going. She had chosen the bike for its cute straw basket, but the frame was heavy and as she approached the village of Bridgehampton, she felt red in the face and desperate for a drink.

It wasn't what Jem would call a village, more a collection of galleries, restaurants and high-end boutiques along a quaint manicured stretch of the Montauk Highway, but it was the nearest outpost of retail civilisation to the beach house. As she hit the intersection of Ocean Road and the main street, she spotted a pretty coffee shop, Barb's Beans, all bleached wood and seaside shabby chic. Perfect; it even had big ceiling fans instead of air con.

The queue was short, the breakfast crowd gone, the caffeine-hungry commuters departed on the Jitney for the city. Jem ordered an iced latte and a glass of water and couldn't resist a poppy seed lemon muffin for a sugar fix.

She crossed to a long bar table at the end of the store

and, one hand holding her tray, tried to hook her bag over the stool, but the weight made it tip. Grabbing for it, she watched almost in slow motion as iced coffee went sideways, spilling across the table.

'Bugger,' she said, grabbing her solitary brown napkin, which was wholly inadequate to mop up the lake of coffee beginning to drip onto the floor.

'Here,' said a voice, a hand passing her a wedge of napkins.

'Oh God, thank you,' she gasped, smiling up a fifty-something man sitting two bar stools along. He didn't smile back at her, too busy airlifting his laptop as the coffee trickled in his direction.

'I'm so sorry,' said Jem, doing her best to staunch the flow. 'I didn't splash you, did I?'

'Don't worry,' he said, standing up and brushing at his chinos with another napkin.

'Oh crap, this is totally my fault,' she said, grabbing more napkins to dab at the man's trousers. He stepped back with a slightly alarmed look. Obviously, thought Jem, cringing inside. When a crazy woman is pawing at you.

'Are you sure it hasn't gone on your laptop?' She felt another flutter of panic. It looked expensive; a top-of-the-range iMac she couldn't afford to replace.

'Still working,' he said.

'And your trousers . . .'

A smile finally crept onto his face. 'My pants are fine.'

Jem felt her cheeks flush. There was a quiet confidence about the man that made her more nervous. His crisp off-duty clothes told her this was someone with money.

'Look, you must let me pay for dry-cleaning. I don't have a business card or anything, but I can write down my number.'

He smiled again and she noticed his blue eyes behind

tortoiseshell glasses. He was handsome in a rugged, out-doorsy way, and for a moment Jem was reminded of *Out of Africa*-era Robert Redford, a little past his prime but still magnetic enough to remind you of it.

'It's fine,' he said as she handed him back a napkin. 'Could have been worse.'

Jem winced. 'I could have destroyed your computer just when you were putting the finishing touches to the great American novel.'

'Chance would be a fine thing,' he laughed, then looked back at her, making Jem feel as if she were being observed and assessed.

'You know there's a British author, Jilly Cooper, who once left her novel on a bus,' she said to fill the silence.

The man nodded. 'She told me that.'

Jem's eyes opened wide as his words sank in.

'You've *met* Jilly Cooper?' she said. 'How come?'

'I'm in the business.'

'Publishing?'

'I'm a writer too.'

'Wow. What sort of stuff?'

'I guess you call them thrillers.'

'Well, I've got time on my hands at the moment; maybe I'll buy one.'

'No, really,' he laughed, his eyes dancing. 'You don't need to buy one of my books just because you've ruined my chinos.'

Jem's smile faded, suddenly remembering why she was talking to this interesting man in the first place. She began to apologise again, but was interrupted by a waitress bearing a mop.

'I'm joking,' he said. 'What were you drinking?'

'Decaf iced latte.'

He turned to the waitress. 'Can you get this lady a refill

when you're done, Em? And another Americano for me.'

'Of course,' said the girl, and Jem noticed the way the young woman seemed nervous and eager to please. She wondered if that was what money did around here. Or maybe it was the twinkle in his eyes.

'I'm Michael, by the way.'

'Jem,' she said, extending her hand.

'Jem from . . . ?'

'London. Well, Cornwall originally. I moved to New York in January; it's my first summer at the beach. But at this rate I'll be blackballed from anywhere that sells coffee before the end of my first week.'

The waitress brought over their drinks and Jem settled back onto her stool.

'London's my favourite city,' Michael said, sipping his drink.

'Really? Why?'

He glanced at her with bemusement. 'You really need an explanation? The history, the architecture, the creative energy, the sense of space.'

'Ah, an Anglophile,' said Jem, beginning to relax.

'I'm from Boston originally. I think every New Englander has a little place in their heart for the mother ship.'

'Where do you live now?'

'Here. Just down the road in Amagansett.'

'All year round?'

He nodded. 'Although God knows why I hang around in the summer.'

'What's wrong with the Hamptons in the summer?'

'The people who come to the Hamptons for the summer.'

'Ouch,' said Jem with a wry smile.

'Well, at least you apologised,' said Michael. 'On the way over here I almost got run over by a gold Bentley with the number plate "PWER HUNGRY". No irony at all.'

Jem was laughing out loud now.

'I'm not joking, it didn't even stop. She was so fixed on going to buy her $20 kale and cashew smoothie, while I was almost squashed on the road.'

Jem noticed the way his eyes crinkled when he spoke. She had a sense he didn't spend much time with people. Join the club, she thought.

'The only time I leave the house in the summer is during the week,' he said, almost in answer to her thought. 'Although I guess I should go away myself. Europe maybe, or South America . . .'

'Well, when we move back to London, you can do a house swap with us in the summer.'

'So you like it here then?'

Jem nodded, feeling a pang of guilt for admitting how much she had enjoyed the weekend, enjoyed the result of the Hollidays' absence from the house.

'I just need to find a job before I lose my sanity,' she said, surprised at how much she was revealing to a complete stranger. 'You never told me what name you write under,' she added, rapidly changing the subject to something safer. 'I can download it onto my Kindle for the Jitney ride back to the city.'

'Michael Kearney.'

She swallowed hard, resisting the urge to say, '*The* Michael Kearney?' He was famous. Well, he wasn't quite Stephen King or Tom Clancy, but she'd certainly seen his books in the racks in the supermarket. And she'd just offered to exchange their two-bedroom cottage in Kensal Rise with him. He probably lived in one of those massive houses with gardeners on Ocean Road.

'So you *were* writing the great American novel,' she asked, looking across at his laptop.

He smiled. 'Writing, yes. Great, no. I generally work

from home, but I'm finding that a little slow going at the moment, so I thought I'd try a change of scenery.'

'J. K. Rowling wrote the Harry Potter books in a coffee shop,' she pointed out.

'Lots of authors do that sort of thing. It's a lonely job. You know your literary trivia,' he added, smiling.

'I'm sorry I didn't recognise you,' she said, looking down at her coffee cup. She realised now why the barista had been so attentive.

'Perk of the profession, relative anonymity. I can phone up a restaurant and generally get a table, but I've never been asked for a selfie.'

He had a great voice, thought Jem, just enjoying listening to him speak. It was deep and rich and considered; it was the voice of confidence and experience.

She noticed that he had finished his coffee.

'I should go,' he said.

'Sure,' she said, disappointed. 'I'm sorry. You know, for disturbing the flow of the writing.'

'I wasn't getting much done.'

He held out his hand formally.

'It's been nice to meet you, Jem. Good luck with everything.'

'And you,' she said, cursing her social ineptitude.

He picked up his laptop and got up to leave, and Jem was surprised at how sad she felt to see him go.

Chapter 5

The first weekends in June fell into a pattern. The group would arrive at the house by six on Friday, and as the weather was fine, they'd eat supper out on the deck: stir fries made with fresh brightly coloured vegetables that Jem or Erica had found at the farm stands, lobster rolls, or pasta vongole laden with freshly caught clams delivered straight to the seafood market in Amagansett.

Jem had gone to yoga classes with Angela and Rebecca on both Saturday mornings, and although she had struggled to keep up with the lithe, experienced Manhattan yogis, she had managed to bend her body into something resembling a pretzel without the rest of the class laughing at her. Saturday nights had meant cocktails at the Topping Rose hotel, a grand white mansion that reminded Jem of a Deep South plantation house, and Nat had also got them on the guest list for a couple of parties that he had assured everyone – perhaps to remind them of his value in the house share in case it had ever been in question – were the hottest tickets in the Hamptons.

But on the fourth weekend of the season, Jem and Nat arrived at the beach house to find that they were the only ones there. Joel and Erica were attending a wedding in the Hudson Valley; Paul and Rebecca were at her parents' in Rhode Island, and although Todd and Angela had not made any excuses, they were yet to turn up.

Jem was already in the kitchen when Nat came downstairs on the Saturday morning, naked except for a pair of pyjama bottoms slung low on his hips.

'What's this?' he asked, rubbing his eyes and eyeing the kitchen in bemusement.

Jem put the finishing touches to the scene: a jug of creamy hydrangeas on the island and candy-striped straws in the Mason jars full of fresh juice.

'Breakfast,' she said, looking up through her fringe before snapping off a series of photos with her phone.

'It's amazing, that's what it is,' he said, threading his arms around her waist.

'Well, Angela did say I should do a blog. There's no job on the horizon, so it will give me something fun and useful to do until I get one.'

She looked up at him and raised a brow.

'What do you think?'

'I love it,' he said, kissing her. 'Seriously. It looks great. But do we actually get to eat it?'

She laughed. 'Hang on a minute and I'll just serve the French toast.'

She turned back to the stove and transferred the fried bread from pan to plate. She hadn't followed a recipe and was nervous about how it was going to taste, but the soft scent of vanilla and cinnamon already had her mouth watering. She sandwiched the stack of warm bread with bananas and blueberries, arranging rashers of hot bacon on the plate and pouring maple syrup in extravagant swirls over the top of it.

'*Voilà*,' she grinned, handing Nat the plate.

'Wow,' he said, sticking a finger into the syrup.

'Uh-uh,' said Jem quickly. 'Just hold it there for a moment.' She snatched up her phone and clicked off a few more pictures.

'Now?' said Nat hopefully.

'Only if you tell me honestly what you think.'

'Of the blog idea?'

Jem nodded.

'I don't know why we haven't thought of it before,' he said. 'You're an amazing cook, you're beautiful, marketable. I could get one of the digital guys at work to help us with SEO. We'll have a book deal in the bag before we know it.'

Jem smiled, but her pleasure was undercut with a slight feeling of alarm. It was good that Nat was so enthusiastic, and he meant well, but it was just like him to start referring to her blog as a joint project the moment it looked like it might actually work.

'I'm not Nigella quite yet,' she said warily. 'But I'm enjoying it.'

'But is it what you want to do?'

'I want to do something, Nat. The fact that we're having fun at the beach hasn't changed that.'

A noise outside, the grumble of a car engine and wheels on the drive, disturbed her train of thought.

Nat frowned. 'Oh no. I was looking forward to having the house to ourselves.'

Jem gave her husband a knowing smile. 'I was wondering how long it would be before a house share wasn't exclusive enough for you.'

They went to the front door and saw a silver vintage sports car parked in the drive.

'Angela?' said Nat in surprise as their friend got out of the car.

'Can you believe Todd has taken up the fucking triathlon?' she began as she strode into the house. 'He's gone to compete in some stupid road and swim race in Trenton and I'll be damned if I have to schlep out to New Jersey to clap from the sidelines.'

She took off her sunglasses and gave them both a kiss on the cheek.

'How are you, darlings?' she said, switching gears from outraged rant to smooth charm in the blink of an eye. 'I was hoping you'd be here. I've got to go to a little party this afternoon – my parents' dear friends' wedding anniversary – and I wondered if you wouldn't mind coming with me.'

'Us?' said Jem, taken aback.

'Why not? I can't just turn up on my own, whatever Todd thinks. And it'll be fun. Well, mostly.'

'Whose is the car?' asked Nat, already leaning in through the open window, running a hand over the cream leather seats. Jem had to admit that it was the sort of car that would suit her husband; standing by it he looked like the star of a glamorous Hitchcock movie.

'My mother's. She said I could borrow it if I stood in for them at the party. Had to go all the way up to Greenwich to pick it up, but isn't it lovely?'

Jem could only imagine what Angela's parents' house was like; probably a double-fronted colonial in the smartest of Connecticut suburbs. But that was Angela's background: private school, skiing holidays, credit cards paid off by the bank of Mum and Dad. It was a world away from her own childhood.

'So why aren't your parents going?'

'They're on a cruise. The South Pacific. It was an awfully long way to come back for a party. So are you in?'

Jem looked down at Nat, now sitting behind the wheel of the car, touching the walnut steering wheel like it was the finest jewel. She didn't have to ask if he wanted to go.

'Cool. Just give us a minute to get ready,' she grinned.

Barely twenty minutes later, Angela was swinging the car into a gated compound just a few miles down the coast, Jem and Nat peering out eagerly.

'Is this the Georgica Association?' said Nat with a note of excitement.

'Uh-huh,' said Angela.

'What's the Georgica Association?' asked Jem.

'Very exclusive, very low-key. There are fewer than fifty houses on the entire compound. It was set up as a summer playground for old-money families in the late nineteenth century. You have to be a member to play on the courts, use the beach . . .'

Angela looked back at Jem.

'I thought your husband worked for *Form* magazine, not the New York Social Diary.'

Jem smiled as they drove through lush emerald meadows, grand houses distant down long driveways, and at the centre, the silvery glint of the Georgica Pond, the salt-water lagoon dotted with the creamy masts of small sailboats. The house itself was tall and white, with high square windows, a more formal style than most of the clapboard colonials you saw on the South Fork.

Leaving the car with a valet, Jem could see why Angela had gone to the trouble of going to pick up her mother's Mercedes; the vehicles parked along the driveway were spectacular, like a glittering display at a car show. Wealth was all relative, she thought. You could have a gigantic yacht with a helicopter pad on top, but there was always someone who had a bigger one, with a swimming pool or a tennis court. It must be tough being this wealthy, she thought with a wry smile.

They were directed to the back of the house, where the gardens were equally clipped and formal, punctuated by fountains and neoclassical sculptures. Around a hundred people were standing on the lawn drinking and talking while a string quartet played discreetly in a white stone bandstand shaped like a Roman temple.

'Thanks for inviting us,' said Nat, taking a glass of champagne from a waiter.

'Absolutely,' said Jem feeling like a character in *The Great Gatsby*. 'We'll return the favour and take you and Todd out for dinner.'

She was aware that supper at her favourite Brooklyn bistro wasn't a fair trade with an invitation to one of the Hamptons' finest mansions, but she was keen to impress that they could give as well as take. Besides, Todd and Angela were her favourite couple in the house and she was keen to see more of them in the city as well as at the beach.

'So these are old friends of your parents?' she added, wondering if her assumptions about the grandeur of Angela's childhood had actually been too conservative.

Angela played with a swizzle stick in her cocktail and nodded.

'Gerald is one of Dad's oldest friends, so we came here most summers. Lots of happy memories exploring these creeks and crabbing in the rock pools.'

She nodded towards the lagoon, a shivering plate of silver in front of them, and Jem followed her gaze. It was quite beautiful. The sloping lawn gave an unimpeded view of the sailboats scudding along like tiny white insects, their taut sails like wings.

'Angela, so glad you could come.'

A genial-looking man in a seersucker blazer and pale blue trousers came over and kissed her on the cheek.

'I wouldn't have missed it for the world. Gerald, these are my friends Nat and Jem. They're in the house with us this summer.'

'Any of you any good at tennis?' said Gerald without preamble. 'My doubles partner has broken his wrist. Big match on Wednesday.'

Jem smiled to herself. She loved how the truly rich were

often so open and inclusive. Angela had brought these strangers into his home, which meant they were instantly accepted as friends – even potential teammates. By comparison, the likes of Joel and Erica, while wealthy by any other standard, tended to be suspicious and competitive.

'I'm game,' said Nat. 'We actually used to live in an apartment that overlooked the All England Club, didn't we, Jem? I mainly play singles but I'll give it a crack if you don't mind a sloppy backhand.'

He's good at this, thought Jem, watching Nat in action, observing him move the conversation back and forth, dropping in anecdotes and subtle references to his own achievements, connections and, ultimately, usefulness. Because while Gerald was friendly and welcoming, that was what mattered in any meeting out here: what could you do for the person you were talking to?

Nat's parents, both teachers, had drilled the importance of education into him; that was how he had found himself at an exclusive school and then Cambridge. But it was the polish and confidence he had found there that was at the root of his success and that would push him higher.

'Happy anniversary, anyway,' he said, extending his hand, which Gerald clasped with both of his. Clearly Nat had made the impression he'd wanted.

'Forty years, isn't it?' asked Jem.

Gerald beamed. 'They flew past. Although I think Marcy probably deserves a medal.'

'And that's what? A ruby anniversary?'

'That's right,' said Angela. 'He planted Marcy a rose garden in the grounds. Ruby-red roses, you old romantic.' She smiled affectionately.

'I try.' Gerald chuckled. 'In fact, I'd better go track her down before some handsome buck like young Nat here tries to carry her off.'

They watched him melt back into the crowd, receiving handshakes and back slaps.

'He seems lovely,' said Jem.

'Nicest man in the world,' said Angela. 'Let alone the Hamptons. No wonder the party is so busy. Oh, I must go and say hi to Muffy Johnson. You'll be all right here?'

Crossing the lawn, Angela greeted a short woman in a pink dress as if she were a long-lost sister.

'Angela seems to know everyone,' said Jem, watching as she ping-ponged from the pink woman to a tall man with white hair, then back to a woman with hair like a burning Kuwaiti oil well.

'She does know everyone,' said Nat in a matter-of-fact tone. 'But I had no idea her parents were so connected . . . God!' He slid his sunglasses down to peer over the top. 'Is that *Spielberg*?'

Jem smiled. 'Don't tell me *you* are impressed with a celebrity spot, Nat Chapman.'

'It's Spielberg, baby,' he laughed. 'That trumps any of the names I might see at fashion parties.'

He tipped his head back and inhaled deeply.

'God, I much prefer parties like this. Older people are less socially anxious, so much less bullshit to wade through. Wouldn't it be great to live like this when we're seventy?'

'We're living like this now, Nat. Well, almost,' she pointed out. 'The beach house isn't as fancy, but it's probably in a better location.'

Nat shook his head and waved his glass towards the water.

'Angela was telling me that lots of people prefer to be on the pond. The thinking is it's safer for families because the sandbar protects it from the ocean.'

Jem gave a half-smile. 'Sometimes I think you'd start eating white bread again if Angela said it was the done thing.'

He looked at her, frowning. 'What are you saying?'

'I just wonder why you care what people think so much.'

'I care,' he said, lowering his voice, 'because what people think is what's going to get me a bigger job and a bigger salary. Agree with what people think and they'll like you, they'll think you're one of them and that you fit in. And when the time comes to find a new editor or publisher, they'll remember that nice young man who cared about their opinion.'

Jem opened her mouth to reply, but was interrupted by a deep voice.

'Hello, Jem.'

She turned and gaped in surprise when she saw Michael Kearney.

'Michael. Hello. Hi. Wow, what are you doing here? I thought you said you only ventured out of the house on weekdays.'

'I make an exception for Marcy and Gerald.'

Jem caught Nat's expression in the corner of her eye. His face was neutral, outwardly interested in this new arrival, but she also saw suspicion and annoyance. Fleeting, but it was there. After all, who could little Jem know who was worth knowing?

'Michael, this is my husband Nat. Nat, this is Michael Kearney.'

Nat extended his hand; not too enthusiastically, she noticed. The handshake of equals.

'Ah yes, Jem said she'd met you in Bridgehampton.'

'Yes, we had . . .' Michael looked at Jem with a twinkling smile, 'a discussion about the best dry-cleaners in the area.'

'I'm a big fan of Jack Garcia, by the way,' said Nat, going straight into mingle mode. 'When's the movie coming out?'

'One of your books is being turned into a film?' said Jem. 'Gosh, that's exciting.'

Michael shook his head. 'Not a movie. TV series. Although television is the new Hollywood apparently.'

'Who's playing Garcia?' asked Nat.

'Not sure yet. At least I have casting veto.'

'Well if you need any help in that department,' said Jem, 'I am happy to audition Ryan Gosling and any of the Hemsworth brothers on your behalf.'

'Oi,' said Nat, gently elbowing her in the ribs. 'You keep away from Ryan Gosling.'

She laughed and took a sip of her champagne, relaxing as she watched Nat and Michael chat. Nat told Michael about his work at *Form*, while Michael revealed that he had once worked for the political opinion magazine *Cover*, only moving into writing books when the publication folded. 'Lots of people loved it, not enough people bought it,' he said. 'And that was the end of that.'

He turned to Jem.

'Talking of which, how's your job-hunting coming on?'

Jem pulled a face. 'It's not. Not really. It's summer, I suppose. Everyone says it's always quiet in summer.'

She thought about telling him about her blog, but even Nat would laugh if she referred to that as employment. She knew it could be months, years before 'The Beach Kitchen' even made a dime, and although she enjoyed it, the chance to make some cash of her own, and not be entirely dependent on handouts from Nat, was still extremely appealing.

'What sort of thing are you looking for?'

'At this moment in time, anything,' she said, filling him in on her experience, her catering company and how much time she'd spent juggling food preparation with the more practical side of running a business: bookkeeping, marketing and promotion.

'You were on social media?' he asked with interest.

'That's how most of the work came in: Facebook ads, the

Twitter feed and Pinterest boards. It's fiddly, but they're all tools you have to use in the digital age.'

Michael looked thoughtful. 'My assistant is on maternity leave at the moment. I was going to manage without one until she's back in the fall – straight after Labor Day ironically – but I can barely work Facebook and I've fallen behind on some admin . . .'

Jem looked at him in amazement. 'You're offering me a job?'

'I only need a few hours a week. Social media stuff that my publishers aren't dealing with, fan mail, that sort of thing.'

'That sounds fantastic,' said Nat, turning to Jem then giving Michael a slick smile.

'I'm not great with Excel,' she said more cautiously.

Michael didn't look concerned. 'I've got people for that. I just need another pair of hands. Someone efficient, organised . . .'

Nat laughed. 'Jem's perfect for that. She's lived with me for eight years. She's used to whipping creatives into shape.'

Michael nodded, but kept his attention on Jem. 'What do you think?'

'Where would it be based?' She didn't want to get rail-roaded into it, wanting to make sure the logistics worked.

'I guess most of it can be done remotely. My current assistant Celine lives in Sag Harbor year round, but she comes to the house a couple of days a week to talk things through, plan my diary . . .'

'The house?'

'My place in Amagansett. I work in a studio in the grounds, but there's also an office, which is where Celine works from.'

'Who does your PR?' asked Nat.

Michael shook his head. 'There's nothing like that to do.

I have an outside publicist and my publisher handles all the heavy lifting on that side of things.'

'No, I was thinking we could work together,' said Nat. 'I have a style column for the *Sunday Chronicle* in London. It's called "I Love Your Style" – interviews with the world's smartest dressers.' He gestured to Michael's crisp white shirt and blazer. 'I think you'd be perfect.'

Jem wrapped her arm around her husband's waist and gave him a diplomatic poke to shut up.

'Well, either way, you should come over to dinner to discuss it further,' said Michael, handing Jem a business card. Just his name, an email address and a number printed on a thick white square of card. A personal card, not something the publicist had given him. She felt flattered and, she had to admit, a growing sense of excitement. Maybe she *should* do it. It'd certainly keep her busy, plus it would be fascinating to see a best-selling writer work at close quarters.

A languid, confident-looking man approached them. He was more typical Hamptons, his jeans, linen jacket and T-shirt the uniform of many thirty- and forty-something men Jem had seen in the pavement cafés over the past month.

'This is my friend Brad,' said Michael. 'Brad is producing the Garcia project. Nat and Jem are locals.'

Jem almost laughed out loud at that. But then they were, weren't they, even if it was only for the summer.

'Locals, huh?' asked Brad. 'I'm looking for a new place near here.'

'Where are you at the moment?' asked Nat.

'I have a house on Shelter Island,' he said, knocking back what looked like brandy. 'Great place, lots of land, but when you have to throw a ferry into the mix,' he pulled a face, 'it's just not convenient.'

'We've got a place in Wainscott, on the beach,' said Nat casually, and Jem could see he was pleased when Brad looked impressed.

'Cool,' said the producer. 'Which end?'

Nat took charge of the conversation, describing the house in glowing terms, telling him about the location and the desirable properties on Ocean Road.

'You mean, near the Pool House,' said Brad looking more curious.

Nat frowned.

'The Pool House?'

Brad nodded.

'Where that girl was killed last summer,' he said, turning to his friend for support.

'You heard about it, didn't you, Mike? She was found dead in the swimming pool of her rental.'

'She wasn't killed. It was an accident,' said Nat, glancing over at Jem. 'She was drunk and drowned.'

Jem could see that Brad wasn't going to let it drop. He was one of those men who had to be right about everything, otherwise it would feel as though he had lost.

'No,' he said firmly. 'I heard there was more to the story than that. Like I got this from a cop or something.'

It was like watching two dogs circling each other.

'Look, I know there wasn't,' said Nat, playing his ace. 'We're actually staying at the house where it happened.'

'Where you're staying?' said Brad, giving a low whistle. 'I hope the realtor disclosed it to you before you signed the lease.'

An uncomfortable quiet descended on the group.

Michael took Brad by the arm. 'Listen, buddy, I need to talk to you about this casting thing.'

Brad looked vaguely annoyed, flashing a look towards Nat, then clicked into business mode as Michael steered him away. 'Excuse us,' he said, already throwing out the names of movie stars as they walked.

Jem and Nat watched them leave, a dark silence between them.

'Well, I got you a job offer anyway. That's good.'

Jem knew better than to tell Nat he'd had nothing to do with it. It was something she'd noticed in a lot of successful people: they had no qualms about claiming success as their own, and as soon as they'd absorbed it into their own myth, it might as well have been chiselled into marble.

'I haven't said I'll do it yet,' she said cynically.

'Why wouldn't you do it?' said Nat. 'It's a great opportunity.'

'For me or you?' she teased.

'Point taken,' he replied. 'But still, even though he's a great contact and he's perfect for my style column, I think working for Michael would be fun. In fact, I don't think this summer could have panned out any better.'

Chapter 6

Jem opened the fridge, took the bowl from the top shelf and put it carefully on the work surface, praying she didn't drop it. She'd never made summer pudding before; hadn't realised it would be such a faff. When she'd offered to bring a dessert to dinner at Michael's – or her job interview, as Nat had taken to calling it – she'd decided to make something quintessentially British, a show-shopping *Great British Bake Off* triumph that would distract from the fact that she had zero experience in book publishing, but as she took the lid off the basin and stared at the soggy pink concoction inside, she was beginning to wonder if it had been such a good idea. Besides the fact that she might poison everyone, she still had to transport the damn thing from Brooklyn all the way to the Hamptons.

Just as she was making a mental note to stop at a deli and pick up a standby dessert on the way, her mobile began to ring. She snatched it up and was surprised to hear Nat on the other end.

'I'm outside,' he said, his voice sounding strange.

'Well you don't have to tell me every step of the way. Get yourself up here. I need a hand carrying a soggy pudding.'

'I can't,' he said. 'Look out of the window and you'll see why.'

Jem went to the window and peered down into the street. She couldn't see anyone until a figure got out of a slick black sports car and started waving.

'Your chariot awaits, Mrs Chapman,' he shouted. 'Grab your bag and come on down!'

Laughing, Jem quickly picked up their bag, balancing the pudding in one hand, kicking the flat door closed and hurrying down the stairs.

'Tell me I'm not getting into a stolen vehicle,' she said as Nat held the door open.

'Not stolen, borrowed,' he answered with a wink.

Jem sat down in the big bucket seat, inhaling that unique aroma of new car: polished wood and leather fresh from the factory. Most of all, it smelt of money. She was immediately worried she'd spill raspberry juice from the summer pudding on the cream leather and end up with a massive bill.

'I told the PR I was doing an interview with Michael Kearney and that we might do it in the car,' said Nat, turning the engine over with a satisfying roar. 'Not a bad idea actually. It could be like a print version of carpool karaoke.'

'But you're not interviewing Michael Kearney,' said Jem, slightly cross that he'd used the occasion to blag something, even something this nice.

'Not technically, no,' he grinned, 'but don't look a gift Porsche in the mouth, that's what I always say.'

Jem laughed, despite herself. Nat gunned the engine.

'And it can do nought to sixty in 3.2 seconds.'

'Well try not to,' she said, balancing the pudding basin on her lap.

As it happened, the trip to the Hamptons took over three hours in the late-afternoon traffic. The V8 engine was no use when you were bumper-to-bumper with a Prius and a mail van. The sun was beginning to set in the melancholy sky when finally they turned off the main road through the Amagansett dunes. It was more discreet out here, fewer obvious celebrity compounds and billionaire estates. Following Michael's instructions, they turned down a dirt track and through an open gate.

'Check that out,' said Nat, switching the engine off.

Michael's house might be modest compared to Gerald's pile, Jem supposed, but it was impressive in a different way, like a sprawling Dutch barn, with fresh cedar cladding, a grey slate roof and windows bigger than they needed to be. It was also isolated and private, nothing to overlook it but the sea and the gulls.

Nat felt silent.

'What's wrong?' Jem said, looking at him.

'It's incredible,' he replied, his voice more subdued than normal.

'You make it sound like a problem,' chided Jem.

Nat kept peering through the windscreen.

'You know, lots of men wouldn't want their wives working for a multimillionaire who lives in a place like this out in the middle of nowhere.'

Jem tapped him on the arm. 'Don't be daft,' she whispered. 'He's a nice guy. Not some sort of sexual predator.'

'He'd better be,' said her husband, getting out of the car. 'Nat . . .'

He held up his hands in surrender. 'Sorry, sorry. He's old enough to be your dad, I know. I shouldn't have said anything.'

Jem felt a prickle of anger and she wasn't entirely sure what had annoyed her the most. That Nat had assumed she would be thinking about Michael Kearney in that way? That her husband had dismissed this new acquaintance as old and not worthy of any attention because of that? Or perhaps, deeper down, because he was right: she had noticed

Michael's blue eyes and was looking forward to being alone with him?

None of the above, she said to herself as they stepped onto the wooden porch and pressed the bell. I'm just on edge; it's a job interview after all.

Jem wasn't sure what she was expecting as they waited. A butler or a maid in fussy uniform? Instead Michael opened the door himself. He was dressed in a T-shirt, khakis and bare feet, his tortoiseshell glasses balanced on top of his head.

'Come in, come in,' he smiled as he led them inside to an open-plan space. 'Make yourselves at home, have a look around. I'm just struggling with pans in the kitchen.'

It was expensively – and recently, Jem thought – finished with wood- and linen-lined walls. There were cream rugs and drapes but this was definitely a masculine house: leather sofas, dark polished wood, the only clutter the inevitable floor-to-ceiling bookcases. The living space had high windows that looked out onto the beach, the ocean so close that Jem wondered if you could actually climb out and jump straight in.

Michael came back through holding two glasses of wine.

'This is a seriously cool house,' said Nat appreciatively. 'You know, we've been to a lot of nice pads since we got out here, but this is my kind of place.'

'Thank you,' said Michael. 'Although I can't really take the credit. I was persuaded to hire an interior decorator and this is what you get when you tell them that you're a guy living on his own all year round at the beach. Dark and zen. Sadly I'm not tidy enough to make the best of it.'

They followed him into the kitchen, which again was stark, with Japanese flourishes. From the absence of clutter on the countertops – just a knife block and a potted orchid; not even a coffee machine – it wasn't a room that saw much use. Jem nodded towards the oven. 'Smells good.'

'Again, not really my work,' said Michael. 'Jackie, my housekeeper, has made us a pie. Apparently all I have to do is steam some beans and broccolini.'

Nat and Jem settled onto barstools next to the central island.

'How did you find this place?' asked Nat. 'I mean, it's perfect for a writer, isn't it? The sea out there, but quiet and hidden away.'

'I was the janitor,' said Michael.

'The janitor?' Even smooth Nat couldn't keep the surprise out of his voice.

Michael laughed. 'I was broke, needed the money. I'd lost my job in journalism, my marriage had collapsed and I knew my savings would last maybe six months at the most. And then a friend said he'd heard of someone looking for a winter janitor at their Hamptons beach house.'

'And it was this place?'

Michael nodded. 'When *Cover* folded, it was a bad time for print media. Everyone was saying it represented the death of magazines, everything was switching to digital. Old guys like me weren't exactly hot property. So coming here as the caretaker and using my downtime to write that novel I'd always promised myself I'd write? It seemed like a good option, the only option in fact. I moved in, lived in a tiny one-room studio – a shack really – out there in the grounds whilst I looked after the big house here. Painted the woodwork, washed the salt off the windows, brushed the decks. And every day when I'd done my jobs, I wrote.'

He gestured towards the windows.

'You're right about the sea, Nat,' he said. 'I wrote to the sounds of the ocean. Some people say they're solar powered, that they work better when the sun is shining, but for me it was the sound of the sea in winter.'

He caught Jem's eye and she smiled at him.

'Well, that and the fact that typing quickly was the best way I had of keeping my fingers warm.'

Jem laughed and saw that even Nat was looking at Michael in admiration. Of course she'd done her research; it was only natural if you were thinking of working with someone. Michael Kearney was the definition of a self-made man. Brought up by a single mum in blue-collar suburban Boston, he'd put himself through college working in an abattoir, graduating top of his year and scoring a reporter's job at the *Boston Globe*. He'd been on the launch team of *Cover*, and when that publication closed, he turned his attention to novels.

'And was that book *Jack Garcia*?' said Nat. 'The one you wrote to keep warm?'

Michael nodded. 'I wrote the whole book in three months. Sent it off to an agent – the next thing I know it's on the *New York Times* bestseller list.'

'And then you bought the house where it all started?'

'Not straight away, no. It took a while, a few more books. But when the owner wanted to sell, I was in a position to buy. The little shack where I started writing is still out there; it's now my office. Only now I get to sleep in the main house.'

'That's a great story,' said Nat appreciatively as Michael spooned out the pie and vegetables where they sat.

Jem was glad of the informality of the occasion. Three of them in a big dining room would have been intimidating, but here in the warm kitchen, conversation was fluid and fun as they discussed the changing face of journalism, the reasons for the failure of *Cover* magazine – too glitzy, too self-indulgent – and a range of topics from politics to the environment. Jem felt as if they'd known Michael for years, whereas this was actually only their third meeting.

As she excused herself from the table to try and salvage her doomed summer pudding and listened to Nat, so at ease in this strange new environment, she felt a stab of guilt. Guilt for the times she had complained about his late nights at the office, and the many social events he had to attend in the name of work. The fact was, without all that networking, they would never have come to the beach house, and they would never have stumbled across opportunities like this one. I could be watching the rain drip down the windows in Kensal Rise right now, she reminded herself.

Offering up a prayer, she tipped the pudding onto a grey ceramic plate – and gasped when it slipped out perfectly. Decorated with raspberries the size of quarters, it actually looked pretty good, and something told her that it was going to taste even better. It was that sort of a night.

After they had finished eating, they moved into the living area, where Michael went to a stylish drinks trolley and poured them both a bourbon. Jem didn't want to point out that she hated whisky of any description, not unless it was in a sauce and dribbled over a sticky toffee pudding, but she felt so chic and sophisticated just being here, talking about films and books and Manhattan life with Michael, that she accepted the glass.

Nat glanced over with a look of encouragement. She knew what he meant: they had talked about dozens of subjects, but they still hadn't talked about the job offer.

'So where does the magic happen?' asked Nat, swilling the amber liquid around his glass. 'Where do you actually write?'

'Just out there,' said Michael, pointing into the darkness beyond the kitchen door. He reached over and flipped a switch, illuminating a pathway through the garden. 'Go take a look if you want to.'

'Can I?' Nat flashed another look at Jem.

'Sure. It should be open.'

Jem watched her husband disappear into the soft darkness.

'What a lovely evening,' she said, meaning both the warm night and the company.

'Thank you for coming,' said Michael. 'And thank you for the dessert, it was delicious – you have real talent. Now, what about your other talents: what do you think about the job? Are you interested?'

Jem gave a wry smile. 'Why do you think I spent two hours hulling strawberries yesterday to make a summer pudding – it's a bribe.'

'I appreciate it, but I don't need to be bribed.' He laughed. 'You said you were looking for a job, and I'm looking for an assistant. You're smart and trustworthy and I think we get on. So far anyway.'

'How do you know I'm trustworthy?' she said, resisting a smile.

'I was an investigative reporter for twenty years. I have a nose for these things . . . plus Nat says you're good at picking up socks.' He held up a hand before she could protest. 'I'm joking.' He laughed.

They ran through the details of how Michael thought it would work out. He suggested that Jem work for him on Mondays and Fridays, which he thought would fit in with weekends at the beach house. Jem felt uncomfortable talking about money, but he pre-empted her, naming a day rate that almost made her cough. Two days working for Michael meant she cleared more than she did in a busy week at Sparkling Jems. It would give her free time to do her blog and put money in her pocket. Lots of it.

'There's also the use of a car. The housekeeper used it for the groceries but she's just bought a station wagon and I don't need it. You might as well borrow it for the summer.'

Jem's eyes were now wide open. A car was Willy Wonka's Golden Ticket in the Hamptons. As dyed-in-the-wool New Yorkers, none of the group had one, and out here they had to make do with expensive cabs, the Hamptons hopper and the bikes in the garage.

'I think I should give you a heads-up, though,' he said, sitting back.

Uh-oh, thought Jem. She knew it was too good to be true. There was a snag, a catch, and by the look on his face it was going to be a deal-breaker.

'I'm interested in the story of your house.'

'Our house?' said Jem, feeling suddenly defensive. 'Interested in what way?'

He crossed one leg over the over and took a sip of his whisky.

'As I said, my background is in investigative journalism. *Jack Garcia* came out of a non-fiction piece I was writing for *Cover* about a guy who was discharged from the marines and disappeared. Rumours were surfacing all over the country of a vigilante who was coming in and sorting out small-town crimes, and the word on the street was that it was this missing marine. *Cover* was pulled before I could run the story, but I thought it was just too good to let disappear.'

'None of the other nationals would take the story so you turned it into fiction,' said Jem. 'I know. I read it on Wiki.'

He paused and looked at her. 'I'm not sure, but I think I might be able to do something similar with Alice Holliday. What do you know about her?'

'She was drunk and fell in the pool,' Jem said, looking out towards the garden, praying that Nat would come back. The situation was becoming quickly quite awkward and she preferred to have back-up to deal with it.

'An accident? Is that what you believe?' asked Michael.

Jem didn't feel comfortable discussing it, not for Alice's sake, but for her housemates; they were her friends after all, and they were real people, not some fictional marine.

'I'm just telling you what I've been told and what I've read on the internet. But honestly, I don't know much more.'

That much was true. After the night at the fire pit, Jem had googled Alice Holliday, partly to see what she was dealing with, sleeping in the bed of a dead woman, but also to see what Alice looked like, to put a face to the name. The pictures she'd found revealed her to be beautiful and fragile. Blonde waves fell to her shoulders, her eyes were cat-like, her cheekbones high and prominent, her skin pale olive. She was exactly the sort of woman men fell in love with and that women were instinctively suspicious of; she looked like a fifties film noir heroine who meets a tragic end.

'I bet you didn't find much, though, did you?'

Jem narrowed her eyes. 'What do you mean?'

'I mean there's not much on the internet about Alice's death.'

Jem had to admit she'd noticed that too. Beyond a few scattered local news reports along the lines of 'Tourist Dies in Beachfront Rental', there was very little, all the stories referencing her drowning but shining no more light on what had happened beyond the story that the group had told her on the first evening in Wainscott.

'What does this have to do with me working for you?' she asked finally, the excitement she had felt just a few minutes earlier having soured to anger and disappointment.

'I want to look into the story,' he said plainly. 'I think there's something there, unanswered questions. There was lots of chatter about it at the time. There still is.'

'It's not a story,' Jem said more fiercely than she intended. 'Alice was a wife, a friend, not some character for a book.'

'Exactly,' said Michael, undeterred. 'Which is why she

doesn't deserve to have her death ignored and covered up.'

'Covered up? It was an accident,' said Jem with an authority she didn't feel.

'Well, I agree that that would suit everyone around here.'

'And what does that mean?' said Jem, feeling her pulse race.

'The Hamptons is one of the most exclusive places on earth,' said Michael. 'It's a smart place. A safe place. Nothing bad happens here, and everyone would prefer it to stay that way. It's good for business.'

Jem wasn't going to let him stop there.

'So what are you saying? That just because no one wants to hear bad news, Alice's death must have been suspicious? That doesn't add up.'

'No, you're right. And I don't know anything for sure.' Michael shrugged. 'Not yet. But I had a dig around the story, spoke to some people. Call it an old hack's instincts, but there's something off about what happened. I want to do some work on it, keep rooting around. Whether it forms the basis of a new book, fiction, non-fiction, I don't know, but I just thought you should know what I am doing if you come and work for me.'

'Or rather that's *why* you want me to come and work for you.' She felt angry and duped.

'No, not at all,' he said.

'Right. So when you offered me a job at the anniversary party, you didn't know where I lived? Is that what you're telling me?'

Michael held up his hand. 'Look, someone pointed Angela out at the party, and when I saw you with her, I put two and two together. But I've been interested in the Alice Holliday story way before we met.'

Jem raised her brow as if to say, *Really?*

'Jem, I was an investigative reporter for twenty years. I

live in the Hamptons. Of course the Pool House was going to pique my curiosity.'

Jem shook her head, disappointed and annoyed. She'd been set up, it was that simple. He didn't want a new assistant, he wanted a mole in the beach house.

But at the same time . . . it *was* strange that the death of a woman as beautiful as Alice had gone almost unnoticed. Jem was not a journalist, but she knew enough about the media through Nat's job to be aware of how easy it would have been to 'sex up' the story. But no one had. Michael was right; there should have been reporters crawling all over this – why not? And she couldn't deny that she wanted to know more about what had happened that night by the pool. Michael's talk about something being off had unsettled her, not least because she had to return to the beach house – to Alice's bed – tonight.

She was about to speak when the cool swoosh of evening breeze announced Nat's return.

'That's got to be the best office on the whole East Coast of America,' he said, striding in from the cold. He gave Jem a wink that said, *I've been out there as long as I can, now tell me you closed the deal.*

'It's not bad,' said Michael, still looking at Jem. 'It's given me a few ideas sitting out there.'

Jem felt uncomfortable under his gaze, but she had already made her decision. However intrigued she was by Alice's story, Michael Kearney had lied to her and tried to use her.

'It's late,' she said, standing and reaching for her bag. 'We should go. Thank you for the food and wine,' she said, pointedly not mentioning the job offer.

'Any time,' said Michael, showing them to the door.

Nat waited until they were safely back in the car before he turned to Jem, expectation all over his face.

'Well?' he said. 'How did it go?'

'Fine,' she said quickly.

'Just fine?'

'Just fine,' said Jem, reaching over to press the engine ignition button. 'Now let's see how fast this bloody car can get us out of here.'

Chapter 7

Manhattan was alive, or at least that was how it seemed to Jem. The sky had been cloudless all day, which in the concrete canyons of the island often translated into unbearable mugginess, but tonight it felt perfect: warmth and energy filling the streets. She had met Nat at his office and hand in hand they had walked the twenty blocks to the gallery on 25th Street. As they weaved through the fashion district, past the shopfronts crowded with rolls of fabric, boxes of buttons, feathers and lace, then down past the swarming hive of Penn Station, she squeezed his hand a little tighter, unable to even remember how she had once been lonely and depressed living in New York.

As they entered the arts district and the office buildings gave way to showrooms and boutiques, Nat hung back, pulling out his phone.

'What are you doing?' frowned Jem, for once keen to get to the launch.

'I'm tweeting about Todd's exhibition,' said Nat.

'Unless it's on social media, it might as well not have happened, right?' she grinned, teasing her husband about his Twitter addiction.

As well as being art director for *HQ* magazine, Todd Carter also had a passion for graphic art, particularly vintage posters. Jem had heard him talk about it many times during their conversations at the beach house. His heroes were Andy Warhol and George Lois, the creative genius behind the iconic *Esquire* covers of the sixties and seventies. It was Todd's view that no one in modern media valued design much any more, so he had taken the matter into his own hands, creating his own art as a sideline. The results were bold and colourful, but also simple and striking. Jem liked Todd as a friend, but she loved his work too, and she was excited that he finally had an exhibition of his art here in Chelsea.

'Come on,' she said impatiently. 'I want to see it!'

Nat grinned at her. 'Okay, okay, I'm coming.'

They turned the corner and Jem was amazed at the scene. There was a long queue of well-dressed arty-looking people crowding the door of the gallery, which had even employed security to control them. Across the narrow street was a roped-off area filled with burly men holding cameras: a sure sign that celebrities and socialites were either inside or expected. Jem felt a rush of pride at her friend's success, but also a little thrill at being one of the rarefied few who had been invited to this exclusive night.

Holding her hand, Nat ignored the queue and walked confidently to the front, flashing his smile at the pretty girl with the clipboard, who simply lifted the velvet rope to allow them to pass inside.

'Look at this place,' whispered Jem. Double-height ceilings and whitewashed brickwork over polished parquet flooring made the space light and airy. The posters themselves were mounted in gold frames, emphasising their credentials, but they hardly needed the help: gathered together at full size, it was a stunning display, and from the little red 'sold' stickers attached to the frames like chickenpox, Jem knew the exhibition was already a hit.

'Come on, let's find the great artist,' said Nat. No one was more at home at these sort of events than Nat, but Jem could see that even he was excited. She supposed he felt the same way as she did: having grown so close to Todd – and all the housemates – during the past weeks, it was almost as if this was their big night too.

The gallery was packed with faces Jem didn't recognise, so she was glad to see Paul and Joel at the makeshift bar, although for a second she had to do a double take, not used to seeing them in their slick city work suits.

'Hey, guys,' she said, taking a cocktail from the bar. 'I almost didn't recognise you fully clothed.'

'Careful, or you'll have our wives asking questions,' laughed Joel, swigging a beer.

'What questions?' asked Erica, coming over to join them. Jem took a moment to admire her look – a black and emerald-green summer dress that fell almost to the floor. Anyone else would have come across as overdressed and try-hard, but the way Erica wore it, with a jangle of brass bracelets on one wrist, it looked as if she was on her way to a *Vogue* fashion shoot.

'Jem's been eyeing Paul's knees,' said Joel with a wink.

Erica looked at him and pulled a face, turning to Jem instead.

'So what happened with you and that author?' she asked.

'The author?' asked Jem, immediately feeling her good mood deflate.

'Angela said you went for a job interview on Friday night with the *Jack Garcia* guy.'

'Michael Kearney,' nodded Jem, wondering who had told Angela. She herself certainly hadn't told anyone in the house about their dinner in Amagansett, not after what Michael had discussed with her. And she'd asked Nat to keep quiet for the moment, putting him off by saying she didn't want anyone to know about it until she'd had a formal offer.

'Yeah, Kearney wants Jem to be his executive assistant,' said Nat proudly, ignoring the glare Jem fired at him.

'That's pretty awesome,' said Joel, nodding his approval. 'Kearney's big news. I heard he's got a new show coming out on HBO or AMC next season.'

'He has a great house too,' said Paul. 'I saw it in *Architectural Digest*.'

'It's amazing,' said Nat. 'He works from an office in the grounds that must have the best beachfront position in the whole of the Hamptons. I could have sat there all evening.'

'Perhaps he'd like to do an "At Home" feature for *Elite*,' said Erica with more interest. 'He's not really on-brand for us, but does he have a wife? Is she pretty?'

Jem tried to swallow her annoyance. 'He's divorced, and anyway I still haven't got anything in writing.'

Nat frowned. 'Still?'

'I'm sure he's busy,' said Joel with more sympathy. 'Those TV things are huge these days. But if you get it right,' he whistled, 'that's some serious change.'

Nat turned to Jem. 'Are you sure he's not waiting for you to get in touch? When we were at the house he said something like "Tell me what you decide".'

Jem wanted to stall for time. She didn't want to bring up the fact that she was going to reject Kearney's offer, here in front of her housemates.

'He was supposed to firm up the package; hours and money and so on,' she said, taking a gulp of her cocktail.

She'd just lied to her husband and she hated it, although the truth was, she hadn't been honest with him about the subject of Michael Kearney all week. After their dinner in Amagansett, she had decided against telling Nat about Michael's plans to investigate Alice's death. She was fairly sure what he would say: Alice's death was an accident and it would suit no one to snoop around the details of the tragedy, least of all the occupants of the beach house, who would surely not want everything dredged up again by a high-profile writer.

Nat had never seemed more relaxed and happy than when he was at the Hamptons house, feeling himself accepted by the group, and he wouldn't want to risk anything that might jeopardise that. Then again, he obviously liked the idea of infiltrating the social circle of a world-famous author, especially one connected in the world of television. Even if it meant upsetting their housemates, he'd be able to justify it somehow. Nat was good at justifying everything he wanted.

No, whether to work for Kearney or not was her decision, and she was going to pick her moment carefully to tell her husband that she thought it was a bad idea. However much she liked Michael, however smart, funny and interesting she found him, however much she wanted the job as his assistant and the perks and money that came with it, the last thing she wanted was to feel used.

She glanced over at Erica, who was still looking at her, no doubt thinking about her 'At Home' scoop with Michael Kearney. Was that how it always had to work in this world? she wondered. Did everyone around here want something? *What can you do for me?*

Michael. Erica. Even Todd had been buzzing round Nat like a moth around a flame, asking whether his magazine and newspaper contacts were going to show up to the exhibition.

Nat headed back to the bar while Paul and Joel melted into other groups, leaving Jem alone to enjoy the real reason they were all there: Todd's art.

It was good, really good, she thought, admiring one

particular print – a graphic illustration of a brick-red Brooklyn town house that reminded her of a cartoon version of their own apartment block. His use of colour was simple but bold – the clever style of the illustration both retro and modern, like an old Hitchcock movie poster updated for the twenty-first century. She wanted to tell him how much she loved it, but she couldn't see him anywhere.

As she looked, she spotted Nat near the bar talking to Angela. She watched them share a joke, watched them laugh, and felt a tremor of something: not quite jealousy, but insecurity and danger, a danger she had felt before, many times before when they were out in public. After five years of marriage, it was easy to forget how popular her husband was with the opposite sex. When they were cuddled up in bed or on the sofa watching a box set, he was just Nat, her smart and handsome husband, but in a crowd, at a party, when sex and desire were as much a part of the atmosphere as oxygen, she was all too aware that he was *hot*.

'I don't know who is the better recreational flirt, Nat or Angela,' said a voice next to her.

Jem turned and saw Rebecca sipping a glass of champagne.

'Recreational flirt?' she asked nervously, noticing that her housemate's smile didn't quite reach her eyes.

'It's a skill,' Rebecca confided. 'Charming the pants off people, making them feel they're the most gorgeous and interesting person in the room, even if it's just to remind themselves that *they're* the most gorgeous and interesting person in the room. They're both so good at it, they're probably having a charm-off right now.'

Jem squirmed a little. Rebecca's arch comments had the effect of making her feel uncomfortable, too naive, too country. Jem liked everyone in the house, but it was Rebecca who made her feel the most on edge. Unlike Erica, who could direct the occasional barb, she was never unkind about anyone, but her cool, androgynous beauty was other-worldly and her sharp intelligence always made Jem feel as if she had to raise her game whenever she was with her.

'Angela is a woman's woman,' said Rebecca as they watched Nat laugh animatedly at something their housemate had said. 'She wouldn't take it any further than a harmless flirt.'

Jem gave a nervous laugh, considering the suggestion behind her comment.

'She'd better not,' she said as lightly as possible.

'Seriously, don't worry about it,' said Rebecca, putting a reassuring hand on her arm. 'This is New York. People come to show off, to let everyone know how great they are. Besides, you are lovely. Remember that.'

Jem smiled back gratefully. Rebecca worked in a gallery, where it was her job to make rich people feel even richer and more tasteful, so that they wouldn't blink at parting with a million dollars for a piece of art; but even though she was a professional at making people feel good, her compliment was still appreciated.

Rebecca's expression stiffened. Her change in mood was instant and obvious, and Jem followed her line of sight.

'David's here,' she said quietly.

'David who?' said Jem, assuming she was talking about one of the celebrities the paparazzi had gathered for.

'Holliday. From the house last summer.' She stopped as if to steel herself. 'Alice's husband.'

Jem's curiosity was instantly piqued.

'Don't you see him any more?' she asked.

Rebecca shook her head, her eyes drifting back from David to Jem.

'Not since the funeral. He's a friend of Todd's, that's

how he came to take the house share, so I'm not that surprised he's here. But still, it's tough to know what to say after everything that happened.'

She paused, and Jem noticed that her unflappability had been ruffled.

'I can imagine it is, but he's still your friend,' she said kindly. 'And it's definitely going to be more difficult for him being here than it is for you guys.'

Rebecca nodded, her pale skin almost translucent. 'I should go and say hello. Don't you think?'

Jem couldn't remember Rebecca ever asking her opinion on anything.

'Sure. Go over,' she said, motioning towards David with her head. 'Go.'

Jem hung back as Rebecca threaded her way through the crowd towards the tall, sandy-haired man, watching her melt into the crowd until she had disappeared and Jem was back to being alone. She was used to feeling an outsider at parties, used to being on the edges. When she first started coming to events like this with Nat, she hated being ignored or avoided, until she realised that she was so unimportant it rendered her invisible – and that provided the perfect conditions for people-watching, a skill she had honed.

A knot of people in her line of vision dispersed so that she could see Rebecca again, and she took note of David Holliday with interest. He wasn't at all like she had imagined. His chinos were not pressed and the shirt under his cord jacket looked as if it was not on its first day of wear. Her first impression was that he looked like a man whose best days were behind him. He had good bone structure, which should have made him handsome, but he looked so tired and worn that you would not immediately describe him as attractive. She guessed his age as around forty, but as that would make him around five years older than the rest of the group, she wondered if the tragedy of last summer had simply aged him.

Her thoughts turned back to Michael Kearney and what he had said about David's wife.

There was a reason Jem hadn't turned down the author's offer to work with him outright: she was intrigued. Intrigued by what had really happened to Alice Holliday, intrigued that so little had been written about it.

She took another cocktail from a passing tray and puffed out her cheeks, trying to expel the thought. No, her first instincts had been correct. It was wrong to get involved. She had to forget about Alice, forget about Michael Kearney and spend more time on her food blog.

She turned her attention to Todd's posters, thinking about art and imagery and her plans for 'The Beach Kitchen', making a mental note to look into web designers and digital retailers where you could buy an off-the-peg site. She'd have gorgeous, mouth-watering photos as the pull for the blog, post three recipes a week and—

'He's good, isn't he?' said a voice, shaking her from her thoughts.

She turned, her mouth open. She hadn't noticed David Holliday approach and felt caught off guard.

'Todd? Yes, he's great,' she gushed. 'Actually, I want to buy this print, but I'm not at all sure I can afford it, not even if he gives me a discount.'

'I like that one too.' He nodded towards the wall. 'It reminds me of the movie *Rear Window.*'

A silence hung between them as they both looked at the poster.

'I'm David, by the way,' he said, offering his hand. 'I thought I'd come over and say hello. You're at the beach house now, correct?' He didn't say it unkindly or with any accusation.

'Yes, I'm Jem,' she said, shaking his slim hand. 'My husband Nat knows Todd. They worked together at *Form*.'

David smiled. 'I have to say, I was surprised when I heard that one of Todd's friends had filled the vacancy.'

'Why do you say that?' she replied with genuine interest.

'Look around. Todd's friends aren't very Hamptons.' He motioned towards a skinny guy with a jet-black pop-boy haircut. '*Todd* isn't very Hamptons. If it wasn't for Angela, the East Village and dive bars would be his stomping ground.'

'I did wonder. When he's wearing his shorts, we tease him that he's the whitest guy in Long Island.'

David gave an affectionate smile. 'You should have seen him as a teenager. Long black hair, big glasses, a thick overcoat even if it was ninety degrees in a Boston summer.'

'So you've know him for years?' said Jem.

David nodded wistfully. 'Childhood friends. Our families were close. I was a couple of years older than him, but we reconnected back in New York. When Julie and Will, the couple before us, had a baby, Todd invited us to join them.'

Us. The word hung between them until Jem felt she had to say something.

'I was sorry to hear about your wife,' she said after a moment. 'I had no idea when we agreed to the tenancy.'

'Don't feel awkward,' said David stiffly. 'I don't blame any of them for going back. People have got to carry on living.'

There was a wobble in his voice as he said it, and Jem put her hand on his arm. She glanced over at the group standing by the bar. Rebecca had joined them and Angela was looking over.

People have got to carry on living.

The housemates had certainly done that, she thought with a sense of guilt. She'd noticed those first few days of the summer season how everybody had avoided the pool area, but the previous Saturday, she'd walked past and seen Angela floating on a giant inflatable. The pool had been cleaned, too, reviving it to a more Hamptons-appropriate bright turquoise, and fresh lemon cushions had been put on the banquette seats outside the pool house. And once Angela had taken that first step towards putting the history of the house behind them, everyone else had followed, so that by the Saturday afternoon they were all congregated around the pool, bare feet dangling in the water, laughing and joking as if nothing bad had ever happened there.

'You know, I thought I'd be okay coming here tonight,' said David sadly. 'But it just reminds me how much I miss her. Alice loved parties, she loved people. She wasn't without her faults – which of us is? But she certainly loved life, lived it to the full. On occasions like this, I think I'll turn around and see her, surrounded by people, laughing, having fun, and then I realise that I won't. I can't. I keep thinking it's going to get better, easier to deal with, but a year on, it still makes me catch my breath when I remember I'm never going to see her again.'

He paused.

'People say it will get better, that time will heal, but it doesn't, not really. You just have to get used to it.'

Jem nodded, feeling a strong and sudden sense of solidarity with the stranger.

'My dad died when I was sixteen,' she said without even thinking. 'A heart attack. No warning, no history of cardiac problems, just gone. My whole life changed in a matter of hours.'

David didn't say anything, as if he had recognised that she wanted to talk about what had happened. And it was true: Jem got to speak about her dad so rarely. She wasn't close to her mother, only spoke to her every couple of weeks, and even then, her mum's life seemed to have moved on so much, to a new world that revolved around her second husband, it was sometimes as though their old life as a family hadn't even existed.

'I miss him every day,' she said, finding comfort in her frankness with this man she hardly knew. 'At first it was hard to keep remembering him because it was so painful. But you have to keep thinking about them, as much as you can, because otherwise you'll forget, and you don't want to forget a single little detail about why you loved them so much.'

David gave a sad smile. Behind the spectacles and the limp fringe, he had a kind face. Jem imagined a more vital version of the man standing before her, and could suddenly imagine what a beauty like Alice would have seen in him.

'So you didn't know about Alice before you took the house, huh? That sounds like Angela.'

'I think it's difficult to talk about,' she said diplomatically. 'You'll know better than anyone that people are scared of saying the wrong thing, so they avoid the subject entirely.'

She looked at him, unable to resist asking the questions she had trawled over in her mind, again and again.

'How did it happen?' she enquired as gently as she could.

David gave an almost indiscernible shrug.

'I ask myself the same question every single day,' he said. 'I ask myself whether it was my fault. Whether things could have worked out any differently if I had made different choices that night.'

'Choices?'

He let out a slow breath.

'We were at a party. We had an argument and she left. I should have gone with her. I should have been a better husband, not one who let his wife leave a party on her own, but I wasn't.'

His words seemed self-flagellatory and his face was creased with sorrow. Jem touched his hand, willing him to stop, but it was as if he was compelled to continue. Perhaps no one had asked him about it before.

'I did follow her eventually, back to the beach house,' he said. 'But it was too late. I couldn't find her anywhere inside, so I went back outside. I didn't even think of looking by the swimming pool.'

'Why not?'

'Alice never went there. She hated the water, couldn't swim. Her sister drowned when she was child, and as long as I knew her, Alice got nervous whenever she was near a pool or the ocean. But the gate was open so I went to look.'

His eyes started to mist with tears.

'She was lifeless under the water. Not floating, not sinking. Just there.'

He took a sip of his drink as if to steady himself and looked directly at Jem.

'You want to know what happened, but the truth is, I don't know. Why had she gone to the pool in the first place? Did she slip? Jump? I just don't know. And sometimes I think that's going to drive me mad.'

He turned back to Todd's artwork and Jem thought of Michael Kearney and his suggestion that something was off with the investigation into Alice's death. Why was Alice by the swimming pool in the first place? Why?

'Do you want to find out?' she said without thinking.

David looked at her. 'What do you mean?'

She felt her heart race with energy. She hated seeing this man in such obvious emotional pain; not knowing what had happened to Alice was quite clearly killing him. But now she had a sudden sense that she could do something positive and help him. That was what had been bothering her the most since she had come to New York. That lack of purpose.

Well, right here, right now, she could change that.

'I have a friend, a writer, an investigative reporter. He might be able to find out what happened,' she ventured cautiously.

'How?'

'He has money, resources, connections. I know he's interested in what happened to Alice. He told me that he thinks her death wasn't properly investigated.'

'Did he?'

Jem nodded. She looked up and saw Nat and Angela threading through the crowds towards her. Her heart was rushing now. David Holliday was well within his rights to think her an interfering rubbernecker. It was his wife's death they were talking about here, not a piece of salacious gossip. And Jem still had a gut feeling – no, a certain knowledge – that the group would not welcome any sort of probe into the affairs of last summer.

'Do you want me to speak to him?' she asked quickly, aware that her husband was almost in earshot.

David took a business card out of his wallet and pressed it into her hand.

'I think we should have a conversation,' he said, putting his wallet back in his pocket as Nat and Angela approached them, flashing Jem a complicit look and turning the conversation back to art.

Chapter 8

Jem's eyes snapped open as soon as Nat's alarm went off. Nat rolled over and tried to put a heavy arm across her hip, but Jem slid out from under him and got out of bed.

'What's up?' he said as she slipped on her robe.

'I've got to get the Jitney,' she said, trying to work out what time the bus would get into Bridgehampton if she caught one within the next hour. Damn, she was already running late. She went to switch on the shower in their tiny en suite, and while she was waiting for the water to heat up, she popped back into the bedroom to gather the clothes she had laid out the night before.

'Hey,' said Nat, propping himself up on the pillow. His hair fell in awkward angles; he looked hung-over. He had thrown himself into the New York way of life, but he still had enough Britishness in him to drink on a school night.

'Any chance of a coffee?'

Jem scooped up her underwear and looked at him disapprovingly.

'You're going to have to make it yourself. I have to be out of the house in . . .' She looked at her watch. 'God, six minutes.'

'Where are you off to at this time? Yoga?'

'I'm meeting Michael Kearney.'

Nat looked immediately more awake.

'You're starting the job?'

She smiled. 'I hope so.'

'What happened? Did he email you?'

'I emailed him,' she said, avoiding his gaze.

Nat got out of bed and came towards her. He was naked, and Jem almost felt the urge to tell him to put on some clothes.

'Come here,' he said, extending his hand.

She took it and he pulled her close.

'Congratulations,' he said, kissing her softly on the lips. 'So you're leaving now? How's it going to work?'

Jem shrugged. 'I don't know yet. I go early on Friday, have a meeting, do whatever Michael wants me to do. I work at his house on Monday. Come back to New York on Monday night.'

'Do whatever he wants you to do, huh?' said Nat, untying the sash on her gown. 'I'm not sure I like the sound of that.' He nuzzled his warm nose into her neck and Jem started to giggle.

'You know what I mean . . .'

He slipped his hands around her waist.

'You're a very clever girl,' he said, pushing his fingers down the curve of her spine. 'I think we need to have a little celebration, don't you?'

He pushed the robe off her shoulders and she could feel his hardness against her belly.

'Nat, I've really got to go,' she said, pulling away as he tried to kiss her again. 'And I've got to have a shower first.'

'I don't mind that,' he said, following her into the en suite.

'Stop it,' she laughed, swatting at him with a towel. 'I've got to catch the Jitney.'

'Get the next one,' he said, and he opened the shower door and pulled her inside.

Jem laid her head back on the headrest of the coach as it drove out of the city towards Long Island. Even though it was early, the Jitney was packed, the excitable chatter of pretty young things in summer dresses and sandals rising above the hum of the engine. Jem had never understood how everyone looked so perfect in New York. Even their casual, off-duty wardrobe, the things they wore for travelling. Behind her, she could hear a banker type loudly trying to chat up a model-looking girl, who confided that she was a waitress. By the time they had reached Westhampton, they had made plans to meet in a bar that evening.

Jem wondered what they might have in common, and who was using who. It was easy to think that pretty girls latched onto wealthy men to help pay their way in expensive places like the Hamptons, but a plain-looking, boorish guy like the one seated behind her would be unlikely to take a beautiful woman for dinner unless he had a solid bank balance to flex. Sex was social currency everywhere, of course, and that was never more evident than in an image- and status-conscious place like New York.

The thought of sex cast her mind back to that morning. So much for getting out of the apartment at six to catch an early Jitney. They'd screwed in the shower, on the sofa, and on the bedroom floor. Their lovemaking had been urgent, intimate and raw, and for the first time in a long time, Jem had felt sexual and desired.

Lately she had avoided giving the lack of sex in her relationship with Nat too much thought. He was busy and tired, coming home late, moving and shaking in the city, networking, forging friendships and alliances, pursuing his career with a determination that he constantly reminded her was 'good for us'. So Jem had got used to the fact that they only had sex a couple of times a month. Frankly she had no idea what was normal when you'd been married for five years and together for eight. Certainly she'd heard her old friends back in Kensal Rise joke about their sex lives going to pot, although admittedly that had been in the context of dealing with teething babies and toddlers who liked creeping into bed with Mum and Dad.

But that morning, it had felt good to feel wanted again, and as she stared out of the window, her face warm from the sunlight, she felt more energised than ever, as if a mistral had blown away the lingering cobwebs of whatever restlessness she had been feeling since she got to New York.

She checked her watch and tried to work out how close they were to Amagansett. They'd already passed through Bridgehampton and East Hampton and she ducked her head to read a passing sign.

'Oh crap,' she muttered, getting up as she realised the stop they were pulling into was the nearest one to Michael's house.

She blew out her cheeks as she stood on the sidewalk watching the coach drive away and squinted up at the white sun; on the air-conditioned bus she hadn't realised quite how hot the day was.

'Now what?' she muttered, checking the map on her phone. Buses were few and far between in this part of the world, one of the many things that kept the Hamptons exclusive. She flipped on to Uber and, noticing the fare-price surging, flipped off again and swung her backpack onto her shoulders. She was Cornish; they walked everywhere – and anyway, it didn't look far.

Her steps were brisk at first and she smiled to herself, noticing how few people there were on the sidewalks once you came off the main drag, but her stride faltered when she came out from under the shade of the trees lining the road, although she wasn't sure if that was because of the heat or because she was nervous about getting to her destination.

Her decision to take the job had been immediate having met David Holliday, and she had emailed Kearney to let him know as soon as she had left the gallery. She could only imagine David's torment at not knowing what had happened to Alice in those last few minutes of her life. He had said that he wished he had made different decisions that night at the beach, but that didn't mean he wasn't tortured by what he had – or hadn't – done. And Jem had been moved by that. She couldn't imagine being in that position and she wanted to help; both for David and for Alice. For the first time in a long time she felt as if she could make a real difference in someone's life.

There was still a nagging sense that what she was doing had the potential to blow up in her face. Jem knew how the housemates – and her husband – would feel about her investigating something they were so intimately wrapped up in. They would not take it well, she was damn sure about that, so her first order of business had to be to ask Michael to be as discreet as possible and to only talk to her housemates when he had some concrete evidence. The group were not unreasonable; they were the Hollidays' friends, and as such, Jem felt sure they would want to know the truth about Alice's death if it helped David deal with his grief.

That was what she hoped, anyway. There was also a very good chance that they might go ballistic and kick her and Nat out of the house. She wasn't even sure she would blame them.

Sighing, she glanced down at her phone to check she was still going in the right direction. She could feel a bead of sweat dripping down her temple and wiped her brow with the back of her hand. She had taken care with her appearance that morning; blow-dried her hair until it curled onto her shoulders, and put on khakis, a crisp white shirt and a pair of loafers. At the time she'd hoped the outfit struck the right note for a can-do, roll-up-your-sleeves assistant, but right now she was beginning to think she looked like a sweat-soaked sack.

'Too late now,' she said to herself. The phone hadn't lied, she was yards away from the gates to Michael's house.

She walked up and gave them a push: locked.

'Great start,' she said, peering through the bars. There was a 4x4 in the drive, alongside a dusty station wagon that she assumed was the housekeeper's.

She pressed the intercom and waited. When there was no reply, she pressed it again.

'Hello? Michael?' she said, not sure if she was speaking to thin air. Frowning, she checked her text messages from him again: no, she was here at the right time and on the right day.

She scrolled down to his number and pressed 'call', but it went straight to voicemail. Becoming irritated now, she switched to messages and sent a text.

Outside right now. Are you there?

She waited a few more minutes, but when there was still no sign of life at the front door, she grimaced and looked around, wondering what she should do.

The house looked different in the daytime. The bright sun made the shingle frontage more bleached and silvery. She had not been outside onto the deck when they had come for dinner, but Nat had talked glowingly of the property's direct beach access – perhaps she could try that way. Not that I have much choice, she thought, following the fence to the right down a cinder path towards the beach.

Nat had been right: there was a set of steps up from the sand leading to a wooden gate at the rear of the house.

But the gate was shut tight – she was no better off back here; there wasn't even an intercom.

Peering over the gate, she saw a square granite pool with a solitary sunlounger, and a wooden building to one side with a large window facing the sea. Was that Michael's office? Squinting, she could make out a dark figure sitting inside. 'Hello?' she called, waving. Michael – if indeed it was Michael – didn't move.

Strapping on her bag, she wedged one foot in the flimsy-looking fence and hoisted herself up with a grunt. An undignified scramble, a scraped shin and she was over. She made a mental note to bring that up with him at some point; you couldn't be too security-conscious these days. Just the other day she'd heard of a celebrity being robbed by a five-man gang, and that had been in a secure compound in the Hollywood Hills with an on-duty security guard. Then again, at that very moment, a secret alarm bell was probably ringing at some high-tech security firm that was about to dispatch attack dogs and armed police to apprehend her. She quickened her pace towards the studio.

'Hello?' she called. 'Is anyone there?'

At first there was nothing but the sound of the waves, and she thought she must have imagined seeing someone in the little house. She approached the door, jumping back in shock when it opened and Michael stood in front of her.

She almost didn't recognise him. He was unshaven, his eyes hooded. Sweat pants and a T-shirt made him look older than usual, and he was holding a tumbler of dark liquid in one hand.

'Oh,' was his immediate response, and Jem knew instantly that she was an unwelcome guest.

'You said twelve o'clock,' she said quickly, to hide her confusion and embarrassment. 'I thought I was going to be late, but actually I'm a bit early. I can come back later, or tomorrow if that's more convenient? Sorry, I didn't mean to . . .'

Michael just turned around and stepped back into the studio. Jem tentatively followed him inside. It was larger than it had looked from the outside, and much more stylish. It was cosy and chic, like a ski lodge styled by Ralph Lauren, with tartan throws on a wide leather sofa and a coffee table made from artfully styled driftwood. 'Twelve?' said Michael, his voice gravelly. 'I thought bourbon pickled the liver, not the short-term memory.'

He put his glass down on his desk and she realised that he was embarrassed.

'I'm not usually like this before lunchtime,' he said, trying for a smile.

'Oh don't worry,' said Jem. 'I used to be a chalet girl, so I've seen everything. Grown men wearing polar bear outfits and drinking Jägermeister at ten o'clock in the morning insisting it was still après-ski.'

She saw he wasn't smiling and immediately regretted making light of it.

'Is everything okay?' she asked. It occurred to her that perhaps this was how Michael Kearney rolled, that this was all part of his creative process. She'd found a long feature about him online in the *New Yorker*, describing his fifteen-year career as a literary hit-maker, a commercial genius who produced bestseller after bestseller, but it had also alluded to drink problems and a spell in rehab.

'Yes. No,' he said.

'Let me make you some coffee,' she said quickly, spotting a Nespresso machine in the corner.

'It's fine, honestly,' he said, holding up a hand. 'I'm fine.'

Jem shook her head. 'I've worked in enough cafés to know that a cup of tea or coffee can always make you feel better,' she said. It was true: during her many months of service at the Pickled Pantry café in Newquay, she had time and again witnessed the restorative powers of the small and simple things in life. Whether people had come in to escape the cold Cornish winter or had arrived fresh from an argument or a disappointment, they always seemed to leave looking happier and with more colour in their cheeks than when they came in.

'Better than losing yourself in a bottle of whisky anyway,' she said. 'Believe me, that's only going to give you one shitty headache by teatime.'

He looked at her and rubbed his chin.

'After our conversation last weekend I didn't think you would be interested in the job any more,' he said after a moment. 'I was surprised when you texted me. But I wouldn't blame you for having second thoughts right now.'

He didn't need to say the rest: that he looked like a shambling drunk. Booze and the poetic soul were a great tradition among American writers from Hemingway to Bukowski, but there was nothing romantic about the man hunched by the window. He wasn't tapping into the truth of the human condition; he just looked miserable and a little pathetic.

'Do you want to talk about the no?' said Jem, concentrating on putting the capsule in the coffee machine. She turned and watched Michael frown at her.

'The no?' he said.

'I asked if you were okay. You said yes, then no.'

Michael rubbed his eyes, then sat down in the chair in front of his desk. It was one of those expensive ergonomic ones that Nat had insisted on buying for his back, even though it looked too big and bulky for a Brooklyn apartment. It looked equally out of place in Michael's beach hut – like a spaceship dropped in the desert.

'I got an email from my daughter Alex this morning,' he said finally.

Jem nodded encouragingly. Michael had mentioned his divorce at dinner but not his children. She was aware of a family from the *New Yorker* piece but knew nothing beyond that.

'Is she okay?' she asked, fearing the answer.

'She's very okay,' said Michael. 'Getting married next month to Chris, a doctor. Extremely nice guy. I met him at the engagement party. It was up in Boston where they both work. It's where the wedding will be too.'

Jem handed him the coffee and waited for him to continue.

'She wants her stepfather to give her away.' He spoke with undisguised bitterness in his voice, then turned to look imploringly at Jem. 'Am I wrong to feel hurt by that? I'm her actual father,' he said as if he was still trying to process it. 'Did she not realise how hurt I was going to be?'

'Did she say why, in her email?' asked Jem.

'There was some explanation. And a lot of bullshit,' he said, standing up, starting to pace around. 'I mean, am I such a bad man, was I such a terrible father, that I deserve this?'

He powered on without waiting for an answer.

'No, you're right. I probably do,' he said, looking across at the bottle of whisky standing on the desk.

Jem perched on the edge of the leather sofa. She felt uncomfortable being here, and seeing Michael like this was a reminder that people often surprised you. On the previous occasions that she had met him she had found him cool, composed, impressive. Too impressive, if the truth be told. Yet this looked like another man.

'When did your wife remarry?' she asked, keen to keep him talking.

'Sixteen years ago. Almost as soon as our divorce was through,' he snorted. 'We separated not long after I started at *Cover* magazine. I thought it could work, me being in Manhattan, my wife and daughter being in Boston. Sarah didn't want to make the move: Alex was settled at school and New York was only an hour's flight away. I thought we could *make* it work . . .'

'It's hard,' said Jem sympathetically. 'Nat and I even thought about the long-distance thing when he was offered his job in New York.'

'It doesn't work with jobs like ours,' said Michael. 'If it was just the work, maybe, but you find yourself going out with your co-workers for a drink to talk strategy, or going to parties, convincing yourself that you're networking, but the truth is you come to enjoy the status that the job gives you, the fun even. Home, a relationship? That's just problems, hard work.'

Jem didn't say anything, thinking about Nat and his constant reassurances that his presence at events and parties was vital to his career.

'Work was full-on. Chicago one day, Sudan the next. My plan of going back to Boston every weekend soon became going back once a month. Looking back, it came down to choosing between my marriage and my career. I chose my career.'

He peered down at his coffee cup as if he were looking down a well.

'I should hate Tony – that's the new husband – but the truth is, he's a good man; in Alex and her mother's eyes, probably an even better man because he's everything I'm not. He's a family man, a provider, but he's always home for dinner. Reliable, solid . . .'

He stopped and looked at Jem.

'Sometimes I ask myself if I would have become an author

if I was still married. I doubt it,' he said, shaking his head. 'I sat in this shed for three months and didn't come out until I'd finished *Jack Garcia*. You can't do that with a family. But when I started to make money, real money, I tried to make it up to her. I bought Alex a car, an apartment when she went to college. It was a beautiful place, two beds, two baths . . .' His face creased in the realisation that all the material things in the world couldn't make his daughter choose him over her stepfather.

Jem wanted to go over, lay a hand on his shoulder, offer comfort. But what could she possibly say? She imagined what was running through his head at that moment. The family holidays, Thanksgivings, picnics, graduation ceremonies. She wondered how many of those he had gone to. How many his daughter had spent with Sarah's new husband.

'No, I didn't choose my career over my marriage. I chose ambition over my family. I chose selfishness,' he said quietly. 'And where does it get you? A spot at the back of the church.'

'Don't blame yourself.'

'Who the hell else am I going to blame?' he said, spinning around.

'I just mean it's never that simple,' said Jem. 'Okay, so you're a man whose marriage didn't work out. You say your career ended it, but would that have happened if your relationship was strong enough? I don't know the ins and outs of your marriage, but you *could* all have moved to New York: people do. And if your wife chooses to remarry, you can't dictate how that is all going to pan out either.'

She paused.

'Look, I know it's easy for me to say, but you should be glad your wife married a good man. That he has been a good stepfather to your daughter. Better that than a bum . . .'

'Better than me, you mean,' he said, looking out of the window towards the crashing waves on the shore.

'No, that's not what I meant.' Jem wondered what Tony must be like for Sarah Kearney to have picked him over Michael.

'You know, maybe it's not such a good idea,' he said finally.

'What's not a good idea?' asked Jem.

'This goddamn book. I mean, a non-fiction book? We both know what that is. A distraction from the fact that I can't write a real one.'

Jem looked at him in surprise.

'That day we first met,' he said, 'I'd been up since six. In here, staring at a blank screen, desperate to think of a new idea. It's why I went down to the coffee shop; thought maybe I'd come up with the great idea there.' He jabbed a finger against his temple. 'I got nothing. Nothing. It's all gone.'

Jem could feel he was slipping into self-loathing and cast around desperately for a solution.

'Well, you don't have to come up with a totally new idea, do you? People love Jack Garcia so much, you could have an entire novel of him reciting the telephone directory and people would buy it.'

Michael looked at her. 'I've killed him off,' he replied bluntly. 'It's how the new book ends. No one knows yet; it's not out until next month. No review copies either, so the death of Garcia is a big surprise. I convinced my editor that we should start another multimillion-selling series; that after sixteen books Garcia had run his course. But the truth is, I'm done. All dried up. There is no next big idea. Nada,' he said, swiping a hand through the air for emphasis.

'But what about Alice's story? That's a great idea. And I can help you.'

He waved a hand. 'No one is going to be interested. I mean, how many books are you going to sell with a story about some depressed housewife?'

Jem surprised herself by how cross she suddenly felt.

'Is that what everything is about with you? Money?' She could hear the words falling out of her mouth but was unable to stop them. 'Your daughter didn't want the cars or the apartment, remember, she wanted your time. And a book about Alice might not sell as many as a new Garcia, but at least it might help David Holliday understand what happened to his wife that night. And that, I think, is more important than your bloody self-pity.'

Michael looked at her as if he was shell-shocked. His mouth opened and closed, but no sound came out.

'Look, I'm sorry,' said Jem, coming over to sit on the edge of the desk. 'But it's nowhere near as bleak as you're painting it. You have your health, financial security, talent. Don't sit there moaning about how you've made the wrong choices. Just go and make some new ones.'

'But how can I?' he said quietly. 'Alex chose him. She chose her other father.'

'Yes, she did. But that's in the past. All you can do now is move forward, doing better than you did before.'

'Move forward?' said Michael. 'I can't even go to the wedding.'

Jem frowned. 'Why not?'

'Why not? The humiliation of it all. Sitting there watching as someone else walks my daughter down the aisle.'

The anger rose in Jem again.

'This isn't about you, Michael,' she said firmly. 'It's about your daughter having a great day. Yes, your feelings might be hurt, I get that. But whatever made Alex choose her stepdad over you, it's time to face up to it. Spend more time with her, go on vacation together, go for a bloody cup of coffee in Barb's Beans. Be her dad, earn it, don't just expect her to give it to you.'

She stopped, knowing she had overstepped the mark by some distance.

'Look, sorry. I just think . . . No, actually it's none of my business.' She picked up her bag and turned towards the door. 'I'll leave you in peace.'

Michael stepped forward. The office fell silent and she could hear the sound of the waves.

'Thank you,' he said. 'You're right. That needed to be said. And most people wouldn't have had the balls to say any of it.'

He puffed out his cheeks and picked up his tumbler of whisky. Jem thought he was going to drain it; instead he leant forward and tossed the amber liquid out of the open window.

'If you still want to work with me, I'm going to have to trust you to enforce a few rules. No bourbon; that can be a start. In fact, no booze of any kind.'

'So you do want to keep writing?' she said.

'I'm due to deliver a book to my publisher at Christmas, so I'd better get on with it, hadn't I?'

'I guess so,' said Jem with a tentative smile.

'So you're the boss,' said Michael. 'What do I do first?'

Jem laughed. 'First, I think you need a shower.'

Michael nodded and stepped towards the door. Then he seemed to think of something and turned back.

'Are you this blunt with all your friends?' he asked.

'Is that what we are? Friends?'

He raised an eyebrow. 'We'll see.'

Chapter 9

The sun was dipping in the sky, and finally the hazy air was beginning to cool. The slanting rays turned the warm stone of the rear of the house peach and the housemates stirred from their places lounging on the deck. Paul had already gone inside, and Nat and Jem were talking about going for a stroll on the sand. Joel was to the side of the house, playing with his paddleboard, while Angela was reading a book with her head on Todd's stomach like a pillow.

Rebecca lounged languidly in an Adirondack chair, adjusting the wide-brimmed hat that almost covered her face. Purring as she stretched, she turned to Jem. It was the first time anyone had spoken in twenty minutes.

'So tell me about Michael Kearney,' she said, peering over her sunglasses. 'What's he like?'

'He's nice. Surprisingly normal,' said Jem, looking up from her Kindle. She didn't want to admit that she was reading one of Michael's books – her third in the Jack Garcia series so far; she was racing to catch up.

'No one with any sort of celebrity is normal,' said Angela, turning over to apply another layer of sunscreen.

'You said he was cool after you met him at the Glenisters' party,' chipped in Todd.

'Sure, but anyone who has any profile has a rampant

ego,' insisted Angela. 'They can't help themselves. We had a psychologist on the show who insists there is a direct link between creativity and narcissism.'

As if to prove the point, Erica interjected.

'By the way, I spoke to my editor, and Michael isn't really right for an "At Home" feature, but I was telling the fashion director about the house, and we thought it would be perfect for a shoot – you know, some sort of librarian chic with Michael hanging around in the background on a typewriter.'

'I'm not sure it's his style,' said Jem honestly.

'No, obviously Michael Kearney wouldn't want a bevy of gorgeous models hanging around his house.' Rebecca smiled cynically.

Jem had to admit she had a point, even though she didn't like the idea of her boss being surrounded by beautiful women hanging on his every word.

'Nat, are you really okay with this arrangement?' said Joel, walking over, half into his wetsuit. 'You know most women around here think Kearney's hot.'

'Yes, the local newspaper once called him "the George Clooney of the literary world",' agreed Erica, reaching up to zip Joel's suit closed.

'George Clooney doesn't seem quite so hot now he's married,' said Angela, as if she were handing down a judgement.

'That's what marriage does to you,' drawled Todd.

'You will always be my Captain America,' said Angela, patting his bare white knee.

'Come on, everyone – Michael's my boss,' said Jem, feeling hot and uncomfortable. 'Can we please not talk about him as if he were a sex object?'

'What else do you want us to talk about over cocktails in the sunshine?' grinned Rebecca, waving her glass towards Todd, who lifted a pitcher to give her a refill.

'You know, I'm going to miss this place,' said Erica, extending an arm like a self-satisfied tiger.

'Don't worry. Labor Day is a long way off,' said Rebecca sagely.

'No, I mean next year.'

'Next year?' said Nat. 'What do you mean?'

'Well, we'll have our own place by then.'

'You're buying in the Hamptons?' said Nat, sitting up.

'Who said the financial sector was in crisis?' said Todd, sipping his cocktail, then lifting the glass towards Joel in salute, 'To the victors, the spoils.'

Joel responded by flipping him the bird with a lopsided grin.

'Didn't you hear?' said Erica to Nat. 'Joel got a great bonus and we're sinking it into a place out near Montauk. Just four beds, maybe five after the remod, gorgeous views up to the lighthouse; it's your basic dream house.'

'Or your basic money-pit nightmare,' said Joel, picking up his board and heading towards the beach.

Rebecca sat up and waved a fan in front of her face.

'Why don't you just rent it out?' she said. 'That way you can still stay here. How is a big, empty house in Montauk going to compare to this?'

'You know I love the summers in this house, and I always thought it would carry on forever,' said Erica, with a slightly smug tone. 'But this new place will be ours. Hey, why don't you all come to us next year?'

Angela shook her head. 'I knew you'd be the weak link,' she said, directing a smile that wasn't entirely good-natured at Erica.

'Well, let's make the most of it,' said Erica, as she settled back to look at Instagram on her phone.

Feeling the sinking temperatures of both kinds on the deck, Jem stood up and held out a hand to Nat.

'Shall we walk along the shore?'

'Sure,' said Nat, throwing a navy sweater over his shoulders. Jem smiled to herself as she slipped a kaftan over her own head. It wouldn't be cold enough for a jumper for hours, but Nat was all about image, and recently he had been going for a weather-beaten preppy look. Assimilate, adapt, become one with your surroundings. If her husband was an animal, he'd be a chameleon.

He reached up to open the little gate and they walked along the worn boardwalk and out onto the warm sand.

'Did you know Joel and Erica were buying a place?' asked Nat when they were a safe distance down the shore.

'First I'd heard of it,' said Jem.

'I mean, how can they afford it?' said Nat. He seemed put out to be the last to hear the news.

Jem smiled. 'Joel is a banker. Of course he can afford it.'

Nat looked unconvinced. 'He's not that senior. A VP at his level can't be pulling in more than a quarter of a mil a year.'

She gave him a sideways look. It was funny how Nat always knew how much everyone was earning, as if he had mentally plotted it all on league tables: who was up, who was down, who was due a promotion or relegation. It was also odd how annoyed he could become about it.

'What's this about?' she teased. 'House envy?'

'Me, jealous of Joel? No way!' he huffed.

'Not even a teeny-tiny bit?'

He paused and dropped her hand.

'I'm not jealous, Jem. But sometimes you have to wonder if you've made the right career choices.'

Jem frowned. 'But you love your job.'

'Yes, but I've got a bloody Cambridge degree, I'm top of my game and yet we've got a two-bedroom cottage in a grotty part of London and a rented flat in Brooklyn. Where's our luxury house by the ocean?'

'About two hundred yards away,' she replied.

'It's a rental,' he sniffed. 'And that's all we are ever going to afford.'

She was taken aback by his bitter tone and felt her own mood sour.

'Nat, you can't have everything.'

'What's that supposed to mean?' he asked, and Jem began to get the feeling he was spoiling for a fight.

'Nothing bad, just that you love your job, it's fun and glamorous and we get to live a life we couldn't otherwise afford. It's pretty good, isn't it?'

'Yes, but what happens when the job stops?'

That made Jem pause. 'Why do you say that? Has something happened at work?'

'What? No! In fact Jeremy – you know, the publisher? – told me they might well be considering me for a wider role in the company very soon.'

Jem glanced over and saw the fire in his eyes. She knew how much his career meant to him, and that she should support him. But still, his blind ambition, his desperation to succeed in New York was making him lose his perspective on what was really important, and as his wife, Jem knew that it was her job to ground him.

'Does it matter really?' she said, the tone of her voice softening. 'I mean, does it matter if it's just me and you and a takeaway in Kensal Rise, which, as you know, is considered very des res these days.'

She took his hand, wondering if this was the right moment to say the words.

'I bet Joel and Erica have a baby by this time next year,' she said, watching his face carefully.

Nat shook his head, not rising to the bait. 'I've always got the sense that no one in the house wants a family any time soon. I've heard them all say as much.'

'Come on,' said Jem, wanting to press the point. 'Joel has too much of an ego not to want to procreate and produce lots of mini Joels. And I saw Erica taking folic acid supplements. I think they're trying.'

Nat fell silent, but Jem knew she couldn't back away from the subject now. Since their morning of lovemaking the week before, things had improved dramatically in that department and they needed to talk about what might happen.

'And what about us?' she said after a moment.

Nat didn't say anything, so she carried on.

'When we talked about moving to New York, you said we should have a baby when we're out here. To get an American passport.'

'I wasn't being entirely serious,' he said. 'As much as our future child would thank us for not having to wait in a mile-long immigration queue every time he came out here, I think having a child for a passport is the wrong reason, don't you?'

She admitted he had a point, but knew she had to pursue the conversation.

'I'm thirty-four next month, Nat,' she said more seriously. 'That's a better reason to start trying for a family, isn't it?'

Nat's face softened. 'Jem, despite what women's magazines try and tell you, thirty-four is still young. It's too soon to think about tying ourselves down. In fact I've been meaning to bring this up.'

Jem looked at him and frowned. 'What?'

He hesitated as if he was bracing himself.

'I think you should go back on the pill.'

She gaped at him. She'd come off the pill eighteen months earlier when they'd had a first half-hearted attempt at trying for a baby. Whilst other friends who didn't conceive immediately were buying ovulation kits, making their husbands wear boxer shorts and going to fertility clinics, Jem and Nat had, well, just stopped trying.

'I thought you wanted a family,' she said, feeling suddenly emotional.

'I do,' he replied frankly. 'But when we were trying last time, that was when we were in London and settled. Right now, I'm so busy and I'm just not sure New York is the right place to bring up a child.'

'There are children being born in New York every day,' she said, hearing a wobble in her voice.

Nat stopped in the sand and turned to look at her. 'Come on Jem, don't do this. There's no rush.'

'Nat, it's hardly a sudden thing. We've been married five years. Surely we don't want to leave it much later.'

'Says who?' said Nat, with obvious frustration. 'Some fertility-scare feature you've read in the *Daily Mail*?'

If she'd expected sympathy from him, she realised she wasn't going to get any.

'I want to start trying again. Soon,' she said determined to stand her ground.

Nat shook his head and looked less sympathetic. 'You're beginning to sound like a bored housewife. I thought you were enjoying the Hamptons. Imagine what it'd be like if we had a toddler. There'd be no house, no parties, certainly no job with Michael Kearney.'

'That's temporary.'

'Maybe not,' he said with feeling. 'Remember, his last assistant is on maternity leave, and you know how often women just don't come back after the birth. *Celine* doesn't exactly sound like she needs the pin money.'

Jem bristled at the implication that whatever job she got would be just a petty distraction to keep the little woman happy. But she knew she needed to press the bigger issue.

'If now isn't the time to start a family, then when is?'

He gave a long sigh and looked out towards the ocean.

'We should just wait. It doesn't make sense while we're in New York. Our flat isn't big enough for the two of us, let alone all the crap you need for a baby.'

Jem could see he'd made up his mind but she couldn't let it drop. She tried a different approach.

'But we're not going to be here forever. It's been six months already. Another year will go by and before we know it we'll be heading back home.'

'You're talking like we have a rigid schedule.'

She looked at him, puzzled. 'But that was always the deal. Eighteen months in Manhattan and then we go home.'

'Jem, we've only just got here. There's the prospect of promotion for me, not to mention another summer at the beach house. Erica and Joel might be off, but that just means we can have their room with the bigger balcony.'

It finally began to dawn on her. How could she have been so stupid?

'You don't want to go home, do you?' she said, a croak in her voice.

He paused. Jem was angry with him, but she could see a hint of his vulnerability, his desperate desire to cling on to everything he had created around him.

'I like it here,' he said honestly. 'Don't you? And what's there to go back to? Rain, stupid house prices and a massive commute? Out here, I'm getting noticed, I really feel I've got a future. An exciting future. *Our* future.'

She thought of Michael Kearney and his confession about ambition poisoning his relationship. She wanted to stop Nat and remind him of everything that Michael had told them at dinner. How traditional media – the magazines and newspapers Nat so loved – was dying. How thirty-five-year-old senior executives would soon become eminently dispensable when there was a new tech-savvy generation coming up behind, digital natives who would work for nothing, who were happy just to get a few 'likes'. And that was without even adding in the fact that they were in New York, the world capital of the brutal and the ruthless. Here, people would chew you up and spit you out without even blinking. Nat's friends – or the people he thought were his friends – would cut his throat if they thought it would get them one more rung up the ladder.

Michael had told them all this, but Nat hadn't heard it, Jem knew that. Nat's unshakeable self-belief and sense of entitlement was his great strength; it allowed him to go up to anyone at a party and immediately tell them how great he was, that they should work together, hand them his card. But it also blinded him to the politics of his industry, the unthinkable notion that a publisher or a director might consider anyone else above him. It was one of the things Jem loved about her husband; he was a charmer, a self-publicist, but he wasn't a back-stabber, and in the shark pool of New York, that made him vulnerable. If Nat was vulnerable, that meant Jem was too.

She chose to stay silent, knowing that it was wise to choose her battles, or at least save them for another time. He slipped his arm across her shoulders, and she let him leave it there as they walked back to the house.

Chapter 10

Jem had never been to Milan or Paris, but this was how she imagined a fashion-week party would look. The Heyse hotel was a swish upmarket affair, one of the few boutique hotels in the Upper West Side, and the bar had a similar feel to the lobby: subdued pink neon lighting, black leather stools, designer cocktails with catwalk prices and a clientele of beautiful thirty-somethings who had Madison Avenue charge accounts and sleek town cars with drivers idling at the kerb outside. To say Jem felt out of place was a mammoth understatement, but she took some comfort from the fact that she was meeting Michael Kearney, who looked completely at home when she spotted him at the bar.

This was a different Michael to the one she had seen on Monday morning; in a pair of chinos and a white shirt that made him look relaxed and tanned, he could have come straight out of the *New York Times* lifestyle pages, and as Jem crossed the room she noticed an attractive blonde to Michael's right unable to keep her eyes off him. She quickened her pace and took the stool beside her employer.

'Hey,' he said, summoning the waiter for the cocktail menu. He put his phone back in his pocket, and Jem wondered who he had been texting.

'So what's it like being back in the city?' she smiled,

casting her eyes over the delicious-sounding drinks but opting for a Diet Coke.

'I used to come up here a lot in the old days,' said Michael, looking around. 'The drinks were about a tenth of the price, though.'

'That was twenty years ago,' she teased. 'Did they even have bars back then?'

Michael smiled and knocked back his drink. 'So you live in this part of town?'

Jem shook her head. 'I wish. Maybe back in the day you could afford Manhattan on a journalist's salary, but nowadays? Fuggetaboutit,' she said, in a very poor imitation of a TV gangster.

Michael laughed. 'I'm not sure your career in the Mafia has much future, Mary Poppins.'

Jem laughed along, enjoying Michael's company. They were now into their second week working together, and they had settled into the sort of relationship of friendly banter and gentle ribbing that Jem realised she had missed since leaving England. Or maybe she was covering her nerves. They were, after all, here to see David Holliday, and despite their positive first meeting at the gallery, there was a good chance he'd had second thoughts about the investigation.

'So where *do* you live?' Michael asked.

'Brooklyn.'

'I forgot.' He nodded sagely. 'All you trendy young things live across the water now. Back in the day we'd call you the Bridge and Tunnel set, and that was not a compliment.'

'Well, now we're paying an obscene amount for the privilege of being outside looking in. You do get the views across to that famous New York skyline – if you're prepared to walk all the way down to the water, that is.'

'Have you been to the open-air jazz club yet?'

Jem shook her head.

'I should take the two of you. That's if you don't mind being seen with a man who remembers swing the first time it came round.'

'You're not that old.'

Jem winced at the way it came out. She didn't want to offend him, especially when the thought of a night out in a jazz bar with great food and better music was an appealing one.

'So what have you been doing since you've been in da Big Apple?' he asked, imitating her cod-Brooklyn accent.

Jem smiled down at her Coke, stirring the ice cubes around.

'Not much, actually.'

'Come on, you must have done plenty. It's the greatest city in the world.'

'I thought you said London was the greatest city in the world.'

He pointed at her. 'You have too good a memory. And don't expect me to be consistent.'

'Nat is so busy the whole time, we haven't really had much time to explore. His job means he has to go out a lot after work.'

'So why don't you go with him?' He looked at her as if he were stating the obvious.

'I do, sometimes. But no one really wants to talk to the wife.'

Michael smiled. 'Tell me it's none of my business if you like, but I say go to everything. Why did you come if you weren't going to throw yourself into New York life?'

Jem smiled to herself. Trust a writer to cut straight to the core of it. The funny thing was, no one else had ever asked her that. Why come to New York? It was like asking someone, 'Do you want to win the lottery?' Everyone assumed you'd simply jump at the chance of spending a few years living somewhere in the five boroughs.

'I guess you don't think it through when the opportunity is presented to you. Nat wanted it so desperately and I think I had this romantic idea of a grown-up gap year. I never got to do anything like that when I was younger; in fact this is my first time in America.'

Michael lifted his glass and chinked it against hers. 'Well, America welcomes you. Now, how long do you plan to stay?'

Jem laughed. 'That's what the immigration guy wanted to know.' She forced a smile, trying not to think back to the conversation with Nat on the beach last weekend.

She noticed the blonde still looking over at Michael, and nudged her boss in the elbow.

'If we weren't going to David's, I'd say it was your lucky night.'

Michael looked surprised, and Jem felt herself blush, realising her words might sound like a come-on.

'The woman behind you. I think she's going to come over. Maybe for an autograph or something.'

Michael didn't even turn. He swirled his drink around his glass and smiled.

'Shame you didn't get here five minutes earlier. You'd have experienced the great New York tradition of prostitution first hand.'

'Prostitution?' she whispered, stealing a glance across at the woman. She was well dressed, not at all like the stereotype; more like a particularly glamorous office worker on her way home. 'She's a *hooker*? How do you know?'

'I spent twenty years haunting bars like this. Besides, just before you came in, she made a play.'

'A play?' said Jem, wondering how enthusiastically he had dismissed her. She didn't know anything about Michael's relationship status; there had been no mention of a significant other, so she assumed he was single, even though it was hard to believe. For all she knew, hotel bar hook-ups might be what he was into.

'I said I was meeting someone,' smiled Michael, as if he were answering her question. 'And she said you could join in for an extra hundred.'

'Welcome to the New York sisterhood,' muttered Jem, picking up her bag, suddenly anxious to leave.

'Now you're getting what Manhattan's all about,' laughed Michael.

David's apartment was on the Hudson seaboard. It was not a part of town that Jem knew. She had no reason to come out here; no one did really, unless they were lucky enough or rich enough to own an apartment in one of the smart condo buildings in this pocket of the Upper West Side. One thing that had always struck Jem was that Manhattan was such an adult place; you never saw children unless you happened to be passing one of the few playgrounds in Central Park. But out here, there were plenty – a girl in school uniform walking a sausage dog, a pair of kids in matching checked shirts racing along the sidewalk on wheelie shoes. There seemed to be more trees too; real ones, with thick trunks and broad leaves, not the choked and gnarled things struggling to breathe in Lower Manhattan.

The Holliday block was a big one – maybe fifteen storeys high, with an awning over the sidewalk, like a hotel on the Upper East Side. The building had a burly doorman with gold-braid epaulettes who directed them to the tiny elevator, which slowly clanked its way to the seventh floor, enough time for Jem to become seized by a flurry of nerves. The problem was that there was no real plan. Jem had emailed David and suggested a meeting, to which David had promptly replied inviting them to come round for dinner. It seemed a friendly enough gesture, but it could just as easily be a trap, a chance for him to rant at them or even to produce legal gagging papers – Jem's mind had been working overtime.

It didn't help that Michael had been so cagey about his investigation. Yes, Jem had been working with him at the house, but she'd had a separate office and had mainly been involved in fan-based admin, replying to enquiries and getting Michael's online presence off the ground. She would see him for just half an hour at either end of the day, and even then he would excuse himself to make a call.

Jem had tried to broach the subject of Alice, of course, especially when this date had been arranged, but Michael had met every enquiry with a terse 'Let's see what David has to say first'.

The elevator pinged and Jem slid the concertina door open, trying not to look at the gap between the lift car and the floor of the corridor. Somehow it seemed to be a metaphor for what they were doing: flirting with danger and not quite joining the dots.

Michael rapped on the door of apartment 19 and Jem was relieved to see David open the door alone and with a welcoming smile.

At least it's not a trap, she thought as he ushered them inside. Not yet anyway.

'This place is huge,' she said as they were shown into a comfortable living room. 'I didn't think anyone in Manhattan had elbow room.'

It was also surprisingly traditional: heavy furniture, Persian rugs over polished parquet flooring, and prints of horses in gilt frames. Jem supposed she had imagined Alice living somewhere fashionable, chic, minimal; somewhere more in keeping with the breezy lifestyle of parties in the

Hamptons and gallery openings. Instead the Hollidays' apartment had the feel of family money, solid, prosperous rather than desirable. The walls were papered with Toile, books were stacked in a neat pile on the coffee table, while a substantial sideboard was covered with photos of David and Alice: a wedding photograph, skiing, on a city break. No pictures, she noted, that looked as if they were taken in the Hamptons.

'Is it so big?' said David. 'I suppose I'm too used to it. It certainly feels as though I'm rattling around since . . . well, now that it's just me.' He clapped his hands. 'Now then, what can I get you to drink? I have all the usual things, and I've opened a rather good bottle of Bordeaux for dinner.'

'A gin and tonic, please. Just a small one, though,' said Jem, wanting to be polite.

Michael held up a more confident hand. 'Water's fine.'

'Oh, I think we can do a little better than that,' said David. 'Something fizzy; I've got a few of those fruity things in the icebox.'

He went through to the kitchen, making clanking and chinking noises. 'I can't remember when I last had people round for dinner,' he called. 'So I didn't think I'd chance my cooking.'

He walked back with their drinks.

'I've had some Chinese food delivered; it's very good, lots of choice – I hope that's okay.'

Jem felt a surge of affection for the man. It was an extraordinary gesture to be so hospitable when you considered that he didn't know either of them and had no real idea what their plans were. They could, after all, be here to drag his wife's memory through the mud, take advantage of a grieving man.

'As I'm sure you know, I'm a lecturer in literature, so I can't tell you how much of an honour it is to have a best-selling author to visit. You must tell me everything about your process; I've always wondered how something truly gets from the spark of an idea to a fully written manuscript.'

Michael answered his questions politely at first, clearly a man used to being interviewed, but Jem could tell he was beginning to warm to the task as David asked more probing questions, taking more time with his answers, rubbing his chin and musing, 'Do you know, nobody has ever asked me that before.' Jem too found it interesting to listen to Michael's approach; he was from the school of thought that preferred spontaneity, creating his characters and a loose framework, then letting them run. 'Some people plot it out line by line,' he said, 'but I find it keeps the characters more real if you're effectively letting them make their own decisions day by day.'

'Fascinating,' said David, and Jem believed he meant it. She didn't imagine that David Holliday usually had much time for a populist writer like Michael Kearney – his bookshelves were crowded with American classics and weighty prize-winning books, with not a single thriller or romance novel anywhere – but if he felt any condescension, he did well to hide it. In fact, he oozed the old-school polish of someone brought up to make people feel at ease, never compensating with the aren't-we-old-pals overfriendliness that Nat employed.

They sat down to dinner at a long formal dining table with expensive glassware and linen napkins, but the food was still served from the white wedge-shaped takeout cartons Jem so loved. It was refreshingly relaxed, but formal enough that it felt a fitting place to begin talking about the real purpose of their visit.

'Before we even start this conversation, I just want to ask if I can trust you,' said David, leaning forward.

'Trust us?' said Michael, sipping at a glass of water.

'Well, you want to look into Alice's story, and so do I, but really what is it for? What is your purpose? A salacious novel? A movie script? A magazine exposé? I think it's only fair that if I'm laying my cards on the table, so to speak, then so should you. That's why I've invited you to the apartment. I always believe that once you have been into someone's home and accepted their Chinese takeaway, it's more difficult to screw that person over.'

'I can understand you asking,' replied Michael. 'But if you want a truthful answer, then that answer is I honestly don't know. Because I don't know what we're going to find. Perhaps it will lend itself to a non-fiction investigation of the facts, or it might be better to fictionalise the story in order to better reveal the true nature of the crime.'

'Crime? Why do you say that?'

Michael shook his head. 'Sorry, old habits. I was an investigative reporter for a long time and often it involved a crime.'

'I remember your work,' said David. 'You did something on the Colombian hostages.'

Michael looked surprised. 'Good memory,' he said.

'Good story,' said David.

Jem could tell that Michael had enjoyed the compliment. He'd said 'old habits', but she could see he was relishing getting back in touch with them. In the short time she had worked for him, she had become familiar with the fan mail, star-struck readers fawning over him, telling him his novels were the best they'd ever read. After the first few times it must lose its meaning, but Jem could see that there was real pleasure both in David's appreciation of his earlier work and in the prospect of getting back in the saddle, doing something he knew he was good at.

'One thing I had, the one thing I think I've still got,' continued Michael, 'is a nose for a story. I remember reading about Alice last year, wondering if there was more to it than the frankly sketchy things in the papers. My instinct was that something was wrong. I didn't have enough facts to decide where that feeling came from, but that was how I felt.'

He paused, as if to collect his thoughts, and then looked directly at David.

'I don't need to tell you that Alice's death wasn't investigated as thoroughly as it could have been. That's the problem with death by drowning. The simplest explanation is that it was an accident. But from what I've heard, it was as if the attending officers arrived with their minds made up that night. Even if they hadn't, it was difficult to pull any print or biological evidence from the pool garden because the area was wet and contaminated. Proof of foul play is always tough in these circumstances, but that was all the more reason for the housemates to have been questioned in depth. In any investigation you're looking for means, motive and opportunity, and yet according to my sources, the police hardly spoke to anyone. Until someone quizzes everyone who might know something about why Alice died, why she was found dead in a swimming pool she wouldn't ordinarily go anywhere near, I don't think you can rule out that it wasn't a crime.'

David looked at him for a long moment and Jem was equally transfixed. She had never seen Michael so animated or passionate. It was a convincing performance, there was no question about that, but all the same she found herself feeling ever more uncomfortable. Because the questions Michael was proposing to ask would be put to her friends, the people she spent her weekends with, the men who stood next to her at the barbecue, the women who swapped make-up and sun cream. There were no two ways about it: it was going to get messy.

It seemed David was thinking the same thing.

'Does the group at the beach house know what you're doing?' He directed the question to both of them, but looked at Jem when he spoke.

'No, not yet. We wanted to speak to you first,' she said.

'They won't like it, you know that, don't you? You probably know them well enough by now to know they're an ambitious lot.' He said it with some distaste. 'All of them have their sights set higher than where they are now. Angela told me once she wants to be a network chief, and I don't doubt that she'll get there. Rebecca will be the next Larry Gagosian if she keeps going the same way. They were all my friends and they were supportive when Alice died, but that all fell away very quickly.'

'Why?' asked Jem.

'Because no one wants to be associated with something like this, no one wants to have a shadow, a question mark hanging over them. That's one of the reasons I was interested in your investigation. Right now, Alice is a question mark, and when there's uncertainty in a closed community like that, what happens?'

'Gossip,' said Michael.

David nodded. 'You're a resident, Mr Kearney, I'm sure you've heard one variation or another. Suicide, murder, government conspiracy; I've even heard some nonsense about a treasure map. In the absence of facts, people create their own. And I don't want that. I want Alice to be laid to rest properly.'

'I've got a question for you,' said Michael, sitting back in his chair.

'A question?' said David with the air of a college professor. Jem could easily picture him in a gown at the front of the lecture theatre.

'The most obvious one,' said Michael more cautiously.

'What if we find out something unpalatable, something you would prefer didn't come out?'

David steepled his fingers in front of his mouth. His face suddenly seemed older to Jem, more drawn, his eyes sunken. In that moment she could see the poison that not knowing had been to him.

'Then at least we can all move on. Believe me, I have considered the possibilities and have done my best to make peace with them all.' He looked up, locking eyes with Michael. 'But make no mistake, this is my life and Alice is – was – my wife. I don't want to give you access if you're just going to showboat and play Truman Capote. I need to know that she is in good hands, so I'll ask you again. Can I trust you?'

Michael nodded without hesitation. 'I was a journalist, so I'm not sure how much you think my word of honour is worth, but I can promise you this: if I look into Alice's life and we find out nothing beyond the fact that it was a terrible accident, then I will hand over everything to you to do as you wish.'

'And if there's more?'

'Then you have my word that I will do my utmost to get to the very bottom of it, and that I will treat everything I find out with respect.'

David nodded and wiped his mouth with a napkin. 'Fine,' he said, standing. 'Thank you for your candour. Now I have something for you both if you'd just like to follow me.'

He led them out of the dining room into the hall. As they walked, he filled them in on the timeline of Alice's death. According to the best estimate of the police, having spoken to the housemates and David himself, Alice left the party at around 8.45, and was discovered by David forty-five minutes later when he went to find her.

'Alice used to call this her dressing room,' he said, changing the subject as they arrived at a box room at the end of the hall. 'I was always getting into trouble for keeping what she called my junk in it.'

He gestured towards a set of dumb bells and a clutch of tennis rackets in the corner. Above them were rows of immaculately tidy rails.

'She had so many clothes,' he said quietly, running a hand over a coat. 'I never understood why she needed so many. Summer clothes, winter clothes, party clothes, gym clothes. She had most of the closet space in our bedroom, but recently I moved everything in here.'

Jem smiled kindly. She knew what he was saying. That he had begun to move on but he couldn't quite get rid of his wife's belongings, not yet.

David noticed Michael clocking the stack of storage boxes with the word 'Alice' written in marker on the sides, and the shoeboxes complete with Polaroid images of the shoes they contained.

'Sorry, it must look a bit like a shrine,' he said apologetically. 'It's not meant to be. It's just I keep most of her stuff here now.'

The three of them stood and looked around.

'I don't know where you want to start, but here might be as good a place as any. It looks ordered, but dig deep and it's all rather a jumble, I'm afraid. Letters, invoices, party invitations, photos, everything she'd hoarded over the years. Her laptop and phone are in there too. Feel free to take those boxes away.' He cleared his throat and turned to Jem. 'So long as you bring them back,' he added awkwardly.

'Of course,' she said. She looked back and forth between David and Michael. 'So we can go ahead? With the investigation, I mean?'

'Oh, of course,' said David. 'I thought that was understood. As I believe the lady in *Jerry Maguire* says, "You had me at hello".'

Jem's confusion must have been obvious, because David continued. 'I knew you were the right person for the job from the moment we spoke at the gallery. I simply needed to hear Mr Kearney say that I could trust you both.'

He turned to Michael. 'It was a very pretty speech, but a yes would have sufficed.'

'Why?' said Jem. 'I mean, why are you trusting us?'

'Because you care, Ms Chapman. And because Mr Kearney gave me his word. That's all that matters in this world, that and faith. Any student of literature will tell you that.'

Still confused, but also excited, Jem picked up one of the heavy boxes and followed David Holliday back towards the apartment entrance.

'One other thing, Ms Chapman,' said David as they paused at the front door. 'My reference to *Rear Window* at the gallery; you have seen that film?'

'Yes, of course. I love Grace Kelly.'

'Keep that in mind when you're going through Alice's things.'

Jem assured him that she would, then they both thanked him for dinner and turned down the corridor towards the lift.

'What was that all about?' whispered Jem when they were out of earshot.

'*Rear Window*?' said Michael. 'Oh, he's trying to tell you that he thinks one of his wife's neighbours killed her.'

Chapter 11

Ever since she had moved to New York, Jem had heard the expression 'Everyone lives in Brooklyn', and these days she was discovering it was true. Everyone lived in Brooklyn, even people Jem wanted to speak to about Alice Holliday's death.

She took her coffee from the counter and carried it – carefully; she'd been super-careful whenever she had a coffee under her control since the incident in Barb's Beans – to a table by the window where she could see everyone coming and going. Tina Baker lived in Brooklyn, and Tina had been one of Alice's closest friends. In fact there was a good chance that Jem and Tina had brushed shoulders in this café or one of the many others Tina posted pictures of on Facebook. According to her profile, Tina Baker only did three things: drink perfect cappuccinos (dozens of pictures in close-up), eat super-healthy meals (ditto photos of glistening sugar snaps and broccoli stalks) and visit the gym (lots of beaming group shots with other toned women in gym gear). At least that meant Jem knew what she looked like, which took a little of the guesswork out of the meeting. Beyond that, she was feeling completely out of her depth.

She had of course asked Michael for advice and he had said, 'You want to know the secret of interviewing someone?

Think about what you would like to know, then ask them that. It sounds easy, but it's hard as hell, because the questions you want the answers to are usually the questions they don't want to answer.'

'So how do I get them to answer?' Jem had asked, her nerves even worse now that the award-winning investigative reporter had described the task as 'hard as hell'.

'Be yourself,' Michael had smiled. 'That's why I'm sending you. Trust me, you'll get more out of her than I ever could.'

Jem appreciated the vote of confidence, but she wished she shared his optimism. Of course, she had done this sort of work before; when she had worked as a waitress back in Cornwall, she had become good at spotting the people who came into the café to talk. The old people, the young mums left alone with a baby all day who came in to get a coffee and just interact with other adults. Sometimes people wanted to unload a worry or share something they couldn't tell anyone else. One girl, a complete stranger, had told Jem that she had just done a positive pregnancy test. She looked young and vulnerable and Jem was just about to commiserate when the woman had practically burst into song with excitement. She was waiting for her husband to come home from work and just had to tell someone her good news.

Tina Baker looked like the sort of woman who loved to talk. Jem spotted her even before she had pushed the door open. Dressed in the latest high-end gym gear, her auburn hair pulled back in a ponytail, emphasising her girl-next-door beauty. The Lycra showed off her toned curves perfectly. Perhaps that was why she posted so many gym shots; Jem doubted the woman looked any better than this in a ball gown.

Nervously she went over and introduced herself, insisting on buying Tina's coffee – she had no idea about the etiquette of the interview, but as Tina was doing her the favour, it only seemed fair. She was right about Tina's love of talking; she didn't have to worry about filling the silence. Before they had even made it back to the table, Tina had told her that she had lived in Brooklyn for five years, having moved here from upstate New York to teach Pilates, which was how she had met Alice. She had also recommended two other cafés for their 'amazing banana bread' and promised to give Jem her recipe for a kale and blueberry smoothie 'just to die for'.

'So you said on the phone you're sharing at the beach house this year,' said Tina when they were finally settled at the table. 'What's the set-up there? I never understood it. Do you share all the food bills and stuff?'

'Mostly we take it in turns to buy groceries,' said Jem. 'Didn't Alice tell you about it?'

Tina shook her head, her ponytail bobbing. 'David and Alice just did one summer there. I only ask because I'm not sure she particularly got on with the others in the house. But what a great house, huh? I saw photos. So nice, I wish I could spend my summer there.'

That set her off on an anecdote about her friend Candice who had done a house-swap with a couple in San Francisco and got home to find they'd been wearing her clothes. 'Took them right out of the wardrobe, can you imagine? Didn't even get them laundered at the end.'

Again Jem found herself floundering. Should she cut Tina off? Steer the conversation back towards what she wanted to ask? Or just wait it out? She chose the last, not that Tina gave her much of an option; she barely seemed to take a breath, let alone pause. Jem waited until Tina took a dainty sip of her coffee.

'You said Alice didn't really get on with David's friends; why do you think that was?'

'I got the impression some of them have their thumbs stuck up where the sun don't shine.'

Jem smiled. She didn't know what Alice had told Tina, but it was possibly a little unfair.

'You know when someone's rich and just wants you to know? I meet people like that all the time at the gym. They're friendly enough, but every now and then you just feel it.'

'Feel what?' asked Jem.

'The cliquishness. Like you're one of them but not really. Alice thought that about the group. They have these close, tight bonds. Old money, Ivy League, went to boarding school together or whatever. You're never going to break into that even if you marry one of them.'

'So you think Alice felt that way? An outsider?'

'Oh Alice was beautiful – she could mix in any crowd – but even she could never crack the beach house crowd. They made her feel who she was – a poor girl from Indiana who barely scraped high school.'

Jem nodded, trying not to show her surprise. She hadn't known this detail about Alice, hadn't known very much at all beyond the assumptions she had made: chiefly that Alice *had* been one of the Hamptons crowd, the typical New York blonde who played down her privilege just enough so that you would like her. She was thinking it through so intently, she hadn't noticed that Tina was looking at her.

'So why are we meeting?' Tina asked. 'Why all the questions about Alice all of a sudden?'

Jem paused, not sure how much she could say. But she needed all the help she could get, and the best way to do that was to get Tina onside.

'I have a friend, a writer. He's not sure Alice's death was an accident. I'm helping him look into it by speaking to people who knew her.'

'Not an accident? You think she jumped?' Tina shook her head. 'Uh-uh. No way.'

She paused and narrowed her eyes.

'Does David know about this?'

'I wouldn't be speaking to you if it wasn't what David wanted.'

Jem let that sink in.

'So what do you think, Tina?

'Alice wouldn't have killed herself, I know that much.' She fixed Jem with a hard stare. 'Now tell me what *you* think.'

Jem was taken aback, didn't know what to say. She wanted to tell Tina the truth, but she hadn't really made up her mind yet. There just wasn't enough information.

'Tina, I didn't know Alice, I can't even make a guess. But I do know David doesn't think she killed herself either . . .' She trailed off.

'And?'

'Well, perhaps it's hard for him to accept that she did, because then he'd have to face the fact that he missed the signs she was unhappy.'

'Alice wasn't unhappy,' said Tina matter-of-factly.

Jem was surprised. 'Really? How do you know?'

Tina looked away and shook her head.

'Tina?' said Jem softly. 'If you know something . . .'

Tina took a deep breath. 'David is a good guy,' she said softly.

Jem observed in a detached way that the machine-gun-prattling Tina who had walked in two minutes ago had completely disappeared. Now there was just this pretty woman who looked like she was struggling with the world's biggest dilemma. And then Jem saw that there were tears sparkling in Tina's eyes.

'Hey,' she said, putting her hand on the other woman's. 'What's wrong?'

'She was happy. I know she was.'

'How do you know?'

'She told me she'd met someone. I could tell she really liked whoever it was. Her eyes sparkled when she mentioned him.'

'Alice was having an affair?' said Jem, eyes wide.

Tina nodded. 'Yes. I don't know who with, but whoever it was made her happy.'

'Do you think she wanted to leave David?'

'I'm not sure. Maybe.' Tina brushed away a tear with an index finger. 'She and David were doing couple counselling. She'd had another affair a couple of years earlier and I don't think David got over that.'

'Did he know about the new guy?'

Tina shook her head. 'I don't think so.'

She closed her eyes before she spoke again.

'Look, Alice wasn't perfect; she liked male attention and yes, she got tempted occasionally. She was confused for sure. At first I think she wanted her marriage to work, but whoever had come into her life just made her glow.'

'And did you say this to the police?'

Tina paused for a moment and looked into her coffee cup, running one perfect nail around the foam at the rim.

'No.'

'Why not?'

'Because I like David and it would have made him look bad. Real bad.'

'Do you think David found out about the affair? You think that's what they were arguing about that night?'

Tina gave her a sideways look. 'Look, it was David who found Alice in the pool. The police seemed to accept that he had nothing to do with her death. But what if they knew that Alice was having an affair, that she was thinking about leaving David . . . They could have arrested him . . .'

Jem let her thoughts dwell on the dinner at David's house. His sadness, his desperation to find out the truth about his wife. She had believed every word of it.

'I don't think David would have done anything to hurt Alice,' said Tina, as if she were reading her thoughts. 'I don't believe that for one second. That's why I didn't tell the police about the affair. It's why I didn't tell David either. It was a no-win situation. David adored Alice. If I'd told him about Alice's affair and he didn't already know, he would be heartbroken. If he did know, he would have felt dreadful, humiliated that other people knew. And I couldn't have that, not after everything he'd been through.'

She turned to face Jem.

'David loved her, you know. He wasn't the most exciting husband, but he did love her.'

Jem thanked Tina and walked out into the Brooklyn sun. She crossed the street and went to sit on a bench under a tree. From her vantage point she could see across a grassy space where people were sitting eating their lunch, a couple of mothers playing with their toddlers.

She pulled out her mobile, scrolling to Michael's number, her first instinct to fill him in on developments. But instead she clicked off the phone, feeling suddenly tired and a little sad. She should have felt proud of her first attempt at investigation: she had formed a much better impression of the subject and discovered a vital piece of information to boot. But she didn't feel proud; she felt ashamed. She had judged Tina on appearances, just like the Hamptons crowd had done with Alice. Just like all those aloof media people did with Jem herself when she accompanied Nat to events. Yes, Tina was beautiful and fashionable and perhaps too concerned with surface, but underneath she had cared enough about Alice and David to lie to the police to protect them.

Just then she saw Tina pushing out of the café, her shiny ponytail swinging behind her, designer bag over her shoulder. She looked like any other Brooklyn gym bunny, the kind you'd dismiss as vacuous and vain. And maybe she was, but Jem felt a sudden pang of jealousy: she wished she had friends like that in New York. She wished she had friends like that anywhere.

She stood up and pulled out her phone again, scrolling to Michael's number and pressing 'call'. She had a feeling they were both going to need friends by the time this was over.

Chapter 12

Letters, bills, magazines, a few books, a snow globe and a musical jewellery box; they were all spread out on the floor of their tiny apartment. Jem looked at them again and sighed. None of it made any sense. None of it got them any further. It was just a collection of things that get left behind when someone dies. It was just stuff.

'Hey. How's it going?'

Jem looked up as Nat walked in, and smiled. He had even started talking like an American.

'What you got there?'

'Just some things Michael asked me to look through,' said Jem, gathering it together and putting it back in the box, feeling oddly nervous. Well, it wasn't odd, not at all: she *should* feel nervous. She was, after all, in the middle of an investigation into the woman who had died at their weekend house, and into the motives and movements of their housemates and friends. And she hadn't told Nat.

'So what are we having for dinner?' he asked, tossing his jacket and bag onto a chair.

'You do know I have a job too now,' she said. 'We might have to start a cooking rota. It's been a long time since we sampled the Nat Chapman school of cuisine.'

'You know what a crappy cook I am,' he sighed, going

straight to the fridge and pulling out a bottle of wine.

'Okay, I'll do a stir fry,' she said, sliding the box behind the door and out of sight. It was true that despite declaring himself a feminist and a metrosexual, Nat expected the little woman to have his dinner on the table when he got home, like some 1950s sit-com cliché. She supposed it had made sense when she had been at a complete loose end, early on in their time in New York, but now it was just habit. Still, she didn't want to make an issue of it. Since their talk on the beach two weeks ago, Nat had been more irritable and short-tempered; she had no desire to get into an argument tonight. And anyway, she enjoyed cooking.

She sliced some onions, threw them in a pan with some coconut oil and diced a rainbow of vegetables to add to the mixture along with a home-made soy and ginger sauce she had already prepared. Quick and easy to make, and she sighed with contentment at the delicious aroma. She carried two plates to the small table by the open window as Nat poured them both a glass from the bottle he'd already made a start on.

'Well this is nice, actually getting to have a meal together, at home, when the sun's still out. I feel like I'm on holiday,' she said. She felt content as the warm, muggy air floated in from the street.

'So come on,' said Nat, spearing a slice of red pepper. 'You've been working with Kearney for nearly two weeks now. Have you formed a view about him yet?'

'Michael? He's smart, fun, he's generous.'

'Yeah, but what about under all that? What's the gossip? We know he's divorced, but he can't be a hermit, not with half of the Hamptons lusting after him. What about girl-friends?'

Jem stopped, her fork halfway to her mouth.

'I've only been his assistant two minutes. I haven't exactly got round to knowing any of the personal stuff yet.'

'Well get on it,' smiled Nat. 'I want a full report on his sex and drugs intake by next weekend. And no more of this "he's a nice guy" stuff.' He mimed a yawn.

Nat was being playful, which was definitely better than being grumpy or sarcastic, but Jem detected an edge under his ribbing and she wondered if he was a little jealous of Michael. After all, Michael's career path was pretty much Nat's dream, every journalist's dream: award-winning writer followed by rich and famous best-selling novelist. And now he got to spend a decent chunk of time with Nat's wife. She'd be worried if he wasn't jealous.

'Hey, I've been working on a new recipe for toffee popcorn,' she said. 'Do you want me to rustle up a bowl each and we can watch Netflix? There's that new sci-fi thing everyone's talking about.'

Nat puffed out his cheeks. 'Can't,' he said. 'I actually left the office early so I could get cracking on that feature for the *New Yorker*.'

Jem felt a stab of disappointment.

'Oh Nat,' she said, hating the nagging tone in her voice, 'I thought we agreed no more freelance. It's so time-consuming, and you work long enough hours as it is.'

'Jem, it's important. I've got to build my brand and—'

She laughed. 'Your brand?'

Nat frowned. 'Personal branding is everything these days. Journalism is going nowhere fast; even your mate Kearney is saying that. So if the industry is shrinking, I've got to try to diversify really hard, really fast.'

'But writing another magazine feature? How's that helping your brand?'

'Jem, this is the *New Yorker*. Do you know how lucky I am that they asked me to write for them? You don't call them and offer your services; they call you. If I turn down this opportunity, I might not get another one.'

Jem knew she was not going to win this argument, and she was actually less annoyed by the fact that he was writing some feature than by the fact that he could bring himself to leave his precious office for the *New Yorker* but not for her.

'Do you know what?' she said, getting up and collecting their plates. 'I have some work to do as well.'

'Are you working by the day or by the hour for Kearney?' he asked.

It was Jem's turn to frown. Like he'd ever cared about her salary before: it was just pin money in his eyes.

'We've said a couple of days a week,' she said defensively.

'Well if you're going to be doing all this extra time, make sure you're billing him by the hour. He can afford it.'

Jem bristled, but she didn't want to completely ruin an already pretty shitty evening. By the time she had filled the dishwasher, Nat had set up shop on the little dining table: staring into his laptop screen, oblivious to her anger. Muttering to herself, she grabbed the box she had been sifting through and carried it into the bedroom, dumping it on the bed and climbing in with her glass of wine.

David Holliday had given them six boxes of Alice's things, which Michael had taken back to Amagansett. But David had called Jem the day after their dinner and said he'd found some more personal stuff they might find of interest, and had couriered it over to Brookyn that afternoon.

Jem's initial rummage hadn't yielded much, she had to admit.

There were no photographs or diaries, no receipts for secret purchases, nothing obviously significant. It just looked like stuff Alice had kept to one side for sentimental reasons – the jewellery box and the snow globe – and a few things that might be useful one day. Jem picked up the books: a beauty and style guide written by a celebrity she had never heard of, biographies of Audrey Hepburn and the Dalai Lama, an etiquette guide and a couple of novels.

She tossed them to one side, letting out a sigh. She was keen to make a good impression with Michael, wanted him to be glad he'd hired her. The previous evening, when she'd called him with Tina's revelation that Alice was having an affair, he had been complimentary and animated, signing off with a heartfelt 'Good work, Jem!' and she wanted more of that. It had been a long time since anyone had shown any appreciation of her work. Her years working in cafés, kitchens and chalets had been pretty thankless, and even when she was making a success of her catering company, she was mostly working for highly strung middle-class housewives who seemed entirely focused on getting the event out of the way so they could post it on Facebook. Those women weren't big on compliments either.

She picked up a magazine and flicked through it, knowing that Alice must have stored it away for some reason. She skimmed over a feature about grand Connecticut mansions, and fashion shoots featuring diamonds and ball gowns, which only hinted that Alice was an aspirational woman. There was a big section of society photos of people who seemed quite alien to Jem – Binkys, Bunnys and arrogant-looking youths who all had 'Jr' as a suffix to their names. She realised that any one of these photos could be significant, or they could be completely irrelevant – there was no way to tell for sure.

The etiquette book was lightly annotated – society events ringed in biro with phone numbers that Jem made a note to contact. One of the novels was a chick-lit bestseller that had been made into a popular movie; another was more literary fare. Jem picked it up frowning.

It was the one item that didn't really fit. She recognised

the title, remembered it had been a smash hit the previous summer; the sort of book that got plenty of buzz and column inches and constantly popped up on her Amazon home page. But it didn't seem to gel with her impression of Alice's personality; plus it looked barely read. She flicked through the pages, the paper thick and crisp in her fingers. Halfway through, a bookmark fluttered out, a slim piece of card that carried the name of a bookstore in New York state: Rivertown Books.

She remembered being in a bookshop with Nat a few weeks earlier – a hip, indie shop, the sort of place Nat liked to be seen in even though truthfully, he preferred to play video games than read. He'd bought the new Pulitzer Prize winner, which Angela had said was excellent, and Jem remembered the assistant had slipped a bookmark inside the cover.

'Nice marketing,' Nat had said, even including the smartly designed card on the inevitable Instagram snap of the book.

'Why did you buy a book in Rivertown?' whispered Jem, looking at the bookmark again – an illustrated picture of the store, along with its logo and address. She grabbed her iPad. 'Rivertown, Rivertown . . .' And there it was: about two hours north of the city, deep in the Catskill mountains. Curious.

She looked at the book again, flicking to the copyright page at the very front. Yes, she had been right: it had been published last year. Turning back to the iPad, it only took her a few seconds to discover the US publication date: 20 June.

She leant back against the headboard and stared out of the window, her mind a whirl. The twentieth of June was only a couple of weeks before Alice died, which meant she must have bought the book in the preceding few days.

And if she had bought it at the Rivertown bookstore in person, she must have visited the Catskills in that last fortnight.

She hopped onto her email and sent Michael a message: *Just looking through the extra box of Alice's things that David gave us. Do we know what her schedule was those last few weeks. Trips away?*

It occurred to her that it might be inappropriate to contact her employer after hours, but she was suddenly anxious to follow this particular rabbit down the hole, wherever it would lead her. Michael had talked about having a nose for a story, and Jem was beginning to understand what he meant: she was *sure* this was relevant.

She took another sip of wine, drumming her fingers thoughtfully on the stem of the glass, then she opened a new message and typed David Holliday's address in, sending him a more carefully worded version of the same message.

She sat back on the pillows, feeling a buzz of excitement. Maybe this was nothing – it was only a bookmark, after all. Maybe someone had simply brought the book back from a trip as a gift and Alice had tossed it into the box, meaning to read it when she had the time. But Jem didn't think so. It felt like something important.

There was a discreet 'ping' and she snatched up the iPad, expecting a terse message from Michael along the lines of 'Can't this wait until morning?' – but the email was from David Holliday: *We didn't go anywhere in June or July beyond the Hamptons. I went to a two-day conference in Illinois 23/24 June. Hope that helps. David.*

The dates fitted. Her heart leapt: it *all* fitted. Even Jem knew that the Catskills had a reputation as a place young New Yorkers went for fashionable mini-breaks and romantic trysts – and Alice could easily have slipped away to the mountains while David was at the conference. Jem imagined her in the throes of a passionate affair, desperate for a romantic overnighter with her clandestine lover.

She picked up the book and stared at the cover, as if she could read the fingerprints smeared on the surface. 'Who did you go with, Alice? Who?'

Chapter 13

All the roads looked the same as they drove towards the Catskills. One winding tree-lined road gave way to another, occasionally passing a flash of water, a pond or stream, but mostly it was trees, trees and more trees.

'Are we still trusting this sat nav?' said Jem. 'According to the screen, the Catskills are still twenty-three miles away and we've been on the bloody road for two hours already!'

Michael glanced over. 'I love how you Brits swear. You use curse words like it's part of the language.'

'It *is* part of the language,' said Jem. 'And a vital part of our culture, along with drinking, Marmite and Bonfire Night.'

'Bonfire Night?' said Michael.

'Don't ask,' smiled Jem.

While Jem had enjoyed the banter, the drive from South Fork had already been unnecessarily long. Michael's slightly eccentric GPS had sent them on a scenic tour of Yonkers, and in frustration they had switched to his dog-eared Rand McNally road atlas, becoming even more lost in the process. Now Jem was reasonably sure they were approaching the foothills of the Catskills – they did seem to be climbing steadily upwards, at any rate – but secretly she wouldn't be too upset if they took another wrong turn, because Michael was such fascinating company. During the journey he had given her an incisive run-down of the Vietnam war and its fallout, discussed the pros and cons of playing golf on the moon and told her a scandalous anecdote about a road trip he'd taken with a once-famous rock singer who, despite being in his twenties, had a kink for women old enough to be his grandmother.

'I've been flapping my gums since we left the dunes,' he said now. 'Isn't it about time you told me the story of your life?'

'There's not much to say,' she shrugged. 'Not everyone can be a top journalist, best-selling author and Hollywood screenwriter.'

'I'm not writing the Garcia script. I'm just consulting,' he said as he shifted his hands on the wheel. 'Anyway, I'm dying to hear about your days as a chalet girl.'

'It's a long story,' she said waving her hand.

'There's plenty of time. Come on, humour me.'

Jem could hardly get out of the car, so with a groan she began.

'I grew up in Cornwall, which is a far-flung corner of England.'

'The land of smugglers and rum and haunted tin mines,' he said knowingly.

'So you've never been.'

'No, but I'd like to,' he smiled, glancing over.

Jem let her eyes trail out of the window.

'It was just me, my mum and dad. Dad was an electrician, Mum stayed at home. She was a great cook – I think that's where I got it from. We were never really close, but she'd take me shopping to the butcher, the fishmonger's, tell me which were the best cuts of meat, the ways to spice up pollack.'

'No brothers and sisters?'

Jem shook her head. 'Only child. I always wanted a brother or sister but it never happened. There was no imaginary friend either, before you ask.'

'So that's how you got into cooking. Through your mom?'

'It was by default rather than design,' she said, glancing back over. 'I flunked my GSCEs – that's like your high school leaving exams – so I was never going to end up as a doctor or a lawyer.'

'You surprise me. I had you down as valedictorian.'

'Not me,' said Jem with a sad smile, remembering her last year at school. 'My dad died just before my exams and everything sort of derailed. My teachers encouraged me to resit them the following year, but I was so cut up by everything that happened, I didn't think I'd ever be ready to go back to school.'

She puffed out her cheeks before she continued.

'I had experience as a waitress, so after a few months of feeling very sad and hopeless, I started doing that in a restaurant in Newquay. I got promoted to the kitchens and ended up as a cook at a local conference centre.' She held up a finger. 'That's a cook, not a chef. I peeled a lot of potatoes,' she laughed. 'I always loved food but kitchens are stressful; there's a *lot* of shouting when your julienned carrots aren't up to scratch.'

'How long did you stick with it?'

'A couple of years,' she sighed. 'Long, long years. Then I read a feature in a newspaper about chalet girls. Mum had met someone new by this point. They were getting married and I felt a spare part in the house. I knew it was time to leave Cornwall, make a fresh start, and getting out of the country for a while seemed the best way to go about it, even if it was a bit extreme.'

'And what *is* a chalet girl exactly?'

'You've never seen a chalet in a ski resort?'

'I'm from south Boston. Never really thought skiing was for people like me.'

Jem smiled. 'Chalets are big fancy wooden houses that look like cuckoo clocks. Chalet girls are basically glorified slaves employed to cook and clean for rich Brits.'

'I'm thinking James Bond meets *Downton Abbey*,' said Michael.

'Not quite. I spent eight hours a day scrubbing toilets and making flapjacks for very self-absorbed families from Hampshire, sorting out lift passes, and cleaning yet more vomit from the loos because Freddy or Giles couldn't hold his drink. But I learnt to ski, tasted snowflakes on my tongue and fell in love with the mountains.'

'How long did you do it for?'

'I did that for seven seasons. Worked my way up to chalet manager, even got hotel work in the summer months.'

'And what happened after season seven?'

'I met Nat,' she said.

'What happened? You shared a chairlift. Eyes met across tangled skis?'

'You can tell you're a writer.'

'Don't believe the hype.'

'Actually he was a guest in one of the chalets. Some reunion for him and his university friends.'

'Is fraternising with the guests allowed?' asked Michael with mock-disapproval.

'Not really, but we couldn't help ourselves. We did the long-distance thing for the rest of the season, then I moved in with him in London.'

'That must have been a shock to the system after so long.'

'Not really. I'd done enough travelling and I was ready to settle down.'

'And the catering business?' prompted Michael.

'My first client was a family who had been at one of the chalets. They must have liked my ginger biscuits. And the rest was word of mouth, pretty much, cooking for dinner parties for the smart people of Notting Hill. Obviously I had to use the staff entrance, but still . . .'

'And do you miss it? The cooking, I mean.'

'I didn't think I would,' she said, remembering the night that Nat had come home telling her excitedly that he'd been offered a job in New York. 'My business was doing well, but I guess after five years of crème caramel I was open to a change. But yes, I do miss it. I love food and I miss people appreciating it, but I think I miss feeling useful and being busy more than the cooking itself. Which is why I love working for you. I guess in September when the season finishes I'll go back to catering. Or at least try to. It was pretty difficult to find anything in New York, if I'm honest. Maybe the Brits still have a bad reputation for their food.'

Michael looked thoughtful. 'You do know you're welcome to stay on after Labor Day. The house is big enough if you need to stay over instead of trawling back to the city.'

Jem raised her brows. They both knew what Nat would think about that.

'Well, I'm happy to do some stuff remotely. Research, emails, fan mail. I don't have to be in the Hamptons to do that.'

'Sure,' said Michael more coolly. 'We'll work something out.' But Jem detected a note in his voice that suggested it wouldn't happen.

The sat nav made a sudden 'bing-bong' sound. 'In one. Hundred feet. You will. Reach your destination,' said the synthetic voice.

Jem turned to look out the window as the trees suddenly

gave way to farm buildings, then a white wooden church. A painted sign passed on their right read: *Welcome to Rivertown, est. 1890, pop. 2942.*

'Bloody hell, we made it,' gasped Jem.

The town seemed to consist of one main street bookended by the church and an elementary school. In between were boutiques, antiques stores and galleries: the Catskills were a magnet for wealthy urban New Yorkers. Rivertown did however also have more workaday premises – a diner, a coffee shop, a kind of post-office-cum-general-store; the town's homespun charm hadn't quite been buried by tourism. Michael parked the car outside the gentleman's outfitters, which, judging by the window display, was attempting a delicate balance between Ralph Lauren bow ties and John Deere overalls.

'There's the bookshop,' said Jem, nodding to the other side of the road. It was sandwiched between an ice cream parlour and a wine store. Michael nodded and strode across, but Jem hesitated. Now they were here, she felt a flutter of butterflies in her stomach. She supposed it was because this was her scoop, the big clue she had stumbled across, and if it turned out to be nothing, she'd have led them on a wild goose chase.

The bell rang as they went inside the shop. It was surprisingly large, with well-spaced bookcases and a series of oval tables holding displays in various categories: 'Classics', 'Crime', 'Biography' and so on.

'Where do we start?' whispered Jem.

'It's a bookstore, not a library,' said Michael. 'And I suppose we start with the evidence.'

He pulled the bookmark from his inside pocket and walked over to the sales desk, where a small man with grey hair was sitting hunched over a laptop. Jem noted he was playing solitaire rather than working on a stock-check.

'Hello,' said Michael, slightly startling the man, who peered up through thick spectacles.

'I was wondering if you could help me . . .'

'You're Michael Kearney,' said the man, his eyes wide.

Jem gave a wry smile. 'So much for undercover.'

'That's the beauty of being an author. You never get recognised. Except by the very observant.'

'Ah, no,' said the man, standing up. 'It's just that we had these life-size cardboard cut-outs of you to promote your last book and they've been in the back next to the coffee machine, so . . .'

'Life-size cut-outs?' repeated Michael.

'Yes, I imagine it's because we've written to your publicity department a number of times. We have an excellent schedule of author events at Rivertown Books and we were hoping to get you along.' The man peered at Michael through the glasses again. 'You're not here for that now, are you?'

'Not this time. I was actually looking for a little expert assistance.' He leant forward. 'Confidentially, I'm doing research for my next book.'

'Here?' said the man incredulously.

'It's a great bookstore,' Michael said.

He held out the bookmark.

'I think this is one of yours?'

'Oh yes. When anyone buys a book we always slip one between the pages. Would you like any more?'

'No thank you. I was hoping you could help me with something. This bookmark was in a book owned by a girl I'm investigating. I think she bought it here a little over a year ago. We just wondered why she came to this bookstore and whether anyone here remembers her.'

'Is this really for one of your novels?' The man's eyes glittered with excitement at the prospect of contributing to the great Michael Kearney's work.

Michael pulled a photo of Alice from his jacket pocket.

'I know it's a long shot, but do you recognise this woman?'

The man took the photo and peered closely.

'Pretty girl,' he murmured.

'You don't remember her?'

He pulled a face and handed the photo back.

'I don't have a very good memory for faces. Sorry.'

Michael nodded, his frustration plain.

'Maybe Mary would recognise her,' said the man.

'Mary?'

'Oh, Mary owns this place.'

'Can we speak to her?'

'She's only in on Monday and Tuesday. Are you in town long?'

Jem could see the disappointment in Michael's face. It had taken long enough to get here. The last thing they wanted was a return visit. And anyway, even if this woman Mary did remember Alice, what else could she realistically tell them? Jem realised far too late the futility of the trip. They had been so caught up in the excitement of finding a clue, they hadn't really considered what that clue might actually lead to.

'This girl you're looking for,' said the man, rubbing his chin thoughtfully. 'Where does she live?'

'New York,' said Michael. 'Manhattan.'

'Just a thought, but Rivertown is a long way from the city. Most people don't do the journey in a day. If she came to the bookshop, it's possible she was here for the weekend.'

Michael nodded his agreement. 'And if she was staying in the area, where do you think she'd stay?'

'You could try the Inn the Woods, fancy place a couple of miles north. Tell them Jimmy said hi.'

'I will,' said Michael, taking a business card out of his

wallet and handing it to the man. 'And send me an email about your author events. I'm sure we can sort something out.'

Chapter 14

Considering that Nat was a walking encyclopedia of all the smart and sexy places to go on the entire east coast of America, Jem wondered why she hadn't heard of the Inn the Woods before. It was gorgeous.

Set in a thick woodland clearing a hundred metres off the main road, it was quaint but modern, an architect's stylish interpretation of a classic mountain shack with an exaggerated Alpine peak to the roof and shutters on the windows, but using minimal materials like slate and fired brick in the construction. In the lobby, a log fire was burning in a suspended black steel fireplace, the bronze flue shooting straight up through the ceiling like a Soyuz-era rocket in a museum. Michael and Jem walked quickly to the reception desk, where an attractive fortyish brunette greeted them warmly. 'Checking in?'

'Wish I was,' said Michael. 'It's an amazing place.'

'I never get tired of hearing that,' smiled the woman. 'The whole place has been a labour of love for me and my husband.'

'You built this?' said Jem in wonder.

'We're city downsizers,' replied the woman. 'Worked in the financial sector for far too long, but we always knew we wanted to escape. Alec, my husband, got laid off from

Wall Street, so we took the plunge. Sold up, moved out here.'

'Incredible. How long did it take?'

Jem could see that Michael was warming up for a full-on charm offensive, so she moved away to give him room. On the far wall were a series of photos showing the construction from timber frame to finished article. She could see the woman from reception in most of the pictures, in shorts and hiking boots, hands protected by thick workman's gloves as she carried planks of wood down through the forest. Must have been damn hard work, but Jem could see the wide smiles on their faces, imagined them planning and designing and building side by side. Now that was a real partnership, she thought, and she felt an almost physical lurch of envy when she tried to imagine Nat having the faith and courage to take on such a challenge. Would he ever be able to step away from the rat race, his constant need for instant gratification? She felt a sadness creep over her. She didn't think so.

Slowly she walked back to Michael.

'Hey, Jem, come and meet Sophie. She and her husband run this place.'

'I've just been admiring the pictures,' said Jem, then noticed that the woman was holding the photo of Alice. Michael followed her gaze and smiled.

'I told Sophie why we're here and she remembers Alice,' he said, the excitement in his voice impossible to miss.

'She was so pretty you couldn't forget her,' said Sophie, leaning on the check-in desk.

'Was she on her own?' asked Jem as casually as she could.

Sophie glanced at Michael.

'Your friend just asked that.'

She hesitated.

'Look, we're a discreet place,' she said apologetically. 'The majority of people who come here are couples, but we don't ask questions about their status, if you know what I mean.'

'Sophie, Alice is dead,' Michael said.

The hotel owner paled.

'She died shortly after coming here. Don't worry, the police ruled out foul play, but still, her family are keen to find out what she was doing in the Catskills.'

Sophie looked nervous. Jem could only imagine what she was thinking. She'd spent her life savings building a magnificent retreat in the woods; the last thing she wanted was for it to be dragged into a scandal.

'I didn't realise. How sad. Of course, I'll tell you what I know.' Sophie shuffled some papers around. 'We hadn't been open long, that's probably why she sticks in the mind. She was with a good-looking guy, but I couldn't tell you any more than that. I might recognise him from a photo if you had one,' she said hopefully.

'That's just the problem,' said Jem with disappointment. 'We don't know who she was with.'

'Of course,' said Sophie, looking thoughtful. 'Do you know the dates?'

'It was probably the twenty-third and twenty-fourth of June last year,' said Michael. 'Could have been a few days either side, we don't know exactly.'

'Then they were here the first month we opened. Just give me a moment.'

She sat down at a computer terminal and slipped on her glasses to peer at the screen. Jem could see the lines of text from the booking records reflected in the lenses as they scrolled past, and she wondered idly how many other affairs were contained in those lines, how many other couples had come here pretending to be Mr and Mrs Smith. Perhaps if she looked hard enough, she might find Nat's name jumbled up there too. It was a thought she suppressed, but if she was honest, it was often there. She trusted him, sure, but that was because she really had no other choice. In her darker moments she wondered if he always was at the parties and launch events he claimed to be at, and whether he was alone. She closed her eyes, shaking her head to clear the thought. It wasn't healthy and it wouldn't lead to anything good.

'Sorry, can't find an Alice or a Holliday, I'm afraid,' said Sophie, looking up from the screen.

'Perhaps the booking wasn't in her name,' suggested Michael.

Sophie nodded. 'Makes sense. Beautiful girl, it's often the guy who pays.'

She concentrated on the screen again and then tapped at the keyboard. Jem glanced across at Michael and their eyes met. She felt hope rising again

There was a low humming sound and Sophie pulled out a piece of paper, laying it in the counter.

'Here you go. These are the details of everyone in the pool cabin between those dates.'

'The pool cabin?'

'We have a luxury cabin set on a little swimming hole just past the main building. It's down a dirt track, very exclusive, very private. I remembered that was where they stayed because they requested meat for the barbecue and it was the first time we'd done it.'

Michael and Jem bent over the sheet, the sense of anticipation between them palpable. Jem ran her finger down the list, looking for any name that might seem familiar. There was a Curtis Briscoe on a one-night stay, with extras amounting to $747, on 19 June. He was followed by a Jennifer Elliot of Trenton, New Jersey, who had paid upfront for two nights. Then there was a Richard Sander. And a P. E. Ellis.

Jem's finger stopped and she looked up at Michael, her mouth open.

'P. E. Ellis,' read Michael, his face blank.

'It's Paul,' said Jem, her voice barely a whisper. 'Paul Ellis. He's one of the housemates. Alice was having an affair with Paul.'

Last summer

Chapter 15

'Yes! Yes! God, yes!'

Alice bucked her hips against his, sweat beading on her naked body.

'Please, baby, please,' she gasped. 'Please.'

Always say please. Always make them feel special, make them feel as if they're in charge. He arched his back, twisted his neck. He was close, trying to prolong it. For her. So sweet.

'Now,' gasped Alice, biting her lip.

He groaned, the noise rising in his throat, the cords standing out on his neck. Primal, fierce. Stupid.

Men. In that final moment when their desire spiked, then flatlined, they all looked dumb, like they were in pain. The sort of look you saw on marathon runners stumbling across the line. Agony and relief, but part of them wondering why they had got involved in the first place.

Alice raised her own voice in a sort of ragged harmony. 'Yessss! YES!'

Her mother had taken a lot from Alice, but one thing she had given her, one glittering gift was a glimpse into the minds of men. 'Remember this one thing, girl,' she had said, drunk one night. 'Remember that men are brought up to believe that women hate to fuck.' Mom had giggled at that, happy in her own wisdom. 'That's how they think about it, Allie. They think we've got to be persuaded into it against our will because it's so nasty. But you know what? That gives us power. You got yourself a little diamond right there between your legs, girl. Never forget that.'

Mom had been a lush but she had been right about that.

Alice lay back on the mattress and looked up at the ceiling before closing her eyes, exhaling softly and trying to regulate her breathing.

'That was good,' said the honeyed baritone voice beside her.

Alice turned and looked at him.

She'd met Adam Pearson running in Central Park about three weeks earlier. They'd flirted between swigs of water, then arranged a race around the reservoir path. He told her that he worked for a fund, but Alice had already found that out. A profile in Bloomberg had described Adam Pearson as a financier on the up, a profile in *Town & Country* had described him and his socialite fiancée Lauren as a power couple of the future.

Alice had worked out pretty quickly that if Adam hadn't entirely regretted his New Year's Eve Tulum Beach proposal to his fashion PR girlfriend, then he was certainly sick of the circus accompanying his impending wedding: the endless hours being dragged to florists, calligraphers and the smartest gift registry departments in town, and the incessant chat about the big day.

She had no illusions that he had fallen head over heels in love with her; she knew she was just a distraction from the thought of getting married – the big full stop to his single life and feeling hot and free.

He rolled over and dropped his head on the crook of his arm.

'I should go. I've got a lunch at Per Se in ten minutes.'

'Does that make me an amuse-bouche?' she said with her best seductive smile.

His spent post-coital expression turned serious.

'I'm really glad we met,' he said finally.

'But . . .' She smiled with resignation, pre-empting what he was going to say next.

'But I'm not sure we should see each other for a little while.'

'I get that,' she nodded. 'It's your wedding in three weeks. Then there's the honeymoon in Maui . . .'

'You do understand?' he said, stroking her cheek gratefully.

She smiled and got out of bed, stretching her arms over her head to elongate her body; might as well give him one last look as a seductive swansong.

'Go on. You better hurry,' she said, turning back to face him and smiling wolfishly. 'If you're going to be in Columbus Circle in seven minutes, you should leave now.'

She watched him give her a long, lingering look up and down before sighing softly in wistful regret.

Swinging his legs out of the bed, he muttered that there was no time for a shower, and pulled on his boxer shorts. As he got dressed, Alice slipped on her dressing gown and, as there seemed little point in chit-chat, waited for him in the hall.

He was still straightening his tie as he came over to kiss her goodbye. She smelt the scent of sex, of her, on his cheek and felt a giddy sense of triumph as she imagined him sitting at his business lunch talking about his wedding. She wondered if his dining companions would be attending the service at St Patrick's Cathedral, and the reception at the St Regis, and would remember him turning up to Per Se a little late, a little red-faced and rumpled.

She closed the door of her apartment behind him and gave a soft smile. She knew she wouldn't see Adam Pearson again and she really didn't mind.

He was good-looking, but not that good in bed. The first time they'd had sex, he'd gone down on her for a few lacklustre seconds and then expected to come in her mouth. It had been better this morning; he'd been definitely less selfish, but then she suspected it was because he knew the big kiss-off was about to come.

But the truth was, Alice had got what she had wanted from him, and now she was glad their fling could be cut short without any protracted awkwardness.

She went back into the bedroom and used a tissue from her dressing table to pick up a condom that had been discarded on the floor. Taking it into the kitchen, she wrapped it in a brown paper grocery bag, which she scrunched into a ball and threw into the trash can. All she had to do now was change the bed linen, air the room, and David would never know.

She flinched in surprise when she heard the rattle of a key in the lock and the sound of the front door opening. Panic made her freeze, but she recovered her poise and went out into the hall.

She saw the sleeve of his jacket first, brown tweed that irritated her skin. Glancing left towards the bedroom, she saw the post-sex tangle of an unmade bed and knew she had to think quickly.

Her husband closed the door behind him and put his briefcase on the parquet floor. She saw him take a second to observe her dressing gown, bare feet and tousled hair.

'Are you not dressed?' he said finally.

Alice shook her head. 'I feel crap. I cancelled all my classes and went back to bed.'

'How are you feeling now?' he said, the trace of a frown appearing between his brows.

'Better. Much better. I was just getting up.'

He looked down at the floor as if he was examining an invisible spot on the polished wood, and when he looked up again, his frown was more pronounced.

'Who was that man by the elevator?' he asked after a moment.

She heard the accusation in his words, and didn't blame him.

'What man?' she said, grateful that the situation could have been more damning; if Adam had left just a few minutes later . . .

'Suit. Dark hair,' he said, taking off his jacket and putting it on the coat rack.

Alice shrugged and gave a pretty laugh. 'I don't know. Just because I'm home some of the day doesn't mean I know the comings and goings of everyone on this floor.'

He didn't come closer. He kept his distance and she kept hers, and she knew she had to lie to him.

She glanced up at the clock in the hall and saw that it was 12.20. Her husband was an English and comparative literature lecturer at Columbia University and spent most of his day on campus. She'd been hoping that Adam would have booked a hotel room for their mid-morning rendezvous, but when he'd refused on account of the check-in/check-out times – like he couldn't *afford* to pay for two nights at the Pierre – she'd invited him over to their Upper West Side place instead, not imagining for one moment that David might catch them in the act.

'What are you doing back so early?' she asked, trying to keep her tone light.

'There's building work going on next to my room. It's too noisy. I was between lectures and just thought I'd come home to do some work.'

She watched his eyes flicker left and right, as if he was

165

trying to piece together what had gone on in his absence. She didn't want to meet his gaze and instead went into the kitchen, where she switched on the coffee machine.

He loitered outside the bedroom door and looked inside with disappointment. He was twitchy, and she half expected him to pick up the duvet and smell it, but he followed her into the kitchen and took a seat at the breakfast bar.

In the soft overhead light he looked particularly boyish and vulnerable. It had always been his charm. After a run of bad boys when she first moved to New York – not just the handsome, penniless chancers who were as much on the make as she was, but the Wall Street traders who only ever seemed interested in a one-night stand – David's appeal was that he was reliable and intelligent, a good man from a good family, and that was why, at the age of twenty-five, Alice stopped chasing the sexy, flashy, exciting members of the opposite sex and married him.

She handed him a coffee cup and made herself an espresso.

'Did Todd manage to get in touch with you this morning?' she asked.

Alice liked Todd Carter. He was an old family friend of David's but was plugged in to a much hipper scene than her husband. Todd's parents had a house in Nantucket and they'd gone there the summer before for his father's seventieth birthday celebrations. It had been the weekend of Alice's dreams. A short flight from La Guardia had taken them to the tiny blue-blooded island. She could almost smell the generations of money and privilege in the air as they had driven past the huge shingled summer cottages that belonged to some of the grandest families in America. The Carters didn't own the biggest house on the island, but it was certainly the prettiest, with honeysuckle that climbed around the double front door and manicured green lawns that smelt of freshly mown grass. For lunch they'd been served tiny lobster rolls by chefs in tall white hats, and for the evening celebration they'd taken a cinder path to the beach, where there'd been a clam bake on the sand with a glorious view of Nantucket Sound.

As soon as it was over she'd wanted to do it all over again, and now she knew that opportunity was close at hand.

'The battery is dead on my cell phone,' said David, sipping his coffee. 'Did he call here?'

Alice nodded and leant against the granite countertop.

'They want an answer about the beach house.'

There was a copy of the *New York Times* by the fruit bowl and he began to flick through it as if he hadn't heard her.

'David, come on. We can't be rude. They want an answer.'

'We've discussed this before,' he said, putting his cup down. 'I can't think of anything worse than going to the Hamptons every weekend. We'd spend six hours stuck in traffic, and sixteen hours asleep. For what? A couple of afternoons at the beach with people I can have a beer with anywhere.'

She shook her head fiercely. 'You're so miserable sometimes, you know that.'

'Believe me, Al. It's overrated.'

'It's fine for you to say that. You've had a lifetime of summers at the beach. What about me? Is it wrong to want to have some fun, rather than spend every weekend in Manhattan, business as usual?'

Her time in bed with Adam had relaxed her, but now she felt all wound up again. David was such a killjoy. She always felt his saving grace was that he cared about her, but now he didn't seem to give a flying shit about how she wanted to spend the summer.

'When school finishes, I thought we could go to England.

I've not been for such a long time and you'd love London, the Cotswolds, Oxford . . . there's lots of places I'd like to show you—'

'I don't want to go to fucking England,' she hissed, stomping to the fridge to pour herself an ice-cold water. As she turned away from him, her eyes closed, heavy with the weight of disappointment.

When she had met David, she had imagined society parties and weekends with friends in Cape Cod and Rhode Island. David might be just an academic, but his contacts were sparkling; the offer of a Hamptons house share was just the latest invitation that had made Alice's mouth water, but what was the point in having the opportunities if he couldn't be bothered to take them?

Her husband closed his paper and looked at her.

'Who was the man by the elevator, Alice?'

'Why do you keep mentioning that?' she said, throwing her hands up in frustration.

David maintained his cool.

'Has he been in the apartment? Did you fuck him?' He spoke as calmly as if he were reading out the television listings.

Alice almost missed her breath.

'How dare you say something like that,' she said, her hand curling into a fist.

David gave a soft snort.

She knew what he was thinking about. The last time. The last time she'd been careless and got caught. It had been two years earlier and he'd found a text, not even that incriminating but just enough that she'd had to admit to the affair.

'I told you it wouldn't happen again,' she said, realising that a high-handed approach wouldn't work.

He shook his head, and when he looked back at her, she could see a tear glistening in his eye.

'What am I supposed to think, Alice? You're undressed, the bed is a mess, there's a man I've never seen before outside our apartment . . .'

She didn't say anything. She could spend the next hour denying it, but deep down he knew what had gone on in the apartment even if neither of them wanted to admit it.

'Do you think about other men?' he asked simply.

'Yes,' she said, the word slipping out of her mouth before she could even stop it.

'Does our marriage make you unhappy?'

She closed her eyes and exhaled softly. She thought of what life had been like before David: the fleapit studios she'd had to live in, with shared bathrooms and junkies in the doorway. Moving up in the world had taken her longer than she'd thought. The dancing dream hadn't happened and the modelling came to nothing. She'd scraped a living as a fitness instructor, retraining as a yoga teacher when she realised she'd meet a superior class of client and that it sounded better to the unreliable young bankers she met in the bars around SoHo. But still . . . still David had saved her.

'I don't know,' she said after a moment.

She realised she had an opportunity here and decided to run with it.

'You work so hard, we don't even seem to see each other any more.'

'Once I get tenured at the college, things will be better,' he said.

'Will they?' she replied cynically.

She paused and looked at him.

'You want to know why I want to do the Hamptons house share? Because I think it will be good for us. You talk about the traffic jams, but at least we'll be together. We can enjoy the sea and the sun. Remember what was good . . .'

David had the decency not to challenge her on her real motives.

'It's not as easy as that,' he said, his expression softening.

'Maybe it is. Look at Todd and Angela. They have a great marriage and you don't think it has anything to do with the fact that they have fun together?'

Her husband looked thoughtful. His natural resting face was a sombre one, and now he looked especially serious.

'How about we make a deal?' he said, and Alice felt her heart beat faster. 'We'll do the house share, but only if we go to counselling.'

'*Counselling?*' said Alice, her initial euphoria about the Hamptons being squashed by the thought of a shrink. 'What do we need that for?'

Unlike most of her friends in New York, she didn't have a therapist on speed-dial. You didn't grow up in small-town Indiana to go running to a shrink every time you had a problem, and the time, the money, the sheer pointless indulgence of it all made her shake her head in refusal.

It was David's turn to look cynical.

'What do we need it for?' he repeated. 'You had an affair, Alice. We never really got over it. I'm not even sure I still trust you, however much I want to. And then you tell me you think about other men.'

She looked at him almost in pity. He didn't know the half of it.

'I love you, Alice,' he said in a voice so quiet she hardly heard it. 'I love you and I want to make it work. Will you just help me try?'

She looked away and felt her teeth bite into her bottom lip.

Did she really have a choice? she thought, wondering what the alternative was. She had a nice life, a life that she enjoyed. Their apartment wasn't the biggest in Manhattan, and strictly speaking it still belonged to David's parents. But it was a good building, in a good area. It passed muster; that was what the rich folk said, wasn't it?

She did love her husband. He provided a security in her life that had always been lacking, that she knew she had always wanted. And it was only a matter of time before she persuaded him that the house in the Hamptons, going to the right parties, having the right friends wasn't just what she wanted, it was a quicker way to get his beloved professorship than spending all his time in a dusty library.

'Let's do it,' she said, already working out what she would wear for her first weekend at the beach.

Chapter 16

David sat in the car, drumming his fingers on the steering wheel.

'I was sure the traffic would have eased off by now,' he said, craning his neck to see beyond the truck ahead of them in the line. To their left, there was another stationary line of 4x4s, and as Alice looked in the rear-view mirror she could see nothing but cars.

'I don't believe this,' she muttered, glancing at her watch and seeing that it was after nine. They were supposed to be at the beach house for welcome cocktails at seven o'clock, but at this rate they wouldn't even get there for breakfast.

The car was stuffy and Alice opened the window for some air. David looked over and smiled.

'I did warn you,' he grinned.

Alice was in no mood for humour.

'Perhaps if you'd got back from Columbia before four o'clock we'd have made it in time.'

'It's pre-registration for the fall intake of students. I had to be there.'

His wife shook her head to register her disapproval.

'Don't worry. We can go straight to the party.'

Alice smiled, grateful that at least David was willing to throw himself into the swing of things.

When he'd agreed to joining Todd and Angela's Wainscott beach share, she'd thought he would be the Grinch, stuck in the corner with his books and papers, complaining that he had to work when everyone else was at the beach.

But ever since their first couples counselling session with Mark Berger, her husband had appeared to keep his side of the bargain, joining in with Alice's enthusiasm when Angela had sent over an email cataloguing the summer events for the house share. As Dr Berger had pointed out to them, compromise was everything in a partnership.

Alice reached over and gave her husband's hand a grateful squeeze, as she watched the light fall from the sky and breathed in the soft breeze coming through the window.

It was almost ten o'clock by the time they drove into Southampton. Alice felt a flutter of nerves and excitement as David looked for a place to park. She'd been to the smart Hamptons town before; shopped in its little boutiques, had breakfast in the Golden Pear, strolled through the streets, soaking up the vibe, with a green juice bought from one of the cafés.

But then she'd been a day-tripper or, the one time over the course of their five-year marriage that David had agreed to come, a guest at a local and very expensive B&B. On both occasions she had never really felt as if she fitted in. She'd often wondered why the area had so few hotels, such expensive taxis and so limited a bus route, but then she realised it was to keep the Hamptons exclusive and keep people out.

Now she felt giddy as the car pulled to a stop. Not with confidence exactly; after all, she still hadn't met a couple of her housemates, and she was definitely feeling anxious about that. No, she felt the comfortable sense of belonging that came with having a summer rental in one of the best locations in the whole of the Hamptons. The house share was all she had worked towards since the day she had stepped off that Greyhound at Port Authority. And now here she was. Little old Alice from Hawkins, Indiana had finally arrived.

The inaugural event of the season, at least for the Wainscott house share, was a party being held at the Southampton Social Club. There was already a mob of people outside trying to get in, and as Alice and David loitered on the pavement, her husband began to look agitated.

She suppressed a smile, knowing that he felt bad about arriving so late. Punctuality was one of David's personal bugbears. He judged people's character by their ability to arrive on time, and Alice had scored points on their first date by arriving fifteen minutes early. She had never told him the reason: that she had wanted to scope out possible escape routes. Instead, he'd been already sitting at their table, checking his watch. She supposed if you'd been raised in boarding schools, then moved seamlessly from those rigid dorms straight into academia, timetables and structure would be everything.

She clasped his hand and walked straight up to the doorman.

'Guest list. Alice and David Holliday,' she said as brazenly as she could.

'All these people are guest list too, sweetheart,' he said pointing to the line.

'I'm two hours late and in so much trouble,' she whispered, hoping her smile struck the right note between wounded puppy and playful sex kitten.

'Go on, get in,' he grinned, pointing his thumb towards the sound of the music.

Alice smiled to herself. The knuckleheads fell for it every time.

'So is everyone going to be here tonight?' she said, taking in the sights, sounds and people as they stood at the bar. It was an eclectic mix, middle-aged men dressed in Tommy Bahamas, beautiful rich kids with their top-of-the-range fake IDs, trophy wives with frozen faces and beach-hair blowouts.

David collected their drinks, wincing at the $32 charge for a Pepsi and a mojito, and shrugged.

'Yes, I should think so. Todd and Angela, of course. Paul and Rebecca. Maybe Joel and Erica, not sure. Last time I saw Joel, he was showing off about working a-hundred-and-twenty-hour weeks, so maybe they're not here. You're not nervous, are you?'

'Of course I'm not nervous,' she said, moving her hips to the sound of the music, her eyes searching out the most interesting-looking players.

'You shouldn't be. There's no reason to feel inferior in places like these, although if it does bother you, maybe it's something you could discuss with Dr Berger.'

Alice rolled her eyes, but then she heard a voice behind them. She spun round and saw Todd and Angela, who greeted them with an excitable squeal.

'Thought you were never going to show, man,' said Todd, embracing his friend.

'David knows that this place doesn't get going until midnight, don't you, darling,' said Alice, giving Todd a kiss on both cheeks.

She was glad they'd seen the Carters first. Todd was one of David's closest friends; younger than him by a couple of years, but they had been thrown together as children and clung to each other in the hell of their East Coast prep school, even though they couldn't have been further apart in temperament; where David was stiff and regimented, Todd was louche and easy-going. The fact that they had remained friends all these years was close to a miracle.

Either way, if Alice liked Todd, she loved his wife. Angela was everything she aspired to be: successful in her own world and seemingly at home in her own skin. She was one of the few people Alice had met through David who treated her as an equal. It was the others she had to win over.

'Alice, how are you?' Angela beamed, grabbing her hand and squeezing it. 'Come on, follow me. We managed to get a cabana.'

'How much is that costing us?' said David with the honesty he could adopt with his oldest friends.

'My treat,' said Angela, sipping a Scotch as she weaved through the crowds.

The outside area was so pretty that Alice stopped to take a picture for Instagram. Strings of fairy lights twinkled overhead and the noise of the DJ faded into the sound of holiday weekend laughter and conversation. There was a row of white cabanas along one side of the garden and she recognised the elegant shape of Rebecca Ellis reclining in a chair in a cream trouser suit, like a character from *The Great Gatsby*.

Alice had met the tall gallerist a couple of times before and had been unnerved by her on both occasions. David had casually described her as being from a Rhode Island sailing family, but she was nothing like the Upper East Side WASPs that Alice saw around Manhattan. If she had to find a word to describe her new housemate, it would be *angular*. Alice didn't know much about art, but she'd been to enough galleries with David in their dating days to compare Rebecca to a Picasso painting – all monochrome sharp lines and unusual symmetry.

She made a mental note to tell Rebecca about her observation one day, suspecting that she would like the comparison. She had already brushed up on a list of topics to discuss with her new housemate that summer: boats, the

Kennedys, and of course art. She felt confident that she could hold her own now that she had the names of a few edgy photographers and lesser-known fashion labels at her disposal.

David slipped into the cabana first and Alice followed him, taking a seat next to Joel, who she had also met before. Angela introduced her to the two people she hadn't met previously – Rebecca's husband Paul and Joel's wife Erica – then poured her a flute of champagne in place of her empty cocktail glass.

Paul extended his hand as she was in mid-sip, and she took it.

She could feel a few drops of cold liquid dribbling down her chin, and she cursed herself for the rare misstep.

'Hello,' he said simply.

Alice put down her glass and forced herself to take a breath. She wasn't sure what had unnerved her more, spilling Taittinger down her green silk blouse, or the colour of Paul's eyes, bright blue even in the low light of the cabana. She'd met incredibly good-looking guys like him before, though, and was determined not to let him see her reaction. Especially with his wife only two feet away, watching her.

'David, Paul is almost as good as you at tennis,' said Todd, lying back in his seat. 'You should sort out a game.'

'Maybe we should organise a ladder,' said Angela, clapping her hands together. 'Winner at the end of the season gets a trophy. We can call it the Wainscott Cup.'

'It's got a good ring to it,' agreed Joel.

'Who knows, in fifty years' time it might be as prestigious as Roland Garros.'

'My wife is nothing if not ambitious.'

David seemed to have perked up.

'Do we have access to a court?' he asked, taking off his jacket.

'Paul, don't you have a client with one?'

'He's got a place on Meadow Lane. He's invited me for a game but I'm not sure that includes a season-long tournament for all of us.'

'Jeez,' said Angela, looking deep in thought. 'I'll have to come up with somewhere else.'

'Why can't the Wainscott Cup just be beach Frisbee?' grinned Todd.

A photographer approached them and asked to take their picture.

'Here, all crowd together,' he said, stepping forward, a flash blinding Alice.

Even though Angela had no doubt paid a considerable amount to secure a cabana for the evening, the group chose not to stay in it.

'It's base camp,' she said, ordering margaritas for everyone. 'We have a shot, we circulate, repeat.'

'Who wants to dance?' asked Alice. Clubs were a part of her pre-David past that she missed. She loved the hypnotic beat of the music, the smell of sweat collecting on the walls, and the kick from the night's first hit of cocaine. Even though she had left that period of her life behind her, she still missed the raw, primal abandon of those crazy clubbing days and wanted to get it back, even for just a few minutes.

'Darling, I'm just going to say hello to Danielle over there,' said David, ignoring her invitation.

No one else seemed keen to take up her offer, so she wandered back inside on her own. All the tables had been cleared away and the lighting had dimmed to almost total darkness. A glow of purple light came from the corner, where the DJ held some headphones to one ear and focused on the turntable as if he were performing surgery.

There was a seamless shift from one track to another, and Alice recognised the song immediately. She felt her whole body come to life as she stepped onto the makeshift dance floor.

Dance had always been Alice's passion. When she was a very little girl, when there had been a little bit of spare money to go round, before her home life had been kicked against the wall, she had taken ballet and tap lessons in the tiny church hall on the main street of town. She'd loved dressing up in her little leotard, and twirling around to the sound of a tinkling piano never failed to make her feel like a princess.

She'd felt that power too as an adult. On the podium, her crop top riding a little higher, her moves slicker and hotter than everyone else's, aware of the wolfish looks of the men around her.

She closed her eyes and started to dance. Song after song until she lost track of the evening and didn't even care what time it was.

When eventually she stopped, the room was full of people and it was hot. Sweat beaded in the space between her breasts and her mouth felt parched and dry. She went to the bar to get a glass of water, and downed it in one gulp.

'You made me feel tired just watching you,' said a voice behind her.

She spun around and met Paul's cool blue gaze.

'I was trapped in a car for five hours. No wonder I can't stop dancing.'

'Don't worry, you've got forty-eight hours at the beach to look forward to. More if you decide to stay on Monday.'

'Is that what you're doing?' she asked.

'I don't know yet.'

Their eyes connected, and Alice felt a prickle of energy so strong she thought she'd been wired up to the speakers. She was used to men responding to her sex appeal, but rarely had she reacted the same way on first meeting a man.

She started to smile, and it made Paul smile too.

'Something funny?' he asked.

She shook her head. 'Not really. I was just thinking how far all this is from the Memorial Weekends I had as a child.'

'No $25 cocktails and cabanas that cost as much as your rent?'

'None of that, no. Although I hear there's a parade on Monday, and that would have been me.'

'Queen of the fair?'

She swirled a finger in the air. 'More likely to be twirling a baton or doing backflips.'

'I'm imagining you in a leotard with a lot of gold braid.'

Imagine away, she thought.

'No leotards. It was a dust-bowl Baptist town. We wore uniforms that covered us neck to ankle; didn't want the men of the village to get tempted.'

It was an out-and-out lie in so many ways, but Alice had learnt that no one wanted to hear the truth. About stealing from her mom's purse to eat, about screams in the night that no one seemed to hear. People felt safe with a fantasy vision of Americana: cheerleaders and jocks, pie bakes and proms. So that was what she gave them, especially here where the ragged myth of the American dream flattered the wealth and reinforced the idea of meritocracy the rich loved to cling to.

'So I guess that's how you got into yoga. David said you're an instructor.'

Alice stuck out her lower lip, pondering. 'You know, I've actually never thought of it that way,' she said. 'But I suppose so. The high kicks led to the ballet, the ballet brought me to the city, and after you've spent five years stretching, a yoga mat is the logical next step.'

The ballet was a lie too, but it set the right tone. Respectable, classical. Highbrow. He wasn't to know she'd given it up at the age of ten, when everything started to go wrong.

'Well, here's to Coach Harris. The gym teacher who set me on the path.'

'To Coach Harris. And to your moves on the dance floor.' Paul smiled slowly, lifting his beer bottle aloft.

'You should join me next time,' she said softly, hearing the tempting siren call of challenge.

'I might just do that,' he replied as she headed back to the cabana as if they hadn't even spoken.

Chapter 17

'Why are you here, Alice?'

Alice shifted herself in the hard seat, thought about crossing her legs, then decided that would send the wrong message.

'Aren't you supposed to tell me that?' she replied after a moment.

Dr Hannah Berger looked like a bitch. Or perhaps that was all part of the act. She sat across from Alice in a far more comfortable chair; crisp white shirt, dark pantyhose, half-moon glasses. And deep lines around a pursed mouth that didn't look like it cracked into a smile very often.

'It would be much more useful if you told me what you thought,' she said.

Alice looked up at the ceiling, took a deep breath.

'I'm here because my husband suggested couples counselling,' she said finally. 'I agreed to it, and when we started seeing Dr Berger he thought I should see someone separately about my personal issues. He suggested you. Quite ironic really: my husband sends me to a shrink who sends me to see his wife to talk about my relationship. It's cosy.'

'Good,' said Dr Berger, her face softening. 'To move forward, we need to listen to other people's thoughts and suggestions. You've shown that you're open to change.'

Alice smiled thinly, knowing already that this was a bad

idea. Strangely, she had quite enjoyed her couples counselling session with David. It had given her the opportunity to air some of her marital grievances; how could he not know that his frequent use of the word 'darling' whenever he was really registering his displeasure irritated the hell out of her? Or that his jackets with the patches on the elbows made him look about fifty?

But this was something else. Alice knew she was going to be under personal attack, and she was not going to allow this woman to break her.

She softened her expression, remembering what she had been practising in the mirror that morning. She knew she needed to appear eager, yet anxious. That was what Hannah Berger would expect in this first session. Some awkwardness, some resistance, but above all else she would expect her to show willing. Alice knew that if she was in any way difficult, it might get back to her husband via Berger's own husband, no matter what the professional ethics code might say.

So she had planned a loose schedule: a few weeks of platitudes and denial, then confusion and anger. Week five, she intended to have some sort of self-revelatory break-through – blame everything on a fictional but abusive stepfather – then wrap it all up with a few touchy-feely declarations of 'finding herself'. She was pretty sure she'd be out of there by August, maybe even earlier.

'But what has actually brought you here now?' asked the doctor. 'It's good that you know you need help, but what was the incident that made you dial my number?'

'We had a deal,' she said simply. 'I'd come to therapy and David would pay for a house share in the Hamptons.'

Hannah Berger nodded and wrote something on a notepad in front of her.

'And why is it important to spend the summer in the Hamptons?'

'I want some fun,' shrugged Alice, taking a sip of water from the glass on the coffee table in front of her.

'Do you think that's what is missing in your marriage?' asked the therapist.

'Is fun missing in my marriage? Yes. Is it missing in my life? No.'

Berger continued with her notes.

'Have you ever had an affair?' she said after a long period of silence.

Alice gave a soft snort. She hadn't expected the shrink to go straight for the jugular. Then again, Hannah Berger looked as if she could turn people to stone with one icy look over the top of those glasses.

She knew she had to tell the truth. To some degree at least. It was obvious why she was here: her husband thought she had issues, and had been at the receiving end of many of them.

'Yes,' she said, taking another sip of water. 'Two that my husband knows about. Half a dozen that he doesn't know about.'

'You've had eight extramarital relationships?' said Berger, trying to clarify the point.

'I wouldn't call all of them relationships,' said Alice, watching Berger give a faint fake smile of encouragement. The frigid bitch obviously disapproved of her behaviour. Alice had met Berger's husband – a business arrangement if ever she had seen one, referring clients to each other – and Mrs Berger obviously didn't know just how addictive, how vital having good sex in your life was.

'How would you describe them?' asked the shrink, putting her notebook on the table as if she had reached a particularly juicy part of the story, the one she didn't want to be distracted from.

'Mostly it was just sex,' Alice replied.

'And that's all you wanted?' said Berger, crossing her legs and observing her. 'What you needed?'

Alice took a moment to contemplate the question. It was an interesting one, one she had already given some thought to after the end of her affair with Adam Pearson. She hadn't enjoyed the sex, or even the banker's company; it was the seduction she had found intoxicating.

From the moment she had let him win their race around the reservoir, and he had casually suggested a commiseratory coffee, Pearson thought he'd had the upper hand. The reality was that Alice had played him every step of the way. She knew exactly what his fiancée would be like. Beautiful but neurotic, controlling and nagging and yet completely under Adam's thumb. A tick-box version of everything Adam had grown up to expect from his future wife; a cookie-cutter version of every other financier girlfriend in town. Even if Adam hadn't gone looking for some light relief from the slowly tightening claustrophobia of his engagement, when it was presented to him he took it enthusiastically, regardless of the consequences.

'If you're asking am I a sex addict, then the answer is no,' said Alice simply. 'Sex is just a side effect.'

'Of what?'

'What I like is the power.'

Hannah Berger began to nod enthusiastically, as if she had struck psychiatric gold. 'This is interesting. Tell me about this power.'

Alice shook her head. Did she really have to spell it out? Could Berger not see how it made Alice feel, seeing photographs of the soon-to-be Mrs Adam Pearson, appreciating how much more beautiful and polished she was than Alice herself, but knowing that when Adam masturbated in the shower, or in bed at night, it was Alice he was fantasising about, not his fiancée.

'I like feeling desired,' she said finally. 'Do you ever feel that, Dr Berger? Seeing a man you find attractive and knowing you can have him. Or even better, knowing he's off-limits, that you can't have him, not yet, but in time he will become besotted, that you will become all he ever thinks about, all he wants, even if it is for a brief moment in time.'

'So you like the chase,' said Dr Berger, her dark eyes opening just a little wider.

'Who doesn't? You must remember how it feels. Seeing the high-school quarterback, thinking he's out of your league, and then he smiles at you at the lockers, and that first sign, that first giddy bite, is all you can think about for a week.'

Like Paul Ellis, she thought, trying to push his face out of her mind as she had been trying to do since Memorial Day. She couldn't forget the complicit looks they had shared over the weekend; nothing so suggestive or flirtatious that anyone would have noticed if they had seen them, but instead something more powerful, slight, yet intimate, as if they had a secret code. An understanding that they were connected now.

'I should go,' Alice said, picking up her handbag.

'We have another fifteen minutes of the session left,' said Berger, looking disappointed.

'This has been more difficult than I thought.' Alice avoided her gaze.

Berger stood up and extended her hand. 'Then you've probably made more progress than you think.'

That could be the problem, thought Alice, and hurried out of the room.

Chapter 18

The next week went quickly. Paul and Rebecca were not at the beach house, even though it was only the second weekend of the season. A work meeting in Dubai had taken Paul out of the country, and Rebecca texted Angela to say that she had gone to the spa, as if that was a preferable option to spending two days in the Hamptons.

'She detoxes four times a year,' Angela confided over a round of margaritas. 'She takes it very seriously.'

Alice imagined she did, although she also appreciated that missing a weekend at the beach house, which at Alice's estimation was costing them almost $1,500 a visit, was no big deal when Daddy owned a yacht.

She curled up from child pose and stood on the mat looking out to the class. Alice enjoyed her job most of the time, but she was glad that particular session was over. Her students had been especially annoying, taking a long time to settle down to their warm-up session, too busy checking out each other's gym kit and boasting about their plans for the weekend at the beach.

She pressed her hands together in a namaste as the class clapped and gathered up their things. Then she took a sip of water and smoothed back her hair.

'Weren't you at the Hamptons magazine party on

Saturday?' asked a voice behind her. Alice turned and saw one of her more annoying students, Darby Green, hedge-fund wife, whose huge diamonds seemed to change every week and who got dropped off at the gym by Escalade even though she made a big deal about being on the Friends of the Planet benefit committee.

'Yes, I was.' Alice rolled up her yoga mat. 'Fun, wasn't it?'

She didn't miss Darby's thin smile, a smile that said Alice was not welcome in her social world, at least not as an equal.

Pure Yoga East was one of four studios in Manhattan and Brooklyn where Alice came to run a class, and until recently it had been her favourite place to work. She loved that the typical clientele were the groomed Park Avenue princesses she found so fascinating. Her twice-weekly Ashtanga classes at Pure Yoga hadn't just been a job; they were an education. She'd listen to the chatter before and after the sessions, and take it all in: the places her students went for dinner, the interior decorators they used, the hairdressers they visited for their three-weekly colour; in fact a considerable portion of Alice's wages had been spent at John Barrett's Ponytail Bar because she'd heard it was where the prettiest girls congregated on a Friday afternoon, and Alice didn't mind admitting she wanted to be part of that particular club.

But since Memorial Weekend, things had changed. As she looked out onto the sea of faces during the class, she recognised several of them not just because they were regulars, but from seeing them around in the Hamptons.

Alice was popular at the gym; her students gushed about how much they loved her, how they owed her for their perky little bums and their strong, elongated necks. But to people like Darby Green, she was still staff, and from the look on Darby's face, it had confused her world and annoyed her.

It had unsettled Alice too. Living in the beach house, she felt as if she finally belonged, and the last thing she wanted to do was upset that apple cart. She didn't want to be Darby's equal at the private estate parties in East Hampton and have her asking for clean towels in the city.

'Maybe see you around the beach,' she said quickly, slipping on her nylon gilet and zipping it up to the neck.

She didn't hang around for a smoothie in the café and instead went straight out onto the street, debating whether to get a taxi or walk back home across the park. Storm clouds were gathering overhead. The one thing Alice loved about New York was its seasonality. Winters were cold and summers were hot, but on days like today, when the heat and humidity were oppressive she marvelled at how quickly and unpredictably the weather could change. The sky was darkening by the second and the vacant lights on the yellow cabs winked off.

'Damn it,' she muttered, knowing that her cotton tote bag was going to get soaked.

She picked up her pace and hurried west towards the park just as raindrops started to fall. Every few feet she stopped and looked around for a taxi, but there were none to be seen. A crack of thunder overhead was the signal for the deluge to begin. The rain came down in sheets and her hair clung to her skull. There was nowhere to shelter either, not on these smart streets; nothing but a tiny forest-green awning outside a fancy condo, which she ran under despite the snooty looks from the doorman hovering inside. She reckoned she could stay here for a few moments before she was moved on.

The rain was so hard now that it blurred her vision. She unzipped her gilet and wiped the water away from her face with the fabric, and when she looked up, towards a grand limestone building on the other side of the street, she could see someone waving at her from inside a doorway.

She narrowed her eyes to see who it was, but the rain was like an impenetrable sheet of frosted glass.

The figure came out from under the shelter and ran across the road towards her.

'Alice!' shouted a male voice over the metallic din of rain on the roofs of parked cars.

She recognised his voice before she could make out his face.

Smiling, she pushed her wet bag further up her shoulder and ran to meet him in the middle of the road, taking his hand to follow him back to where he had come from.

The pane of glass in the revolving door was steamed up as they pushed their way into the building. Once they were inside, Alice and Paul stood motionless for a moment and then started to laugh in unison.

'My white knight,' she said, wiping the corners of her eyes, hoping that her mascara hadn't run. 'I thought I was about to get moved along by the doorman over there for loitering.'

'Well, we can stay here until the rain eases off,' he said, looking over her shoulder at the street and then moving his gaze straight back to her.

Alice couldn't stop smiling at the good fortune of seeing him.

'Where are we?' she asked, hearing the tap-tap of shoes across the hallway. A smart concierge was coming their way.

Paul held up a bunch of keys.

'The penthouse belongs to one of my clients. It's a remodelling project I've been working on.'

'Nice place,' she said, looking around, unable to hide the

fact that she was impressed. The marble floors and walnut walls whispered discreet elegance, a building where you didn't get change from twenty million dollars and could only get past the co-op board if you had a surname that mattered.

'So what have you done to your project?'

'Want to look?' he asked, touching the small of her back to lead her to the elevator.

The doors shut, and the lift went up.

'What did you say to the concierge?' she asked, watching the hand of the restored art deco dial move as they went up.

'I told him you were the decorator and we were going upstairs for a meeting.'

'How many Upper East Side decorators do you know that wear yoga pants on the job?'

'I don't think he noticed,' Paul said as the bell pinged their arrival on the top floor.

'Still an old-fashioned key,' he grumbled as he fiddled around the lock. 'But this time next week it will be biometric fingerprint access.'

'The world of the twenty-first-century millionaire,' said Alice, gasping as the door opened onto a huge atrium.

'Billionaire,' corrected Paul, as Alice followed her nose into a drawing room twice the size of her entire apartment, with arched windows that looked out over the rooftops and towards the park.

The clouds had begun to part as quickly as they had gathered, and soft grey light spilt into the room.

Alice put her hand on the glass and looked outside.

'Do you think the billionaires who live here ever stop and remind themselves how lucky they are to have this place?' she said, feeling his presence behind her.

'They've never lived here,' he shrugged. 'They get people like me in to rip everything out and spend millions putting it all back together again while they rent somewhere two blocks away for another million dollars that could have funded fifty kids to go college.'

'I bet they didn't even choose the colour of the walls, or the kitchen, or that lamp over there,' she said, moving around the room to take it all in.

She ran her hand along the plastic sheet covering the bus-size sofa in the middle of the room, imagining how beautiful it would look when the giant chandelier was switched on and the light from the thousands of teardrop-shaped crystals illuminated it all.

'I've loved the apartment for them,' said Paul, watching her. 'I've spent two years on it, opening up all the rooms, restoring the features and the floors.' He indicated the polished parquet.

'Then the apartment is lucky,' said Alice as Paul moved a step closer.

'What do you think?' he said in a voice so low she could hardly hear it.

'I think I want it,' she whispered, closing her eyes, feeling his breath on her face as he brushed his lips against hers.

They didn't need to say anything else. Words were meaningless, the deal already done that first night at the club in Southampton. She'd known that at some point he would kiss her, and she would kiss him back, an inevitability that was pointless to discuss or deny.

He unzipped her wet gilet and it fell to the floor. He kissed the bare shoulder exposed beyond the thin straps of her workout top whilst she unbuckled his belt.

She rubbed his hardness with the palm of her hand and he groaned softly, then she lifted her top over her head and half naked they kissed again, more intensely now, his hands in her hair. She moved her lips across his chin, wanting to feel the roughness of his stubble on the inside of her mouth. She kicked off her shoes and peeled down her yoga pants and thong in one movement.

Turning her around, he unclipped her bra, and when it fell free he put a hand on each breast, moving his thumbs over her nipples as she tipped her head back in pleasure. His hands moved down the curves of her body, pressing against her hipbones, and he pushed himself against her until there was no space between their skin.

She could hardly breathe. She wanted him now, she wanted to feel him inside her; every inch of her wanted to be consumed by him.

Spinning back around, she held his face between her hands and kissed him urgently. They fell back onto the huge sofa, a soft landing on the feather cushions. Somewhere the sweet, sharp, burning sensation of her skin rubbing against the plastic wrap registered in her consciousness, but as Paul's mouth connected with her nipple she gave a breathless laugh from the pure satisfaction of his touch.

She spread her thighs and he held his cock, pushing its thick velvety tip into her, softly at first, then deeper and more urgently. They moved together, her hands grabbing at his hair, her nails running down his back, and her soft moans turned to desperate cries of desire. Pleasure pulsed between her thighs; he filled her completely and yet she still wanted more. She opened herself wider for him, and he responded; her sweet, tight climax exploded and fired white heat to every nerve ending in her body. And as she lay back and looked at the crystal chandelier, Alice realised that in a unknown billionaire's half-empty apartment, she had just had the best sex of her life.

Chapter 19

First Avenue wasn't exactly Queens, but it was gritty enough for a woman in heels. Only two short blocks east of Bloomingdale's, First stretched north and south, a tangle of ten-dollar nail bars and by-the-slice pizza joints; there was even a hardware store boasting a range of vermin control devices. Edgy, yes, but this was still uptown Manhattan, so between the 'real people' stores were cupcake bakeries and tofu tagines and juice bars like Organic Planet.

Alice crossed the sidewalk and pushed inside. The interior was suitably distressed: stripped wood, reclaimed sheeting and a giant blackboard chalked with today's specials. Spirulina greens, Moroccan flatbread; ethnic and expensive, the perfect combination for this part of town. Here you got wheatgrass smoothies with a taste of mean-streets grittiness. Oh, and it had been mentioned in *Vogue*, so it was safe.

'So hard to get a table here,' said Tina, rising to air kiss Alice. 'Luckily Jennifer – you know, my nutritionist? – she knows the owner. They're in a cat pool.'

Alice suppressed the urge to ask about the cats. Presumably everyone was doing the cat-pool thing right now, and asking about it would reveal her ignorance. Instead she ordered an echinacea shake and looked around. Hipsters, anorexics, fifty-somethings in gymwear and Harry Winston eternity rings. All was right in society.

'So tell me everything,' said Tina, tapping Alice's hand impatiently. 'How is the *house*?'

'Tina, I love it. The very first time I went, I honestly never wanted to leave.'

'And?'

Alice couldn't stop herself from smiling. 'It's amazing. Seriously. Not absolute beachfront, but it does have a cute little boardwalk that takes you straight there, and from our room – wow! – there's such a view of the sea.'

Tina let out a little squeal of delight and Alice couldn't help laughing. Moving in Manhattan society, it was easy to forget that there were people out there in the world who derived genuine pleasure from someone else's good fortune. Like herself, Tina was a yoga teacher, and although she was definitely more haute hippie than the mung-bean version, she was fun and kind-spirited; not for the first time, Alice thought she needed more people like Tina in her life.

'Tell me about the kitchen. I'm imagining it being the size of our entire apartment, all white marble and chrome. Does it have pans hanging over the stove?'

Alice nodded, grinning. 'I'm afraid it does. Not that I think anyone has ever cooked there.'

'No one cooks? Then what do you eat?'

'They BBQ. Or we go out for dinner. Next weekend apparently we're having catering.'

'Catering? Like a party? You must think you've died and gone to heaven.'

Alice thought about Paul Ellis and couldn't resist another smile.

* * *

'So what are you up to this evening?' asked Tina when they had exhausted the Hamptons gossip. 'I got class passes for a Barrecore workout if you fancy it.'

Alice shook her head.

'Come on. It's an amazing class.' Tina sipped on her green smoothie, watching Alice as if she would not let her off the hook. 'I've not seen you properly in ages. Let's make a night of it.'

Alice sighed. She longed to have a fun, girlie night out and tell her friend about David almost catching her with Adam; about the real reason why she loved the house share so much, more than she'd ever imagined. But she couldn't. Even Tina needed to gossip.

'If you must know, I'm going to see my therapist,' she said quietly.

Tina smiled. 'You have a therapist? I thought you were the only person in New York who didn't. '

'Well I do now,' said Alice, not meeting her gaze. 'Couples counselling.'

Tina paused and sipped her matcha smoothie.

'Is everything okay?'

Her concern was heartfelt. Tina was the only person Alice could really talk to, the only person she had shared any real confidences with. She knew about Alice's past in Indiana, her frustrations with her marriage to David, and had always made the right sympathetic noises, even though she was a nice middle-class girl from Albany who'd moved to the city to be near her photographer boyfriend Joe, with whom she had nothing but everything in common.

'Yes, of course. Why wouldn't it be?' Alice shifted un-comfortably.

'I just wondered why you're doing counselling. Has something happened?' She ventured the words softly.

Alice shook her head and didn't look at her.

'Alice, I'm your best friend . . .'

'I know. But there's nothing to tell you. We've been married five years. We live in New York. This is what couples do.'

'It's not what you do. Not unless you have to.'

A silence hung between them and Tina tried to catch her gaze.

'There's someone else, isn't there?' said Tina finally.

Alice didn't reply. She didn't find lying difficult, but with some people it wasn't easy.

'Who is he?' said Tina. Her words weren't hard or accusatory. Just a question from a friend who wanted someone she cared about to be honest with her.

'He's just a guy,' Alice said, feeling her cheeks flush.

'Is it serious?' pressed Tina.

Alice felt herself smile. She didn't how to describe what was going on with Paul Ellis. All she knew was that she couldn't stop what was happening between them.

The empty Upper East apartment had become their unofficial meeting place. Since their first encounter two weeks earlier, they'd been back half a dozen times; snatched moments between Paul's appointments and Alice's yoga classes, whenever they could get away. There were no beds in the apartment – not yet – but it hadn't bothered them.

They'd fucked on the granite countertops and on the floor of the cream-carpeted walk-in closet. Standing up against the de Gournay papered walls, and bent over the wide arms of the sofa; even outside on the terrace in the soft glow of the million light bulbs that illuminated Manhattan. She had no idea what the concierge thought or how their neighbours explained away the banging coming from the empty penthouse.

'You really like him, don't you?' said Tina quietly.

'He's amazing,' Alice whispered back.

'But you're seeing a counsellor because you want your marriage to work?' ventured Tina.

Alice tried to dial back her emotions. She was annoyed with herself that she had allowed her friend to tease the information about Paul out of her. Tina was not the sort to openly judge her, but she knew that her friend liked David and would not approve of Alice's betrayal of their marriage.

'I just need some time to work everything out.'

She felt her mobile vibrate in her pocket. She pulled it out to read the incoming text message.

I need to see you.

She knew who it was from and she needed to see him too.

'I've got to go,' she said, collecting her things together and stretching over to kiss her friend goodbye

'Be good, okay?' said Tina as a parting shot, and Alice waved over her shoulder as she left.

She paused for a moment on the street. Hannah Berger would have to wait this afternoon, she decided as she called her therapist's office to cancel her appointment, then texted Paul back to arrange when and where to meet.

Chapter 20

Alice took a cab to the address he had given her, trying to ignore the butterflies in her stomach.

This isn't like you, she thought. You're the predator, the seductress. You eat men alive. As she watched the city slip by beyond the window, she thought about her conversation with Tina and wondered if what she had said to her friend was true. Did she want to save her marriage? Was it even worth saving?

Why did you marry David Holliday? She could almost see Hannah Berger's lined face leaning in, asking the question.

Because David was steady. Because David had money and respectability. And because he had prospects – Alice could push him up the social ladder, hanging onto his shirt-tails. The rich irony, of course, was that he saw her the exact same way: a pretty girl from the wrong side of the tracks who could be improved. She was a project, a fixer-upper. In his mind, David was a Victorian philanthropist, saving a fallen woman and working – via science – for the greater good. Alice wasn't interested in the greater good. She just wanted a house in Wainscott with beach access.

The taxi was weaving its way through Chelsea now. Crowds of suits and high-end dresses, presumably heading to a gallery opening or a restaurant. Amazing how this area had somehow become the heart of arty Manhattan. Twenty years ago it would have been no-go, home to junkies and working girls, the gutters overflowing. Now there were galleries and artfully distressed bars wherever you looked.

They continued south and stopped on Gansevoort Street. She looked up at the High Line overhead and smiled at the schmaltziness of it all. She hardly ever came here; there was no need to. If she wanted to see nature, she went to Central Park. Not even in the early days of their marriage had David ever suggested a walk on New York's elevated park.

Her cell phone buzzed again.

I can see you. I'm up here.

Alice felt aroused as she took the stairs. She liked the fact that he was waiting for her; watching her.

Perhaps sneakers would have been a better bet, she thought, looking down at her feet, her court shoes squeezing her toes together. Usually she would wear cute little pumps or trainers. She always went for a sexy, feminine look when she was meeting Paul. A little sundress, or denim shorts worn with a T-shirt and layers of colourful fashion jewellery. Girlie, playful, fun – and that was precisely the point. It was the opposite of Rebecca.

She followed the formula; that was what she did, right? Tick the boxes, be the opposite of the thing he was running from. Laugh, smile, giggle. Rebecca, it seemed to her, was uptight and joyless. Alice had certainly never seen her smile – not a real smile – and she'd never heard her laugh. She'd asked around. Rebecca's preppy crowd were serious, rigid; they followed the rules. So it was simple to flip that around. Be fun-loving, witty, flirty.

'Hello,' said a voice as she looked up.

'You scared me,' she laughed, putting a hand to her chest.

Hell, he looked good. Jeans, a T-shirt and a suit jacket, and his stubble had grown just a little bit longer in the two days since she had last seen him.

'Wow, it's pretty amazing up here,' she said, taking a moment to admire the view.

The High Line had once been a part of New York's subway system, or rather an overground railway that ran up the west side of Manhattan. Built in the thirties, it had fallen into disrepair but had now been developed into a public space, with wooden walkways laid over the tracks and trees planted along the route. Here, at its most southerly point, it stopped abruptly, with nothing but a glass wall separating the platform from the ground twenty metres below.

'Do you never come up here?' he said, his eyes trailing out over the Hudson.

Alice shook her head. 'I don't know why. It's incredible. If I had a friend coming from out of town, this is where I would tell them to come.'

'So where is home?' he asked, touching the small of her back to lead her north.

Alice paused for a moment, knowing which version of her life she was going to tell him.

'Hawkins, Indiana,' she said finally. 'Population 2342.'

'That's a very specific number,' he laughed. 'Does it include you?'

Alice smiled. 'That sign has said the same thing for an awfully long time. When my dad left I always wondered if someone would change it. But they never did. I don't suppose they did me the honour either.'

'Your dad left home?' he asked, a frown knitting his brows.

She carried on walking without replying. Hannah Berger had started to ask these questions, and she hadn't told her about it either.

Paul took her hand, and she gulped hard as she felt his palm against hers.

'Don't,' she whispered, glancing around, wondering who might have seen it.

'Why not?' he asked simply.

'Doesn't Rebecca work around here?'

'Ten, fifteen blocks away. She's at an auction.'

'But someone else might see.'

'They won't. I doubt Rebecca's friends come up here.'

Alice felt herself relax. Everything he did was with a quiet self-confidence that she didn't just find attractive; she also trusted it. If he said they weren't going to get caught, then she believed him, and the fact that he was willing to take the risk made her feel giddy.

'Hot dress, by the way,' he said, glancing sideways at her grey shift.

This was the outfit that Alice usually wore to meet Dr Berger. It was her most sensible outfit, although even she had to admit that it was cut a little low at the chest and a little short in the skirt. It wasn't the sort of thing that she usually wore to meet Paul; she had gone straight to the High Line rather than go home and change, so she was glad that he liked it.

'It's my meet-the-therapist dress,' she said, surprising herself that she had just admitted that to him.

'I'm sorry,' he said, stopping on the walkway. 'Is that where you should have been?'

'I think being with you is going to be a lot more thera-peutic,' she said vaguely. She stopped short of giving him any more details about Hannah Berger and her and David's couples therapy. It was hardly sexy – and besides, it would make Paul ask questions. The last thing Alice wanted to tell him was that her husband didn't trust her. She didn't want him to think there had been other men, because standing here on the High Line, it felt like there had never been anyone else. Just him and her.

She wondered where the night was going to end. They were just a stone's throw from the Standard hotel and a dozen cool bars where they could go and drink and dance and feel horny. She didn't know how long Rebecca was going to be out – David had suggested that it might be as late as eleven – but if they checked in somewhere now, they could have a couple of hours in bed before they had to go home.

'What are you smiling at?' he asked, squeezing her fingers.

'I was just wondering if we're ever going to end up in a bed,' she said, shaking her head with a smile.

'I know,' said Paul more soberly.

Alice looked at him. 'I didn't mean it like that. It's fun at the apartment.'

For a second she remembered herself naked on the bathroom floor. Paul between her thighs, his tongue stroking her clitoris for what seemed like forever. Fun didn't even cover it.

'Do you think you can get away?' he said after a moment. 'Away?'

'We could go somewhere for a night. I have a few out-of-town meetings pencilled in. It wouldn't be difficult to stay away longer than I need to.'

'I'd love to,' she said slowly. 'I'm not sure how easy that's going to be, though.'

'This was never going to be easy,' he said, dropping her hand when a second look from a passer-by made them both edgy.

He was right about that. Over the past two weeks they'd had to make some rules, and sticking to them had been no mean feat. No sex at the beach house – at least not together.

That was rule number one, but there was temptation every-where. Paul only had to appear on the deck in his swimming trunks and Alice had to make her excuses and go to another room.

'I'll make it happen,' she said, feeling a spike of determin-ation.

'Do,' he said, with a look of such intensity that it made her shiver.

The route along the elevated park alternated between sparse boardwalk and more lush vegetation. The air was fragrant and Paul pointed out the various flowers and plants as they passed them: moor grass, and asters of every size and hue. As they walked, Alice could hear the muted sound of New York traffic in the distance, and every few hundred feet she went to the edge to admire the sight of the city spread beneath them, the long avenues of lights and shop-fronts, and the tail lights of taxis funnelling into the distance.

'The thing I love most about this place,' said Paul as the sun started to fall out of the sky and the crowds began to thin, 'is that it shows what you can do if you use your imagination. Fifty years ago this was just a run-down bit of track; now it's a park in the sky.'

'Who'd have thought it,' smiled Alice, wishing that she was able to think big, creative thoughts.

'Everything you can imagine is real,' said Paul, looking at her again. 'Picasso said that apparently, but my art teacher used to remind me of it every time people in my home town laughed at the idea of me becoming an architect.'

'People laughed at you for that?' said Alice, imagining who would do that at the sort of fancy prep schools the group went to. She realised that she knew very little about Paul's background, and it occurred to her that maybe they were more alike than she'd first thought.

'I'm from small-town Pennsylvania,' he shrugged. 'You

wanted to build stuff, you learned a trade: carpenter, brick-layer, construction. But I didn't just want to build; I wanted to dream it and make it happen, from the ideas up here,' he tapped his head, 'to the world out there.'

He started to tell her about his past. His scholarship to the local college, thanks to the encouragement of his single mum, Julia, then a transfer to Columbia and an internship at one of the biggest architectural practices in the world. He'd found a mentor, a household-name architect, a man from a similar rust-belt background, and now worked alongside him on prestigious projects that were changing skylines in New York, London and Dubai, as well as on high-end residential work.

She didn't know if his openness about his own past was a cue for her to share more about herself. There was only so much she could say. That was what happened when you created a new fiction for yourself. She didn't want him to question things that she'd mentioned at the beach house; things she'd lied about in conversation. She might have said she grew up on a small farm in Indiana, but the reality was a run-down house on the edge of town. There were no grounds; just the local woods where the middle-school kids were too scared to go because of the stories of monsters and bogeymen.

Never did she think she couldn't lie because one day she'd be holding hands with Paul Ellis in an urban park at sunset, sharing their fears and hopes and dreams and talking about the experiences in their lives that had shaped them.

'You wanted to know about my dad,' she said finally, looking straight ahead. 'He left home when I was nine.'

'What happened?' said Paul simply, willing her to continue.

She took a breath, not quite believing she was going to tell him this. No one knew the full story of her childhood;

not even David. Perhaps, in time, Paul could be her one confidant.

'My sister died when I was eight. She was younger than me. It was a cold winter and there was an accident.' She shivered at the thought of it. 'My parents didn't have a good marriage to start with, but after that, it never recovered. Dad was always a heavy drinker, but Mom started drinking too. The rows got worse. And one day he just left and never came back. I haven't seen him since.'

Light was beginning to fall quickly from the sky. They were approaching a part of the High Line called the Chelsea Thicket. The trees were thicker there, and the branches of the oaks and beeches on either side of the walkway stretched out and touched each other so that it was like walking through a tunnel of crisp green leaves. Early in the day, Alice imagined, it would be a pretty, shady spot, but now, with the sun sinking behind the city's skyscrapers and the cat's-eyes along the path twinkling on, it was cool and a little eerie.

'Your sister. What happened? Do you want to talk about it?' asked Paul.

She thought about it for a moment and then nodded. It was funny how he knew her body so intimately and yet he didn't know anything at all about the things that had scarred and shaped her.

'Mom had just come home from work, but she was busy, distracted, and we ran off to play,' she said slowly. She remembered very little about her early childhood, but she could remember that day as clearly as if it was yesterday. 'There was a lake close by. Sometimes, in the winter, we went skating on it, but the temperatures had started to warm up and the ice had begun to thaw. It thawed into a big jigsaw puzzle of icy slabs, and me and my sister thought they looked so pretty we'd play hopscotch on them . . .'

A single tear began to run down her cheek, and she wiped it away quickly.

'We only jumped between four or five blocks. I made it back to the side of the lake, but my sister slipped and fell in the water. I grabbed a stick and held it out to her, and for a second she held onto it, but she was cold and her hands were so tiny . . .' She puffed out her cheeks. 'I screamed and screamed, but there was no one around. I kept trying to reach her but it was impossible. Within two minutes, she was gone.'

She shook her head, feeling cold.

'Don't tell me it wasn't my fault because we shouldn't have been allowed to go there by ourselves,' she said, stopping and looking at him. 'I was older than her; I should have looked after her.'

'But it wasn't your fault. It was an accident.'

'So now you know,' she said. 'If you ever wonder why I don't go near the pool or into the sea, that's why. I'd rather we didn't talk about it again.'

Paul put his arms around her and kissed the top of her head. She closed her eyes, and for the first time in a long time felt happy and safe and at peace.

'Do you mind if we don't go to the apartment tonight?' she said into the soft linen of his jacket.

'Let's just walk,' he said, and Alice knew the evening had been better than any session with Dr Berger.

Chapter 21

The dining room looked like a spread from *Vogue Living*. The table was laid with bone china, linen and glistening silverware, all carefully arranged to show the dark polish of the Chippendale table, the one real heirloom David had inherited from his grandmother. Soft lighting accentuated the brown and cream tones; candles were a big no-no, according to Tina. Far too 'noughties boho', apparently.

Alice seriously doubted the dinner guests would spot the subtlety, or even notice the ambience she had worked all day to achieve. Even if they did, she knew they wouldn't mention it. Tonight's dozen visitors were all from David's work crowd: academics, administrators, a couple of friends from other colleges, all of them careful to maintain some bullshit notion that they were cerebral and intellectual and therefore couldn't be aware of their surroundings. Or retain any basic common courtesy. I mean, thought Alice, if you visited a friend's home, you said a few nice things about the drapes or the furniture, didn't you? It was just *polite*.

She took a breath, checked that her place mat was straight. Be cool, she told herself. It's just a dinner party. And so what if she wanted to be somewhere else across town, spending time with someone else? There would be time for that. All she had to do was get through tonight first.

She looked up from her asparagus, suddenly aware that she had been asked a question. Susan was looking at her. Grey hair, beads. Some sort of weird sandals, probably ethnic. Alice gave a smile and answered.

'No, I don't think I ever read that book.'

'But surely in college?' said Susan, reaching for the wine. 'Wasn't Bellow required reading?'

'I studied dance,' said Alice, feeling David's eyes on her. 'Ballet.'

A lie, of course, but so old and worn, it was seamless. Susan splashed cabernet noir into a Baccarat glass, a drop of the red liquid beading on the wood. Only a deliberate act of will stopped Alice from mopping it up.

'Yes, of course, but wasn't *Herzog* on every shelf, whatever your major? At Yale, people would bring copies to parties instead of wine. I think I spent most of my sophomore year discussing that damn novel. Crazy, right?'

Alice watched her sipping from the glass she had spent two weeks tracking down from a supplier on the East Side. Susan had no idea how 'now' Baccarat was. David had told her not to bother. 'Wouldn't know Wedgwood from Walmart' was his assessment, but that was just his reverse snobbery in play. *My friends aren't socialites, they don't care about the tableware, their minds are on higher matters.* Right. Susan Jeffers was a friend from the literature department at Columbia, sure. But she was Boston Brahmin through and through. She would no more shop at IKEA than she would wear heels to work.

She looked over at David, deep in conversation with Elliot Lowell, dean of admissions and all-round creep. She had the feeling David was avoiding her gaze.

'What *did* you read in college?' pressed Susan. 'Tell me you're not a Hemingway apologist?'

Leave me alone, you bullying bitch, thought Alice. I get

that you don't like me, but can't we talk about reality TV like everyone else?

'I always find American literature a bit dull,' she said finally, feeling the volume in the room lower. It was like someone had suggested the earth was flat.

Susan snorted incredulously. 'Dull? My dear . . .'

'I think what Alice is saying is that *Herzog* is a little turgid,' interjected David. 'You have to look at the work in the context of its creation and remember that Bellow was going through a divorce. He wanted us *all* to suffer.'

This was of course David's idea of a joke. There were polite smiles around the table, but more to hide their embarrassment, Alice thought. The poor pretty wife getting out of her depth again.

'An Anglophile, then?'

Alice looked at Susan. Christ, can't you leave it alone? she thought. Yes, I'm the idiot wife, I get that's my role. But why make such a big deal about it?

And then, like flicking on a light, Alice understood. Susan, with her greying bob and her mannish uniform of shirts and slacks, was hot for David. She almost laughed out loud. So *that* was why she always tried to belittle Alice at dinner parties, her passive-aggressive digs and academic in-jokes. She was trying to tell David – no, tell everyone in David's life – that Alice was beneath him, that he could do much, much better. Like her, for example.

'Anglophile?' said David with a forced laugh. 'Darling, tell Susan what you said when we went to see *The Merchant of Venice* last month.'

'I said Portia should have married the Prince of Morocco.'

The table laughed with relief. A joke they could all share. But Susan wasn't prepared to let it go.

'I don't understand – why?'

Drop it, Susie, thought Alice wearily. He's not going

to sleep with you. Not with that wardrobe.

'Portia's already rich, right?' she said, trying to hide her irritation. She knew she was playing a role here, the dumb-but-pretty wife, so she kept her language simple. 'She has her father's money, plus she's supposed to be the most beautiful woman in the land. Adding a foreign title and all that Moroccan spice would have made her the most powerful woman in all of Italy, right?'

She glanced at David, saw his approval. He was enjoying her performance, like a parent watching a young child stutter through a piano recital.

'The Prince, well, you've got to think he's only into the money – probably got other wives to worry about too – so then Portia can shack up with Bassanio during the week and no one needs to lose a pound of flesh.'

More laughter and an indulgent smile from David. He raised his glass to her. 'Round one to Alice, I think.'

Susan's face had drained.

'As for Herzog,' continued Alice, speaking before the other woman had time to open her mouth, 'David's right, it *is* turgid and not a little self-serving too, but surely the whole point of the story is to show that placing intellectual ideas over real life is just a form of bondage, and only by letting academic pomposity go does Herzog find authenticity and begin to live a life of real meaning.'

She stood up, carefully placing her linen napkin next to her plate. 'Now, who's ready for dessert?'

By the time the guests had all gone, David was drunk. 'A roaring success, even if I do say so myself,' he grinned from his position slumped across the sofa. Sometime after coffee, he had taken the unprecedented step of bringing out his prized collection of brandy, and he was now gesturing with a glassful.

'Did you hear the jealousy in their voices when I told them about the beach house? I could have sworn Abe Rice actually turned green that we had been invited to the Wendalls' party. And you' – he pointed at her, closing one eye – 'you were magnificent.' He stumbled over the last word, but didn't seem to notice. 'Everyone said so, even Elliot and it's hard to get him to notice anything beyond his damned spreadsheets.'

Alice smiled, unable to stop herself feeling self-satisfied. She was glad she'd done her homework; skim-read a few of the American classics on David's bookshelves and checked out Google to find out what people were saying about them. She'd even enjoyed the exercise; she wasn't a reader by any stretch, but Paul was also keen on books, and if it was going to impress him, then maybe she should keep ploughing through David's literature collection.

'Come over here,' said David, stretching out a hand. 'I want to see you.'

She knew what he meant – they had gone through this particular script many times before – but she hesitated. She was tired and she had a headache coming on, but then she remembered that on the rare occasions that David got horny, it always worked in her favour. Afterwards he felt manly and guilty in equal measure, which in practice made him pliant, suggestible, sometimes even generous.

'What do you want to see?' she whispered, going to stand in front of him.

David looked up at her, a smile playing on his lips. She imagined he thought it was seductive, but in fact he looked like a teenager who had just discovered porn.

'Your legs.'

'You want to see my legs?' said Alice, unzipping the back of her skirt so it fell to the floor with a rustle. She felt powerful standing there in just her high heels, panties, hold-ups and a cream silk blouse.

'More,' said David, taking a drink of his brandy. His eyes were glassy and she could smell the alcohol on his breath even from this distance.

'More?' she said, unbuttoning her shirt slowly, suggestively. For a moment she was reminded of her time with Paul at the apartment. She'd done this little routine for him too, and she felt vaguely traitorous going through the same motions for David now.

Duty calls, said a voice in her head. She pointed at David's belt and whispered, 'Your turn.'

He started to laugh and put down his drink. He unbuckled his trousers and kicked them off, then sat there in his boxer shorts, arms stretched out along the back of the sofa.

'Are you going to be a good boy?' she said, kicking off her shoes and kneeling down in the space between his legs. 'Are you going to do whatever I say?'

'Oh yes,' whispered David as she unfastened the fly on his shorts and released him.

Chapter 22

The first time Alice had seen a dildo, she had assumed it belonged in the kitchen and had tidied it away in the drawer next to the wooden spoons. Momma had hit the roof, especially when Alice had told her she had washed it first. Apparently soap suds wouldn't do Momma's pussy no good. It was a phrase that had stuck in her head, often popping up when she was in the shower.

But the phallic sex toys in XD'Or didn't look much like Mom's dildo. That had been cheap rigid plastic, like someone had melted down a bunch of Barbies. No, these things were works of art; they looked like they had been designed by a sculptor, and perhaps they had.

XD'Or was the socialite's erotic outlet of choice that she had heard being whispered about in the Hamptons. Tucked away just off Madison, it had a discreet but chic frontage, somewhere between high-end spa and Parisian patisserie. No one actually wanted to be seen going in or out, especially not by their husbands, but society women exchanged whispered anecdotes and gushing recommendations about their visits to the store. XD'Or was legendary.

Alice could see how it could be a guilty pleasure. It was unashamedly naughty – it was after all selling sex toys – but also reassuringly stylish. The racks of lingerie were high-end and delicate, the various bottles of lube and massage oil were packaged like they'd come straight from Estée Lauder. Even the vibrators were presented like objets d'art: raised on their own plinth and spotlit from above.

Despite herself, Alice could actually feel herself becoming aroused as she walked around the store. It was less the proximity of so many erotic implements, more the anticipation of using one of them. Not for the first time in her secret life, the illicit thrill of doing something forbidden was almost more of a rush than the sex itself, much like the incessant texts that she and Paul exchanged, using dedicated accounts and burner phones like cut-price spies – they were always careful not to be explicit because everyone had heard tales of affairs and flirtations becoming public after they'd been sent to the wrong number.

'Can I help you at all?'

The assistant Alice had seen hovering at a discreet distance finally stepped forward. *I'm Sandy*, read her name badge. She was mid-forties, shapely without being out-and-out pretty. Just attractive enough to give the impression she knew how to use these things, but not so beautiful that she was a threat. Sandy was perfect.

'Do these actually work?' asked Alice, holding up a small plastic egg.

'Ah, the Ben Wa balls. You usually use them as a pair. The idea is that they slide around against one another. They're kind of retro, sort of a *Boogie Nights* kind of vibe.' She smiled without embarrassment.

'Now if you're looking for hands-free, technology has definitely moved on,' she continued, stepping across to another stand. She picked up a squat piece of baby-blue plastic that looked like an overgrown dummy. 'You pop this in and' – she squeezed the sides to show that it was pliant – 'it moulds itself to you. You can walk around all day no problem. But the big difference is this.' She held up an iPhone. 'It looks like you're checking your emails, but with this app you can trigger it wirelessly.' She slid a thumb over the phone's screen, and Alice gasped as the dummy-plug began to buzz. 'Love eggs for the twenty-first century,' nodded Sandy.

'I was actually looking for something a little more conventional,' said Alice.

Sandy beckoned her over to the far side of the store. Here was a shelf of a dozen or more dildos and vibrators, each sitting on a scarlet silk cushion. 'I'll leave you to get acquainted,' she said and disappeared.

Wow, thought Alice, running her fingertips along the row. Things have come along since Momma's kitchen drawer. She felt like Goldilocks as she picked up each one: too big, too small, too pink, too many bumps . . .

And then she saw it. Now that one was just right.

It was around ten inches long, sleek and polished, possibly steel, although it didn't feel cold to the touch. It looked like a 1950s vision of a futuristic space rocket and she just knew that Paul would appreciate the design.

In the event, it had been easy organising a night away from the city with Paul. David had a Hemingway conference in Illinois he had to go and speak at, and although he had invited Alice to go along with him, he hadn't made a fuss when she said she should probably stay in New York and let him concentrate on his work. He hadn't questioned it; after all, as Mark Berger had said in one of their joint counselling sessions, it was vital that couples trust each other.

Paul had suggested they go upstate to a little hotel he knew. 'It's basically off-grid,' he'd said, 'but it's still very luxe.' Alice was imagining a Ralph Lauren hunting lodge, although she didn't much care as long as the bed was big enough for her planned itinerary. An itinerary that now included this. She held the vibrator up, feeling its weight. She smoothed her hand over the end, imagining how it would feel pushing inside her, Paul's intense eyes on her face, seeing the pleasure he was giving her, turning the dial up another notch. She glanced over her shoulder to make sure Sandy wasn't looking and twisted it on. Mmmm. It bucked in her hand, sending an electric tickle up her arm.

That's good she thought. Really good.

Turning it off, she glanced at the price tag and felt her heart drop. How much? She looked at the card, then back at the vibrator. How could they charge *that*? She closed her eyes and tried to recalibrate. When it came to money, she had never been able to shake off her upbringing. Back then, whatever cash she had had always been like sand slipping through her fingers. Now that she was rich – or comfortable, at least – she had to keep reminding herself she could go into Bloomingdale's and buy a lipstick without budgeting for months before and after. It was still an alien concept to her.

Even so, this purchase was different. She couldn't charge it to any of her cards; David was thorough about checking the statements every month. So it had to be cash. Mentally she counted the bills she had in her wallet. It would be enough, but it wouldn't leave much. She'd have to think of some scam to wheedle more out of David. Maybe something to do with the dinner party? Yes, that would do it – the caterers had submitted an additional invoice that had to be paid in cash. He wouldn't question it; domestic affairs gave David a headache.

'That one?' smiled Sandy as she rang it up. 'An excellent choice.'

'I just had to have it,' said Alice as she picked up the discreetly packaged gold bag and stepped out into the street. She had made it sound like she was making conversation, that she was happy with her purchase, but she meant it literally. She needed the vibrator, needed to give Paul something new, something he wouldn't get anywhere else; certainly not at home.

She caught a glimpse of herself in a store window as she walked back up Madison and stopped, looking at herself anew. What did Paul see when he gazed at her with such hunger? Sure, she had curves where Rebecca was pretty much up and down, and she was sun-kissed blonde where Rebecca was pale and gothic-looking. Was that it? Was it just that Paul wanted something new? That was how Alice operated after all, her simple formula. If he's unhappy with what he's got, give him the opposite. If he has fat, give him thin. If he has quiet, give him loud. And even if he's not unhappy, even if he seems content to paddle along with the familiar, men are always men, they all have the same flaw: hard-wired to their primordial urges, doomed to spread their seed as wide and as far as possible. Any man's going to get bored with one set of tits: a pearl of wisdom not from her mother this time, but her friend Carolyn, comforting Alice when she had caught an early boyfriend going down on some slut after ball practice.

Sighing, she walked on, back towards their apartment, feeling the weight of the bag in her hand, swinging it as she went. Usually she would take a cab, but tonight she wanted to think, to plan. Alice had always been good at that. Plans, charts, maps drawn in her head. Perhaps she should have been a bank robber, she thought with a smile. It would certainly have played to her strengths: conspiracy, disguise and a desire to take risks, to name just a few.

So what about Paul? That was the strange thing. Usually Alice had planned her movements four or five steps ahead. With Paul, she was just reacting, taking it as it came. Which was why she had chosen to visit XD'Or – she needed to get back in control. But that was the other thing about Paul: she didn't know how to behave. She became giggly and moon-eyed, like a schoolgirl in the first flushes of love.

Love. Was it really love this time? Was that it? Yes. That was what she wanted to say; she wanted to spread her arms and scream it at the sky. YES! She was in love. It was crazy, it didn't make any sense, but it was true, as true as anything Alice had felt anyway.

She looked down at the golden bag. All the more reason to get this right, to hook him, reel him in. She felt butterflies at the thought. She knew it was a risk; up until now their lovemaking had been pretty vanilla. Sure, it had been frantic and dangerous and forbidden, but it had followed the basic porn formula: kisses, rushed foreplay, fuck. Sometimes she went down on him, sometimes he went down on her. Nothing adventurous, nothing kinky. And everyone had a kink.

She looked at the faces of the people passing her on the sidewalk. A businessman in a grey suit, a woman in low-slung jeans, an Asian guy with a back-to-front baseball cap. Ordinary people, the kind you'd see in any city, but what did they like when the lights went down? Did they go on top? Did they like to watch? Giving pain, taking it? Would they appreciate a silver dildo that cost more than a brand-new laptop? She smiled to herself. Who wouldn't want a gift like that? Nothing says 'I love you' better than a steel vibrator.

She was approaching her building now and opened her purse to find her phone. She wanted to check her messages to make sure David hadn't done something crazy like leave his office early. It would be just her luck to choose the day he was waiting by the door to carry a bag from XD'Or into the apartment. She didn't want to have to waste it on her husband.

'Hey, stranger.'

Alice jumped, and in her surprise she dropped her purse, sending the contents spilling across the sidewalk.

'Oh shit,' she muttered, bending to scrabble it all back into the bag.

'Here, let me.' It was only when the man bent down to help that she finally saw his face. And froze.

'Nick?'

'The very same,' he grinned.

But it wasn't. Or rather, it was the same Nick Vlautin she had known, but he had changed. God, he had changed. That Nick had been handsome, with a lopsided smile and unruly hair, a lean rock-star look to him. This Nick had got old. The leanness had turned to haggard, the hair still long but thinner, lank, the cheekbones hollow – the sign of someone who had done way too many drugs. He handed her the purse and they stood up, regarding each other, both lost in the past for a moment.

'Well . . . surprise!' he said, with forced levity. 'Bet you didn't expect to see me again, huh?'

No shit, Sherlock.

'How are you, Nick?' said Alice.

'All the better for seeing you,' he said, showing her his once-perfect white teeth, now uneven and discoloured.

'What a coincidence,' she said guardedly.

'No coincidence,' he grinned, rubbing his hands on his jeans like they were sweaty. 'Thought it was time I looked you up. Catch up on old times.'

'Look, Nick, it's good to see you,' she said, moving towards her building, trying to hide her panic. 'But I have an appointment across town. Maybe you can give me a call and we can catch up next week?'

He looked awkward, embarrassed, his eyes changed then, his expression hardened, and she saw the lines the years had scored in his face. She saw the hunger, too, that determination to make a buck. Nick had been a friend, a champion for a while, but he had always been driven by his own needs, his own selfish agenda. And Alice immediately knew why he was here.

He stepped in front of her, shaking his head.

'No, Alice,' he said firmly. 'We need to talk, and we should probably do that now.'

Chapter 23

The deli was almost empty and Alice could see why: the vinyl covering the booth seats was cracked and there were smears on the countertop where the tired-looking waitress had half-heartedly wiped it after the last suckers had left. The menu wasn't exactly a crowd-pleaser either. Written on the grease-yellow whiteboard behind the counter, the specials were 'eggs', 'eggs and ham' or 'meatloaf'. In a town driven by the organic, the fresh and the new, it was like an ink blot someone had forgotten to erase.

'This place remind you of anywhere?' said Nick as he slid in across from her. Alice immediately knew what he meant. The Pie Palace, 54th and 9th. 'Fresh like Grandma's House' was the motto on the window. Alice had been seventeen, broke and scared, working twelve hours a day to scrape rent, when Nick had swung through the door, wearing Ray-Bans in the middle of November.

'Coffee, black,' he had said, pushing the shades up to reveal dark-rimmed brown eyes. 'And whatever you got, sweetness,' he'd added, pointing at Alice, 'sprinkle some of that on top.'

Nikolai Vlautin wasn't like the boys from Indiana. The name was a giveaway of course: Russian Jewish via Ellis Island, he was brash, loud and opinionated, almost a checklist for things that would make you stand out in small-town Hicksville. Not that Nick minded standing out: he wore a biker jacket and a T-shirt with the word 'Fuck' printed on it. He always carried a camera with him, but put himself centre of the frame. He'd go shoot the bums on the subway, or the whores on Canal Street; even the grouchy cops in Times Square. Everyone loved Nick, called him a crazy kid. He had a charm, a persuasiveness that could disarm anyone. And Alice had been his easiest mark.

'We're a long way from Hell's Kitchen, Nick,' said Alice, ordering tea with lemon and ignoring the waitress's sneer. 'And you didn't come here to reminisce, did you? Why don't you get to the point?'

'I'm disappointed,' said Nick, tapping his pockets. 'I thought you'd want to hear all about my life.' He pulled out a nicotine vaporiser. The waitress made a 'uh-uh' gesture with a finger and pointed at the No Smoking sign, which had been amended with a sharpie to read 'Vape Too!!!' Nick held the tube to his lips and made a kissing noise. 'It's empty, sweetheart,' he called. 'Doctor says I got to keep using it, though. Says it's a nipple substitute.'

That was classic Nick – always trying to shock, make an impression, bending the rules to suit himself. But still – it *wasn't* the old Nick. His eyes were dark, sunken; he looked like he needed a decent meal. Plus he was nervous, jumpy, his knee constantly jiggling under the table. The old Nick would have been leaning back, both arms along the back of the booth, far too cool for school.

'So tell me about your life, Nick,' said Alice as the waitress brought their drinks. 'I'm guessing you're CEO of Microsoft by now.'

'Hey, no need to be like that,' he said. 'What, because your life has turned out so goddamn peachy? Sure, I saw you in that society magazine, at some party out in the

Hamptons, you and your stiff husband up at Columbia.'

Alice looked at him sharply.

'What, you never heard of the internet, babe? It ain't hard to find out anything about anyone any more.'

'That's how you found where I lived?'

Nick raised his eyebrows and leant across for the sugar. 'I still have friends.'

Alice wanted to ask more, find out what he knew, whether he had been following her for years, but she knew it didn't matter. The important part was that he had found her.

'So what now? What's the big plan this time, Nick?'

Nick had always had plans. Big, crazy plans that, coming out of anyone else's head, would have sounded grandiose and unrealistic. But he made you believe. And for a girl fresh off the Greyhound, that was exciting – no, it had been more than that; it had been life or death to Alice.

'You know what the plan is, babe,' said Nick. 'You're a smart cookie, you always were.'

'Not that smart, obviously.'

The day she had left Hawkins, her friend Chloe had handed her a map of Manhattan with a big red circle inked in the middle. That, Chloe said excitedly, was the Barbizon, on the Upper East Side. Some rich old woman had set it up as a sanctuary for smart, streetwise girls arriving in the city, a kind of safe house where they could crash while they found their feet. Its roll call of former guests – Liza Minnelli, Candice Bergen, even Grace Kelly – had appealed to Alice's romantic side.

The circle on the map had been a forty-minute walk from Port Authority bus terminal, and when she got there, Alice had seen the dark windows, the polished steps of just another expensive hotel and known immediately it was a mirage, just some stupid story teenage girls told each other.

There was no sanctuary. So she rented a locker and slept sitting upright at Grand Central, then hit the want ads, lucking into the job at the Pie Palace on the third day. If she lived on pie crusts and coffee, she found she could just about make rent at a hostel in Midtown sharing six girls to a room.

After a month of cold nights and cockroaches, the romance of the Big Apple had just about worn out. That was when Nick walked in. For Alice it had been like when Dorothy woke up in Oz: like someone turned the lights on.

Now she sipped her tea and looked at the man sitting across from her. He was grey, like a child had scribbled over all the good parts. Funny, wasn't it, how life could do that to you. It made Alice feel desperately sad, even though he'd clearly come to shake her down.

'I've often thought about you, you know,' she said honestly. 'Wondered where you were, how you were doing.'

'And?'

'What do you mean?'

Nick smiled. 'You always had a hell of an imagination, babe. What did you decide I was doing? Doctor, lawyer, Indian chief?'

'I guessed you were probably in jail.'

He flinched visibly at that, looked away. When he turned back, his eyes were blazing.

'We do what we have to do, don't you remember that, Alice? That was our code. Whatever it takes.'

He reached into a pocket and pulled out a slim black flash drive. He placed it on the table and slid it across to her with one finger.

'You want to take a stroll down memory lane, it's all in there.'

Alice looked down at the thumb drive. She didn't need to plug it into a laptop; she knew exactly what was on it. She had told Nick of her dream to become a model, and Nick had told her he was going to make it happen. He was that certain. To say that there were stars dancing in front of Alice's eyes didn't even come close. She had spent her teenage years hearing she was trash, shit, a dirty whore no better than her mother, and now here was a handsome native New Yorker telling her she was going to be the next Cindy or Eva, or Lynda Carter from *Wonder Woman*. And he wasn't going to stop at the catwalk; he was going to take her to Hollywood – 'You can dance, right? And the camera already loves you. It's a cinch, babe. I got connections in Century City, it's all gold.'

But first they needed eight-by-tens, they needed a show reel. They needed to show the real Alice.

She closed her hand around the flash drive, the sick feeling spreading from her stomach as she remembered that hotel room, the camera already set up, the bed stripped. She could still hear the lock clicking, could see herself turning, the look on Nick's face. Whatever it takes.

She still couldn't believe she had let it happen. Then again, she wondered if her momma ever wondered how it had taken six short months to go from electrical store clerk to town hooker.

'Whatever it takes,' repeated Nick, disturbing her from her thoughts, clenching his hand around hers. The flash drive cut into her palm, but she refused to cry out.

'You trying to guilt me up?' he spat. 'You trying to pull at the old heart strings? Well fuck you, Alice. You've done well for yourself, married that rich motherfucker, now you can pay me. Twenty grand or it goes viral.'

Twenty? Anger rose in Alice and she wrenched her hand away.

'I'm only a goddamn yoga teacher! How the hell do you think I'm going to get twenty thousand dollars?'

'I don't give a shit. Sell your jewellery. Go turn tricks in the alleyway, for all I care. But if I don't get my money, your face will be all over the World Wide Web. Your choice.'

She looked at him, shaking her head.

'What happened, Nick? You were always so . . . so good. Why don't you do real photography or film-making? Like you used to?'

He sneered, his face wrinkling.

'You think I didn't try? You think they hand a directing job to a junkie two-time loser? Grow up. The only people willing to let me roll a camera were down in the valley. Skin flicks. Same old, same old. Problem is, everyone does what I do now – everyone can. Anyone with an iPhone and a girlfriend willing to spread her legs.'

He looked at Alice, and she felt nauseous.

'Twenty Gs, end of the month. Think of it as an investment in your future,' he said with a casual shrug.

Alice looked down at the memory stick.

Otherwise I won't have one.

This summer

Chapter 24

The pie sat steaming on the table, but Jem couldn't lift her fork.

'Not hungry?'

She shook her head and looked up at Michael.

'It's just so . . .'

She trailed off and looked out of the window. The diner was cute: all stripped pine and red and white checked tablecloths, which she suspected was genuine local decor rather than tourist-pleasing Americana. It sat at the end of Rivertown's main street, giving them a view of the lit-up shopfronts as the sun dipped behind the hills. It was almost six already.

'It just feels so wrong. I know Paul. Or I thought I did; we've certainly spent almost every weekend together and I just can't believe it.'

'Believe what? That a good-looking guy had an affair with a good-looking girl he was sharing a house with?'

She glanced back, annoyed at Michael's glib tone, but of course he had a point. Put a bunch of people in a confined space and sexual tension was inevitable; an entire industry of reality TV had been built on that one human truth.

'But Paul? He seems so straight, so ordinary.'

'I hate to play the cynic here, but Paul Ellis is handsome and rich and women in that part of the world make a career out of marrying well, then marrying again, moving up a notch from wealthy to rich to billionaire as they go.'

Jem wanted to object, but there was no denying the logic. She had seen enough beautiful women on the arms of warty, squat men twice their age; couplings were as much an economic transaction as a love match.

'We don't know that it had anything to do with that,' she said lamely. 'Tina told me Alice was in love, remember.'

'Maybe,' replied Michael sceptically. 'And maybe it was mutual. But the why doesn't really matter, does it? The fact is that Alice and Paul were having an affair.'

But the why *did* matter to Jem. She wanted Paul and Alice's relationship to have been a grand passion, a head-over-heels love affair that took them by surprise but couldn't be denied. She wanted it to be some pulpy written-in-the-stars romance; otherwise it would ruin her own love affair – with the beach house. Because for all her misgivings, she had been happy there. It was a beautiful house and an amazing setting and the housemates had accepted her as one of them, at least for the duration of the summer. It had been sunshine and laughter and barbecues, but this revelation had thrown it all into shadow. Perhaps she didn't know Paul; perhaps she didn't know any of them.

'So what now? Are you going to speak to him?'

'Paul?' Michael shook his head. 'Absolutely not. We need to keep this quiet until we know more.' He looked at her sternly. 'Seriously, Jem. When you see him this weekend, don't say anything about Alice.'

The waiter came over and asked if they wanted anything to drink. Jem didn't like drinking in front of Michael, who had made a real effort to stop, but she couldn't help ordering a large glass of wine.

She waited until it came and took a fortifying sip before she spoke.

'What do you think happened that night at the beach house?'

'That's what we're trying to find out,' he said, spearing a potato.

'Come on,' said Jem, laying her palm flat on the table. 'I live in that house.'

Michael looked at her directly. His gaze was so cool and intense, she felt as if she were under a spotlight.

'I don't believe Alice fell in the pool. I don't think she jumped in either, unless things with Paul had really turned sour.'

'So what? You do think she was pushed?' said Jem in a low, steady voice.

Michael nodded. 'We should consider that.'

'But if she was pushed . . . that's murder,' she said, saying the words that hadn't yet been vocalised.

'Or manslaughter.'

Jem felt a shiver of fear.

'It's not the most logical explanation for what happened,' she said, desperately trying to think. 'I get it that no one wants bad things to happen in the Hamptons, but murder is murder and the police aren't going to let that slip under the radar.'

Michael didn't look convinced. 'The easiest explanation for Alice's death was that she slipped, but it doesn't make it the correct one.'

'Do you have any evidence to suggest otherwise?' Jem felt her breath quicken; she was surprised at how unsettled and panicky she was feeling.

'Death by drowning almost always happens as a result of an accident, you're right about that. Alice couldn't swim, she was scared of the water, she had high levels of alcohol in her bloodstream . . . so it does all stack up.'

He stopped and swirled his Pepsi around his tumbler.

'Homicidal drownings are almost impossible to prove, unless there are signs of violence: strangulation, throttling. David has a copy of the autopsy report. I've been through it, and there were no bruises or marks to suggest a struggle.'

'Which suggests it wasn't murder,' said Jem, taking another swig of pinot gris. 'What about suicide drownings?'

'Also very difficult to prove, unless there's a note or they have weighted themselves down. There was nothing like that in Alice's case. Also, in a lot of suicide cases, the victim is often naked or removes some clothes, but she was fully dressed, other than her shoes.'

'So why don't you think she just slipped?' said Jem, daring herself to hear the answer. 'I'm not talking about the town gossip, but real evidence.'

Michael paused.

'David said he found Alice in the water when he went back to the house to look for her. He jumped in the pool to try and save her, but it was too late. In his statement to the police he said that Alice's body was around two metres from the side of the pool, but that's a long way if you've slipped.'

'Or her body floated away. Or maybe she tried to swim to reach the edge and went backwards, not forwards,' said Jem.

'Perhaps.'

'Michael, it's thin.'

'There were footprints by the pool. Footprints that matched Alice's shoe size facing away from the water, not towards it.'

'Which means what?' said Jem, trying to piece all the information together in her head.

'Think about it. If you slipped into a swimming pool,

would you fall backwards into it? It's unlikely. Unless you were pushed.'

He beckoned to the waitress for the bill.

'Footprints were largely discounted from the investigation because the area was contaminated. When David found Alice, he called the police, the paramedics, then his housemates, who got to the pool garden within minutes. You can imagine what it was like: water, sand, prints, hair from half a dozen people, all of whom had a right to be there.'

'Exactly,' said Jem. Michael's words had unsettled her, his undisguised accusation that Paul had pushed Alice into the pool, had killed her. 'What's that expression about the simplest explanation being the best one?' She knew she was on shaky ground. Michael was her boss, he was rich, tough; he had no real need for her help and could easily dispose of her services. But she knew she had to speak up.

'You might want Alice's death to be a murder-mystery, you might like the idea of solving it,' she said cautiously. 'Certainly it's a change from writing another Jack Garcia, and I get that you might be a little bored of that . . . But don't make what happened at the pool that night into something it's not.'

Michael looked at her directly.

'Maybe you're right,' he said finally.

Jem sat back in surprise.

'I am?'

'Every single day I miss being a reporter. You've seen that film *Spotlight*? The *Boston Globe* investigation team who discover the scandal about abuse by the Catholic clergy?'

She watched his hand ball into a fist.

'It was based on a true story, Jem, and I knew those reporters. And sure, they won a Pulitzer Prize, but boy, I bet what felt better was discovering the truth. That's why I became a reporter. Why a part of me still wants to be a reporter. Not just for the buzz. But because you're doing something that matters.'

He kept his eyes locked on hers and Jem could feel the force of his passion for his old professional life.

'Perhaps I am looking for things that weren't there in the circumstances surrounding Alice's death. Perhaps I want to find some explanation that appeals to the dramatist in me, the author who wants a better story than the fact that it was a tragic accident or the hack who wants to expose a cover-up. But we're doing Alice's memory a disservice if we don't consider it. If we don't look into the possibility that she was pushed. Because we've just found someone who had motive.'

'Paul,' she said quietly.

'They had an affair, but it can't have been easy. Tina said Alice was in love, but what if Paul didn't see it like that? What if she made things difficult for him? People do things in the heat of the moment, Jem. Perhaps he tried to call it off, perhaps they argued.'

Jem didn't want to think about it. She could only imagine how difficult it must have been keeping their affair under wraps when the housemates were all so close. Perhaps the deception had got too much for Paul, and he tried to break it off. But if he had pushed Alice into that pool, he would have had to watch her drown. She squeezed her eyes shut, unable to prevent her mind creating the macabre tableau: Alice splashing desperately, crying out, reaching for the side. Paul standing on the edge, looking down. Watching her die.

She couldn't believe he would do that.

'We need a witness,' said Michael after a moment. 'It's the only way we can move forward. Plus we need to drill down exactly where Paul was between the hours of eight and ten p.m.'

'I thought you'd read the police statements. He was at the party.'

'So says his wife,' said Michael.

'So he has an alibi. After all, one night in a hotel doesn't make him a murderer,' said Jem. She just couldn't make the leap. Paul was her friend, her housemate; she refused to see him as a killer.

Michael got his credit card out of his wallet to pay the bill.

'We don't know,' he said simply. 'But one thing is true: this *is* the job. We have to look at every possibility, every suspect, every angle.'

Jem was keen to get some air.

'It's getting late, I'd better ring Nat,' she said.

She excused herself and walked out to the porch. She dialled Nat's number and stood there impatiently. She just wanted to hear his voice, just wanted to latch onto something real.

'Hey, babe,' said Nat as the line connected. 'What's up?'

In the background Jem could hear music and raised voices.

'Where are you?'

'Oh, some launch thing. New kind of shoes, I think?'

'You don't even know?' said Jem, with surprise.

Nat spent every evening at these events, saying they were so vital to his career, and yet he couldn't even tell her why he was there.

'Shoes, definitely shoes. Anyway, Dolan wanted us all here, the brand's a major advertiser. You okay? Line sounds different.'

'I'm in the Catskills,' she said, waiting for a reaction. 'With Michael.'

She wanted to tell him everything: about Alice and Paul and the cabin in the woods, but it was too difficult to explain on the phone, especially when she hadn't given him any indication of what work she was doing with Michael.

'Cool, cool,' said Nat. 'Hey, Lonnie!' There was a rustling, then muffled voices, before Nat came back. 'Hey, sounds exciting.'

'I just wanted to tell you I'm going to be late back.'

'You're in the Catskills right now?' said Nat, finally grasping it. 'You're not thinking of driving back in the dark?'

'Of course,' she said.

'Why doesn't Michael spring for a hotel?' said Nat. 'He can afford it.'

Jem frowned, annoyed but not sure why.

'Stay upstate overnight?'

'Why not? I'll be here till late and I've got an early meeting tomorrow. No point in rushing back on those mountain roads, babe. I'd worry.'

'Right,' she said coolly, wondering why he was so keen for her not to hurry back to Manhattan. 'I love you,' she added, feeling a cool chill in the summer evening air.

'I love you too,' he said as she ended the call.

Jem hesitated before she went back into the restaurant.

What? You're getting upset because he trusts you now? she scolded herself.

She went back to the table. Michael had slipped on his sports jacket.

'I didn't realise it was so late,' he said, looking at his watch. 'I've phoned Sophie at the inn and they've got rooms if you don't fancy the drive back.'

She thought of the cabin in the woods, the cosy, romantic luxury that had drawn Paul and Alice here, and imagined herself checking in with the handsome, famous author, drinking whisky in front of a roaring fire, or sitting under a star-crusted sky talking about love and life. No, that wasn't appropriate at all, she decided, wondering once again why Nat, somewhere in Manhattan at some noisy, splashy party, didn't seem bothered whether she came home or not.

'What do you say?' Michael asked, catching her eye and making her feel self-conscious.

'It's not far back to the city,' she said, looking away and picking up her bag. 'No need for a hotel. We'd better get moving.'

Chapter 25

'Oh, I like it here,' said Todd, stepping out of the car. Across the parking lot, a leggy blonde was leaning into a silver convertible Mercedes, her tight trousers leaving little to the imagination. 'Good choice, Erica.'

'Hey, eyes right, Grandad,' said Angela, swatting her husband on the arm. 'You'd never be able to afford her.'

Erica walked across, trying to smile, but Jem could tell she was on edge: in fact she'd been jumpy all morning. They had driven down to Montauk in convoy to have lunch at the Surf Shack, the hottest new hangout in the Hamptons. Erica had spent most of the weekend telling them how difficult it had been to secure a table for eight: Leo DiCaprio had been DJ-ing by the pool last Sunday. It was hands-down the place to be right now, and as the lunch tables were usually full of high-flying celebrities and super high-spenders, the fact that Erica had managed to wangle a reservation through a friend in PR was a very big deal.

Jem was nervous for other reasons; this lunch was going to put her face to face with Paul for the first time since she had found out about his affair with Alice.

'Where are Paul and Rebecca?' asked Nat, as if he was picking up on her thoughts.

'Rebecca just texted,' said Joel, glancing up from his

phone. 'She had to run an errand in town. They'll be here in ten.'

Erica rolled her eyes, while Jem gave a sigh of relief, wondering if it was too late to feign a stomach bug – or simply run.

'You okay?' asked Nat, putting his arm around her. 'It's only lunch,' he smiled.

'Just got a bit of a headache,' said Jem.

'Here,' said Angela, rummaging in her purse and handing Jem a plastic vial, 'take one of these and have a cocktail, it's like magic.'

Jem smiled her thanks.

'Come on, let's get by that pool,' said Todd, turning towards the entrance, ignoring Erica's objections. 'We can't stand in the parking lot all day. We'll tell the clipboard Nazis the others are coming; it'll be fine.'

Jem followed quickly. She didn't say she would have been quite happy for Paul and Rebecca to be refused entry, but even if they did make it in, at least she could choose a seat that put her at the other end of the table to Paul. So far she'd managed to avoid him all weekend, persuading Nat to come out from the city on the Saturday morning rather than the Friday night, and once they had got to the Hamptons she had gone running, read in her room and busied herself cooking an orange and pistachio polenta cake, all of which had kept her on the periphery of the group.

'I can see why you're moving to Montauk,' said Nat to Erica as the model-grade greeter showed them out through the restaurant. The place reeked of money, from the sleek minimalism of the pool – all slate and glass, like a designer fish tank – to the cool wealth of the other guests, the men casual in open-neck shirts and twenty-grand watches, the women in boho beach wraps and discreet diamonds. The map might have said they were in Montauk, but it was a world away from the sweet village everyone called 'The End' because of its position at the far edge of Long Island. Jem had driven out there midweek, to escape a particularly muggy day in the city, and had enjoyed the slightly more relaxed vibe at Kirk Park beach – families with ice boxes, dads struggling with parasols, kids playing with rubber rings. There was a wildness to the area she loved too, the high cliffs and seagrass around the lighthouse, the crashing waves; if she squinted, it was almost like a summer's day at Porthmeor in St Ives.

But not at the Surf Shack. Here people were dressed to be seen: designer shades, hair extensions and dye jobs from the most exclusive Manhattan salons. Jem felt positively under-dressed in her T-shirt dress and gladiator sandals.

Still, the others seemed happy to be there. Nat, predictably, was in his element, his eyes twinkling with pleasure at being allowed inside this rarefied enclave. Todd, as usual, was taking it all in his stride, ordering champagne for the table.

'Here they are!' he cried.

Jem's heart sank as Paul and Rebecca skirted the pool towards them. Rebecca had swapped her trademark trouser suit for a long sundress and looked happy and relaxed. Paul was wearing chinos, loafers and a white shirt unbuttoned to show a flash of chest. Jem looked away, trying not to picture him in that cabin with Alice.

To her relief, Paul immediately launched into an anecdote about a building project he was working on, and the women huddled together to talk about a minor local scandal involving a billionaire hedge-funder who had dumped his wife in favour of his masseur. The two groups stayed separate as their food arrived: dressed salads for the women, seafood for the men. Jem relaxed, smiled and laughed in the right places, but her eyes kept straying across to Paul.

Despite herself, she could see how easy it would be to fall for him. His eyes were striking and his smile, though infrequent, was dazzling when it came.

All weekend Jem had wondered who had seduced who and how easy it had been for them both to be unfaithful in their marriages. David had struck her as decent and upright, but he was certainly not in the same league as Paul when it came to sex appeal. Similarly, the other women always spoke of Rebecca as being some pale beauty, but Alice was more obviously attractive and sexual. Jem had seen her Instagram feed; her teeny-tiny outfits: tight shorts that had clung to her ass, bikini tops that left little to the imagination. Her wide smile and thick honey-coloured hair. How had the affair begun? wondered Jem, not for the first time. Perhaps it had simmered for weeks, long, lustful gazes over the Friday-night cocktails; or had it been a crazy spur-of-the-moment thing? She had imagined Paul in the pool one evening, swimming lengths, his tanned physique sleek in the water. Alice had come outside to get some fresh air, cradling a drink, watching Paul from a safe distance. And she imagined their eyes suddenly meeting. A spark that lit the tinder.

'Jem?'

She looked up, suddenly aware that Rebecca was staring at her. 'Are you okay?'

'What? Yes, I think so.'

'Looks like you zoned out there for a moment,' said Angela. 'Maybe shouldn't have had the pill and the fizz together.'

Jem smiled uncertainly. 'Maybe you're right.'

'Shall I get you some water?'

'No, it's okay, I think I'll just have a little walk down to the beach. Need some of that sea air.'

She glanced across to Nat, hoping he'd join her, but he

was clearly not going anywhere. He was sitting in the middle of the circle of the men, leaning back in his chair, glass in hand. He obviously felt he was exactly where he was supposed to be: at the centre of these movers and shakers. For Nat, the Hamptons project had been a roaring success.

'Don't go too far,' said Angela, like a mother hen, as Jem walked away from the table.

Jem waved and shook her head. 'Just going to sit in the shade.'

She walked down a flight of steps and out onto the sand, perching on a low outcrop of rock. The Surf Shack was in a little bay with steep sides sweeping around to the landmark of the Montauk lighthouse. Here and there in the distance you could see the rooflines and walls of beach houses, the weekend homes of the rich and powerful. It seemed absurd that she should have been feeling so tense all weekend, not when there was such beauty and peace just a stroll away. She wondered for a moment whether it was worth getting so stressed over. After all, Alice was dead and nothing any of them could do was going to bring her back. Perhaps it was better to let sleeping dogs lie; it was hard to see how much good could come from it.

'Everything all right?'

She looked up, almost gasping in surprise. Paul was bending over her, holding out a bottle of water.

'Yes . . . no,' she stuttered. 'I mean, I'm okay, thanks.'

'Rebecca said you'd headed this way; thought I'd check on you.'

He sat down next to her and Jem accepted the bottle, taking a nervous sip.

'Sorry, didn't mean to break up the party. Not used to heat, I guess.'

'Ah, I was wondering why we hadn't seen you much this weekend.'

'Really?' she said, feigning innocence. 'I've been baking. I want to start a blog but I need some content. Takes longer than you think.'

Paul nodded. 'Angela told me about it. I can't wait to see it. You're an amazing cook.'

'Thank you,' she said awkwardly. She had never been good at accepting praise, but this had taken on a surreal quality: compliments from a man she had recently been thinking of as a cold-hearted murderer.

'It's not just the cooking,' she said, keen to fill the silence. 'It's the styling, the photography. I always seem to get random crumbs floating into the shot.'

'You should get Photoshop,' said Paul. 'That will fix things like that easily enough. I've got it on my Mac back at the house. I'll show you how it works.'

She smiled her thanks and took another gulp of the water, feeling paranoia rise. Had Paul come out here because he was being kind, or had he suspected something? Did he know? Did he know she had been asking about Alice? Had Tina told him? But no – Tina hadn't known who Alice was having a relationship with.

She must have been quiet for a few moments, because when she looked up, Paul was watching her with concern.

'It's not scary, you know,' he said with a smile.

'What?' asked Jem, her heart beginning to race.

'Photoshop.'

'Of course.'

Maybe he was just being nice. Maybe Paul *was* nice.

A voice in the head reminded her of the Inn the Woods. He had taken Alice up to the cabin; so discreet, so duplicitous. Where had he told Rebecca he was that night? At a design convention? A business meeting in another state? Had Rebecca been suspicious? Had she checked his cell phone or smelt the clothes in his overnight bag, looking for the unfamiliar scent of someone else?

'You sure you're all right?' asked Paul. Kind, caring Paul. Paul luring Alice out to the pool, telling her that he wanted to talk, that he wanted to make up, then shoving her, watching her flail in the water. Watching her die.

'I know, Paul,' she whispered.

'Sorry? You know what?'

'I know about you and Alice.'

She couldn't look up, couldn't see his reaction. All she was aware of was the brightness of the sun on the sand and the dryness in her throat. And relief. Relief that she had let it out.

'Alice?' said Paul.

Finally Jem looked at him, saw the confusion, but saw something else behind it. Panic? Fear? Could it be anger? In second-rate movies, when the heroine confronted the murderer, Jem always shouted at the screen, 'What are you doing? He'll kill you now!' But she couldn't stop. Not for anything.

'I know you had a relationship with Alice. And I know about your trip to the Inn the Woods.'

His eyes flashed. 'What are you talking about?'

'You know exactly what I'm talking about,' said Jem, forcing her voice to stay even. 'The Catskills, Paul. The cabin.'

She turned to look at him, daring him to deny it.

He swallowed, and she could see him wondering if he could continue the lie, wondering how much she knew. He let out a long breath.

'How do you know about the cabin?' he asked.

Jem shook her head. 'Does it matter how? The point is, I do. I went up there, Paul. I saw it.'

'You went up there? Why?'

It was a straightforward question – the obvious question.

But Jem didn't have a ready answer. After all, Michael had told her to keep quiet, asked her not to speak to Paul; she couldn't tell Paul about Michael or the book.

'David asked me to look into Alice's death,' she said finally. 'He wanted to know why she died.'

'*Why* she died?' said Paul. 'You're suggesting she died because of me?'

There was no anger in his voice, only confusion and sadness.

'I'm not suggesting anything,' she said as evenly as she could manage. 'I'm just telling you that I know about your relationship with Alice, and if David decides to pursue the reasons behind her death—'

'Why would he do that?' snapped Paul. 'It was an accident, Jem. It was awful, awful for everyone, but what's the point of dredging up speculation and blame and . . .'

His voice trailed off and he wiped his mouth.

'All right, I liked Alice, and she liked me,' he said, rubbing his hands on his trousers. 'And yes, something happened. We bumped into each other in the city and . . .'

He shook his head.

'It was a one-off at first. That's what I thought, anyway, but before I knew it, I'd got sucked in. Things are easy to start, but not so easy to finish.'

'You broke it off?'

'Yes, of course. I love Rebecca,' he said passionately. 'She's my wife. I've never done anything like that before and I was ashamed of myself. I didn't want my marriage to break down, so I ended it with Alice. It was over after a matter of weeks.'

Now that the box was open, Jem wanted to know everything.

'How did Alice feel about it? How did she react to that?'

It was another moment before he spoke.

'She wasn't happy,' he said quietly. 'She said she wanted us to be together.'

'And that wasn't an option,' said Jem, a statement not a question.

It was easy to see how it had all played out. Infidelity was a line you had to cross; once the taboo had been broken, she could imagine how Alice had been seduced by Paul, the idea of a lifetime with him. And making a choice between the charming, movie-star-handsome Paul and the older, plainer David . . . she wasn't at all surprised at which way Alice had jumped.

'She kept calling me up, crying, drunk. But I told her it was over.'

He stood up, brushing sand from his trousers, and turned to look at her.

'You're not going to tell Rebecca, are you?'

And that was when Jem knew what kind of man Paul was. There was no pleading in his voice, no sense that he cared about Alice, or David's pain. No, his question was a challenge, a warning. All he was concerned about in that moment was himself.

'Will I tell Rebecca?' she repeated. 'No, not if I can help it. But whether you tell your wife that you had an affair last summer is another thing.'

Her words sounded braver than she felt. Paul laughed, brittle and cruel.

'The last thing I need from you, Jem, is a morality lesson.'

She frowned. Morality? Was he accusing her of something? Dishonesty, perhaps? She hadn't exactly been upfront about her work – no, her collusion – with Michael. But was that as bad as Paul's adultery or whatever lies he'd told about Alice's death?

He was smiling now, a mocking smile.

'Before you start questioning the honesty between myself

and Rebecca, perhaps you could tell me if *your* husband told *you* about his own little liaison?'

Jem's world slid sideways. It was as if a trapdoor had opened and she had fallen through it. She couldn't grasp onto anything and she was falling, falling, her safe, normal world tumbling about her.

'Liaison?' she managed. 'Who is this supposed to be with?'

She suddenly thought of Angela. Nat did seem to hang on every word she said, and Jem had never felt comfortable seeing them huddled together at parties, dissecting the latest gossip.

Paul's smile grew wider.

'With Alice, of course.'

Alice.

Jem narrowed her eyes at him, her head spinning. It was as if he was talking in a foreign language. How could he be talking about Nat and Alice in the same breath?

Paul chuckled, seeing that his words had hit home.

'Alice was so pissed with me, so pissed that I could break it off with her, she went on a revenge mission. And she chose your husband to use as a weapon.'

'No,' said Jem, but it came out as a croak.

'You wanted us all to be honest, Jem, but how does honest feel now? It was at one of those parties that Nat likes so much. The drinks were flowing and Alice was a very beautiful, seductive woman. You can imagine how easily it happened, can't you?'

Jem looked at him with hatred. The bastard was enjoying this. She had always detected something niggling between Nat and Paul. Not hostility exactly, just a prickliness that she had put down to clashing male egos. But perhaps it wasn't the usual alpha male dick-swinging; perhaps it was rivalry of another sort: rivalry over a woman.

'Nat wouldn't do that,' she said, sounding more sure than she felt. She wasn't going to let Paul see just how much he had rattled her, that it was feeding into every insecurity she had about her husband.

'He would, Jem – and he did. I saw it happen.'

'Bullshit,' said Jem. 'This is just something Alice told you to make you jealous.'

'Oh yes, Alice told me,' sneered Paul. 'One of the many times that sad lush cornered me, drunk out of her mind. She told me that if I didn't want her, there were plenty of men that did – like Nat. She told me how much Nat wanted her, how he'd already had her, again and again.'

'Stop!' cried Jem, putting her hands over her ears and clenching her eyes shut.

When she opened them again, she saw that Paul was still watching her.

'This is what happens when you start poking into things that don't concern you, Jem. You uncover things that are better left alone.'

Jem wanted to respond, to tell him she would go to Rebecca, scare the crap out of him. But she couldn't seem to get the words out.

'We welcomed you into our group,' said Paul, his voice heavy with menace. 'Don't abuse our friendship, digging up things that should stay in the past. Alice is dead, but there are people still alive who can be hurt.'

'Is that a threat?'

'Just a statement of fact. You think you can blackmail me, threaten to tell Rebecca? Well, consider your damn husband's position. He's here because we allow him to be. That can all change' – he snapped his fingers – 'like that.'

'And is that what you said to Alice? Did you threaten her too?'

Paul rounded on her, pushing his face close to hers.

'Why don't you ask me what you *really* want to ask?' he growled. 'You know you want to. Did I kill Alice?'

Jem's face must have betrayed her shock, because he barked out a mocking laugh.

'Oh, you don't seriously think I haven't heard the rumours? Come on! They've thought up every angle, from pool orgy gone wrong to Satanic sex cult.'

He made a beckoning motion with his hands. 'Go on, ask.'

'All right,' said Jem. 'Did you kill Alice?'

He glared at her, his very being radiating anger and disgust. Then he closed his eyes, his shoulders sagging, as if all the air had gone out of him.

'No,' he said. 'No. I never hurt Alice. I might have been an idiot, I might have been unfaithful, and yes, perhaps the reason she was drinking so much the week she died was because of me, because I rejected her, broke it off. But I didn't hurt her. Not in the way you're suggesting. I would never do that. I can see you don't believe me. Well, that's up to you to decide. But think about this. Why are you looking at me as a suspect? Because I have motive? Because I wanted to keep Alice quiet about the affair?'

He smiled grimly.

'But I'm not the only one who fits that description, am I? Maybe you should start looking a little closer to home.'

Chapter 26

Jem couldn't breathe. She tried, but no air seemed to reach her lungs. It felt like a giant hand was pressing on her chest, squeezing everything inside.

Just a panic attack, she told herself. Just the shock.

She looked back towards the Surf Shack, searching for Nat, hoping he was watching, that he'd come running. Then she remembered, and felt another squeeze in her chest.

'Oh God,' she gasped, forcing air in, out.

He wouldn't come, not when there were other women by the pool. In, out, breathe.

He was probably trailing his hand over Rebecca's pale skin right now. God, *breathe*!

Finally she managed to force air down, felt her chest loosen. In, out. Her vision cleared and she looked back towards the restaurant, just as Paul crossed the pool area.

There was Rebecca, touching him affectionately on the shoulder, Paul putting his arm round her waist, a peck on the cheek. And that was when Jem knew: Paul would never tell his wife about what he had done. Never.

And neither will I.

No, she could never tell Rebecca about Alice and Paul, not without everyone finding out about Nat's infidelity.

Infidelity.

What a word. So polite, so innocuous. And yet it meant the end of everything.

Breathe.

Jem blew out her cheeks and turned towards the ocean, grateful at least that she was alone. She walked down the sand, numb and shell-shocked, and stared out towards the horizon, wondering how far it was to the coast of England. How could this be happening? This time last year, she had been living in a cute little cottage in London, blissfully in love with her devoted husband, surrounded by friends and familiar things. And yet it had all been a lie, hadn't it? Her devoted husband had been over here, having an affair with a beautiful American socialite. How could Jem compete with that?

She watched the waves lapping at the shore, wondering how deep the water was, wondering if this was how Alice had felt that night as she had stared down into the pool. Wondering if a few simple steps, one foot in front of the other, would take all the pain away. But the pain never disappeared, did it? It was just transferred to the living. To your family, who wished you had confided in them; to your friends, weighed down with guilt because they hadn't seen the signs. She thought of the grey pallor and drawn features of David Holliday, still tortured by his wife's death. Did he know? Did he suspect his wife's infidelity? Did it even matter to him?

Alice.

Nat and Alice. Could it be true?

Of course it could. In her heart of hearts, Jem knew that everything Paul had said was true. Nat was vain, easily impressed, obsessed with surface. He was shallow, that was the truth. He lived for parties and clothes and any opportunity to show off to strangers. Yes, he was charming and good company – all those things were positives – but it made him vulnerable to temptation. Not booze or drugs, but flattery. Pay Nat attention and he was yours; that was why the fashion PRs spent so much time wooing him. It worked.

Jem had seen it happen again and again at parties and events: women would flirt and he would flirt back. It was easy to see how he could have stepped over the line from flirtation into an actual affair – in fact it had been Jem's secret fear all those nights she had sat at home waiting for him when he was out at some important event or launch. She had tried to tell herself she was just being paranoid, that Nat loved her and always came home to her in the end. But love would only get you so far when the champagne was flowing, beautiful, connected women were beckoning to you and your wife was at home baking cupcakes.

She brushed at the tears running down her face, barely noticing them as she half walked, half stumbled along the beach, wanting to put distance between her and the house-mates, oblivious and laughing back at the restaurant. To them, it was just another great day in the sunshine; they were completely unaware – and probably uncaring – that her world was cracking down the middle.

Eventually she reached the point where the sand ran out and the headland jutted into the sea. She sat on a rock, turning her wet face up to the sun, screwing her eyes closed, trying to piece it all together.

'Maybe you should start looking a little closer to home.' That was what Paul had said, trying to imply that Nat could equally have been involved in Alice's death. But that part Jem didn't believe.

Nat was an idiot. But he wasn't a murderer. Lying was one thing, but he just didn't have the self-discipline for crime. He was too sloppy, far too scared of people thinking badly of him. Still, he had been in New York around that time, hadn't he? A two-week secondment to see how the Americans worked, meet the major players. He had fitted in so well they had offered him a full-time job, and Jem could only imagine how he had gone about that. Parties, cocktails, anecdotes, small talk, all the things Nat was best at. He liked to tell people the bigwigs had been impressed by his ideas and creativity, but Jem had seen him in action often enough to know that they probably liked how he handled the advertisers, how he had a knack of getting brands to throw money his way.

She squinted at the gulls spiralling above her and struggled to remember the precise dates of Nat's trip and how they tallied with the date of Alice's death.

She was certain that he had been back in England by then. Certain. But how certain, exactly?

That night at the beach house when the group had first mentioned Alice's death, there had been no suggestion that Nat had been present. Not at the house, not at the party, but was he in the country? If he was, he'd have been in Manhattan, barely two hours' drive away.

Now that *is* paranoid, she thought to herself, although she wasn't sure of anything any more. She felt weary, weak, all energy sapped. She wiped her eyes and inhaled deeply, tasting the salt on her lips. How could she be somewhere so beautiful and yet be so miserable?

She had a sudden thought that she should phone Michael. He always made her feel better, always spoke such sense. But what would she say? 'Hi, Michael, my husband's been shagging your murder victim. How's your day been?'

Michael would only tell her to leave Nat. That was what men always said. They were quite happy to sleep around, play the field like some oversexed dog, but they were always hard-line moralists when it came to other people's relationships.

'Hey!'

A voice behind her made her twist, shading her eyes. Her heart jumped; was it Nat? Paul? She didn't want to see either right now. No, a female silhouette.

'Erica,' she said. Not Nat, not Paul, but not so much better. She could only imagine what Erica would think about this whole mess. Roll her eyes and tell her that she'd brought it all on herself, most likely. She might well be right.

'You okay?' Erica asked as she walked over, her sandals swinging from one hand.

'Sure,' said Jem, wiping her face. It was a vain gesture; her eyes must look red and swollen. At least she wasn't wearing make-up – the hot days in the Hamptons only called for a slick of lip gloss – so she was spared streaked mascara, but still, she didn't doubt that Erica could see she had been crying.

'You sure?' A softer tone, more concerned.

Jem tried for a smile.

'I just came out for some air. It's a bit full-on for me today. But thank you for the invite,' she said quickly, not wanting to appear ungrateful.

'Sure.'

There was a pause as Erica sat on the rock beside her, a second when Jem wondered which way Erica would jump. A show of faux-sympathy, perhaps. Find out what was wrong, use it as social currency: 'You'll never guess what I heard . . .' Laugh at the simple wife with her cheating husband: 'Who can blame him?'

Instead, Erica leant over and handed Jem a bottle of flavoured water.

'Tell me what you think of that,' she said. 'They're doing a big PR push; I might be doing some consulting for them.'

Jem had a tentative sip. It was horrible, like day-old chewing gum.

'Vitamin K Bursting Verbena,' said Erica. 'That's what they're calling it. Tastes like mouthwash, right?'

Jem giggled despite herself.

'Mouthwash,' she agreed, handing it back. 'If I was being charitable, I'd say peppermint and lemongrass. But those are flavours that clash. Mint needs something softer, fruitier . . .'

Erica smiled, nodding. 'You're good at this.'

'What?'

'Well, you understand flavours. I've seen you in the kitchen, a splash of this, a dash of that. You instinctively know what works together and what doesn't.'

Like me and Nat, thought Jem, grimly.

Erica put a hand on her shoulder.

'Is everything okay?'

Jem glanced at her, then shook her head quickly. She couldn't stop the tears, and they spilt down her face.

'Oh honey.'

Erica's face softened and she pulled Jem into a hug. For a moment Jem felt reassured by the sweet smell of her hair and the warmth of her arms around her.

'What's wrong?' said Erica, pulling away. 'And don't even think of saying nothing,' she chided, giving her a stern look.

Jem hesitated, and then, realising how alone she felt, knew that she needed to talk about it.

'It's Nat,' she said, so quietly she could hardly even hear herself.

'You had a fight?'

Jem squeezed her eyes tight. If only it were that simple. Of course she'd been angry with her husband before. More than usual lately, she thought sadly, thinking about his flippant attitude towards starting a family, the way he seemed to prioritise his work life over their marriage. But this was something else.

This was about their marriage suddenly feeling like a sham.

'I don't know if I trust him,' she said finally.

'Why don't you trust him?' asked Erica quietly.

Jem shook her head. 'Rebecca warned me once. That he was a great-looking guy and a consummate flirt and that I should be careful.'

'She should know. She's got a great-looking husband herself. Add a good job and polish and connections . . . that makes someone hot, desirable.' Erica pulled a Kleenex from her tote and handed it to Jem.

'You can be desirable and . . . honest, can't you?' said Jem. 'You don't have to act on it.'

Erica snorted. 'This city is ruthless, Jem. People come here to get what they want and they don't care who they have to step on to get it. It takes a strong man to turn all that temptation down. I mean, why not have your cake and eat it? It's the American dream, right?'

'How do you know so much about it?' Jem asked, curious.

'Because I live with a man just like that,' Erica replied.

'Joel? You don't think Joel has been tempted, do you?' Jem chose her words carefully. Erica was being sympathetic right now, but she was exactly the sort of woman who might turn on you if you assumed too much. But Erica looked as crestfallen as Jem felt.

'Joel works in finance,' she said, twisting the strap of her bag distractedly. 'He's not the CEO of Goldman's, but that doesn't matter. It makes him popular with a certain type of woman in New York, the sort who think he's fair game even if he has a ring on his finger.'

Erica looked bleak, haunted, and Jem could only wonder what had happened in the past to make her that way.

'But look at you,' she said. 'You're beautiful, successful.

What's that Paul Newman quote about not going for hamburgers when you have steak at home?'

'Maybe Joel thinks the steak's not quite as juicy as it was when he first ordered it from the menu.'

There was a moment's pause, then both women burst out laughing. For Jem it felt good, but when the smiles faded, Erica looked even sadder.

'Do you know, I spend two hours a day in the gym to look like this,' she said. 'I haven't eaten cake since twelfth grade. When we go to a dinner or a party, I hate even going to the bathroom in case someone has their eye on my husband. And they're just the women I don't know about.'

'You know about others?' asked Jem. She knew she was prying, but she needed to hear. Erica nodded.

'I know Joel has slept around, but it's not just that.' She drew a breath and looked out to sea. 'You know, Angela can't understand why we want to leave the house share, why we want to get our own place. I love the beach house, I love the group. But I'm not sure I'll ever be okay with Joel and Rebecca's relationship.'

Jem couldn't keep the astonishment from her face.

'Joel and Rebecca? I thought they were just old friends from school or somewhere.'

Erica gave a soft snort. 'Close friends. Too close, maybe.'

Jem looked at her more closely, unsure if she was joking. Irony was one of Erica's big stock-in-trades.

'You don't think anything has happened between them, do you?' she asked, but Erica just shook her head sadly.

'I don't ask any more, it's not worth it. He'll deny it, he always does.'

She paused.

'It's okay when we're in the city. Joel works like a demon, he's so competitive. So I know he hasn't got time to see her even if he wanted to. But out here, it's different. I have to watch them together every damn day. Their closeness. The way they can communicate with just a look. That's why I need to get away.'

Jem couldn't think of anything to say, so instead she put a reassuring arm around Erica's shoulder. At first Erica resisted, then she relaxed into it and they sat there lost in their own thoughts for what felt like a long time.

Finally Erica pulled away and smiled gratefully at Jem.

'Do you want to come and see it?' she asked.

'See what?'

'Our new house, of course. It's not too far from here. Unless you want to get back to the Shack?'

'I'm not sure anyone will notice we've gone,' smiled Jem.

It was a short walk back to the road, then Erica led Jem along a sandy path through the dunes. 'It faces the next bay,' she said as they walked. 'We can't go in yet, but you'll get an idea.'

They climbed a slope, then turned a corner and Erica stretched out an arm.

'There it is,' she grinned. 'The house that Yonex built.'

'What's Yonex?'

'Joel had a good bonus last year and made a ton of money from a trade. Together we could afford it. Just.'

'Wow,' said Jem. The house was like a centre spread from *Architectural Digest*. Modern and box-shaped, with sharp lines of concrete and glass, it jutted out of the hillside as if it was reaching for the sea.

'There's a pool on the terrace at the back, of course,' said Erica proudly. 'And the views of the sunset, well, I hope you'll come and see.'

'Erica, it's amazing. You must be so happy.'

The redhead nodded. 'It makes up for a lot, I will say that.'

Jem looked at the dream house, feeling envy and sadness

at the same time. It was undeniably beautiful, the kind of house anyone would die for, but would it really replace honesty and a genuine relationship? What would it take to remove the stone from her own heart? Could any possession or lifestyle really do that? Clearly people in the Hamptons thought so: the whole place seemed based on the assumption that more was better.

They walked back towards the Surf Shack, neither woman hurrying, neither wanting to break the spell of the view and their fragile, unlikely friendship.

'So who's going to take your place in the house next year?' asked Jem.

'I can't imagine they'll have any problems filling the space. Why, do you know anyone?'

Jem laughed. 'Even if we're still in New York, which I doubt, I don't think any suggestion of mine is going to carry much weight.'

'Angela loves you guys,' said Erica seriously.

'Does she?'

Erica nodded. 'Really. She's always saying what a breath of fresh air you are.'

She smiled.

'You have no idea how rare it is in this world to have someone speak their mind. That's why I wanted you to see the house, to make sure it wasn't just some overhyped Hamptons crap.'

'Erica, it's an amazing house. You don't need me to tell you that.'

'You'd be surprised how insecure this environment makes you.'

They were approaching the rear of the Surf Shack now, and Jem's smile faded.

'I wish I knew what to say to Nat right now.'

'Tell him how you feel,' said Erica.

Jem gave her a sideways glance and pulled a face.

'I'm terrified that if I tell the truth it'll mean . . .'

'That it's over?' Erica touched Jem's arm. 'Maybe, and maybe not. But take it from me, it's worth the risk. I wish to God I'd told Joel how I really felt ten years ago, instead of keeping quiet and letting it happen. Now?' She looked towards the restaurant. 'Every day you die a tiny bit more.'

She turned and kissed Jem on the cheek.

'Good luck,' she said softly and walked towards the bar.

Chapter 27

Jem pretended to be asleep on the journey home. She put her head back against the seat and closed her eyes; Nat didn't object. All she could hear was the whirr of the air con and the occasional bleep from Nat's mobile phone, but her mind was alert, turning Paul's words over and over in her mind.

It was dark as they turned into the drive of the beach house; what had begun as a late lunch had turned into cocktails by the pool, the group making the most of their time in the rarified surroundings of the Surf Shack.

'Alone at last,' said Nat, parking up. Jem wondered at his tone. Did he have any idea what she was thinking? Probably not. When she had returned to the restaurant, she had forced herself to be sociable, to keep what she knew to herself, but it had been exhausting and she was glad to scc that the windows of the house were blank; everyone had already left for the city, citing early meetings or preparation for the working week.

As they stepped into the kitchen, Nat was whistling to himself, rummaging in the fridge for an open bottle of wine. 'Want some?'

Jem nodded. She had been avoiding alcohol most of the day, not entirely trusting her raw emotions, but now she felt the need for some Dutch courage – at the very least something to soothe her frayed nerves.

Nat, on the other hand, seemed entirely relaxed. She supposed he'd see today as a huge success: they had chalked up a visit to a hot new place, basked in both the sun and the reflected glory, and now he'd come back to this gorgeous empty house. Nat was a sociable person, but he was not a natural sharer; something to do with being an adored only child, perhaps. He certainly prized exclusivity over everything else. But to Jem the big house felt over-large and lonely without anyone else there. The odd nights she had spent out here during the week, she'd huddled in their room, lights blazing, doors locked. Exclusivity meant distant neighbours; privacy meant no one to hear you scream.

'So where did you and Erica disappear to?' asked Nat, sitting at the breakfast bar, flipping through the pages of a magazine.

'We went to see her new house. It's just the next bay over.'

Nat looked up. 'Really?' Now he was interested. 'What's it like?'

'It's lovely. Very modern, great view and just the right size.'

'The right size?'

'You could easily have a pool party, but it's not so big that you'd feel as if you were rattling around.'

Nat nodded thoughtfully. This was information he could use as gossip or just file away in the drawer labelled 'relative status'. He turned back to his magazine.

'What were you talking to Paul about?'

Jem glanced at him. She hadn't realised he had noticed.

'Nothing much,' she said after a moment, stalling. She didn't miss her husband's frown.

'It didn't look like nothing to me,' he said, looking up. 'It looked a bit . . . heated.'

Jem searched his face. Was this concern for her, or for himself? She felt as if she were standing on the edge of a cliff, the soil crumbling beneath her toes. What should she say? Pretend they were talking about a design exhibition or something in the news, scuttle back from the precipice? Or take a step forward, tell the truth and risk everything she had come to rely on?

'I was talking to Paul about Alice,' she said.

He raised his eyebrows with disapproval.

'I can see why it was heated,' he said. 'Probably not a wise subject to bring up.'

'Why?'

'Because it's sensitive, of course.'

He flipped over another page, as if he had said all he was going to, but Jem couldn't leave it there.

'Sensitive why? Because Alice died?'

Nat looked at her. 'Don't you remember what everyone said the first night we got here? They felt awkward about doing the house share again. There's obviously still a lot of guilt tied up in this place.'

Guilt. It was a good word; but whose guilt?

'I think it's important to talk about her,' she said. 'We can't pretend it didn't happen, that Alice didn't exist.'

Nat took another swallow of wine. It was obvious he would rather Alice had never existed.

'Why didn't you tell me about her before we came here?' Jem said. She didn't want to bring it up again, but now it was more important than ever.

'I don't know,' he said, irritation edging into his voice. 'Because it's hard to talk about.'

'Why hard? I thought you said you'd never met her.' She held up a finger. 'No, hang on, you did meet her *once*, didn't you?'

'What's this about Alice all of a sudden?'

'I'm just trying to understand why you'd bring me here without telling me that a woman had died in the pool.'

He looked at her like she was crazy. Perhaps she was.

'Jem, we've been over this. What happened was sad, tragic. But life moves on.'

'Tell me about the time you met her. The once.'

He hesitated but knew he had to say something.

'It was when I came over to New York last summer. Todd took me to some sponsored event. A polo match. All the housemates were there.'

'What did you talk about?'

He puffed out his cheeks as if it was a tiny detail, not something worth even mentioning. And in that moment, Jem hated him. Hated how convincingly he could lie. He looked up from his magazine, glancing across at her impatiently.

'I can't remember what we talked about, and I certainly don't see why you're getting so worked up about it all.'

'Paul told me,' said Jem, stopping him mid-flow.

'What? Paul told you what?' He was shaking his head now, looking utterly perplexed. It was almost convincing.

'About *Alice*, Nat. About you and her.'

'What about me and her?'

'That you slept with her. That you were fucking her, Nat.'

'This is ridiculous! You've spent too long working with that writer,' he said, his voice on the edge of exploding. 'I thought he wrote thrillers, but now it sounds like he's getting you to come up with crappy romance plot lines. This is just fantasy!'

'Fantasy? I didn't make this up – Paul told me, Nat.'

'And how the hell would Paul know anything about me?'

'Because Alice told him. To make him jealous.'

She watched the words sink in, saw him pale. The penny had dropped. She nodded.

'Yes, Nat, Paul was sleeping with her too.'

Nat seemed to stop in his tracks. The room suddenly felt dark and cold.

'Paul was sleeping with Alice?'

Jem looked at him, examined his expression. If he was faking it now, then he was in the wrong business; he should have been an actor. He looked genuinely stunned.

'Did you sleep with her?'

'No. Paul is just jealous. He's fucked up his own marriage and now he wants to spoil everyone else's. Do you really believe him?'

Jem could see him shifting gears, saw him decide to go on the attack.

'Jesus, Jem, don't you know me at all? You really think I'd cheat on you?'

'I don't know what to think,' she cried.

'You'd trust what Paul says over your own husband?'

Jem paused, feeling that crumbling edge beneath her feet again. To tell him that, she had to tell him everything, to admit her own deceit. But the time for lies and half-truths was over. If there was any hope for their marriage, they had to get it all out in the open.

'I believe Paul because he *had* to tell me the truth,' she said. 'I forced him to confess because I had found evidence that he was having an affair with Alice.'

'Evidence?' Nat said fiercely. 'What, are you some sort of detective now?'

'Michael wants to write a book about Alice,' she said simply, doing everything she could to hold it together. 'He doesn't believe her death was an accident, so he – we – started looking into what happened. That's how we found out that Alice and Paul had been together – and that's when Paul told me about you.'

'You've been spying on us?'

Us. Jem had guessed he would get defensive, but this stopped her dead. He was siding with the housemates, putting himself in their camp.

'Is that why Michael hired you? So you could snoop around?'

'Yes,' she said honestly. 'He was going to work on the story anyway, but he asked me to get involved because I was so close to Alice's friends.'

'And you said yes so you could impress him.'

Jem frowned. Nat wasn't actually accusing her of anything, but a suggestion of something unpleasant was there.

'I got involved because I saw how much David Holliday loved his wife and how much he was suffering,' she said. 'I offered to help Michael because I knew that it could help David.'

'Well I hope you're happy with what you've done.'

'I am, actually, despite all this. Because working for Michael has given me a purpose, and you know what else? It's stopped me thinking about my own marriage.'

'What the hell is wrong with our marriage?'

'Haven't you been listening to anything I've been saying? You've been sleeping with another woman, isn't that enough?'

'I didn't sleep with her!' he yelled.

Jem frowned. The look on his face wasn't anger, it was frustration.

'So what, then?'

He pulled a face, looked away.

'She came on to me. At the polo, she practically threw herself at me.'

'And of course you told her to stop . . .'

'I swear to you, Jem! I did not have sex with her. Maybe we kissed, a quick kiss, but when she came on strong, I pushed her away. *That's* why I didn't tell you about her; not because we were having an affair but because I wanted to forget all about last summer.'

Jem stared at him, seeing the desperation in his eyes, wanting to believe him, but remembering how smoothly he had lied only minutes before. And then it came to her: in the end, it didn't really matter what had happened between Nat and Alice, whether they had kissed or had sex; it was the lies that did the damage, the poison in the well.

'You have to believe me, Jem,' he said, reaching out to her.

'I don't know what to believe,' she said, willing herself to stay strong.

'Don't blow this out of proportion. I love you. We have a great marriage.'

'Do we?'

Nat frowned, and Jem exhaled softly as if a fog was beginning to lift. Suddenly things had become clear; the reason behind all those little doubts and frustrations she'd had with her life in New York. Yes, her lack of a job and friends had made her miserable, but it was her marriage that had made her feel sad and lonely.

Nat had changed. Sure, he had always liked the finer things in life – a great meal, a luxurious hotel, a good bottle of wine – but the higher he climbed up the career ladder, the more influential he became, the more his character quirks felt like vanity and shallowness. Yes, Jem still loved him, she just wasn't sure if she always liked him any more.

'Nat, we've been papering over the cracks for months now,' she said quietly. 'Maybe it started before we even came to America. Coming out here was just a distraction, something to blame it all on, a way of avoiding what was really going on.'

'And what's that?'

She took a deep breath, knew she had to keep going, get it all out.

'We've been avoiding each other. You stay late at parties, go on press trips, I stay at home playing the martyr, but actually I'm happier when I'm on my own.'

'That's not true.'

She didn't look at him.

'Don't you remember when we could just have fun taking a walk in the park? We used to love spending time together, holding hands or watching some stupid rom com on the sofa. Now you treat me like your housekeeper.'

'Jem, I—'

She held up a hand.

'I went along with it. I was the domestic goddess to your alpha male. But I've discovered that it doesn't make me happy.'

'What does make you happy then?' he said, his voice heavy with spite. 'Michael Kearney?'

She ignored the uncomfortable barb.

'Are you happy with our marriage, Nat?'

'I know we want different things sometimes, but . . . aren't you?'

Jem walked to the window and looked out into the darkness.

'Here we are, in paradise,' she said, almost to herself, 'and yet I feel as if I've taken a wrong turn and ended up in the last place I want to be.'

'Millions of women would give anything to live the life you're living.'

He said it so matter-of-factly, she almost had to agree with him. But she couldn't.

'You think I should be grateful? Living with a man who's barely there, a man I can't trust, a man whose main concern is impressing a bunch of vacuous rich morons?'

'It's my *job*!' he said, eyes wide. 'I spend my time with those vacuous morons to secure us a future!'

Jem shook her head, weary. Even now, even after she had caught him in a dirty little lie, he didn't get it. He didn't think there was anything wrong in what he had done, not really.

'You spend time with them because you *like* it. And you'd rather be with them than with me – that's the truth.'

When he didn't respond, she picked up her bag and headed for the stairs.

'I'm going to bed,' she said. 'Try not to wake me when you come up.'

Chapter 28

There were twelve rows of fifteen, five bumps in each cluster, arranged in a pattern that reminded Jem of a fishing net. She had been lying awake since dawn, staring at the ceiling, her eyes following the humps and contours of the ancient Artex, counting and re-counting the grooves as more were revealed by the growing light.

Maybe I've finally cracked, she thought, only vaguely alarmed. The prospect of a spell in a loony bin, drugged and restrained, seemed almost appealing right now, when the alternative was to confront such a stark, miserable reality.

Nat was lying beside her, breathing softly, his warm body inches away but miles distant. Despite her parting request, he had come up hours later, fully drunk, muttering heartfelt apologies and begging forgiveness. Jem had turned over, but had never really got back to sleep. When she hadn't been examining the minutiae of the ceiling's texture, she was going over and over everything Paul had said, looking at every angle, every word, trying to fathom some sense from it. Then she would loop back around to Nat's denial. 'I didn't sleep with her,' he had insisted. 'Maybe we kissed.' Was that true? Had it been a flirtation gone a little too far? And did that even matter?

Yes. It did matter. Nat was a liar; he had treated Jem and

their relationship as an afterthought, and she wasn't entirely sure their marriage would survive. That was the truth. But she still had to know. *Had to.*

Gently she lifted the sheet and rolled off the bed, freezing halfway to the bathroom when Nat moaned and turned over. Hearing him settle, she moved quickly, snatching up a few clothes and shutting the door quietly, almost smiling at the grim irony. She was sneaking out of the house like a guilty lover after a night of indiscretion. How many times had Nat made an early-morning move just like this? An early meeting, a gym session, *I'll call you, babe*.

Safely in the kitchen, she switched on the kettle and shook her head. She had been torturing herself like this since dawn and it hadn't got her anywhere. Now she needed to stop chasing her tail and do something about it, otherwise she knew she would come unglued. And she knew just where she could start: Michael's.

Heart jumping, she turned to see Nat leaning against the kitchen door frame, dressed only in pyjama bottoms, his hair raked at all angles, his eyes unfocused and dopey. On any other occasion she would have thought he looked adorable, maybe even dragged him back up to the bedroom, but this wasn't any other occasion.

'Hello,' she said non-committally, turning back to the kettle and swearing inwardly. She had wanted to get out of the house without another confrontation. The last thing she wanted was to go over it all again when she was still feeling so raw.

Nat nodded towards the solitary coffee cup on the countertop.

'I wanted to beat you to that,' he said.

'Breakfast in bed?' she said, unable to keep the note of sarcasm from her voice.

'Well, maybe we could go out for breakfast.'

'You need to get back to the city,' said Jem.

'I was going to call the office, tell them I'll come in at lunchtime.'

'That'll go down well.'

'I don't care,' said Nat, stepping forward and putting his hands on her shoulders. 'I want to be here with you.'

Jem shook her head, shrugging him off.

'Nat, just go to work.'

He looked surprised, hurt.

'We need to talk.'

'We talked last night – now I think we just need to let things settle.'

The kettle clicked off, sending steam clouds into the air, but Jem didn't move towards the coffee mug. She didn't think she'd be able to swallow right now.

'Let's go out for dinner then. Tonight. What about that Italian you like on Park Slope?' He was pleading now, needy and shaken. He wasn't used to not getting his way.

'Please, Nat. Just go to work,' said Jem, moving to the other side of the room and putting things into her bag. 'I've got things to do too.'

'I love you, Jem,' he said quietly. 'I love you so much.'

She turned to look at him, pathetic and lost. I should go over, put my arms around him, tell him we'll work it out, she thought. But she couldn't.

As she zipped up her bag and grabbed her keys, Nat moved between her and the door, holding his hands up in front of him.

'I made one mistake and I will never do it again. All I want is to be with you and make you happy. And if that means leaving New York, going back to London, then let's do it.'

She looked at him in surprise. She supposed she should have anticipated it, but she hadn't thought he'd suggest something so drastic.

'Let's go home and have a baby,' he said.

She waited for her heart to swell, to fill with warmth. A few weeks ago, it was all she had wanted to hear, but now she just felt even more confused.

'We'll talk later,' she said, not looking at him.

'Great,' he said, more brightly. 'If you don't want to go out, I'll cook dinner.'

Jem picked up her bag and left the house. She closed the door, careful not to slam it. She had the sense that everything around her was delicate, that if she made the wrong move, stepped in the wrong place, cracks would appear and spread right and left until everything crumbled and fell.

It wasn't until she was in the car, the house receding in the rear mirror, that she finally let her breath out. Her whole body was shaking, tense and rigid. 'Don't cry, don't bloody cry,' she whispered, glancing in the mirror again, as if she might see Nat running behind her, begging her to come back. There was nothing except empty road.

Michael answered the door in shorts and T-shirt, earphones hanging around his neck. His arms looked strong and muscular under his sleeves and all she could think about was getting a reassuring hug. She knew that if she told him everything that had happened, he would say the right words to help her fix it.

'Is everything okay?'

'Fine,' said Jem, walking into the house, all business, a voice in her head reminding her that sharing her personal baggage with her new boss was not the answer. 'Why shouldn't it be?'

'You don't usually get here before nine,' he said, looking at his watch. 'I was just going to go for a run. Shall I wait?'

'No,' said Jem, appreciating the opportunity that had just presented itself. 'You go, I've got plenty to catch up on.'

Michael frowned, like he wasn't convinced. And why would he be? After their night in the Catskills, he couldn't have been sure she was even going to come back. 'Okay then,' he said finally. 'Get yourself a coffee and I'll see you in half an hour.'

The moment the front door closed, Jem ran outside to the office. It was as if someone had clicked a stopwatch on. Half an hour was nothing given what she needed to do, but she could only do it while Michael was away.

She felt guilty, duplicitous. She was sure Michael would disapprove; after all, they had settled into an easy and trusting relationship, to the point where he would leave her alone in his multi-million-dollar home, and she wasn't being entirely honest with him. But she had to find out if Nat was telling the truth about Alice. Had it been just a drunken fumble, or had it been the full-blown affair Paul had suggested? She felt sure the evidence would be here, in this studio.

The filing boxes David had given them were stacked up on the table, but Jem ignored them, dropping her bag on a chair and sitting down at Michael's desk, flipping open Alice's laptop.

She waited as it booted up. Okay, how to do this? She had to approach it logically.

If someone was going to have an affair, how would they communicate? How would they arrange their trysts? Not via love notes and scented letters; in the twenty-first century, it was email and text. Alice's home page appeared: dozens and dozens of files, seemingly randomly scattered across the screen. Jem had of course looked through the computer before, but she hadn't been in possession of the information she had now. Before, they had been looking for unusual behaviour, not messages from Nat. She felt sure she would have noticed if her husband had been mentioned, but then when you weren't actively looking for something, it was easy for the eye to skate over it.

She opened Alice's email application and clicked on the search box, typing in 'Nat'. She paused, her finger poised over the return key. Was she ready? Did she really want to know?

She tapped her finger down, holding her breath as the screen scrolled upwards with dozens of results. Her eyes danced left and right, quickly scanning the entries, but she could see immediately that Nat – her Nat – wasn't there. The search had returned dozens of results: Nat, Nathan and Natalie were surprisingly popular names in Manhattan. Alice's friends, yoga clients, even a mention of actor Nate Parker – someone had been to see *The Birth of a Nation* at some hip art-house cinema in the Village – but nothing relating to Nat Chapman.

She rearranged the emails into date order, checking all Alice's communications around the time Nat had been in New York the previous summer: still nothing. But there *was* something else. It was true you didn't see things when you weren't looking for them. When Jem had looked at the emails the first time, she had read everything to and from Alice relating to the housemates and her other friends. There were gossipy snippets from Erica and Angela, gushy messages from Tina strewn with exclamation marks, even a few clipped communiqués from Rebecca. And dozens of emails from Paul.

'How could we have missed this?' she whispered, clicking one open and reading it, unsure about what she would find.

Hey A,
    How's things? Great to see you at the weekend – was fun!! Ping me about that venue we were talking about. Maybe tonight?
    Paul

She frowned, opening another. They were all in the same breezy tone, two friends exchanging quick notes, easy to explain away, nothing suspicious. Unless you had the key piece of information: that these two people were sleeping together. She clicked back to the 'sent from' view of the inbox. When you saw the emails all together, it was like seeing the jigsaw completed. Paul had sent Alice a message almost every day during the month leading up to her death.

Except they had tailed off after the date they had been at the Inn the Woods, stopping altogether five days before the fateful night. Why? What had happened?

There might have been an answer in Alice's responses, of course, but Jem already knew that was a dead end. Alice's 'sent messages' folder was empty; or rather, it was missing altogether, as if someone had deleted it permanently.

She looked at her watch. She'd been sitting here for twenty minutes and Michael would be back any time. She looked around the office, her gaze falling on the filing boxes. There was nothing much in there, just papers and receipts and ticket stubs. Potentially there might be a clue like the Rivertown bookmark hidden in one of the boxes, but certainly nothing she could find in the next five minutes. She puffed out her cheeks, trying to think.

It was ironic that the last time she had gone through Alice's things, she was searching for the identity of the mystery man. Now she was looking for a connection to her own husband.

She closed the laptop and looked around for Alice's phone. David had given it to them along with her computer and the boxes. Again, they had already been through the messages, but hadn't found much of interest.

'Where is it?' she muttered, expecting the office door to open at any minute.

The last time she had seen the phone, it had been sitting

on Michael's desk. But that had been days ago, and Michael's desk was in a constant state of flux; cluttered with coffee cups and papers, nothing ever in the same place twice. Jem had tried gently to suggest he tidy it, get some system in place, but every morning when she arrived, it was covered again with papers, magazines and tottering piles of books.

Just then there was a sound from outside: a door closing – almost certainly Michael's back door.

Crap.

Impulsively, Jem grabbed the desk drawer, pulling it open. And there was the phone, right on the top. She grabbed it and slid it into her pocket, then turned to face the door, closing the drawer with her hip.

'I'm back,' said Michael, stepping into the office. His face was flushed and he was rubbing his neck with a towel.

'That was quick,' said Jem.

'I'm fast,' he smiled.

She bent to pick up some papers, then turned away, not wanting Michael to see the telltale bulge in her pocket.

There was a sofa along one side of the room. Michael got a soda from the fridge in the corner, offered one to Jem and sat down.

'At least we can get an early start,' he said thoughtfully. 'I had a couple of interesting conversations over the weekend.'

'Oh yes?' said Jem, thinking she could say the same thing.

'Turns out there was a drum circle outside your beach house on the night Alice died.'

'A drum circle?'

'It's a party. Music, dancing drums, drugs . . . a young person's thing,' he grinned. 'I asked around. Spoke to a guy called Yeti. He seems to be the ringleader around here for things like that.'

Jem leant against Michael's desk and folded her arms.

'So what did he say?'

'He reckons they were on the beach between about eight and ten. Then most people moved on to a house party in Bridgehampton. I asked him if he heard paramedics turning up at the house, sirens, noise, but he says he must have left by then.'

'Between eight and ten. That's when Alice died.' She felt uncomfortable just saying her name. Things felt different now that Nat was part of the puzzle.

'He didn't see anyone going into the house, but he took a few photos during the evening,' said Michael, forcing Jem to concentrate. 'Do you want to see them?'

She nodded and went to sit next to him on the sofa, her leg pressing against his.

Michael pulled his phone out of his pocket.

'Here we go,' he said, pulling up a picture.

The quality of the photo wasn't amazing, but she could just about work out what was going on. Lots of half-naked young people with tattoos, and such long hair she couldn't work out which were the girls and which the boys. It looked fun and carefree, and for a moment she wished she were ten years younger. She remembered all the fun nights in resort bars, huddled in corner booths with ski instructors, other chalet girls and tankards of cold beer. No decision ever seemed more serious than who they might go home with that evening and whether they would get up in time for work the next morning.

As she studied the photo, however, she couldn't see how useful it was except to paint a picture of what that evening would have been like. She and Michael had already walked the length of sand between the beach house and The Shells, the great oceanfront mansion a few hundred yards away, where the group had partied the night Alice had died, and Jem had tried hard to visualise how it had been; imagined

Alice with tears on her face, perhaps, running from the ball like Cinderella, dashing across the very dunes they stood on and along the beach.

What she saw in the photograph was less dramatic; just another night on the beach. Dark skies, silver sand and a crowd of people illuminated by the flames of a bonfire.

The beach house was just in shot, and Jem asked Michael to enlarge the image.

'You can't really see anything,' she said, peering at the wooden fence and the grey silhouette of the house.

'But look here,' he said, pointing to a man in the shot. At first Jem couldn't make out what he was doing, but then she saw that he was taking pictures.

Michael flipped to another image.

'He's taking photos here too. And look where his camera is pointing.'

'You think he might have taken clearer pictures of the house?' said Jem.

Michael nodded. 'I've tracked him down and he's agreed to meet me in the city. I'm in town anyway for some industry dinner. Why don't you come?'

Jem wasn't sure if he meant to see the drum circle photographer or to the dinner.

'Sure,' she replied, deciding he could interpret it however he liked.

They both fell quiet and Jem stood up.

'Are you sure you're all right?' said Michael, looking at her with concern.

'Honestly, I'm fine,' she replied, feeling flustered. She was not a natural liar, and she could see that taking the phone from Michael's drawer could amount to theft.

'You can tell me, you know.'

She paused, and then decided that she could at least concede one truth.

'I had a row with Nat last night.'

'Do you want to talk about it?'

She gave a soft laugh.

'What's so funny?'

'My male friends in England would never ask that,' she said.

'It's taken me ten years of therapy to be comfortable talking about feelings.'

'Another cultural difference,' she smiled. 'The only time you'll find a British guy on the couch is with a beer can and a PlayStation console in his hand.'

She stopped before she could say anything else. She found Michael easy to talk to – and that was the problem. She didn't want to tell him why she'd argued with Nat, because then she'd have to tell him how she'd found out about Nat and Alice, and he had specifically warned her not to say anything to Paul Ellis.

No, she couldn't tell him all that. Not yet.

'Now how about we don't do any work today,' said Michael, getting to his feet.

'But I've come to work.'

He grinned. 'Well sometimes you just need to know when to say screw it,' he said.

Michael disappeared to make a call and then they got in his car, driving out through the dunes with the windows rolled down. Jem liked this time of day, when the dew had all been burnt off and the air blowing in and ruffling her hair was warm but not yet hot. Neither of them spoke as they drove, each tied up in their own thoughts, each distracted by the sudden changes in the scenery, from the wide-open twinkling blue of the sea to the flashing green rows of farmland.

They approached the Lobster Roll restaurant – the iconic roadside seafood café, where Michael had been promising he would take her for lunch – but drove straight past, heading for Montauk.

'Are you going to tell me where we're going?' Jem said, wondering whether they were heading for the lighthouse. She had only been out to the tip twice and had loved the feeling of space and the sense that she was at the end of the world, but the thought of going there alone with Michael made her feel a little unsettled.

Michael turned right at a sign labelled 'Ditch Plains'.

'The beach?'

'Surfing,' he said, glancing over.

'Surfing!'

'Celine, my other assistant. Her brother Leo has opened a surf school somewhere along here. I've been promising to go and take a look for months. I think we could both do with a complete distraction.'

'I've not got a swimsuit,' said Jem, feeling self-conscious.

'Don't worry, it's sorted,' he said pulling into a car park.

Considering it was a Monday morning, the beach was busy. School was out for summer and the conditions at sea were perfect.

Jem felt her shoulders sag with pleasure as she got out of the car.

'Hi,' said a good-looking man coming towards them. 'Are you ready?' He was about her age, with sun-bleached hair and a deep surfer's tan and the word 'Leo' embroidered on his board shorts.

Before she could even ask about a bathing costume, he threw a big black bag that had been over his shoulder onto the ground. He pulled out a wetsuit and gave it to Michael, then handed Jem a plain black costume – size ten, a perfect fit.

'Michael said you needed this.'

For a second, she imagined Michael discussing her figure

with his friend. How had he described her? she wondered. Petite? Athletic? She couldn't imagine Michael using more locker-room descriptions, but you never knew, and she didn't want to dwell on it.

She took a wetsuit and went to change in the bathroom, meeting Michael as he came out of an adjoining stall.

'Can you zip me up?' he asked, turning around.

Jem nodded, but felt awkward as her palm pressed on the join between the black neoprene and his tanned, warm skin.

They collected their boards from Leo's roof rack and went down to the beach.

'Have you done this before?' asked Leo as Jem looked longingly out across the surf. Thoughts of Alice Holliday, her husband, the beach house were forgotten as she imagined the cold water on her face and the rush of white foam crashing over her body.

'A very long time ago,' she said quietly, stretching her arms above her head. The sound of laughter and waves washing up on the shore was making her feel heady.

Leo was explaining to Michael the art of popping up. He was a quick learner; his running was obviously working and had given him the athleticism of a man twenty years younger.

'Do you mind if I just hop into the water for a minute?' said Jem.

'Sure,' said Leo. 'We can jog to the shore as part of the warm-up.'

Jem put her board under her arm and started to run, drawn to the surf like filings to a magnet.

'Hey!' shouted Leo, running to catch her. 'We've got a ton of stuff to learn first.'

'As I said, I've done this before,' she shouted back over her shoulder.

As soon as she hit the water and lay on the board to paddle out, she felt a different person; she felt like the old Jem. Surfing was the thing she had in common with her dad. It was what had brought him down to Cornwall from Leeds before Jem was born, and every weekend, from when she was about ten, he would take her to Fistral Beach to learn to ride the waves. Surfing was one of the things that had drawn her to the mountains too. She'd worked out pretty early on that she was not the standard chalet girl who had been brought up on skis and considered Klosters a second home. But surfing and winter sports – skiing and snowboarding – were not so far apart, and every time Jem went down a black run, she knew her father was watching her from up above, giving her the thumbs-up.

She positioned herself in the water and waited for the moment, letting one wave go by and then another. She had always loved the instinctive element to surfing; it was a guessing game with nature, and when she felt the water behind her begin to swell, she knew this was the one, paddling furiously, jumping onto the board and letting the wave carry her to shore as if she were dancing on its crest.

'I bloody loved that,' she shouted, shaking the water from her dripping hair.

'So you don't need the surf lesson, then,' grinned Michael.

Leo slapped her on the back.

'I think we've got a new recruit for the dawn patrol.'

'Dawn patrol?' said Michael.

'Very enthusiastic surfers who get up in the middle of the night. You can count me out of that one,' she said, enjoying the banter, imagining herself for a moment up before the birds.

'Do you still want to do this today?' Leo asked Michael.

'I think we'll save the beginner's lesson for another time,' he laughed.

'Don't do that on my behalf,' said Jem. 'I could do with the refresh.'

'I'm not sure you do,' grinned Leo, picking up his bag. 'Mike, why don't you drop the boards and wetsuits off at the office later.'

Michael and Jem flopped down on the sand. Michael glanced over and caught her eye.

'I didn't know you surfed.'

'I grew up by the coast. I was a tomboy. My dad moved to Cornwall just to be near the surf; he did his best to make sure his family enjoyed it as much as he did, although he could never get my mum in the water.'

'So you've not been out here all summer?'

Jem shook her head and felt cross that she had allowed that to happen.

'Does Nat not surf?' he asked in surprise.

'No. Although we did go to Biarritz once. He bought all the kit: the best board shorts, the reef sandals, possibly even a necklace with a shark's tooth on it. We spent most of the weekend in the bar listening to the manager tell us how great his hotel was. The price you pay for getting it for free.'

'You should bring him here,' said Michael, stretching his legs out in front of him.

Jem shrugged. 'I'm not sure he'll be interested,' she said quietly. 'Not unless he thinks he'll find the CEO of Louis Vuitton here.'

'That's entirely possible,' smiled Michael.

Jem resisted the urge to shake her head. The past few days had been like tugging at a thread that threatened to make everything unravel. Finding out about Nat's infidelity with Alice was one thing, but as it forced her to look harder at her marriage, she wasn't sure she liked what it was throwing up.

'It's funny,' she said finally. 'We came out here because

he said it would be an adventure, because we needed to have more experiences together. But we seem further apart than ever.'

'You're going to have to work on that,' Michael said, as if he was speaking from experience.

'Why did you get divorced?' she asked simply. He had touched on it before, that morning she had found him drunk in his office, but suddenly she wanted to know more.

Michael looked at her. 'I worked and travelled a lot. Sarah – my wife – stayed at home. I came home and talked about work. She'd tell me about her day, the school gate, her mom friends. Neither of us knew the people the other was talking about; neither of us really wanted to know. She thought I was a workaholic; I wondered why, when our daughter was at school all day, she didn't want more from her life than shopping and golf. Truth was, no one was right or wrong, better or worse; we just didn't respect each other's choices. We didn't get what made each other tick. We drifted apart without even realising it had happened.'

He paused. 'In the end, she had an affair. I was angry at first. Almost angry that she had beat me to it. And then she told me she wasn't sure if she had ever really loved me.'

'Ouch.'

Michael smiled ruefully.

'Brutal, yes, but at least it was honest, clean. I didn't have to spend months wondering what I could do to make it better. Boom, it was over, and maybe it was easier to take. And when the dust settled, I knew it was for the best. Tony was her golf instructor and they have loads of things in common: cruises, and bowling night, and afternoons at the driving range. The little things count for a lot in the big picture of a relationship.'

An elderly couple walked hand in hand in front of them along the shoreline.

'Have you ever thought of getting married again?' asked Jem.

'Yes,' said Michael without hesitation. 'I still believe in marriage, despite everything, so yes. If I met the right woman.'

'So why haven't you? I mean, Angela said she'd read you were the George Clooney of the literary world.'

He laughed. 'I must have missed that one. These days it's usually "pulp fiction has-been".'

'Don't dodge the question,' said Jem. She was intrigued to know the answer, feeling a distant dart of envy for the woman who might eventually marry him.

'It's difficult,' he said. 'I'm not a monk, I've dated a few women since the divorce, but out here? It's hard to know whether it's my glittering personality they're interested in, or my glittering bank balance.'

Jem looked at him.

'Really? You think they were after your money? How do you know?'

'It's little things,' he said. 'They want meals in the best restaurants, vacations in the best resorts. I mean, there was someone at the start of summer, someone in New York. I said let's meet for lunch, she got us a table at Per Se and within five minutes had ordered a four-thousand-dollar bottle of wine.'

'So she blew her chances of being the next Mrs Kearney,' smiled Jem, trying to picture the woman, the sort that he dated.

'I'm more of a burrito and beer kind of guy, and none of them noticed,' said Michael with a grin.

He kicked a clump of sand with his toe.

'Speaking of burritos, when are we going to see your blog?'

'Don't ask,' said Jem, waving a hand. 'I've made a lot of

food, photographed it. But building a website, downloading my pictures, writing up recipes . . . I don't have time to do any of that seeing as I'm working so hard for the international bestseller Michael Kearney . . .'

Michael didn't say anything. She meant it as a joke, but she hoped that she hadn't implied she resented her work in any way. She didn't. It had energised her.

'Speaking of which,' she said, pulling her phone out of her tote bag and taking a picture of him squinting in the sun. 'There, we can download that. Show your fans your human side.'

'My human side?' he laughed, his eyes sparkling a more intense shade of blue than Jem had ever noticed before.

'You're a world-famous author. That's intimidating. I think they'd like to know you can't surf for toffee.'

'Can't surf for toffee?' he said, raising a brow.

'We really do have everything in common with America nowadays, except, of course, language.'

'You're right.'

'Not my words. Oscar Wilde's. But you still can't surf for toffee.'

'Then are you going to stop yapping and start teaching me?'

'Come on,' she grinned, and they got up and ran laughing into the water.

Chapter 29

The rain had finally begun. Fat splatters were hitting the sidewalk, *tat-tat, tat-tat-tat-tat.* It had been threatening for hours, the dark sky seeming to lower itself onto the city, squatting above the buildings, the air thick as cream. Summers in New York. Jem had always imagined them to be like the opening credits of *Saturday Night Fever*: John Travolta swinging down the street in stack heels, disco chirping in the background, all sunshine, medallions and pirouettes. But the reality was hot, sticky and claustrophobic, the glass and concrete reflecting the unbearable heat until you found yourself hanging out in Duane Reade just because it had awesome air con.

Jem flipped up her collar and ran. Until now she had been dragging her feet, drawing out the time it took to get home, but now it was either dash for the building or hope for the best under a tree, and it was obvious it was going to be a deluge. She made it inside the front door just as the skies finally opened, hammering the streets with a downpour that bent the thin Brooklyn trees, formed waves in the gutters and sent little fountains shooting up from the manholes.

She stood in the doorway watching it in wonder. She had only seen rain like this once before, on their honeymoon to the Caribbean, when it had been blissful blue skies all day, broken only by a flash storm that always arrived at about three o'clock in the afternoon, coming down so hard it was impossible to see to the other side of the street. It would last for ten minutes, then the clouds would melt away, revealing the yellow sun, which invariably dried up every trace of the storm by four.

She wasn't sure this one was going to pass so quickly.

She climbed the stairs more slowly than usual, not wanting to go home. Nat would be back eventually and she knew he would want to talk.

Although surfing had meant forgetting about her worries for a couple of hours, away from Ditch Plains she was more confused than ever. How she felt about Nat, what she wanted from the marriage, even where she stood on Alice herself.

Over the past few days she had fallen out of love with Alice Holliday; even if she hadn't been sleeping with Nat, Alice had certainly been cheating on her husband and quite probably looking to upgrade from David to Paul. She was a schemer and a liar and clearly not at all the victim Jem had imagined. But Jem had to face up to why she had so identified with this elusive woman. For all her happy memories of her carefree childhood in Cornwall, she had shared one thing with Alice: she had worked damn hard to escape small-town dreariness, to find herself a bigger, more exciting life. She had moved to the big city and had her head turned by someone glamorous. Someone with good prospects, a catch. Nat.

Jem had never warmed to the gold-digging women of the Hamptons, all those sleek blondes with their toned bodies squeezed into teeny-tiny shorts, but in reality she wasn't so different. She had grabbed Nat and held on for dear life. That was the truth of it. She hadn't stolen anyone's husband, but she had wanted everything Nat Chapman could give her and she had taken it gladly.

At the final landing – their landing – Jem paused to look out of the window. Everything looked dark and cold, the streets of Brooklyn just a blur of shapes and colour through the rain-dappled glass. A low rumble of thunder made her shiver, and she looked up at the solitary bulb flickering overhead, wishing it gave off a little more light. She put her hand in her bag, but stopped when she heard a noise coming from inside the flat.

For a moment she froze. She curled her hand around her keys, the cold metal warming in her palm as she listened hard.

Perhaps she was mistaken; perhaps the sound was coming from the street, but a shiver of danger made Jem feel nervous and on her guard.

Hearing nothing else, she slid her key into the lock, pushing the door open slowly. She caught a whiff of something cooking and felt a calm wave of relief.

Roast chicken with rosemary, an aroma that reminded her of safety and cosiness and home.

Which was exactly why Nat was cooking it, she thought cynically.

'Is that you?'

Jem glanced at her watch: barely seven. The earliest he had made it home in months.

'Hi,' he said, stepping into the hallway, oven mitts on his hands. Jem noted that he was wearing the blue shirt she liked. 'I made chicken.'

A dish he had cooked on their first date in London. She hadn't slept with Nat the week they'd met in the Alps; some romantic ideal about wanting to test that she wasn't just another notch on a public schoolboy skier's bedpost. She'd flown back to England after a month of two-hour daily phone calls, desperate to know if they could take their fledgling relationship to the next step. Nat had picked her up at Heathrow, whisked her back to his tiny studio in Notting Hill, and cooked a delicious roast that was abandoned after twenty minutes for the siren call of the bedroom.

Roast chicken – a meal designed to seduce, impress and now, it seemed, say sorry.

'Smells good,' she said, aware that her voice sounded clipped and forced. But then why shouldn't it be? Nat had confessed – no, Jem had forced him to admit – that he had been messing around with other women, perhaps worse. Should she let him off the hook just because he had made an effort in the kitchen?

'How was work?' he asked, turning back to the steaming pans. Jem noticed the use of the word 'work'; he definitely was making an effort. He had never treated her job seriously before, referring to it as 'your thing with Michael'.

'Fine.'

'Anything interesting?'

'No, not really.'

She knew this was how marriages started disintegrating. Little white lies, half-truths. Evasion. But then what could she say? 'I played hookey from work and went surfing with Michael. We had fun and talked about his failed marriage, which doesn't sound so different from ours.'

Instead, she turned to hang up her coat, wanting to hide her face.

'Perfect timing,' said Nat, removing the chicken from the oven. 'Aren't you going to take a picture of it?'

It was a gentle joke, but Jem still found herself bristling. Nat had always hated the way she liked to snap a shot of her food in a restaurant, complaining that he had to wait while his food went cold.

Oblivious, he carried the chicken through to the tiny

two-seater dining table, already set for a meal: tablecloth, polished silver, an open bottle of wine and a vase of pink lilies, too big for the table. Again Jem bit her tongue. The flowers were all part of Nat's clumsy apology, but all she could think was that she hated the smell of lilies, always had, and that he should know.

'They're lovely, but I'll just move the flowers to the side,' she said diplomatically. 'Otherwise we'll be getting hay fever.'

Nat nodded, then jumped forward eagerly to pull out her chair. Jem couldn't help laughing; it was such a formal gesture, so out of place in their cramped apartment, where there was barely room to sit.

He lit two candles and dimmed the lights so the room was soothed in the soft saffron glow of the flames.

'You can leave the main light on, Nat. It's fine.'

'Let's do this properly,' he said, glancing at her anxiously. 'Sorry, I'm not great at this,' he said, sticking a knife through the crispy brown skin of the bird. Jem could tell from the smell and texture of the chicken that Nat had done a good job with the roast, but he couldn't carve it to save his life, the white meat coming away in chunks. Jem itched to take over, but she knew this was his moment, that he was trying his best – too little too late, perhaps, but he *was* trying. It was something.

Finally, after fussing with vegetables and wine and napkins, Nat sat down and they began to eat in silence. Jem had been worried he would propose a toast, 'to us' or 'to new beginnings', but at least he had spared her that. It was hard enough sitting here when all she wanted to do was run, run and never look back.

'So how is Michael's project coming along?'

Jem put down her knife.

'Nat, I don't think we should talk about this,' she said. 'It's too awkward.'

She could see he wanted to object, perhaps declare his innocence regarding Alice again, but instead he nodded.

He didn't say anything for a moment, just played with his meal with his fork.

'Will you at least tell me why you decided to get involved; you said you spoke to David Holliday?'

Jem really didn't want to discuss it, but then Alice was the elephant in the room, and how could they move forward if they never mentioned her?

'I met him briefly at Todd's art launch; you saw us together, remember?' she said. 'I think he was just glad that someone was interested in talking about Alice beyond "I'm sorry for your loss".'

Nat nodded, clearly wanting more, so she continued carefully.

'When we went to Michael's for dinner, he told me about his interest in Alice's death and that he wanted to look into it. Initially it made me uncomfortable. That's why I didn't accept his job offer immediately.'

'You could have told me,' sniffed Nat, not unreasonably.

'But when I met David, and saw his grief, I knew I was in a position to help him. I introduced him to Michael, we went for dinner and David gave him his blessing to proceed with the story, provided he told him everything he discovered.'

'Dinner? Where?'

'At David's place.'

Another silence, the implication being: why did you never tell me this before?

'I see,' said Nat pointedly.

'When I heard David talk about Alice, saw how hard it had hit him, I couldn't just sit around doing nothing, Nat, I couldn't.'

'I can see that,' said Nat with a small shrug.

'If something like that happened to me, I'd want people to find out everything they could,' she continued, but Nat cut her off.

'But you hardly know David Holliday and you never even met Alice. Why do you care so much about what happened? Why can't you accept it was just a tragic accident, like everyone else has?'

He didn't say it unkindly. Jem wondered if he was sucking up to her, keen not to antagonise her further.

'I'm involved now,' she said, looking at him. It was the only way she could explain it to him. She knew she couldn't give up now – not when it was getting interesting, not when she felt they had touched on an uncomfortable truth – Alice's affair with Paul.

'So what does Michael think happened to Alice?' There was a note of cynicism in his voice, but Jem chose to ignore it.

'He doesn't know. Yet.'

'But he thinks Paul could be involved?'

'As I said. He doesn't know. But this is what he does for a living. What he used to do anyway. He's good at it and I imagine he'll take it as far as he can to find out the truth.'

Nat changed the subject, and she was glad to ask him questions about his day. There were lots of things she wanted to say to him; she wanted to tell him about the exhilaration she had felt surfing, she wanted to ask him how serious he was about returning to England. But it felt safer to keep things light and impersonal: gossip from his office, and their friends back home.

'Jem . . .' he began, but she was already standing, putting her napkin on the table.

'Listen, that's enough for one night,' she said, uncomfortable in the intimacy of the candlelight. 'It was delicious, but I've got a few things to do.'

Nat gazed at her, clearly wanting – needing – to say more, to get his own closure. But she wasn't going to give him that satisfaction. After a moment, he nodded.

'Sure, I'll clear up here,' he said, picking up the plates. Another first; wonders will never cease, thought Jem. 'Then I could do with an early night. I'm meeting Todd at seven for a Barry's Bootcamp session, so I'll have to leave at six.'

'Todd is going to Barry's?' said Jem with surprise.

'I know,' smirked Nat. 'Angela is giving him a hard time about his beer belly.'

She smiled, imagining Todd in the darkened room, the music blaring, furiously trying to keep up with the city's fittest gym bunnies.

'Look after him,' she said, her mood softening ever so slightly.

Nat paused with the dishes held awkwardly in front of him, his usual confidence nowhere to be seen.

'By the way, I've managed to get a few days off work in September. I thought we could go somewhere.'

Jem didn't say anything, so he ploughed on.

'There's an inn up in Maine, it's supposed to be lovely in the fall. And I'll be paying for it, so it's not a freebie.'

He was so vulnerable, so desperate, Jem almost melted. But only almost.

'Maybe,' she said finally.

'But I thought you wanted to see the leaves turn,' he said.

She smiled, not at his invitation but at the thought of London in the autumn, the trees in the parks turning a hundred shades of orange and bronze and the early fizz of Christmas in the air.

'It wasn't an affair,' he said quietly. 'With Alice, I mean. It was just a kiss, you have to believe me.'

Jem shook her head. 'That's the problem, Nat,' she said. 'I don't.'

He looked at her intently, and then as if he had realised he should leave the subject for another time, put the dishes by the sink and went into the bedroom, having the good sense to leave her alone.

Jem walked over to the window, staring out at the street. It was past nine o'clock and completely dark. She could just make out the yellow streak of a cab passing beneath a street light. The city seemed so empty, so free of people. Wouldn't it be so much better if everyone just disappeared? Wake up one morning and – poof! – they'd all gone. No more bad relationships, no more disappointments, just space and time and loneliness. Did it matter that it was 'just a kiss'? Or did that make it worse?

She suddenly recalled watching a movie when she was a kid, Julia Roberts in *Pretty Woman* saying something about never kissing on the mouth, because it was more intimate than screwing. At the time, aged twelve or thirteen, Jem had thought that idea was stupid: of course having sex was more intimate. But now she understood. Sex could be perfunctory and impersonal, while a kiss; now that took feeling. You had to mean it.

Then again, she thought, looking across to the box of Alice's things sitting in the corner of the room. Do I really want to find out he's been having a full-blown affair?

Nat had closed the bedroom door behind him and she could hear the mumble of a video game through the wall. Jem crossed to the sofa and took Alice's phone from her bag, looking at it before she switched it on. It glowed in the dim light as it came to life.

She had to know. If she was ever to forgive her husband, she had to know the extent of his relationship with Alice.

Jem had checked Alice's phone once before, but this time she was looking for something else, something she might have missed. A connection to Nat, not Paul.

The first thing she noticed was the battery indicator bar. Only 20 per cent of charge; she needed to move fast. She tapped on the envelope icon, scrolling through Alice's text messages, front to back. Nothing from Nat, but then there was nothing from Paul either; text messages were the simplest things to erase.

The battery bar was ticking down and Jem needed to keep looking, although her hope was already fading. If Alice had had the foresight to delete messages, the chance of finding anything useful was slim at best.

'What else?' she murmured. Apps? She tapped on a couple of social media applications, but there wasn't anything much there. Alice posting gushing comments and pictures of random parties; Alice using yoga equipment; a stretched-arm selfie of the housemates early in the season: all very standard. She turned to Alice's photo album: more of the same, just a wider selection. Parties, gyms, selfies in yoga gear, selfies in party wear, selfies taken in the mirror.

She switched off the phone and debated whether to go to bed, but the thought of lying next to Nat made her flinch.

She turned on a lamp and walked over to Alice's box. Setting it on the table, she opened the lid and put the phone inside. Michael was coming into the city tomorrow; she would give it to him then. Maybe she wouldn't even need to explain that she had taken it from his office, although a voice in her head told her she had to be honest.

She picked up Alice's jewellery box and opened it. She'd had one just like it herself, and the haunting tinkling melody took her straight back to her childhood. The little ballerina turned in time with the music, so slowly and sweetly it was almost hypnotic. Jem imagined a young Alice receiving the box for a birthday or Christmas; she imagined her wide-eyed and innocent before life had conspired to make her otherwise.

The ballerina stopped turning and Jem frowned. She tried winding the box up again, but still nothing.

'Bloody hell,' she muttered, giving it a shake. She could hear something rattling at the base of the box. She took out the rings and tangled necklaces and shook it again. There was definitely something in there, and she couldn't help but wonder what it was.

She used a pen to prise the pink satin base off the wooden frame. Underneath, trapped between the base and the box, was a thumbnail-size card; she recognised it instantly as an SD memory card.

She picked up Alice's phone and looked at the empty memory card slot. Her heart started thumping hard when she realised it was the same size.

She switched the phone back on and popped the card in, checking the power as she did. There was only 12 per cent left, and she wasn't sure she had a compatible charger that could juice it up.

She tapped on the videos file, and there was a pause, followed by the word 'Loading . . .'

And then there they were: dozens of new videos. More videos than had been on her phone.

At first it was pretty much like the photo file. Clips of people standing around talking at parties. Shots of people getting out of cars; the fronts and backs of grand houses. A film of two women and a man Jem didn't recognise dancing badly to what sounded like Madonna's 'Material Girl'. A boat trip and a pod of dolphins swimming in the ocean, followed by a clip of Todd falling out of a canoe and the sound of Angela laughing hysterically off-screen.

Then it changed. Paul began to appear. Footage of a party much the same as all the others, only in this, instead of just filming the general ambience, Alice had zoomed in on Paul, lingering on his face. Then Paul on his own, walking down a busy Manhattan street, waving at the camera and laughing. Paul in a park, sitting on a bench, clowning around with a pair of sunglasses. Paul in bed, sleepy and grinning lazily; Alice giggling – Jem recognised her voice now – off-camera. There was Paul in the shower. Paul in the garden at the beach house, painting the fence in his shorts, just as he had been that first day they had arrived. And then there was Alice herself: wide mouth, white teeth, happy, laughing, a beautiful ghost from the grave.

The Paul and Alice clips were still interspersed with more straightforward party shots: a charity auction chaired by some white-haired TV presenter; an odd, shaky clip of Joel boasting to another man about some investment he'd made, fuzzy and indistinct off to the left. That one was strange actually; it looked like one of those movies where you film your feet by mistake, like it had been shot without Joel knowing. But then there came another shot of Paul, and another, each so intimate, so charged with a tingling teenage blush of excitement, that Jem began to feel as if she were intruding. Still she persevered, needing to know if Alice had filmed Nat in similarly compromising positions, but as the movies went on, she knew she wasn't going to find anything.

Alice had been in love with Paul, that much was clear. No, that wasn't strong enough: Alice had been head over heels, she was *crazy* in love. The loving, lingering way she filmed Paul when he was asleep or just sitting in the sun reading told her that here was a woman who only had eyes for one man. Yes, she might have grabbed hold of Nat too, but more and more Jem felt convinced by Nat's account, and by Paul's assertion that Alice had only made a play for Nat to make him jealous.

But the more she watched, the more she felt a growing, sinking sense of sadness. For Alice, this had been a grand passion, something real. For Paul? At best, a distraction from his chilly wife; at worst, some conquest to amuse himself over the summer break. No wonder the movies stopped abruptly straight after a near-pornographic clip involving a vibrator shot in what Jem recognised as the double bed in the Catskills cabin. Clearly that was when Paul had decided it was all getting too risky and had cut it off. And that, for Alice, had been the beginning of the end.

Jem set the phone down, closing her eyes with an all-consuming sense of sadness.

Alice had been a victim after all, a victim of unrequited love.

She got up and made herself a coffee, jolting to attention when she heard her own mobile beep. Grabbing her mug, she stretched over to her bag and pulled the phone out, surprised to see a message from Erica.

Hope you're feeling better. Will bring you some beauty goodies next weekend. E x

She put the phone down with a soft snort. Some people surprised you in a good way, she thought, thinking about her developing friendship with Erica. Before their heart-to-heart at the beach she had found her housemate a little bit spiky, but now she realised that Erica was as insecure as she herself sometimes felt in the Hamptons.

Yonex. Yonex. A word Erica had mentioned the previous day lurked in her consciousness.

Repeating it out loud, she picked up Alice's phone.

Six per cent battery life. With trembling, anxious fingers, Jem switched back to movies and scrolled through until she found the footage of Joel and his companion. She listened hard to the dialogue between them, pressing the phone close to her ear.

'Pyani is coming after Yonex,' said the other man.

'For sure?' said Joel.

There followed something inaudible, then she heard Joel speak again.

'Makes sense. What's the target offer?'

'Twenty-five dollars cash. Better start thinking about buying some options, my friend.'

Jem took a moment to think. She wasn't exactly sure what it meant, but instinct told her she had just seen and heard something significant.

The sound of the video game had gone quiet in the bedroom and Jem wondered whether to disturb Nat and show him the clip. Whatever she was thinking about her husband right now, he was smart and informed and she knew that if she told him everything, if she showed him the video, he could help her connect the dots.

'The house that Yonex built'; that was what Erica had said when she had taken Jem to see the house in Montauk. Nat's laptop was on the table. Jem flipped it open and typed 'Yonex' into Google.

Yonex Shares Rocket in Surprise Merger Announcement

The unexpected announcement of tech sensation Yonex's merger with Indian giant Pyani caused a huge rise in their share price Monday, with the value jumping more than 30% in less than an hour of trading.

'So Joel grabbed himself some of that windfall,' she murmured, as the battery bar tweeted angrily to indicate that the phone was about to shut down.

Quickly Jem returned to that odd scratchy footage of the two men, the film that had seemed so out of place among all the selfies and party clips. It began with a swooping shot of painted toes in a pair of expensive-looking sandals, then whirled up to a close-up of some leaves: Alice getting herself in position, presumably. It was as if she had shot the footage through a porthole, but Joel's face was still clear to see. He was smoking a cigar, talking to a dark-haired man Jem didn't recognise.

'No more house shares for you next summer,' said Joel's friend as the footage ended.

The phone ran out of battery in Jem's hand, and for a moment she just looked at it. Then she glanced at her watch. She didn't know Michael's habits post-sundown, but she was willing to guess he was working five nights out of seven.

She looked back towards the bedroom door, then picked up her own phone, flipping through her contacts book to find Michael's number.

'Come on, come on,' she muttered as the line rang, imagining him either hard at work or feeding a burrito to one of those nameless ladies he'd been so coy about dating.

'Jem? Everything all right?' he said.

'Yes, absolutely,' she said, trying to sound as professional as possible. After their enjoyable surfing trip, the last thing she wanted was for Michael to think this was an inappropriate late-night call; that she had read too much into his suggestion to have some fun.

'I think I've found something,' she said, keeping her voice quiet.

'Okay,' he said. She heard a noise in the background and imagined him putting on his glasses and picking up a pen.

'First things first,' she said, taking a breath. 'I have to tell you, I did something wrong today.'

He waited for her to continue, and the silence made her feel more guilty and embarrassed. She looked towards the bedroom door again, praying that Nat had fallen asleep over his console.

'I took Alice's phone, this morning. I took it from your office.'

She was about to tell him why, but stopped herself. She didn't need to explain herself – not yet, not unless she had to. She didn't want to make this situation more complicated than it was already, and dragging Nat into proceedings, linking him directly to Alice, would do exactly that.

'I know I shouldn't have done it, and I'm sorry. You have every right to be angry,' she said, her voice an urgent whisper. 'But I found a memory card in the additional box of stuff that David brought round. It slotted inside Alice's phone and there were videos on it that weren't on her mobile, videos she must have deleted but kept on the memory card. I found something interesting.'

'Go on . . .'

She breathed a sigh of relief that he wasn't going to pursue her theft of the phone.

'Alice had taken a video of Joel talking with a friend. That friend was tipping him off about a company being sold.'

She couldn't replay the video, but she told Michael, word for word, everything she could remember.

'Insider trading,' said Michael after she'd finished.

'I've heard of it, but what actually happens?' asked Jem.

'It's acting on confidential information that can affect a share price. It's generally illegal. The SEC will come down on you. Martha Stewart, various Wall Street kings, they've all gone down because of it. It's very difficult to prove, but that video is actual evidence.'

'Maybe he didn't act on the information . . .'

'Maybe,' replied Michael. 'Quite a coincidence, though, that he's just bought himself a beach house in Montauk. They're generally above Joel's pay grade in the scheme of things.'

He paused.

'Who's the friend? Do we know?'

'No,' she said, feeling a surge of energy as she thought of Nat meeting Todd the next morning. 'I don't know now. But I have an idea how I can find out.'

Last summer

Chapter 30

They checked in at a boutique hotel in the middle of nowhere called the Inn the Woods, and as they hopped on a golf buggy to a cabin in the pine-studded grounds, Alice thought she had died and gone to mini-break heaven. It was exquisitely designed, with granite tiles, sofas draped with soft fur throws, a wood-burning stove, even a circular bath made from wood, and as the bellboy explained, it came ready-loaded with champagne and steak so they never even needed to leave.

When they were alone, Paul took her face between his hands and kissed her tenderly.

'What do you think?' he asked, with an expression that told her he was satisfied with his choice.

'I think I want to stay here forever,' Alice giggled, already feeling the panic of sadness that within twenty-four hours they would be back in the city.

'I'm hungry. What about you?' he said after a moment.

Alice would much rather have gone straight to bed or tried the bath out for size, but she'd heard her stomach rumble too and agreed they should kick off the trip with lunch.

There was a barbecue pit outside, and Paul got to work

grilling the steaks that had been left for them in the cabin's tiny kitchen. Alice laughed as he disappeared in a cloud of smoke. Paul had lived within a ten-buck cab ride of Central Park most of his adult life; she wasn't at all sure he'd ever touched a barbecue before, but then men loved burning meat, didn't they? It filled them with manliness and testosterone, which was exactly what she had in mind.

'You want it rare?' he shouted as she packed a wicker picnic basket.

'I'll have it any way you want,' she replied playfully as she went outside and kissed him.

'Want to go and find a nice spot to eat?' he said.

Alice nodded and walked away from the cabin and the smoke towards a clearing. She saw a line of sparkling water, and although she shivered, she found herself being drawn towards it.

The bellboy had told them there was a pond, which had made her a little nervous, but it was certainly a beauty. It was not large; Alice could see the rooftop of the main hotel on the opposite shore. The sun shone on the water, sending bronze ripples scudding over the surface, and the soft breeze made the leaves of the trees brush together in a gentle, reassuring whisper.

The place was pretty, she had to admit that, and as she walked towards a short wooden pier, she felt a calm that she had not felt for a long time near water.

She brought out a blanket and unrolled it on the jetty. Sitting down, she unpacked the basket. She looked back towards the cabin and knew it would all be perfect, if it weren't for the neat little plastic stick digging into her thigh.

She put her hand in her pocket and pulled it out.

She'd kept the flash drive close to her from the moment Nick Vlautin had given it to her, knowing that she couldn't do anything with it until she'd worked out how to resolve the situation.

Unfolding her fingers, she looked at the USB stick, imagined watching the movie. Part of her wanted to see it, to see herself, that young girl, watch the look on her face. Did she look scared? Had she been forced into it? Had Nick beaten her, made threats? No. She had done it because he had asked her to. Because he had held her face and told her what she wanted to hear: you're the most beautiful woman in the world. Alice had lain down in that hotel room under the blinking red light because that had been the last – the only? – time she had been in love, the last time she would have done anything for a man. *And look where it got you.*

Twenty thousand dollars. Twenty fucking grand. For some women she knew, that wouldn't be such a big deal. They had trust funds, personal wealth, access to investment portfolios or assets they could liquidate. Rebecca, for one. Alice was willing to bet Rebecca could write a cheque for ten times that amount then go for a manicure, get straight on with her day.

But for Alice, it was an anvil chained to her neck, threatening to pull her back down into the black depths. She looked into the shadows under the pier, her mind lost in the past.

Alice hadn't just lost her sister that afternoon by the lake. She'd lost her innocence. When Rose Buckle went under the ice, her feet getting stuck in the knots and weeds tangled in the freezing cold water and pulling the child down to her death, Alice's heart broke in two.

Stickle Pond was an old quarry pond and had been a popular swimming spot once, but like everything in Hawkins it was tired and neglected and no one from town came down there any more.

No one except Alice and Rosie. The Buckle girls had

never been taught to swim, but it was a place they could go to escape the tight confines of home, escape the shouting and arguments. It was a place they could go to have fun. They didn't have skates, but when the ice was thick, they tied magazines to their shoes and tried to glide across the surface, pretending they were figure skaters like the ones they'd seen on the TV, with their elegant dance moves and pretty chiffon costumes that Alice thought looked like tiny clouds.

It was a tough year, the year Rosie died. One day her dad just took off; he said he couldn't stand all the weeping. There were four in the Buckle family and then there were two. But Alice and her mother were glad to see the back of him. Alice would say that her father drank away his sorrows, but then he was always a heavy drinker, and if he felt the depth of grief that Alice felt then he never showed it.

New boyfriends came and went for her mother. Looking back, Alice wondered if she was looking for love, but she never found it in the string of losers that she dated. And when she lost her job at the electrical store, she started turning tricks to pay the rent.

Alice kept out of the house. Puberty kicked in and she fell in with a bad crowd. She slept around and discovered drugs; drugs that made her forget. They were too expensive for her to buy herself, so she found boyfriends who could supply them. Bad boys like Nick Vlautin, who for a few moments made her feel excited and happy and loved.

A couple of supportive teachers took her to one side and tried to get her back on the straight and narrow. They suggested a dance scholarship to the local college; although she had given up all formal training many years before, they thought she had a good chance of winning one. But Alice didn't want to hang around Indiana any more. She didn't need a high-school diploma or a degree certificate; she needed to reinvent herself and change her past so she could change her future.

And although moving to Manhattan hadn't immediately been the answer to her problems, meeting David Holliday was. He wasn't her type, and that was precisely the point. She'd had to change her strategy completely to get where she was now, and she was not going to let the likes of Nick Vlautin drag her down now.

She looked down at the flash drive. Then she tipped her hand forward, watching it spin end over end, disappearing into the water with barely a plop. Goodbye, Alice, she thought, as she closed her eyes and exhaled deeply. Goodbye, Rose.

She could tell even before he'd reached the pier that Paul had nuked the steaks. There was a strong smell of charcoal and the meat was still steaming as he approached her carrying a wooden platter.

'You been letting off fireworks?' she grinned.

'What can I say? Man make fire,' he said, making a grunt like a movie caveman.

Considering Paul's evident culinary shortcomings, they had quite a feast, helped immeasurably by the fact that they had found a great deli in Rivertown, the last town in the hills on the way in. They had picked up tubs of salad, hummus and some great crusty bread, not to mention stocking up on wine. No one was going to starve.

They ate in pleasurable silence for a while, enjoying the sunshine and the quiet. When they were finished, they sat back and sipped champagne from crystal goblets. Alice listened to the birds, the wind, tried to let her tension drift away. She was in a spot, that was true, but she was here in an amazing bolthole with a man she was head over heels for – and she had him to herself.

'You read any of this?' asked Paul, picking up the book Alice had put in the picnic basket.

'First few pages. It looks pretty good.' She was glad she had popped into the cute bookstore in Rivertown while Paul had been agonising over his choices in the deli.

Alice didn't read much. She liked the occasional spy thriller or romance on her sunlounger, but David frowned on anything so low-brow, so she had to hide them in her lingerie drawer then unload them to goodwill as soon as they were finished. All the novels on their shelves at home were literary or so-called classics, almost always by sinewy, rugged Americans: Hemingway, Mailer, Kesey, Faulkner. The book Paul was holding was somewhere in the middle. *The Dark of Night* by Randall Carver, the latest *enfant terrible* on the literary scene, was a psychological thriller with a sheen of intellectual credibility. Over breakfast a couple of weeks before, David had read aloud its glowing review in the *New York Times Book Review*, and grudgingly said that he might give it a try.

Those first few pages had made Alice's eyes roll with their self-consciously overwritten prose, but that wasn't the point: the book was a prop and she had brought it outside so that Paul could see it. It said, 'I'm clever and interesting'. It also said, in a much more subtle way, 'I have a brain too, so don't underestimate me'.

The fatal error in this kind of relationship – and Alice had made this mistake before – was to be regarded as a plaything. If the guy just saw you as an oversexed air-head, you were dead. He'd take what you were offering, then disappear – why wouldn't he? No, the key to seduction was always the element of surprise. He thought you were just beautiful, but you turned out to be clever; he thought you were just rich, but it turned out you were a great artist.

And that, not the sex, was what kept a man on the hook: the sense of spending time with a real person rather than a glorified blow-up doll. You had to remember that these men were alpha. They expected the rewards, but they also wanted a challenge. So no nagging or demanding – they got enough of that at home; rather intrigue, fascinate, even irritate. That was what made them come back wanting more.

'And what are *you* reading at the moment?' she said, making it sound casual, as if it hadn't all been planned days ago.

'Read? I don't have time to read. I'll probably just wait for the movie and watch it on the plane.'

Alice turned to face him. 'Okay, tell me your favourite movie.'

'Of all time?'

'Of all time, only you're not allowed to say *Citizen Kane* because I won't believe you, and you can't say *The Godfather* either because it will be disappointing.'

Paul grinned. 'But I love *The Godfather*.'

She rolled her eyes.

'Do I have to go to the mattresses with you?'

There. She saw the eyes widen, the little smile of pleasure. Men were so easily pleased, so easy to manipulate. When had he last come across a woman who could quote a movie back at him? When had he met a society girl who had even *seen The Godfather*? Now Alice was special, interesting. She was worth getting to know better.

They lay back on the deck and watched the clouds drift across the expanse of blue.

'Why didn't I meet you years ago?' he said with a soft sigh.

Alice almost punched the air in triumph when she heard not only the contentment, but the regret.

'Why do you say that?' she asked, taking his hand.

'Having fun. Being myself.' He spoke in a voice so quiet she could hardly hear it.

Alice nodded without looking at him. She knew what he was saying. Paul had made the Faustian pact too. He'd made compromises when he'd married the frosty, patrician Rebecca, who was as much his type as David was Alice's. Somewhere along the line, poor kids from gritty working towns made romantic choices that satisfied their ambition rather than their hearts.

'When did you meet Rebecca?' she asked after a moment.

She didn't normally like asking about the wife, never liked to break the spell. But she knew it was as good a time as any to make Paul think about the choices he had made and whether they were still relevant.

'We met at college. Columbia. I met Todd and Angela there too. I was friends with Todd. He'd been dating Angela from day one. Rebecca was her friend and she fixed us up.'

Alice resisted the urge to make a tart remark. Instead she shifted her position, balancing on her side so that she could look at him.

'I wish I'd met you before too.'

'Before what?' he asked.

'Before David,' she said simply.

He turned to face her and stroked her cheek.

'You make me happy.'

Alice nodded, although she could not ignore the churn of anxiety in her stomach. She had found a little piece of heaven here, yet she felt as though she was teetering on the edge of a clifftop, the wind pushing at her back, the ground crumbling beneath her feet.

Nick Vlautin. The contents of the flash drive.

The first film might be explained away as a Kim Kardashian-style home sex tape – two lovers who'd just pulled out a camera and decided to have some fun. But the rest of it? It was porn; a series of short, grubby skin flicks that Nick had sold to his low-life friends to make some cash. And although Alice could console herself that she looked quite different then, unrecognisable with her bottle-red hair and curvier pre-yoga body, if she didn't pay him the twenty thousand dollars she didn't doubt that Nick would tell everyone who mattered exactly who it was that had the starring role in the tape.

What would Paul think if he ever saw it? David? Her friends at the beach house? She shivered despite the heat of the day.

'Are you okay?' said Paul, disturbing her thoughts.

'I'm good,' she said, pasting a soft smile on her face.

Paul leant forward and brushed his lips against her. It wasn't foreplay, it was a kiss of tender emotion. It was a kiss that said, 'This could go further'. A kiss that spelt pure danger for Rebecca.

For a minute, on the long drive to the Catskills, Alice had wondered whether to tell Paul about the sex tape. It was dirty and gritty and there was a side of Paul's lovemaking that suggested it would turn him on. She'd also thought about asking him to lend her the money to pay off Nick Vlautin; call it a loan, an investment, disguise it as something else, then find a way to pay it back when the danger had passed. But she knew now that that would kill whatever they had here stone dead. Money and sex just couldn't be part of the equation.

She'd been with rich guys before she'd met David, taken their handbags and their jewellery, let them pay for the spa breaks and the treatments. They'd say they were gifts but they never meant it. They saw it as payment. It was a transaction for services rendered, tied up in a red ribbon, a way for the man – the client, really – to feel better about the whole thing. It was just like paying the driver or the pool guy or his secretary. But she knew that Paul would see it as a shakedown: 'Twenty grand or this gets back to Rebecca.' None of the dating manuals ever listed blackmail as a way to get a man to go down on one knee.

She felt another wave of anxiety. *One knee*. Was that what she wanted; where she longed for this love affair to go?

Her mind created a ridiculous tableau of Paul kneeling on the porch of the cabin, a ring clutched in one hand. Ridiculous was the word, wasn't it? He was already married – and so was she. Be realistic: they had been together a handful of times. Hardly the basis for any sort of relationship, let alone something as drastic as a double divorce followed by a million-dollar society wedding.

But Alice had fallen for Paul. She shouldn't have, it was an impossible situation, but the fact was she wanted to be with him all the time, not just snatched moments, or the odd night in a woodland cabin when he could convince his wife he was at a conference. All the time, permanent, till death us do part. That was what she wanted more than life itself. But Paul was classy. Paul was smart. He was a man who had chosen an upper-crust WASP like Rebecca to improve his own social position. He wasn't going to throw it all away for a girl from the wrong side of the tracks who'd made porno flicks to pay the rent.

'Let's go back inside,' she said, sitting up and tossing back her hair. 'Let's read and drink champagne and be happy,' she purred, her eyes drifting to the pond and imagining the flash drive sinking to the bottom. Nick Vlautin wanted twenty thousand bucks to make her past stay hidden, and she was more determined than ever to find the money.

Chapter 31

Art was bullshit: that was what Alice had learnt. Or rather, art was just one of those things that rich people loved, like sailing, speculating in junk bonds or driving cars that cost more than a house. Like all society pastimes, it was designed to impress other rich people and keep the rest out. You needed money to buy it, you needed a particular kind of education to understand it, and most of all, it was the sort of undertaking where you got to show off. That was why Picassos and Hirsts had exchanged hands for such insane amounts at auction in recent years; it wasn't about the paintings or the sculptures, it was about swinging dicks.

And there are plenty of dicks here tonight, thought Alice as she walked slowly around the gallery. Millionaires, a couple of billionaires, even a movie star; they were all here for the annual party for the Gugualian East. The heavy-hitting Gugualian studio, the gallery of choice for Warhol and Bacon and now a new generation of art stars, had a glittering opening in their purpose-built East Hampton space every June. It attracted only the wealthiest and the best connected; people had been known to beg and bribe for the shiny blue tickets.

David fitted into the 'connected' category by virtue of having shared a dorm with Leo Cutler, the current head curator at the main gallery, two blocks from the Guggenheim. Alice was always grateful for the invitations, but she had to admit she was surprised by these favours: had David been more fun when he was at school? Maybe he'd been a secret hell-raiser; why else would he engender such loyalty from old friends?

Clearly he has hidden depths, she thought, looking across to where David was standing with Todd and Angela, evidently discussing the merits of a Tracey Emin collage involving a picture of a butterfly and a naked man.

The Gugualian East was essentially a sawn-off version of the Manhattan gallery. The high ceilings and white walls had been replicated here, the East Hampton facility's smaller dimensions made up for by a large sculpture garden out back. It was still a wildly impressive space, though, with each of the works given a whole wall or corner to itself, all the better to admire it in isolation. Tonight there was a late-period Matisse, a Georgia O'Keeffe skull, one of those Jeff Koons balloon dogs; all crowd-pleasers, all of them worth millions.

Alice walked over to where Erica and Joel were standing with Rebecca, admiring a painting of a stick man. She almost laughed out loud; the picture represented everything she hated about the pomposity of the art world. A stick man! It was worth hearing what Rebecca had to say about it, though, even if Alice was still narked that Erica and Joel were here. David had impressed upon her that it was a very exclusive event, but obviously it wasn't that exclusive if Rebecca had managed to get everyone in.

Rebecca looked particularly formidable tonight, she thought as she approached them. Her cream trouser suit made her look longer and leggier than usual; her mouth painted with scarlet lipstick reminded Alice of a splash of blood in the snow.

Erica kissed her on the cheek and nodded towards the painting.

'Rebecca was just explaining the significance,' she said as she sipped her champagne.

'You mean it's not just a stick man,' Alice grinned, resisting the urge to join in and say something pretentious. It suited her to downplay her cleverness in front of Rebecca. She didn't want her to see her as a threat.

'The artist is trying to deconstruct a human being to its simplest form,' said Rebecca knowingly.

'Or maybe it's reminding us girls that men are just plain simple,' quipped Alice.

Erica laughed and Rebecca surprised Alice by joining in. She was not known for her sense of humour. In the house, she was usually the one with her nose in a book or a magazine like the *New Yorker*. She ate very little too, picking at her salad in a cool and restrained way that made her seem joyless.

'Where's Paul tonight?' Alice tried to say it as casually as she could. She'd asked Todd and David and Angela, but no one seemed to know and she felt on edge, checking the door constantly to see if he was coming in. She needed to know, and after five weekends at the beach house since their affair began, she was confident enough of her deception skills to ask his wife the question.

'He's working. Again,' Rebecca said with a roll of the eyes. 'Between both our workloads at the moment it's amazing we ever see each other. If he doesn't make our anniversary dinner on Wednesday I'm going to kill him. I've managed to get reservations at Spring and I'm going on my own even if he can't make it.'

Alice managed a conflicted smile. On the one hand she hated the thought of Paul sharing a celebratory dinner *à deux* with his wife; on the other hand, she liked to imagine him in a stuffy restaurant wishing he was eating steak on the lakeside dock in the Catskills. It had been the most perfect day: lying in the sunshine until the temperature cooled, then making love in the queen-size bed. They'd got up to finish the last of the champagne and take a bath together in the circular tub, then gone back to bed, snoozing and screwing until the sun rose again and they had to get back to the city. Beat that, Rebecca, Alice thought as she sipped her cocktail.

'So is David going to be buying anything tonight?' said Joel.

Alice turned to look at him. Joel was fine at the beach house, but put him in a high-society environment like this one and he became the worst kind of swinging dick: the high-flying banker who made six figures a year but was bitter and grouchy because he was surrounded by other people making ten times more. Everything was a competition with Joel; tennis, gossip, vacations, they all had to be better than whatever you had. Alice could stomach it most of the time, but this chafed at her: a dig at David for not being one of them, not being a big spender.

'Well I know he was looking at that Dali drawing,' she said airily. 'But we did just get an etching by – what's his name? Did a famous book about horses?'

'Stubbs? You mean *The Anatomy of the Horse*?' said Rebecca, raising a brow in approval.

'That's it. David loves his stuff. Don't mention the print to him, though,' she said quickly, not wanting to get caught out. 'It's a present; he's not supposed to know about it yet. I set it up with a dealer in Lennox Hill.'

'See, Joel?' said Erica, looking meaningfully at her husband. 'Alice knows what her husband likes and goes out of her way to get it for him. That's nice, isn't it?'

Joel glared at her, then lifted his half-full glass. 'Going to the bar,' he said. Rebecca followed him.

'Men!' said Erica when they'd gone. 'Joel's such a . . .' She seemed to rein herself in for a moment, then looked away. 'I do envy you, you know,' she said quietly.

'Envy me?' said Alice in surprise.

Erica took a long swallow of her wine, then gestured towards David on the other side of the room.

'You envy me for *David*?'

'Look, I've known David for years; he's steady, cute, reliable, and that's cool, isn't it? To know who your husband is – to know *where* he is.' She looked at Alice. 'And you love each other whatever your faults, that's the important thing, right?'

Alice could feel her hand tightening on the stem of her glass. 'Yes,' she said, keeping her face as neutral as possible. 'I guess that's what you aim for, sure.'

She touched Erica's arm, softened her voice.

'Is everything okay? What's happened?'

Erica's mouth tightened and she gave a slight shake of the head.

'He forgot our anniversary.' The word 'forgot' was dripping with sarcasm.

'Oh crap.'

'It's not even that he forgot,' said Erica. 'It's that when I called him on it, he just shrugged, like it wasn't a big deal.'

She took a ragged breath and blinked hard.

'I mean, it's not like I've caught him fucking the nanny or something. It's just . . . he doesn't seem to care.'

'About you?'

'About anything except his damn *job*,' she said with angry emphasis. 'Has he ever once asked about my day? Does he even know what I do? All he ever talks about is how the other partners are doing, or how Jimmy Welch just got a bonus for some stupid deal. It's like I'm invisible.'

Alice nodded gravely. She wasn't thinking about David.

She was thinking about Paul. It had been three days since their secret getaway in the Catskills, and beyond a couple of replies to her texts, she had heard nothing from him. He certainly hadn't mentioned that he wasn't coming to the beach that weekend and every scenario had passed through her head: she had done or said something wrong, she'd been too sexually adventurous in bed and the vibrator from XD'Or was one step too far. Perhaps he'd lost interest; perhaps Rebecca had found out or he feared she had; or maybe he had just been really busy. That was the problem with an affair: you had no rights. You couldn't ring him at home or work, you couldn't just turn up for lunch. Unless it was mutually arranged, it wouldn't happen – and there was no way to find out why.

Alice knew it was crazy to feel rejected after just a few days, but that was how it was. There had been fire and passion and a connection like she had barely ever felt; and now it had gone.

'That was a really sweet present you got for David, by the way. The drawing,' added Erica. 'Rebecca was telling me what she's got for Paul. A 1973 Mustang, can you believe it? He's going to look like fricking Steve McQueen driving around Brooklyn.'

Alice tried to smile but she felt the gallery walls closing in on her. If Paul wasn't coming to the party, she needed to get out of there; the last thing she wanted to do was coo over expensive presents that his wife had bought him.

Her eyes darted around the room. Rebecca was deep in conversation about another ridiculous painting and she couldn't see David anywhere. Excusing herself from Erica, she looked in her bag for a cigarette. She was a very occasional smoker, but when she found out that Paul liked a couple of American Spirits a day, she kept a packet in her bag for them to share, and boy, did she need one now.

She walked out into the sculpture garden, grateful that there was a good place to hide. Alice was cynical about the art world, but there was something quite majestic about the works out here: the life-sized ceramic cows painted in a rainbow of colours, the giant mirrors and the polished steel spheres that reminded her of the Ben Wa balls she had seen at XD'Or; there was even a huge spoon the size of a subway carriage that threw dark shapes across the lawns. She went to the far reaches of the party and sat behind an enormous bronze of a theatrical mask, lighting a cigarette and inhaling deeply.

She wondered what her friends at the yoga studio would think of her now. A tobacco habit, though frowned upon for years by most of society, now had a kind of forbidden glamour about it; if you were a smoker, you were part of a slightly racy secret society, a mildly oppressed minority. It was like the high-school lunch room all over again: the smokers all sat together and had an air of solidarity. They also had the best gossip, which was why, when she was out of David's line of vision, Alice would sometimes join in.

She blew grey smoke up to the sky. It was a clear night and the stars washed the black ribbon between the lights of East Hampton and the sea beyond. You certainly wouldn't see anything like that in Manhattan; if you looked up there, you were lucky to see the blinking light of a traffic chopper. It was amazing that they were only a couple of hours' drive from the claustrophobic avenues of the city. It was so calm here, so peaceful. If only that serenity could translate into Alice's head.

She could hear voices approaching and stubbed her cigarette out. It would be just like David to come looking for her, and he'd only get suspicious if he found her skulking around the sculpture garden, reeking of cigarette smoke. For all his vagueness and seeming lack of interest in her life,

Alice could recognise the controlling side to her husband's personality. He wouldn't let her wear high heels above a couple of inches, and off-the-shoulder dresses made him pissy. Alice could live with that, but she couldn't live with him rifling through her purse, hoping to catch her with a pack of cigarettes or a telltale lighter. Get into that sort of habit, there was always a chance he'd take it into his head to look through her phone messages.

She decided to stay hidden until the voices had gone. The noise rose in volume: two men, one talking, then sudden, slightly subdued laughter. One telling the other an off-colour joke, she guessed.

At least it wasn't David, she thought, wondering whether to pop up from behind the bronze. She peeped through the eye hole in the mask, but she couldn't see much, though her ears pricked up when she heard a name – 'Erica' – then 'bitch'. Ever so slowly and quietly, she edged to her left, where the foliage thinned out. It was Joel and another man; from their body language, they knew each other well.

They were sitting on a bench, and Alice could see them clearly in side profile. In light of her conversation with Erica, she wanted to find out what they were saying, and as long as she kept behind the wide expanse of the sculpture, she knew she could listen to them undetected.

'I tell you, there's no pleasing some women,' said Joel, his voice clear above the faint background party noise. 'We have a great house share, but still she goes on and on about our own place.'

'Same with Anna and her horse,' said his friend. 'Co-ownership is no good any more, she wants her own, but have you seen the cost of stabling in the Hamptons? I said, you'll only see the fricking thing a dozen weekends a year, but now she's throwing words like "unreasonable behaviour" around.'

'Man, I wish I was single sometimes.'

'Too right. Who's that new chick at the beach house? I wouldn't mind a piece of that.'

Joel laughed. 'Figures. She's got that cheap look about her I know you like. Rumour has it David picked her up in some brothel, so if you fancy a pop, I rate your chances.'

Shithead, thought Alice, feeling her cheeks burn red.

'You're joking, right?'

Alice tuned back into the conversation in front of her.

'There's no way I'd tell her a thing about that money. Anna has a hair up her ass about ethics.'

Joel laughed. 'Ethics are for pussies.'

There was a long silence. Alice peered through the eye hole and watched Joel light a cigar.

'So. Quid pro quo,' said his friend. 'Here's something you'll be interested in. Play it right, you'll get Erica her own beach house.'

Joel popped three smoke rings into the air.

'What you got?'

Alice frowned, her instincts telling her that she was listening to something private and juicy. She clicked the camera on her phone and started recording their conversation. She wanted to retain every word of what they were saying and didn't want to take any chances with her own recall.

'Pyani is coming after Yonex.'

'For sure?' asked Joel.

'I'm working on the contracts now.'

'How close is it to a done deal?'

'It'll take a few more weeks to close it, but it's definitely going to happen.'

'Pyani and Yonex . . .' Alice peered through the eye hole again, this time bringing her camera with her to capture them on film. 'Makes sense. What's the target offer?'

'Twenty-five dollars cash. Better start thinking about buying some options, my friend.'

'Call options.' Joel smiled and blew another smoke ring into the cool air.

'No more house shares for you next summer,' laughed his friend as the two men walked back to the party.

Chapter 32

The beach was silent save for the slight ripple of a breeze over the sand. Alice sat on the edge of the dunes, hugging her knees. Sunday morning, just a couple of hours after dawn, and the golden stretch between her and the water was mercifully deserted, serene. Back in Indiana, Sunday was a busy day: church with friends and relatives, shooting and hiking, even just hanging around the 7-Eleven talking bullshit. Out here, it was a nothing day. Stores all closed, eating late, driving back to the city, just a pit stop before the working week ticked around again. Which was another reason why Alice loved the house share. She could slip out of bed – David tutting and grumbling in his sleep – and wander along the sandy boardwalk down to the water, the light still grey, the day not quite yet formed.

She sniffed the air, tasting the salt and the earth. It was clean and empty and, just for now, all hers. Even the pair of gulls wheeling overhead seemed to be keeping quiet, intent only on riding the warm updraught, black eyes searching for the silvery glint of fish. Just like me, thought Alice, her eyes scanning the green water beyond the beach. Everyone was hunting for something around here. Money, security, a better job, a new nose, a house in Montauk; everyone wanted something, no one was ever truly happy with what they had. It was the human condition to want more. Maybe when you were retired, sitting on a porch somewhere, all you wanted was the sun to shine. But right now, Alice needed plenty of things. Most of all she needed money. She slid her hand into the pocket of her jacket and pulled out her cell phone.

After the party at the gallery had broken up, they had all headed back to the Wainscott house. Joel had been in an upbeat mood – no great surprise after the conversation Alice had witnessed – and had opened a bottle of champagne, even going so far as to press a glass on David and ask his opinion on Impressionism. Seeing that it was shaping up to be a late one, Alice had feigned a headache and slipped up to their room. Lying in bed listening to the sounds of laughter below, she hadn't slept. Instead she had offered up a prayer of thanks to whoever had dropped this opportunity into her lap just when she needed it.

Alice was not a banker or a financial wizard, but she recognised an illegal share tip-off when she heard one. The question was how to use the information. In an ideal world, she could take advantage and buy shares, turn them into a sizeable profit, pay off Nick. But it wasn't an ideal world, it never had been – not for Alice, anyway. In order to make money from Joel's friend's tip, she needed capital to invest. And right now, she didn't have enough. David had a distaste for the world of finance and there was no way he would play ball. Besides, he would want to know where the information had come from; he was also maddeningly law-abiding. Paul? No, she had the same problem as before. Even framed as an investment opportunity, it was too much commitment too soon; he'd be tying himself to Alice and she sensed that would be a bad move right now. So what could she do?

This.

She stood up as she saw the figure round the headland. Brushing the sand from her dress, she began to walk across the beach, her bare feet sinking into the sand. She watched the figure in the distance getting closer, the shimmer on the water making her lift her hand to shade her eyes, turning the movement into a half-wave when she saw him turn towards her. She walked closer, her heart beating in her chest. She hadn't felt nerves like this in a long time, but she knew the stakes. She had to make this work, or the house of cards she had so carefully stacked could come tumbling down.

Joel returned the wave, then went back to paddling. He was already tall, but standing on a paddleboard he looked like a giant. She knew he was putting on a show, even if it was just for himself, flexing his muscles as he pulled left then right, his wetsuit tied around his waist. And she could imagine the dialogue going on in his mind: why is Alice out here so early? And all alone, too. Click, click, the cogs in his mind would be whirring, coming up with the only possible answer: she's here because she's hot for me. All men thought that way. Many of the women that Alice met at the yoga studio seemed to be in a constant state of self-loathing: my ass is too big, my tits are too small, I have so many wrinkles, if only I could lose eight pounds. Men were the direct opposite, believing utterly in their own attractiveness and overlooking their pot bellies, baldness or drooping jowls. A mother's love obviously went a long, long way.

'Hey,' she said simply as Joel skidded towards the beach and splashed down into the water. She noticed how he pushed his chest out as he picked up the board. *Look at me, look how manly I am.* She almost laughed. If he really thought that was why she was here, he was in for a shock. She felt the nerves rise again, then reminded herself of the things Joel had said about her, his speculation that she'd met David in a brothel, and her resolve hardened. *Cheap?*

After the conversation she was about to have with him, he'd think she was cheap at half the price.

'You're out early,' he said.

'I didn't think anyone else would be up. You all had a late one last night.'

'Oh yeah, sorry about that.' He chuckled as he hefted the paddle and began walking back towards the house. 'Hope we didn't disturb you. Got a bit of a hangover, but getting out on the water clears the head.'

'You did seem in good spirits last night,' said Alice. 'Were you celebrating something?'

Joel stuck his lower lip out. 'No, nothing special,' he said.

God, you're a terrible liar, thought Alice.

She let him walk a few steps, then stopped.

'Joel, I know.'

He turned, genuinely confused.

'You know? Know what?'

'The tip-off from your friend. Yonex. Call options are a very good idea, by the way. Maximise the profit and all that.'

Shock crossed his face as the penny dropped, and he flushed.

'Call options?' he stuttered.

Alice had only spent a few minutes googling what they were and still didn't understand them properly. But she wasn't going to let Joel know that.

'I heard everything, Joel. Yonex, the Pyani takeover. Your friend is doing the contracts on the deal. Naughty, naughty boy for telling you.' She held up her cell phone and smiled. 'So I thought I should record the whole thing.'

His eyes opened wide, then flicked to the phone. Measuring the distance.

'Don't even think about it,' said Alice, slipping it back into her pocket. 'I've uploaded it to a secure server.'

He stomped his paddle down into the sand, a little boy robbed of his favourite toy.

'You don't even know what you're talking about.'

'Oh, I think I do.'

'Bullshit. Perhaps if you worked in the finance sector rather than a yoga studio, you'd know we were just talking shop.'

'Talking shop? It's insider trading, Joel, and I think the SEC will agree with me.'

'You bitch,' he spat.

'Not really,' she said, making her voice as calm and level as possible.

She thought of Nick Vlautin and their grubby little room. She thought of the flash drive at the bottom of the pond in the Catskills. Nick had started calling the yoga studio and leaving messages for her, and she knew it would only be a matter of time before he really twisted the thumb screws. And she thought of Paul and what they could have together.

'I've just caught you out, and you don't like it.'

He looked at her for a moment.

'What is it you want, Alice? Because I doubt you're here to take the moral high ground.'

'I suppose you're right,' she said with a casual shrug. 'I don't give a crap about what you've done, and I don't really want to report you to the SEC or your boss – Martin Rouse, I believe? Not unless I have to.'

'So you do want something?' he said, his bravado unable to mask the note of fear.

'A hundred grand,' she said, the words falling out of her mouth before she could stop them. She'd only been going to ask for twenty, but she was moving too fast to stop now.

'A hundred grand?' gasped Joel. 'I'd rather—'

'You'd rather what?' She held the phone up again. 'You'd rather go to jail? Lose your job, your licence, your reputation? And of course you're aware that if you trade via an overseas company, you'll have moved the money across borders, and that constitutes international money laundering. The FBI have the power to seize all your assets – *all* of them. You'd come out of jail to nothing. I'm not sure you'd even qualify for welfare,' she added with a confidence she didn't feel.

'Fuck you,' Joel hissed.

She nodded, the smile fading.

'You'd like that, wouldn't you? But I don't think it's going to happen. I prefer intelligent men. Now, I'd like bank drafts, easier to dispose of than cash. Plus I'm sure you can appreciate we don't want a paper trail.'

He glared at her.

'And I want it by the end of next week.'

'This isn't going to happen, Alice,' he said, his voice barely a growl.

She turned on him, surprised by her own fury.

'Oh yes it is, Joel. In fact, this is what's also going to happen. You will be extra nice to me and David. We will be your best friends all of a sudden, and if I hear that you have said even one negative thing about me or anyone close to me, I will make you wish you'd never been born so fucking greedy. Are we clear?'

He kept glaring at her.

'Joel? Are we clear?'

He looked down at the path, at her sandy feet.

'Yes.'

'Good. Then I think you can go and surprise that lovely wife of yours with a cup of coffee in bed.'

She turned and walked back towards the house, leaving him standing in the sand.

Chapter 33

Central Park was the perfect cover for a spy. At 12.52 on a Wednesday lunchtime, the paths and benches were crowded with people holding takeout sushi and subs, killing time or walking briskly to their next meeting. Alice adjusted her sunglasses and smiled to herself. People in New York never paid attention to each other unless they were actually mugging them. She had read a study on it in the *New Yorker* or somewhere. The human brain can't deal with all that variety, all those faces, so it shuts down, filters them out, like so many trees in a forest. To anyone passing she was just another smartly dressed office drone on her lunch break, sitting on a bench, coffee in hand, texting a friend.

They had no idea that she was a woman with a secret. She was in love. No, make that wildly in love. Head over heels. And she was about to have another of her secret assignations. Her heart jumped at the thought. She stood and smoothed her skirt, then left the park and crossed the street. The Olympic Architects office was housed in the Six West building right on the corner of 56th and Park, but she wasn't going there. She turned left onto Fifth, half a block up: the Reload Gym, the latest spot to be if you wanted to be seen to be exercising. She checked the time on her cell phone, then announced herself to the pretty blonde receptionist behind the counter.

'Alice Holliday, yes, hi.' The girl held up a finger. 'I'll just call Jake now; do you want to wait in the café over there,' she said, buzzing her through the glass barriers.

Alice smiled professionally as she went to sit at a table by the juice bar. She only had to wait a couple of minutes before a lean thirty-something with a Reload Gym T-shirt joined her.

'Jake, great to finally meet you,' she said, extending a hand.

'Me too.' He asked the barista to bring them two coffees, then sat down. 'Liz speaks very highly of you. She said you'd be interested in taking some classes here,' he said cutting to the chase.

The personal training and gym instructor world was a small one, and Jake Johnson, manager of the Reload, was the brother-in-law of Alice's friend Liz, owner of a small chain of Pilates studios on the Upper East Side. Getting a meeting with him was easy, and although Alice didn't actually want a job at Reload – with her existing class schedule and time out to see Paul, there was little space in her working week to add anything else – she liked to network, to see what opportunities were out there, and besides, today was an important day to come and visit.

She pulled her résumé out of her bag and gave it to him. 'I do Hatha and Ashtanga yoga, but I don't know if Liz has told you about a ballet-yoga-dance fusion class I've created. It's incredibly popular and I could adapt it to offer Reload something unique.'

Jake skimmed through the résumé and nodded his approval. She knew that every gym manager was looking for the next hot thing – the new Barrecore or Skinny Bitch Collective that they could pitch as hip and exclusive – and she doubted that Reload was any different.

'You know we don't have any openings at the moment,' he said between sips of coffee. 'But maybe you can come and take a one-off class, I can have a look, and we can take it from there.'

'I've love to,' Alice gushed. 'All my details are on my résumé if you want to call me to set it up.'

She looked about her with interest.

'In the meantime, do you mind if I have a look around?'

Jake glanced at his watch and looked awkward.

'I've got another meeting in ten minutes, but if you're happy to have a wander around yourself, then go for it. If you've got your kit with you, feel free to try out the equipment.'

Jake disappeared into the back office and Alice got up to walk to the huge window that overlooked the gym floor. She could see Paul even from this distance; his body just that bit bigger and more toned than everyone else's. He had a male trainer – she was glad about that – and she took a moment to admire him being pushed to his physical limit.

By her reckoning, he had just a few minutes left of his session. She knew what time her lover came here every week. He'd told her when they'd scheduled their meetings at the penthouse apartment, and although she'd been a tiny bit miffed that his training session seemed to be a priority above all else, at least she knew where he was at a certain time each week, and now it was coming in handy.

She went to the changing room to get ready. It was her best gym kit: a tiny mesh bra top and a pair of cropped shorts that left little to the imagination.

She stopped at the end of the corridor, just below the sign reading 'Men's Changing Rooms'. There was a small seating area and she perched on a chair, casually checking her cell. She studied herself with the camera. There was no denying she was looking hot. She flipped back to messages.

Nothing new from Paul – of course – so she began to scroll back through old texts from him. *Can't wait until tomorrow; Let's do that again; Meet me at the Park Avenue project at twelve.* Out of context, they were bland, friendly throwaway things, but when you knew they were part of the dialogue of a secret love affair, they began to glow with passion and meaning.

She was so engrossed, she almost missed it when the door swung open.

'Hey there,' she called.

Paul turned slightly, then did a double-take.

'What are you doing here?' he said, glancing furtively up and down the corridor.

'Can you believe they're desperate for me to run my yoga fusion class here?'

'Here?' he said, with a slight tremor in his voice.

'Don't worry. We won't clash. Not unless you want to,' she grinned.

Paul frowned. His hair was still damp with sweat.

'Follow me,' she said, touching his hand. 'I've been told I can look around. Check things out.'

Paul looked hesitant, but followed her into one of the treatment rooms.

It was dark inside; just the low golden light from a Himalayan salt light.

'Alice, what are you doing?' he said, turning to face her.

She tilted her head to one side, and held out her hand.

'I don't know. What do you want to do?' she whispered.

She pulled him towards her and brushed her lips against his.

'I've missed you.'

'Al, I've got to get back to work. Why don't we meet tomorrow? At the apartment.'

'Aren't you bored of the apartment?' she asked, starting

to feel aroused. She could feel his warm breath on her face and leant in to kiss him again, biting his lip softly with her teeth.

This time he responded, and slowly she pushed the fabric of his shorts down over his hips, then slid to her knees, running her hands down his body until they reached his hardening cock.

She knew how much he wanted it. He had already stepped back and leant against the treatment bed ready to receive her, and she was more than ready to give him a bit of pampering.

Alice knew what day it was – Paul and Rebecca's anniversary – and she imagined where he'd be in a few hours: at the swanky Midtown restaurant being given the keys to a Mustang by his rich wife; a wife who thought she could throw money at their relationship rather than address his real needs.

Well, Alice was going to give him an anniversary present he wouldn't forget.

She slid a gentle fist around his cock and took him into her mouth. Paul moaned softly and grabbed her hair to pull her head closer. His pubic hair tickled her face and she inhaled deeply, feeling drunk on the scent of him. His hips were beginning to rock in time now as she moved in and out, and she felt herself becoming turned on by the power: now *she* was in control.

He groaned again and there was a loud *click* behind them. They both froze as the door to the treatment room was pushed open.

'Shit,' muttered Paul, pulling back, his cock coming out of Alice's mouth with a pop. A cool gust of air blew into the room as he staggered forward and slammed the door shut, turning the lock.

There was a sharp rap on the door. 'Who's in there?' said a voice.

Alice giggled, imagining a confused therapist who had almost got an eyeful of Paul's impressive manhood. Paul muttered some platitudes through the door, then turned to face her.

'We should go,' he said quickly.

Alice looked him up and down; in just a T-shirt and trainers, she couldn't take him seriously.

'Don't you think I should finish the job in hand?' she purred playfully.

He pulled his shorts over his wilting erection and looked flustered.

'Alice, you didn't lock the fricking door. We could have been caught just then. I have colleagues, friends that come to this gym.'

'So do I,' she said, her eyes challenging his.

'Then imagine the shit storm I . . . *we* would find ourselves in if we'd been caught.'

Alice couldn't believe the anger coming off him. After all, she had only tried to engineer a little alone time for them. But she could see it would be a bad idea to feed his fire. She watched his shoulders sag and she felt a moment's panic that she had pushed him too far.

'I'm sorry,' she said after a moment. 'It's just that I had a great time in the mountains and we haven't seen each other since. I needed to see you.'

She wondered how he would feel if she told him the truth. That the idea of him celebrating his anniversary with his wife tore her heart in two, and without his presence, even a single text acknowledging her existence, it felt as if all the oxygen had been sucked out of the air.

He stepped forward and stroked her cheek.

'I'll call you, okay,' he said, the tension shimmering between them.

She closed her eyes and nodded, concentrating hard to

lock his fleeting touch into her consciousness.

'Now I've got to get changed and go back to work.'

He unlocked the door and slipped out, and she could hear him muttering some excuse to the person outside. As their voices faded away, she slid down to the floor and started to cry.

Chapter 34

'Isn't she a beauty?'

David handed Alice his glass and strode over to the pony, slapping its flank.

'There's a pretty girl,' he muttered, stroking its neck. 'Aren't you a lovely thing?'

That's more than he's ever said to me, thought Alice, draining her own glass and looking around for a waiter. This was the Hampton Polo Cup, after all. It was undoubtedly one of the biggest social events in the calendar, and champagne houses fell over themselves to add their name to the programme and hand out samples. You only had to wait two minutes and a handsome resting actor would be along with a tray. Never one when you wanted it, though, was there?

She watched David fussing over the horse and tried to swallow her irritation. He liked to tell a story about being taken to a pony club as a boy and falling in love with the beasts. The punchline was that he had no balance and a fear of heights, so had never taken to riding, but that hadn't stopped his fascination with the animals.

Alice had never liked horses. Little girls were supposed to love them, of course. They were supposed to read *Black Beauty* and stick pictures of sleek stallions on their bedroom walls, begging their parents for a pony for Barbie come birthday time. Alice hadn't had that kind of childhood, of course; Momma liked a different kind of riding. And Barbie was as alien to pre-teen Alice as beer bongs had been to David. It was remarkable that they had managed to make their marriage work for so long.

'Leave the poor animal alone, David,' called Todd, walking over. 'I've got twenty bucks riding on the Chandon team. I don't want all that petting to make her soft.'

David laughed, but reluctantly allowed the groom to lead the horse away.

Alice saw the affectionate smiles pass back and forth between the two men. Unlikely though their friendship was – Todd the social extrovert and David the dour bookworm – it was genuine and unshakeable. Alice felt a stab of jealousy. Not only did her husband save his affection for four-legged creatures, the most meaningful relationship in his life was with another man. It wasn't so much that she wished to be the object of his affections; it was more a case of straightforward envy. She had never had that sort of friendship with anyone. In fact, she wasn't at all sure she had ever had a real friendship, period. Sure, she'd had love affairs, some of which had been passionate and all-consuming, and she'd had girlfriends like Tina to gossip and giggle with, but the former had all been based on lust and the latter on circumstance. The moment she'd moved on, to a new location or new social scene, the old friends had been dropped completely.

She drained David's glass too. Today really wasn't the day for dwelling on her failings; she had enough to worry about already.

She trailed along as Todd and David walked back past the long line of fenced-off white marquees filled with corporate lunch guests, their laughter and boasts mingling with the tinkle and scrape of silver on china.

The real action, as ever, was on and around the polo fields themselves. In the distance, they could see the in-crowd standing at the edge of the grass. The women, all in simple summer dresses and big hats, were huddled in groups whispering about the way the latest Argentine polo star filled his jodhpurs and competing over who had the most explosive gossip. The men all wore chinos and open-neck shirts and were talking money, both on and off the field.

Todd had flippantly mentioned some off-the-cuff wager, but Alice doubted there was anything casual about it. Fortunes had been betted on the outcome of the matches here; she herself had overheard a hedge-fund manager offer his newly imported Bentley as the prize in a wager on which side would score the next goal. When it went against him, he shrugged, handed over the keys and turned to his neighbour to ask for a lift home. She would have been surprised if the guy's heart rate had faltered for even a beat.

'Alice,' said Todd, waving to a tall man in a cream linen suit. He was lean and handsome, and his carefully trimmed stubble did nothing to hide his cheekbones. 'Have you met Nat Chapman? He's over from the London office having a look at how we do things here.'

'It's all polo matches and champagne,' smiled Alice, always glad to meet a good-looking guy.

'Remind me to come out here more often,' Nat grinned.

'That accent,' said Alice with a mock swoon. 'I might have to get you to talk to me all day.'

'I'm going to have to disappoint you there,' said Todd, slapping his colleague on the shoulder. 'Nat has to go and work his *Downton Abbey* magic on some of the advertisers.'

'And there was me thinking the fashion sponsors were trying to get us drunk,' said Nat, flipping his sunglasses down off the top of his head.

'Speaking of which, who wants a drink?' said Todd. He disappeared towards the champagne bar, leaving Nat and Alice alone.

'So you work with Todd on the magazine. I've still not really figured out what he does there.'

'Todd is the art director. A bloody good one too,' said Nat with admiration.

'But what does that actually entail?'

'He decides on the look of the magazine, the fonts, the photography. He overseees all the visual side, really.'

'And what do you do? Back in England. Are you an art director too?'

Nat shook his head. 'I'm the style editor. I don't do the fashion shoots but I look after the rest of the lifestyle coverage and liaise with the advertisers to make sure everyone is happy.'

'Be kind,' said Alice, trying to work out if the good-looking Englishman was straight. The way he'd been scoping her out a minute ago, she was pretty sure he was, but you never could tell.

'Be kind?' He frowned, not understanding what she meant.

'I get nervous around fashion types,' she said in a theatrical whisper. 'I always think they're judging me.'

'They probably are, but you'd pass muster,' he smiled.

'So what do my clothes say about me?' she challenged him. 'If you were judging me.'

He looked her up and down – her blue and white gingham sundress, and the navy ballet flats she'd worn specially to stomp the divots, *Pretty Woman*-style.

'I judge a woman by her shoes,' he said flirtatiously.

'So what do mine say about me?' she asked, twirling her foot in the air.

'Classic Chanel pumps. Elegant but playful. I'm guessing you like your own way too.'

'You think I'm a diva,' she smiled.

'I'm looking forward to finding out,' he said as Todd came back with their drinks.

Under normal circumstances, Alice would have enjoyed a good flirt, but her heart started beating faster when she saw Paul arrive. Rebecca had turned up to the beach house alone the previous evening, and although she had told Alice that Paul would arrive in the Hamptons in time for the polo, Alice hadn't been sure he'd show.

'Darling, there you are,' said David, slipping his arm over his wife's shoulders. 'Rebecca and Paul are here; we should go and say hello before the match starts.'

Alice felt a strange comfort in being by her husband's side as she went to greet her lover. Paul looked relaxed as he and Rebecca greeted them.

'Great dress,' said Alice honestly, taking in Rebecca's black and orange shift. She had never seen her wear anything other than a trouser suit or a long kaftan, and she had to admit she looked fabulous.

'Thank you,' said Rebecca. 'It was a present from my gorgeous husband. He didn't forget,' she said with a soft, conspiratorial look that was like a knife in Alice's stomach.

Alice had decided to get drunk. Well, if she was honest, that had always been the plan. What else was she supposed to do? Play happy families with David and ignore the fact that Paul seemed to be doing exactly the same bullshit thing with Rebecca? Paul wanted to be with her, not his wife, Alice was sure of that. You couldn't fake that sort of connection; she had seen it in his eyes. But like all men, Paul was weak.

'So fucking weak,' she muttered into her glass. It was her fifth, maybe sixth drink since Paul had arrived; they seemed to just appear in her hand, beautiful young waiters bringing them just as she was getting thirsty.

A roar went up from the crowd as Changi Mendez leant dangerously low out of the saddle at full gallop, whipping his stick in a full circle to slam the ball square between the uprights. Alice made sure she shouted her approval with everyone else on the touchline; it was important to maintain the illusion of normality. To anyone watching, she was having a wonderful relaxing day watching the polo, enjoying the sunshine and the hospitality. That was just as she wanted it, until she was ready to make a move.

She needed to get Paul at the right moment, make him remember why he had come to her in the first place: because his marriage had run its course. Sure, Rebecca would still be the easy option, the boring, safe option. With Alice he had passion and excitement and stimulation, but choosing her was difficult; it would cause all sorts of upset. If you were a strong woman, you had to accept that men didn't always know what was best for them. It was a woman's job to gently help them make the right decision. Unfortunately Paul hadn't given her the opportunity to show him how much better he would be with her. She was furious with him, she could admit that, but she was experienced enough to know that anger was useless right now; she needed to be more subtle.

Knowing that all eyes were on the game, she slipped away, skirting the stands and heading for the marquee bar. As she had guessed, there was Paul, talking to Joel of all people.

She smiled to herself. At least that problem had been dealt with. Alice had cornered Joel at the house, and in a whispered, tight-lipped conversation, he had at least

347

confirmed that the money was on its way. 'Blood money', he had called it. Alice had retorted that he should think of it as an investment in the future. After all, if Erica didn't get her own Hamptons cottage, Joel could well be looking at a ruinously costly divorce as well as jail time.

'Gentlemen,' said Alice sweetly as she walked across. Joel scowled and picked up two glasses from the bar. 'I'd better get back to Erica,' he said.

'Yes, you better had,' said Alice.

She waited until they were alone, then touched Paul's hand, stroking one finger up to his wrist.

He flinched, spilling a few drops of wine. 'Shit,' he muttered.

'Don't worry,' she whispered. 'I can lick that off for you.'

Paul grabbed a napkin and shook his head at her. 'Don't, Alice,' he said. 'You can't keep doing this.'

'Doing what?'

'Behaving like this.'

'Like what? Like we're together?'

'Follow me,' he ordered, leading her around the back of the marquee.

It was quiet back here. Just a line of Range Rovers and the occasional groom. Alice smiled to herself, thinking of Paul taking her over the bonnet of one of the fancy 4x4s, her screams of passion disguised by the roar of the society crowd.

'Good. Now we can talk,' she said, playing with her necklace suggestively.

'No, we can't talk. Not when Rebecca is in earshot,' he hissed.

'What do you expect us to do? Ignore each other?' she replied. 'Because believe me, nothing is going to signal the fact that we're fucking each other quicker than that.'

She gave a soft sigh of regret. She wished she could take back what she had just said. She didn't want to debase their relationship in any way. All she wanted was for Paul to know how much she cared about him.

His expression softened and he closed his eyes.

'Alice, I didn't mean for it to end up like this.'

'Like what?' she asked, sensing danger.

'Look, you have to see what an impossible situation I'm in. *We're* in. I'm *married*, Alice. I can't jeopardise that, not right now. If Rebecca found out, I'd be left with nothing. I'm sure you feel the same about David.'

'What do you mean?' she said, feeling her chest tighten. 'It's not an impossible situation. Difficult, yes, but what we have together is worth it. It's worth the risk to see where all this takes us.'

'Alice, I'm saying it has to stop.'

Alice stopped breathing as she took in what he had just said.

'Where has this come from? The cabin, the mountains, we were so happy . . .'

'I'm not saying it wasn't—'

'Is this because I turned up at the gym?'

'No,' he said, shaking his head.

She grabbed his hands and pulled them together as if in prayer.

'Paul, please. Think about what you're saying. We are so good together.'

'I owe my career to my wife. She was the one who introduced me to everyone, and I certainly wouldn't have got a job at one of the best practices in the city if it wasn't for her contacts.'

'It's your talent that has made you successful, not Rebecca.'

'Rebecca wouldn't just divorce me; she would *ruin* me,' he said, his blue eyes wide with fear.

'And that's it? You're finishing it because of the *money*? You'd rather stay in a loveless marriage than lose your client base?'

'Who says it's loveless?' said Paul simply.

Alice let go of his hands and looked down at the floor.

'All I want is for us to be together,' she said, her voice cracking with emotion. 'Can't we just go back to the way we were?'

Paul didn't say anything.

'Please,' she whispered. 'I love you.'

'I can't,' he said, taking a step away from her before turning and walking back into the marquee.

The matches went on forever. There was a ceremony to present the cup, the teams lining up like royal guards to collect the trophy from the sponsor's wife, and as the temperature dropped and the afternoon faded to evening, the hospitality tent was converted into a pleasure palace complete with DJs and ice luges.

By now it looked like the tail end of an expensive wedding: discarded champagne bottles and abandoned Chanel bags on the wine-stained tablecloths.

The dance floor was packed. Alice had no idea where David and the rest of her housemates were, but she could see Paul at the vodka bar at the far end of the marquee talking to someone she didn't know.

'Yay, go me,' she whispered, then stumbled as her toes caught in the carpet. She dropped her wine onto the floor and swore. She couldn't even rely on that.

She wasn't finished with Paul but she knew she needed some fresh air to sober up. She went outside into the cool evening, kicking off her shoes and walking away from the marquee. It was dark now, and she wasn't really sure where she was going, but looking around, she headed towards the players' changing rooms on the opposite side of the field. She enjoyed the sensation of the grass on her bare feet, and did a pirouette to remind herself that she wasn't too drunk.

The pavilion was illuminated by two small hurricane lights that released a soft, reassuring glow. Alice sat on a bench and pulled the packet of cigarettes out of her bag, noticing that her hand was trembling.

She bit her lip and let her eyes trail over to the party; the outsider looking in. Two weeks ago she'd had everything; she'd been confident, sexy, in control of her destiny. And now here she was, miserable and shaking, sitting alone in the dark. Tears began to drip down her cheeks. She put down the cigarettes and found a shred of tissue in her purse.

'Are you okay?' said a voice in the dark.

She looked up in alarm. It was Nat Chapman. Tall, handsome British Nat, his face a mask of concern.

'I saw you heading this way, I was worried.'

'I'm fine,' she said brightly. 'Just got a headache. And you can see the stars out here.'

He came and sat beside her on the bench. Noticing the cigarettes, he picked them up.

'Do you mind?'

'Let's be naughty,' she said, lighting up for him.

Alice didn't feel like great company right now, but as she inhaled deeply, she forced herself to perk up.

'You're going to have to explain the rules of polo to me, because I still haven't got a clue,' she said, folding one slim leg over the other.

'I bet hardly anyone here today understands the rules,' he said, pointing towards the hospitality tent. 'It's about networking, contacts. It's not a game, it's social currency.'

'The sport of kings,' she said, repeating something she had heard earlier in the day.

'That's right,' he said, looking impressed.

He began to give her a brief overview of the rules, explaining chukkas and high-goal, bumps, ride-offs and the line of the ball.

It was Alice's turn to be impressed. Unlike her husband, Nat Chapman wore his intelligence lightly and had the mental agility to explain alien concepts in a simple way.

'So what do you think of New York?' she said playfully.

'I could live here,' he said, stubbing out his cigarette. 'In fact I'm going to try and make that happen.'

She glanced at his left hand to see if there was any sign of a partner, someone who might make that move more difficult, but his ring finger was empty.

'Well, when you come, you must look me up. I'm Alice Holliday, and if you look, you will find me.'

'I'll do that,' he said, not taking his eyes from hers.

The strap of her sundress fell off one shoulder, and the mood between them was suddenly charged. Nat reached across and replaced the strip of fabric. His touch made her shiver as all the anger and pain she felt about Paul crystallised into hot desire for this man sitting next to her.

For a moment neither of them moved, and then, slowly, Nat leant forward and kissed her, his tobacco- and wine-scented lips brushing over hers, testing her response.

'Wow, that was quick,' she whispered.

'I didn't know there was a speed limit around here,' he smiled, kissing her again.

'I'd better get in the driver's seat then,' she said breathlessly, some distant thought deciding that Paul Ellis could go and screw himself.

'Come here,' he said, and she straddled him on the bench. She held his face and kissed him again, softly at first, then growing in intensity and passion. His breathing was ragged now and she could feel him growing hard under her.

She tipped her head back as he stroked and kissed her bare shoulders. As she closed her eyes, she imagined herself in a glossy movie, imagined herself being watched, although the eyes that she wanted to see her were Paul's.

She moved her hips slowly, grinding herself down onto him, wishing the fabric that separated them would disappear. Arching her back, she raked her fingers through her hair as he ran his hands greedily over her breasts and down to her waist to steady her. Her cheeks had flushed and she was ready for sex.

'I know enough about polo to think there's somewhere more private in there we could go,' she whispered, nodding towards the pavilion.

Nat's body slumped back into the bench as if he had snapped out of a spell.

'Shit,' he muttered, dropping his hands to his sides.

His sudden retreat startled her.

'What's wrong?'

'We shouldn't be doing this, Alice. Your husband is over there. And . . . and I'm married.'

It was the second time she'd heard those words in less than an hour, and she was sick of them.

'Maybe you should have remembered that five minutes ago,' she said, sobering up instantly. She pulled her straps back onto her shoulders, then climbed off his lap.

'I'm sorry,' he said awkwardly.

'Don't be,' she replied. Her eyes trailed towards the party, imagining Paul making small talk with his dry, dull wife, and knew that Nat had served his purpose.

Wiping her mouth with the back of her hand, eliminating all traces of Nat's smoky saliva from her lips, she straightened her dress and composed herself.

'We should go back to the party,' she said, taking a deep breath and letting it out.

Nat touched her affectionately on the shoulder. She appreciated the gesture and smiled.

'Better not mention this to anyone, right?' she said.

Nat gave a complicit snort. 'And we should probably lay off the drink for the rest of the night.' As if the champagne was to blame for their behaviour.

Alice was only half listening; she'd pulled her phone out of her sundress pocket and was texting Paul.

Meet me at the pavilion now. Urgent.

'When are you going back to England?' she asked as she and Nat walked slowly back towards the marquee.

'I've only just arrived. I'm here for another week or so.'

They walked on in silence, the noise and light of the party getting louder and brighter. After a minute, Nat stopped and looked at her.

'You should probably go on ahead,' he said.

As Nat hung back, Alice increased her pace, willing Paul to come out of the marquee. *Where are you? Where are you?*

She was just a few feet away from the back entrance when a door opened and she saw her lover standing there. At first it was just his silhouette, but as he stepped out into the dark, she could see his face, his expression unreadable as he looked at her, then glanced behind her to where Nat was standing.

She pulled herself up a little taller, and gave him a sly and knowing smile.

'Good evening, Paul,' she said as she brushed past him, her bare arm skimming the cool cotton of his shirtsleeve.

'What did you want?' he said as they moved back inside the tent and she closed the door behind them. She glanced back through the window and could see Nat still outside, motionless in the dark.

'You know what I want, Paul,' she whispered in his ear.

'But if you're not enough of a man to give it to me, then I've found someone who can.'

Chapter 35

The dress fitted her like a second skin. Black silk mixed with Lycra, it shimmered and clung in all the right places. Alice had always concealed her curves, keeping them in reserve until they were needed. Tonight, she thought, is going to be an ambush.

She smoothed the material down over her ass, then pushed up her breasts, leaning into the full-length mirror. Just the right amount of cleavage, but also just the right amount of chic. It was easy to wear something revealing, but it took guile and self-awareness to choose something that gave just a tantalising glimpse of what lay beneath.

Tonight was the big party at the Dobermans' and every man in the place would have his eyes on her. She wasn't sure if Nat Chapman was still in New York, but if he was, and if he had wangled an invite to the party, he would be kicking himself, wishing he hadn't run off like a scared schoolboy. Maybe even David would sit up and pay attention for once. But most of all, she wanted Paul to see her. It's all for you, she thought, taking one more look at her reflection. It's always for you.

'Is that what you're wearing?' said David as she walked into the living room.

'Yes. Don't you like it?' she said, watching him give her the once-over.

'Isn't it a little tight?' he asked with a faint note of disapproval.

'I don't know about that.' She smiled playfully. She knew he preferred her to wear clothes on the conservative side of things, but she hadn't missed the way his eyes had lingered on the dark line of her cleavage. If she'd managed to stir David's limp libido, then the dress was on the right track. 'It's black, smart,' she continued. 'I heard the Dobermans' party was quite formal.'

David gave her a chaste kiss on the cheek and straightened his tie.

'I suppose so. All sorts of heavy hitters are supposed to be going. Possibly even the governor.'

He stepped closer and lowered his voice.

'Bearing that in mind, I think it's best all round if you refrain from drinking tonight. We don't want a repeat of the polo, do we?'

Alice bristled inside, but an argument this early in the night would be a misstep. It would put her on edge and make David tense. And tonight was all about ticking the right boxes.

'I know,' she said, running a hand down his arm. 'I'm still embarrassed about that. You should never have left me alone, you know that.'

She saw he liked that: begging for forgiveness, asking to be controlled.

'I'll just hold a glass as a prop, but I'm staying sober as a judge tonight.'

'Not Judge Wiseman, I hope,' said David, his face softening. 'He's always drunk.'

Alice laughed pleasantly, scoring another point.

She picked up her bag and they went out into the hall.

Erica and Joel were coming down from their bedroom in the adjoining wing of the house.

'You two are in good spirits,' said Erica with a smile. Alice was pleased to see that she was wearing a tight white off-the-shoulder dress; Laurent, she was almost sure, hip, stylish, but in a battle of sexiness, Alice was always going to win. She could certainly feel Joel's eyes tracing her curves. He might hate her for blackmailing him, but it didn't seem as though his dick had got the message.

'Well Todd and Angela went over earlier and Paul and Becca are coming straight from the city, so it's just the four of us,' said Erica.

Joel held up his cell phone. 'Car's here. Let's go.'

The Dobermans were practically neighbours to the east, but nobody wanted to walk along the beach in their finery. It was a four-minute drive, looping back onto the main road to swing around the big dune sitting between the two houses. From the muffled music and raised voices, it was clear the party was already in full swing.

'Will you look at that?' said David as they walked up the drive.

According to the estate agents, the house was one of the finest in the Hamptons, and in daylight hours it was certainly striking; but at night Alice always thought it looked like a Scooby-Doo house, with its arched windows and chimneys that stretched into the night sky. Worth ten times the house-share property, she could only imagine what it would be like to live in. Alice liked the nice things in life, but it was so big she imagined wind blowing through the long corridors; she would feel quite spooked if the property was hers.

'What does Dickie Doberman do again?' said Erica with undisguised envy.

'Heads up Blackhill Capital.'

'Which is what?'

'Hedge fund. One of the most successful on Wall Street.'

Alice looked thoughtful. 'Remind me, Joel, what does a hedge fund do?' she asked, as if she genuinely had no idea.

Joel didn't look at her. 'It's an alternative investment vehicle that deals with slightly risky forms of trading, although it's the job of the hedge to try and eliminate that risk.'

'With what? With information?' she said innocently.

'It's complicated.' Joel clearly hadn't missed her oblique references to their secret.

'You seem to know a lot about it,' said Alice with a thin smile.

The party was being held in the grounds to the side of the house. What the garden lacked in absolute beachfront location, it made up for in theatrical whimsy. Statues of mythical beasts lined the perimeter; in the middle was a swimming pool – water gushing in from the mouth of a stone dragon – and at the far end there was a guest cottage even more gothic than the house itself.

'It looks like a mini-castle, somewhere a wicked witch would live,' noted Alice.

'You should know,' muttered Joel, so low only Alice could hear. He took Erica's hand and led her towards the pool, where most of the guests were gathered in front of a long bar.

'Shall we?' said David, offering Alice his arm with a formal bow.

She made a mental note to keep track of Joel's movements. He had still not delivered the money, and tonight was a perfect opportunity to get him alone in one of the many nooks and crannies to ask him exactly when she could expect to see it.

She was running out of patience, and so was Nick

Vlautin, who had paid her an unannounced visit only two days earlier.

'Tick, tock, Alice,' he'd said to her as they had discussed the matter outside her building. 'You've got until Monday to wire me the cash. If not, I'm afraid we're going to have to go viral.'

'Isn't it magical?' she said now as she and David walked down the stone steps towards the pool. Blue fairy lights had been strung from every tree, creating a twinkling shimmer on the water, and the waiters, dressed inevitably like medieval servants in tights and tabards, completed the look.

'Yes, I suppose it is. And it's fitting that you look like a princess tonight,' said David between sips of a glass of champagne he had picked up en route

Alice glanced at him in surprise. That wasn't his view of her outfit back at the beach house. Then again, alcohol always did make her husband more affectionate.

'It's been a pretty good summer, hasn't it?' he added wistfully. 'I wasn't sure about the house share at first, but I think it's worked out, don't you?'

You don't know the half of it, she thought, remembering her passionate trysts with Paul Ellis.

A waiter passed with a tray of cocktails and she eyed it with longing. She had promised David that she wouldn't drink but she felt so on edge she needed something to fortify herself.

Needless to say, she hadn't seen or heard from Paul since the polo match the weekend before. She'd sent him countless messages on their disposable phones but he hadn't replied to any of them, and she still couldn't get her head around it. Could he not see how perfect they were together? Had he ever had better sex than their intense night in the cabin? Could he not see that they were almost in perfect symmetry; they were two paper dolls cut from the same sheet who found themselves joined once more. That was unique and special and could not be overlooked.

Feeling unsettled, she excused herself from her husband and went back inside the house. She found the downstairs bathroom and locked the door, then grabbed the side of the vanity unit with clammy hands and looked at her reflection in the mirror.

She hadn't come this far to be knocked back from getting what she wanted now.

Opening her bag, she pulled out a tiny wrap of cocaine from the silk-lined pocket. She racked it out on the cool marble, then rolled up a dollar bill and snorted the white line.

Just like old times, she thought, waiting for the buzz of the imminent high. Immediately her back straightened and her anxiety ebbed away. She felt strong now, in charge; ready to ask for what she wanted.

As she opened the door, the noise of the party engulfed her. She grabbed a cocktail and stepped back outside.

The night air seemed warmer and more inviting than it had just a few minutes earlier. She was alert now, and for a second imagined herself as a panther pacing around the forest. A famous TV host caught her eyes and smiled wolfishly, but she had no time for distractions.

She could see Erica talking to the host's beautiful wife, and that meant Joel was around here somewhere too. After a moment she saw him coming towards her, coming into the house. He hadn't seen her, so she kept out of view until he was almost upon her.

'Joel,' she said, springing on him. 'We need to talk.'

'Not now, Alice,' he said, carrying on walking.

She put her hand on his arm and squeezed tightly.

'I said we need to talk.'

Joel looked around and shook his head.

'I don't want to hear it,' he hissed.

'Of course you don't,' she said, feeling emboldened by the hit of cocaine. 'When am I getting my money?'

Joel pulled her to one side, out of earshot of the party guests.

'I will get you your money,' he growled. 'Just not yet.'

'I need it by Monday,' she said, feeling her heart start to race. He couldn't procrastinate any longer. She had to play hardball with him because Nick Vlautin had run out of patience.

'Or what?' said Joel simply. She could see the muscles in his jaw tense. His eyes were narrow, angry slits.

'Or you don't get to buy your house by the beach,' she whispered, swaying from side to side as if she were singing a nursery rhyme.

'You're high. We should talk about this another time.'

'You're very smart, Joel. Perceptive. If you're that clever, you will know what is good for you and you will deposit the money in my account by Monday morning. To make it easier for you, you can give me twenty thousand dollars then and the rest at the end of the week.'

He moved his face closer to hers, so close that she could see her own reflection in his black pupils.

'Do not speak to me again at this party. Do you understand?'

He turned on his heel and walked away.

'Fuck,' muttered Alice when he'd gone. She was beginning to wonder if getting the money from Joel had been such a good idea. She liked to plot and plan, but she hadn't seriously thought this one through. She liked the beach house, could see herself spending every summer there; hell, even David loved it.

She didn't doubt that she could get her relationship with Paul back on track, and in time they could mischievously co-exist at the beach house once more. But the business with Joel was more problematic. Joel could make things difficult and had already spent the entire weekend glowering at her. She consoled herself with the thought that when he did make his big trade, he and Erica would be gone from the house.

David waved at her across the crowd, but she had no intention of going over and getting embroiled in some boring conversation about politics or literature. The only person she wanted to see was Paul, and as if some silent call had been answered, she caught sight of him by the gazebo.

Sensing her opportunity, she took another cocktail and downed it in one so the alcohol burnt the back of her throat. She steeled herself, then groaned when she saw her husband coming towards her.

'There you are,' he said, sounding a touch piqued. 'I waved but you seemed to have no intention of coming over.'

'I'm not at your beck and call, David,' she said, feeling irritable.

'Where have you been?'

'Exploring the property,' she said distractedly.

David let out a sigh of disapproval.

'I thought you wanted me to come to these Hamptons parties,' he said with slight superiority. 'But when I do come, I hardly ever seem to see you.'

'We're not joined at the hip,' she said, looking over his shoulder to make sure she didn't lose sight of Paul in the crowd.

'We don't have to be, but sometimes I wonder if you're avoiding me.'

'Avoiding you?' she repeated, giving him a moment's attention.

'I know you like these parties, these people,' he said

carefully. 'But see them for what they are. Don't waste your time seeking validation from them.'

'What's that supposed to mean?'

'Alice, darling, you know what I'm saying. Take it all at face value. These things are fun and frivolous, I know, but you don't have to neglect your husband for them.'

She wasn't sure if there was a threat in there somewhere. She wasn't in the mood to find out.

'Don't get needy on me, David. You know I'm a people person. I like meeting new friends, contacts.'

'Are you all right?' he said after a moment.

'Why shouldn't I be?'

'You seem strange. Edgy.' He examined her face and shook his head.

'What's wrong?' she asked.

'You might want to wipe your nose properly after you've shovelled cocaine up it,' he said with unveiled disapproval.

'Spare me the lecture, David.'

'You are my wife,' he hissed. 'Walking around a party with powder up your nostrils. Do you want to humiliate me?'

'I am having fun, David. Try it sometime.'

She couldn't waste any more time with him, and although she expected him to call after her, he let her go. She hurried through the crowds, past the pool towards the gazebo, grabbing a glass of champagne on the way. She was relieved to find Paul still there, nursing a drink, looking up at the house.

He spun round when he heard her approach; Alice was disappointed when he didn't smile.

'Hey,' she said, stepping towards him. 'You admiring the place?'

He nodded and knocked back his Scotch. 'It's good to see it at close quarters,' he said, concentrating hard on the roof.

'Up close and personal. Just how we like it,' she said

coquettishly. 'Where have you been all weekend?' she continued, trying to kick-start the conversation. If he was playing hard to get, it was working. It was taking every ounce of willpower Alice possessed not to just grab his face and kiss him.

'Busy.'

His economy of words was brutal, but she knew she could coax him round.

'I've missed you. I've missed you all week. I've missed the apartment,' she said with a smile. 'My vibrator's been having to work overtime, I can tell you.'

'Alice, stop it.'

'Stop what?'

'I told you the situation at the polo. Things haven't changed.'

'We should at least talk about it,' she said, refusing to give up.

Paul looked round at the gazebo. 'In here,' he ordered.

She liked it when he was masterful like this, and smiled to herself as she put her glass of champagne down and locked the door behind them. For a moment, the stillness engulfed her. Her breath seemed to echo around the confined space and she felt herself getting slowly aroused at the thought of what they could do in here, so close to the rest of the party, so close to David and Rebecca, and yet locked in their own little world.

'All right,' Paul said, turning to face her. 'What do you want to say?'

'What's happened, Paul? You haven't spoken to me properly in a fortnight and I miss you. I miss us.'

'I've told you, Alice. This can't carry on. What part of that statement do you not understand?'

'Why not?' she said passionately, grabbing his arm.

'We're both married,' he said, shaking her away brutally.

'We knew that from the start. We knew it wasn't going to be easy.' She touched him more gently. 'Just tell me you don't have feelings for me and I'll leave you alone.'

'I doubt that,' he muttered.

Alice pressed her lips into a thin line.

'We are in a relationship, Paul.'

'It was fun,' he said, lowering his voice. 'And it got out of control.'

She felt her breath quicken in panic. This wasn't funny any more. She didn't want to play games; she just wanted him to tell her that he loved her and that he was going to leave Rebecca. She didn't care if that took weeks, or even months. She just wanted some sort of reassurance from him that it would happen and they could be together.

'You're in denial, Paul,' she said, feeling emotional.

'I'm not the one in denial. You have got to stop texting me, calling me. Why are you leaving messages with my secretary, for Chrissake?'

'Because I want to talk to you.'

'There's nothing to say. It's over.' His voice was quivering with anger.

'You're pissed with me, aren't you?' she whispered.

'I will be if the drunken messages don't stop.'

'You're pissed because of what happened at the polo.'

'What do you mean?' he said dismissively.

She snorted. 'You know . . .' Her eyes challenged his. 'I didn't want anything to happen with the English guy,' she said in a low voice. 'But he was showing me attention. Lots of attention. I was angry with you and I wanted to make you jealous.'

'Alice, it's none of my business what you do with other men.'

She barked a laugh. 'You *are* jealous, admit it.'

Paul gave a cold smile. 'I'm not, Alice. I have a wife, who

I'm in love with. Your marriage might be a train wreck, but mine isn't and I want to keep it that way.'

'You mean after you've had your bit of fun,' she spat.

'Alice, stop.' His voice was gentler now. 'Please don't do this.'

She saw a window of opportunity.

'I love you, Paul,' she whispered.

'Alice, no . . .'

She held the hem of her dress and peeled the tight Lycra up over her hips. Underneath she was naked, exposed. She knew he loved it when she was like this, sensual and provocative; loved it when she lifted her skirt in the elevator of the apartment, when she let his fingers wander inside her in those stolen few seconds as they rode to the top floor. He loved the danger as much as she did, the frisson, the anticipation of getting caught; the wantonness of her laying herself open and available for her lover.

'I want you,' she whispered, but there was a tremor in her voice and his cold, dismissive look of disgust told her she was wasting her time.

'Pull your skirt down, Alice. I think we're done here.'

She scrabbled at the fabric, trying to recover some dignity. Hope turned to fury.

'You don't know how to fuck anyway,' she hissed, spittle foaming around her mouth. 'You probably prefer men. Is that it, Paul? That's why you can't handle a woman like me, why you scuttle back home to your transvestite wife. Is that what you do, Paul? Fantasise that she's a man? Is that what you like?'

Paul was already at the door and unlocking it.

'I fucked Nat Chapman, by the way. I know you saw us together. After I'd fucked him in the polo pavilion. At least he showed me what a real man can do.' She could hear her own voice growing louder and louder.

'Grow up, Alice,' he spat.

'I'll tell Rebecca,' she screamed, feeling a sob fill her throat.

But he was gone.

Alice sank down to the cold concrete floor. She tried hard to keep her emotions contained, but despite herself, tears trickled down her cheeks and she let out a low moan of anguish. As her hand squeezed into a fist, the sound from her chest grew louder until it was an animal howl. She had no energy to even get up; the pain was too much to bear. He had robbed her of her life force and left her broken. But she also knew that she could not stay here.

Crawling on her hands and knees, she forced herself to stand. There was no way she could return to the party; she just wanted to be alone. She would go back to the beach house.

This summer

Chapter 36

Green. Why did the smoothies always have to be green? Jem looked at the tall glass, running a finger along the beads of condensation clinging to the side, and pulled a face. There were black bits swirling around inside; it reminded her of the goldfish tank she'd had as a child, left uncleaned for a couple of weeks.

'Think of it as medicine,' said Todd. 'Hold your nose and try not to think what's in the glass.'

'What *is* in it?' asked Nat.

'Kale, cilantro, wheatgerm, apple and grape. Concentrate on the apple,' smiled Todd, mopping his red face with a towel. 'Nothing in there but apple.'

Jem grabbed the glass and knocked the smoothie back in three faltering gulps.

'See?' said Todd. 'Don't you feel better now?'

Jem grinned. 'I don't think any amount of fibre's going to help my thighs. That was so tough I'm not sure I'm ever going to be able to climb stairs again.'

'Admit it. You loved it,' said Nat, beaming at his wife. 'In fact I'm going to the desk to ask about Wednesday.'

Jem felt guilty as she watched him disappear towards reception. Guilty that her husband thought she was there to work harder at their marriage, to start doing things together, when she'd put herself through the punishing class for other motives.

She pulled her phone out of her bag

'Hey, Todd,' she said as casually as she could. 'Do you know who this is?'

She had prepared for this, having already pulled up the footage from Alice's phone, the clip of Joel talking about Yonex. She had stopped the frame on a shot of Joel's mystery companion. Todd and Angela knew everyone who was anyone in New York society. If the guy was at a party with Joel, the chances were that Todd had met him at some point.

His answer was immediate. 'It's Ed Dunston, a friend of Joel's. Why?'

Jem had her cover story ready and slid into it easily.

'Nothing much. I was talking to him at some party. He recommended a hotel in the Caribbean but I didn't write it down. I'll ask Joel for his email or something.'

Todd stood up, still mopping his brow. 'Only a Brit could think about leaving a sweltering New York summer to go somewhere even hotter.'

Jem left Nat and Todd and, with the entire morning to kill, headed off to the New York Public Library. She read the papers, spent some time online, then curled up in the corner of the true-crime section with an Edgar Allan Poe Award winner that had caught her eye.

At a little after twelve, she walked out into the sunshine, taking a moment to inhale the fresh air and feel the warmth on her face. She was about to head uptown when her mobile started to vibrate in her pocket. She put the phone to her ear.

'Jem. It's David.'

'David.' She was surprised to hear from him. Although they had exchanged a few emails over the past couple of weeks, they hadn't had any meaningful contact since the dinner at his house, and in hindsight, Jem wondered if they should have kept him more in the loop.

'How's it going?'

Although it was a reasonable question, it was one that she was completely unprepared to answer.

At dinner, David had suggested that he wanted to know the unvarnished truth behind Alice's death. But how much did he really want to know? That his wife had had a passionate affair with Paul Ellis when she was in couples counselling to save her marriage? That she had also possibly had sex with Jem's husband as a misguided revenge tactic when that affair had finished? Or that she was potentially extorting money from Joel, because she knew about his insider dealing? Did David Holliday really want to know any of this, especially when it didn't lead anywhere concrete? More to the point, was it Jem's job to tell him?

'I'm just about to meet Michael, actually,' she said, deciding to tell him what they were doing rather than what they had found out.

'Good. I wonder if he has anything to report.'

'We're going to see a photographer. Apparently he was taking pictures of the beach house the night of the party. It's a long shot, but maybe he took one of Alice arriving back at the house so we can confirm she was alone.'

There was a long pause.

'Are you okay?' asked Jem, imagining how traumatic it must be for him. She ran over what she had just said, wondering if it was too blunt or insensitive.

'Was the information I gave you the other day useful?' he said more crisply. 'You asked if we went away at all in June and July.'

'We were just making a timeline of her movements.'

'And has that been helpful?'

'We'll see.'

'You will let me know how it goes today? With the photographer.'

'Are you sure you're okay?' she asked, noting an edge to his voice. It was so difficult to know over the phone how people were feeling.

'This is just more difficult than I thought it would be,' he said after another moment.

'I know,' said Jem as reassuringly as she could.

'Can we meet?'

'Of course,' she replied. 'It's probably best if we wait until after we've seen the photographer. Or until I've got something to tell you.'

'Todd told me there's a party at Rebecca's gallery on Thursday. Perhaps I can see you there.'

Jem nodded. 'I'll call you,' she said.

The arrangement was to meet Michael at his hotel, the Four Seasons, and as Jem got nearer, she became more nervous. She'd admitted to him that she had taken Alice's phone, but she had only told him half the story.

The Four Seasons rose from the sidewalk like a Roman temple. The flags on either side of the giant door fluttered in the breeze; yellow cabs and black town cars ejected well-dressed guests outside. Jem never felt as if she belonged in places like this, but it was impossible not to feel a surge of power as she pushed her way through the revolving doors.

She had already texted Michael a few minutes earlier, and he'd said he'd meet her in the lobby. Her eyes scanned the luxuriously decorated space, absorbing the refined hush, the frantic noise of Manhattan just a few feet away on the other side of the door.

She felt a hand on the shoulder and spun around, half expecting it to be security come to escort the interloper out of the building.

'Michael,' she said with relief.

'We should go,' he said, glancing at his watch.

Jem was glad they didn't have to loiter in the hotel lobby; before the Hamptons, she didn't know anyone who'd hang out in these sort of places, but now, she couldn't be sure who she might see, and who knew what assumptions they might draw seeing her with Michael Kearney.

He stepped into the road to hail a cab, narrowly missing a blacked-out town car, its horn blaring.

'Damn, I'm too old for Manhattan,' he laughed, falling into step next to her. In his casual navy shirt and chinos, Michael was almost a negative of Nat with his carefully chosen designer wardrobe. It looked like he had rolled out of bed and thrown on whatever he found on the floor, yet he still had a commanding presence, something about him that made you look twice.

Jem flopped back in the black vinyl seat and Michael gave the driver an address.

'So, I know who the guy in the video is. The one who gave Joel the tip.'

Her employer looked at her expectantly.

'He's called Ed Dunston,' she said, lowering her voice. She doubted the name would mean anything to the driver, but you never knew. 'I've checked him out, and guess what. He's general counsel at Yonex.'

'You're a quick learner,' Michael said, impressed. 'The food industry's loss is investigative journalism's gain.'

'So you're staying at the Four Seasons tonight,' Jem said, blushing at the compliment.

Michael looked back at her.

'I've interviewed a lot of people in that bar. Always

promised myself I'd stay there one day. So when I started selling a few books, instead of getting a place in the city, I'd just book myself in there. Sentimentality has cost me a fortune over the years.'

Jem laughed. 'You sure about that? Come to my flat in Brooklyn and see how much bang for your buck you get in the New York rental market. I think it might be cheaper checking into the Four Seasons.'

The car stopped as it got snarled in traffic.

'So did everything get sorted with Nat?' asked Michael after a minute. He didn't look at her; instead carried on gazing out onto the Manhattan streets.

'We're talking. That's a start.'

Jem's phone beeped and she checked her messages, half expecting another apologetic missive from Nat, having received several from him over the past day.

Instead it was Angela.

Sun's out and I'm off early! Manhattans in Manhattan? x

Her instinct was to turn it down; she'd been invited for after-work drinks once before and she'd enjoyed meeting Angela's witty and interesting friends, but that was before she'd started working with Michael, before she'd found out about Nat's unfaithfulness, before collaring Todd so sneakily that morning, which made her feel embarrassed, even now.

But after a moment's thought, she knew that the smart move would be to go, however awkward that made her feel.

Where and when? she texted as the car pulled to a stop.

They had reached the corner of 67th, and Michael suggested they get out and walk the rest of the way. They were in one of New York's most expensive residential areas. The houses were tall, elegant; relics of a bygone age when cars were a rarity on the streets and gas lamps lit the sidewalks. Of course, Manhattan being an island, real estate had always been at a premium, so a great many of the properties had been built as apartment buildings.

'This is it,' said Michael, looking up towards a tall limestone building. 'Riordan House. Kind of swanky for a hippy drummer, isn't it?'

After asking around Yeti's contacts, Michael had found out that the photographer at the drum circle was an 'artist dude' called Alex, who apparently had 'like a fifty-grand camera' that he used to take candid photos of the parties on the public beaches of the Hamptons, posting them on his website and on social media as some sort of art project. Yeti had warned Michael that the guy was 'like, a total stoner', but it hadn't taken much to track the mystery photographer down. Jem had been expecting a druggy artist to live in a walk-up garret in Alphabet City or one of the high-rise blocks near SoHo; certainly somewhere more bohemian than one of the smartest co-ops on the Upper East Side.

The doorman directed them to the lobby elevator, which had polished bronze doors. Inside, Jem was tickled to find that the lift car was equipped with a red velvet seat.

'A bench. In a lift,' she giggled, sitting down. 'I feel like the Queen. How does this Alex guy afford it? Is he a famous photographer?'

'Family money, I should think,' said Michael. 'Alex's name is actually Chase Alexander. Call me cynical, but I'm guessing Chase lives rent-free and buys his fifty-grand cameras with his trust fund. The important part is that everyone at the drum circle said that if anyone had any footage of that night, it would be Alex.'

Apartment 1006 was at the far end of the corridor from the elevator bank, and Jem found herself holding her breath as they walked; the elegant surroundings seemed to demand it, and Michael's knock on the door sounded unnaturally loud in the hushed passageway.

The man who opened the door was another surprise. He was gorgeous. Mid-twenties, sun-bleached hair, he looked almost airbrushed, like he'd stepped straight from a Ralph Lauren advert.

'Hey, you Michael?' he said with a lazy grin. He shook hands and turned to Jem, who could only open her mouth.

'Alex, man,' he said.

'I'm Jem,' she said, extending an awkward hand.

'Cool, cool,' said Alex, ushering them into the apartment.

Jem saw immediately that Michael had been right in his assessment. This was not a home that had been decorated by a surfer, even one who looked like a supermodel. Polished wood, delicate *objets d'art*; it was achingly tasteful, but the taste of a well-travelled sixty-something socialite, not someone who wore board shorts around the house.

'So you don't live in the Hamptons full-time?' asked Michael, wasting no time in fishing for information.

'I like to hang out there as much as I can in the summer,' drawled Alex. 'My folks have a place in East Hampton. Rest of the time I'm here or in Santa Barbara. I'm doing a masters at USC. You guys want a drink?'

They followed him into a kitchen twice the size of Jem's entire apartment. This too was tastefully designed, with a central granite island, but Jem could tell from the clutter of jars and tarnished copper pans on the range that it was used often for cooking. Alex switched on the coffee machine and took a seat on a bar stool.

'After you rang, I googled you,' he said to Michael. 'Sorry I didn't recognise you when you called. I don't have time to read much old stuff.'

Jem suppressed a smile.

'So you're a model as well as a photographer?' said Michael. 'I googled you too.'

'Sure, sometimes.' Alex shrugged. 'I'm in town for some castings this afternoon actually. I'd rather be at the beach, you know? But it's worth it for the contacts with photographers. I worked with Testino last week; I think I drove him mad asking about filters and stuff. The plan is to assist someone like Mario when I finish college.'

Jem liked Chase Alexander. It would be easy to dismiss him as an over-privileged poseur, but he had an easy charm about him, and though he could clearly have spent his days sitting on Daddy's yacht, he was at least pursuing his passion.

He turned back to the coffee machine and passed Jem an espresso.

'So you took some pictures at the drum circle last summer?' she asked.

'Always taking pictures, man,' he grinned. 'But you're welcome to look at anything I have.'

He opened a laptop on the kitchen counter and began clicking on folders. 'I had a quick look when you called, but I wasn't sure which drum circle you meant. I was with a girl who really liked that whole scene, so we went to a lot. She's in a band, Hopefully Forgiven. You heard of them?' he asked, directing his attention to Jem.

'Yeah,' she lied. 'They're great.'

'And you're doing a book on the Hamptons scene?'

Michael stepped forward to peer at the computer screen.

'Yes, a woman died at one of the beach houses about this time last year. I'm following the story.'

Alex looked up. 'You're not working with the police, are you?'

'No,' said Michael. 'This is just research for a novel.'

'Cool.' He shrugged. 'I just had to ask because there's always some weed going around and I don't want to get anyone into trouble.'

'I totally respect your privacy,' said Michael, sounding stiff and formal.

Jem could already see that she had underestimated Alex; his photos were impressive. She pointed to a colourful action shot of a surfer carving through blue water.

'That one's great,' she said.

'Thanks. That one's for my friend Grey's "Big Waves" blog. Pretty cool, huh?'

He looked up at Michael, his blue eyes seeming to assess the older man's face.

'You know, I could take your picture,' he said. 'You've got great bone structure. Do you need any publicity shots or anything?'

Jem could see that Michael was wrong-footed by the compliment. 'Uh, sure,' he stuttered. 'Jem sorts those things out.'

'Oh. You're his assistant?'

She nodded back.

'Cool,' said Alex with a wide smile. 'I thought you were together.'

Jem felt herself blush, and lifted her coffee cup to try and cover it, but Alex was concentrating on the screen, flicking through images of sunsets, surfers and pretty girls until he came to one of a dreadlocked man playing the bongos. Jem could make out the glistening sweat on the man's skin, the texture of his thick matted hair. Chase Alexander was good. Jem had never been to a drum circle, but looking at his photos, she could feel the fun and energy of what it must be like to be there. As he clicked through the shots, she saw the sky getting progressively darker; in the earlier shots there was a spectral, milky luminescence to the beach, but as the sun set, the sky was streaked yellow and violet.

Michael was leaning forward, examining each picture carefully.

'Do you have any more of the beach facing away from the sea, with the houses in the background?'

'Here you go,' said Alex.

In the picture, dusk was falling and the lights of the beach house were glowing against the purple sky.

'I remember taking that picture. That house is kinda gnarly and weather-beaten, but it looked so cool in the background.'

Jem nodded in agreement. Its charm had always been that it was more faded than the other houses. The peeling fence, the bushes that twisted away to the side; to Jem the flaws made it more real, and Alex's picture had caught that.

'That one,' said Michael, his finger raised. 'Can you make it bigger?'

Alex pulled the photo onto the desktop and dropped it into an editing package, immediately stretching it across the screen.

'There,' said Michael. 'Can you see in the window? That's someone's silhouette.'

Jem nodded in agreement. She had thought it was the back of a chair, but there was definitely someone there.

'Do you know what time this was?'

'Yeah,' said Alex, opening an info box. 'Taken at 21.02. I'm pretty strict about making sure the time and date are right on my photos; it can be crucial when you're doing stuff like surf competitions.'

Jem tried to think. David Holliday had said that Alice left the party at around 8.45. It was a ten-minute walk back to the house. 'It fits the timeline,' she said, excitement creeping into her voice.

'If it's more pictures of this house you want, I took quite a few in that direction. People were dancing around the fire and the house in the background gave it scale.'

He flipped through the shots: pretty girls in bikinis,

blankets draped around their shoulders; a small child dancing with an older man, the giggles practically bubbling from the screen; an old black man beating on a conga drum, his eyes closed in concentration. Finally he stopped and pointed.

'Here you go. These were taken ten minutes later. Look how amazing the house looks when the sky is this colour.'

In the foreground of the shot were the silhouettes of people dancing on the beach, fingers of shadow behind which reared the beach house. Alex had obviously shot off dozens – the advantage of using digital film; you were only limited by memory – and as he clicked through, the scene jerked and moved with the dancers, like a strobe.

'Stop!' cried Jem, but they had all seen it. One photo was different: a square of white had popped into the centre of the shot; the rear gate had opened, the light from the house spilling out. And there was something else, a shape caught in the doorway. Jem had stopped breathing.

'Make this one bigger too,' ordered Michael, but Alex was way ahead of him, manipulating the photo so that the bright white of the gateway filled the screen.

It was unmistakably a figure, a person stepping through the gate.

'What's the time on this photo?' asked Michael.

'Twenty-one ten.'

'That's twenty minutes before David Holliday found Alice in the pool,' said Michael, his eyes on the screen. 'And it looks like Alice wasn't alone.'

Chapter 37

Angela had suggested that they meet in the bar at the W hotel on Lexington. Jem told Michael where she was going, and they agreed it was best for her to act as normally as possible with her housemates until they knew what was happening.

Although it was almost five o'clock, the heat of the day was still fierce and Jem was glad to get off the sticky New York streets. She weaved through the hotel towards the bar – Whisky Blue. One of the first things she had done when she had arrived in the city was visit the Bliss spa next door, but she had never come here for drinks, and was surprised by the dark snugness of the room, which reminded her of a gentleman's drinking den in a Scottish castle rather than a place for girlie cocktails.

She spotted Angela instantly, tucked away in a leather booth; she was on her phone and didn't see her approach.

'Look, either you get him to the studio by seven or you can forget any coverage . . .'

Jem hung back, not wanted to intrude, but Angela looked up and waved her to sit down.

Trying to ignore Angela's conversation, glad not to be on the receiving end of it, she got the bartender's attention. Part of her wished she could tell Angela where she had been that afternoon. Like Michael, her friend had that no-nonsense confidence about her that made you believe she could find a solution for anything, and Jem felt sure she would have an intelligent theory if she saw Alex's photograph of the beach house the night of Alice's death.

After their visit to Alex's apartment, she and Michael had found a diner for a debrief, but there hadn't been much to discuss beyond speculation. The frustrating thing was that Alex hadn't been shooting the house itself, so the shape in the doorway was fuzzy and indistinct. It could have been Paul, Joel, or Elvis Presley for all they knew. The excitement at finding a piece of evidence soon ebbed away as they realised that it didn't get them very far unless they could identify the figure.

Angela hung up from her call and they exchanged air kisses. 'You're looking amazing as usual,' she said. 'How do you do that?'

Jem was about to say something British and self-deprecating when she noticed that Angela had already moved on with her conversation, pointing out a talk show host apparently in rehab who was sitting nursing a whisky in the corner.

'What have you done today?' she asked bluntly, as she sipped her cocktail.

'I've been working with Michael.'

'He's in the city today, is he?'

'He's in town for an industry awards ceremony. Apparently he's up for a gong.' She didn't miss the pride in her own words and wished she was going with him to the ceremony at the Waldorf Astoria. Michael had mentioned it again that afternoon, but she'd already accepted Angela's offer of cocktails, and besides, she didn't want to look as if she was point-scoring with her husband.

'Todd said he saw you at Barry's Bootcamp this morning. I don't know who I was more surprised to hear was there, him or you.'

'I won't be going back. My muscles feel as if they've been put through a mangle.' She smiled, but it disguised a flutter of nerves as she remembered her conversation with Todd at the gym.

The waiter brought over her drink and she took too big a sip.

'Joel and Paul will be here any minute,' said Angela, checking her watch. It was dropped in casually – too casually – and Jem was immediately on edge.

'Really? I thought it was just us.'

Jem didn't think she had ever seen Angela look anything other than fully confident and in control, but at that moment she appeared uncomfortable, embarrassed even, playing self-consciously with the straw in her glass.

'Todd told me about the picture, Jem,' she said, finally looking up at her.

Jem's heart started to beat fast, the flutter of anxiety now full-blown panic.

'The one of Joel's friend?' she said. 'Oh, I was just curious. As I told Todd—'

'I know what you told Todd,' said Angela, her voice shimmering with coldness. 'What *I* want to know is how a photo from last summer is on *your* phone.'

Jem knew right then that she had been caught out. Angela was no fool; in fact she was as sharp as a knife, intimidatingly smart, and right now, Jem was withering under her interrogational gaze.

'Angela, what's the problem?' she said, trying to stop her voice from faltering.

'The problem is that you seem to be asking questions. Paul tells me you've been probing his friendship with Alice too. That's why we thought we should all sit down and talk about it. To clear the air.'

Jem looked at her sharply, but she could instantly tell

that Paul hadn't told Angela anything like the whole story. More like 'Hey, so I flirted with Alice, why pick on me?' sort of thing.

'I spoke to David Holliday at Todd's launch,' said Jem, raising her chin. 'We talked about Alice and I said I'd ask if anyone had seen anything. Angela, David's torn up about this. I only wanted to help.'

'No, you wanted to impress Michael Kearney,' Angela said.

Jem closed her mouth. She didn't really have an answer for that one.

'Why did you really show Todd the photo?'

'I just wanted to identify everyone Alice met last summer,' Jem said, hoping her white lie would stave off more questions.

Angela gave a weary little sigh. 'How did you think this was going to end, Jem? This isn't a game, something to occupy your attention in between traybakes.'

'Is that what you think of me?' Jem said, sensing that the damage was already done and at least she could defend herself.

'You have to drop this,' Angela said urgently. 'The beach house isn't mine, but I'm protective of it. Protective of my friends, the people who live with me under its roof. We're a team, a family. I'm not going to let someone ruin what we've got.'

'So you should care about Alice and what happened to her,' said Jem passionately.

'Alice is dead and a childish investigation isn't going to bring her back.'

'David needs closure,' said Jem, but Angela cut her off.

'Don't pretend this is about David; you barely know him. Todd is his best friend, he cares about him more than any of us, and all you're going to do is hurt him with these ridiculous accusations about Paul.'

'And are you so sure they are ridiculous?'

'Let it go, Jem!' cried Angela, before glancing around and lowering her voice. 'Do you want to spoil this for everyone. For your husband?'

Jem frowned. 'What's that supposed to mean?'

Angela looked at her directly.

'You should probably talk this over with Nat,' she said. 'We don't want things to turn sour. You might be indifferent to life at the beach, but I assume that being social in the Hamptons, knowing people, being invited to things is important to Nat – and to his job.'

'Is that a threat?' Jem couldn't believe this was coming from someone she had, only half an hour ago, considered a friend.

'Not a threat,' said Angela. 'Just the way things are over here.' She shrugged her shoulders as if to say 'take it or leave it'.

Jem was about to reply when Joel and Paul walked in. Their expressions were serious, grim. Paul looked at Angela, who just gave a nod. Clearly they had all been planning this little ambush together.

Paul sat across from Jem, Joel to the side of her. Jem wanted to disappear through a trapdoor; her cheeks were burning hot and a puddle of nausea was collecting at the base of her throat. She was prepared for them all to round on her, and she steeled herself by downing the rest of her cocktail.

Paul spoke first, and she was surprised that his voice was less belligerent than it had been during their last conversation.

'Jem, we don't want you to feel we're strong-arming you; we're all friends here and we want to keep it that way. But you have to see there's no up side to this. Alice is dead, we can't change that.'

'And I suppose you'd prefer it if nobody ever mentioned her again?'

'Jem, please,' said Angela.

Jem could feel herself getting even more riled. She looked straight at Paul.

'I assume you've told them about you and Alice,' she said.

There was a short silence before anyone spoke again.

'Look,' he glanced at Angela and Joel, leaning forward and lowering his voice, 'I made a mistake. Over a year ago and we should let it lie.'

'It's not about you, Paul; this is about Alice.'

'Oh, don't be such a hypocrite,' said Angela, her face turning hard. 'You've been running around the beach all summer with Michael Kearney. Don't pretend you don't know what people are saying about you.'

Jem swallowed. 'I'm his assistant,' she said.

'Is that what people call it these days?'

Jem looked at them one by one: Paul acting the injured party, Angela outraged that someone should rock her cosy little boat, Joel at least having the decency to look troubled if not guilty. She truly had no idea whether any of them had been at the house that night, whether they had been involved in Alice's death, but what was certain was that they had brought her here to intimidate her, to threaten her – to threaten her husband's career, in fact – to make her feel frightened and small.

'Just tell me. Do you want to find out the truth about Alice or not?' she asked, struggling to keep her voice from shaking.

'Alice fell and drowned,' said Angela in a way that left no room for argument.

Jem grabbed her bag and stood up.

'Screw you,' she said.

Three faces looked at her in disbelief, and she experienced a moment of triumph. There was fear in their expressions too. They had come here to intimidate her, but the truth was they were scared of her, and of what she might do.

Chapter 38

It was raining hard when Jem came out onto the street, the sticky humidity giving way to a violent summer storm.

'Dammit,' she muttered, her happiness at having stood up to the bullies melting away as she contemplated the soaking she was about to receive. She couldn't stay in the bar, not after that parting shot, and she'd been in New York long enough to know how quickly cabs disappeared in the rain. The sky was pewter, the air heavy and close; it didn't look like it was going to stop any time soon. She took a deep breath and ran, her thin jacket held over her head.

Within a few steps she knew it was hopeless: she was going to get drenched. Her jacket was wet through and floppy, the puddles were splashing up her legs and her shoulders were heavy and cold. Still, she was committed now, dashing across the street and under the awning of a furniture store. It wasn't much cover – a small waterfall was gushing into the street from the gutter overhead – so she looked around for something better. *There.* A red neon sign announced *The Organic Bakery*, along with a picture of a coffee cup. Perfect: she could grab a soy latte and wait it out, or at least dry off a little.

'Jem.'

For a moment she thought the rain drumming on the awning was playing tricks with her ears.

'Jem, wait!'

She turned and was amazed to see Joel running across the road, his hair plastered to his face.

'I need to talk to you,' he panted as he arrived under the awning, his shirt soaked.

'I thought we just did,' said Jem, uncomfortable at being pressed into a tiny space with him.

'I need to talk to you alone,' he said, wiping the rain from his face and glancing back across the street as if Angela might be watching.

'Fine,' said Jem, nodding towards the bakery. 'Let's run.'

She splashed along the pavement, Joel hard on her heels. By the time they burst in through the door, she could feel water squishing between her toes. It was like she'd stepped into the shower fully clothed.

The girl behind the counter looked at them in surprise, as if she hadn't noticed the downpour outside.

'Latte, please,' said Jem. 'Two, actually. We'll sit by the window.'

She had expected the place to be heaving with refugees from the storm, but it was almost empty. Clearly no one else was crazy enough to brave the deluge. She took a chair opposite Joel and tried her best to push her dripping hair from her face. The girl brought the coffee over and they sat for a moment, sipping. Jem wondered if Joel felt as awkward as she did. Probably not: Wall Street people seemed born with thicker skin.

'So Todd told me you'd seen a picture of me and my friend Ed at a party,' he said finally.

'You don't need to be so coy,' said Jem, looking up under her fringe. 'We both know what we're talking about here.'

'Do we?'

Jem looked at him, wondering how much he did know, what he had done. She didn't doubt he'd indulged in insider dealing, and perhaps Alice had been blackmailing him to keep quiet about what she knew. But despite his jock-macho posturing, Jem had always seen Joel as something of a wimp, not someone who could hurt a friend. Then again, none of them seemed capable of that.

'I think I can guess what happened,' she said, finding an odd comfort in the rain lashing down the window pane. 'Alice saw you and Ed talking at the party about a share price tip. She recorded the whole thing on her phone.'

'So I had a conversation with a friend about a business deal. What's the problem?'

'The problem is you acting on that information. You bought shares in the company – and that's very illegal.'

'I'd love to know how you're such an expert on my investments.'

'Erica told me about the Yonex trade.'

He looked away, pressing his lips together in irritation.

'This is none of your business, Jem.'

'Did Alice blackmail you? Did she threaten to tell someone what you were up to?'

She looked at him. It was a bluff, but Joel flinched like he'd been slapped, and instantly Jem knew she was right.

'I have the footage, Joel. Alice put in on a memory card and hid it.'

Joel looked down into his coffee before he spoke again.

'You know, if I'd been five years older, I would have been swimming with the big boys. They had it easy ten years ago: the economy was booming, the money was just pouring in. I would have the yacht and the town house, Erica would be on the board of the Met and I'd be king of the world.' He shook his head. 'Five years. I was just born at the wrong time.'

'So you thought you'd cheat the system,' said Jem quietly.

Joel looked at her, his eyes fierce. 'Insider trading? What a crock of hypocritical crap. Those rules are just there to protect the massive profits of the biggest players. No one gets hurt, all that happens is that the corporations and their lawyers make a couple of dollars less. It's bullshit.'

'It's still illegal, Joel. You can still go to jail.'

The defiance left his face. He looked crushed, haunted. Jem supposed that if he had known about the existence of the footage, he must have lived in constant fear that it would one day resurface.

'How much? How much were you going to pay her to keep quiet?'

Joel glanced at her, then away again, ashamed.

'One hundred thousand.'

'Wow,' said Jem shocked by the amount.

'I know what you're thinking,' said Joel, looking up. 'One hundred thousand reasons to get rid of her.'

'People might say that blackmail is a pretty good motive for murder. I know that's what Michael is thinking.'

'But I was going to pay her!'

'Did you?' asked Jem.

Joel shook his head. 'But she slipped – the police said so.'

Jem moved her head closer to his. 'Someone followed Alice into the beach house that night, Joel. We've got a photo that proves it.'

'And you think that person was me?'

Was it arrogance or innocence? wondered Jem. Was Joel simply unable to believe that he'd been caught out, or was this confusion genuine?

'I was at the Dobermans' party all evening. Until David phoned Angela and told us all to come back to the house.'

Jem pressed her hands on the table.

'Joel, I'm just saying what the police are going to say. It

was a busy party, the grounds are huge. You could have slipped away and come back. Someone was photographed going into the beach house at ten past nine. David didn't raise the alarm until after nine thirty.'

Joel gazed at her, his irritation plain.

'You do know the police interviewed us all after Alice's death? We all had alibis, dozens of witnesses.' He shook his head, his eyes pleading. 'I swear to you, I had nothing to do with Alice's death. You have to believe me.'

Jem nodded slowly. 'Then who did?' she asked, flashing him a challenge to help her.

Joel's head dropped forward.

'You have to get rid of the video of me and Ed.'

'I don't have it.'

'Jem, stop fucking around. This is my life. Erica will be devastated. I could end up in jail.'

'Joel, I don't have the video. It's on a memory card in her phone. And Michael has the phone.'

'But you can get it for me.' Joel looked at her, licked his lips. 'I know something. Something that might help you. If I tell you, will you get me the memory card?'

'Just tell me what you know, Joel.'

He took a deep breath.

'That night? The night of the party, Alice cornered me. She seemed agitated, upset. She said she needed the money right away. She seemed desperate. I said I needed more time but she said she had to have twenty thousand dollars by Monday. She was very specific about it.'

'What did she need it for?'

'I don't know. She didn't say. I've spent the last year thinking about it, but all I know is that she needed that exact amount for something that couldn't wait. Monday was a deadline for her in some way.'

He looked at her hopefully, his eyes glistening.

'You have to get that memory card for me,' he said. 'Erica's pregnant. I *can't* go to jail.'

Jem closed her eyes. It was never just one lie, was it? And it was never just one person who was hurt by them. The ripples went out and out, catching everything in their wake.

'I should go,' she said, standing. Joel grabbed her hand as she walked towards the door.

'Delete the footage, Jem, please,' he said desperately. 'Find a way. Or my life is over.'

Just like Alice, she thought, pushing out into the storm.

Chapter 39

The rain continued all the way back to Brooklyn, but it had eased to a steady drizzle by the time Jem reached the apartment. She was glad to find it dark and quiet; after the day she'd had, her nerves were on edge and she was in no mood for a repeat of Nat's overtures. She went straight to the bathroom and stripped off her damp clothes, dropping them in a pool on the floor. She turned the shower up as high as she could stand and stepped in, never more glad of the American approach to water pressure, loving the hot jets washing the rain and the stress of the day away. She shampooed her hair, then slicked it back off her face and turned off the jets, feeling a little calmer.

Wrapped in her towelling robe, she went over to the bathroom mirror, wiping her hand across the condensation, her reflection appearing like an abstract painting through the opaque mist. What a bloody mess, she thought to herself.

She thought about Erica, pregnant and excited about moving into her new Montauk home. She thought of her standing on a sun-dappled porch holding her baby, both of them crying as Joel was bundled into a police car. She thought of Nat, so happy at the Hamptons, so eager to get back to the beach house every Friday night – mixing cocktails by the pool, basking in the compliments about his excellent mojitos – and although it was more difficult to be sympathetic about him after what he had done, he was still her husband and they had been happy.

She went into the kitchen and opened a bottle of red wine, pouring herself a carelessly large measure that she tipped down her throat. She didn't even like red wine, it tasted sour on her tongue, but still she drank it.

She froze, hand around the glass, as she heard the key in the lock, and darted into the bedroom to get changed, feeling suddenly too exposed in her robe.

'Anyone home?'

She heard the sound of something clattering on the table.

'I'm just in here.'

Pulling on jeans and a T-shirt, she scraped her hair into a ponytail and went back into the living space.

'You're early,' she said.

'The new me,' Nat smiled, slipping off his jacket and slinging it over the back of a chair. She noticed that it was bone dry.

'Got a company car home,' he said, as if that was the sort of thing he usually did. 'So what have you been up to today? Did you go back to Michael's?'

'No, he's in Manhattan.'

'Has he got a place here?' he said, sitting on the sofa with his arms stretched across the backrest.

'He's at the Four Seasons.'

She heard emotion catch in her throat. It came from nowhere and she felt powerless to stop it. She just wanted things to go back to how they'd been, but she knew everything had changed irrevocably: her relationship with Nat, the arrangement at the beach house, her feelings towards people she had considered friends. What frustrated her most was that she had brought all this on herself; had she said no to Michael's offer of a job, she'd have busied herself with her blog and had a happy summer at the beach.

As for her husband, he had been the greatest source of personal disappointment. It was easy to blame his infidelity on the seductive Alice leading him astray, but how easily had he succumbed to temptation; had he even initiated the kiss himself? Had Jem not been a good enough wife? Had their sex been too infrequent and too bland?

She turned to the kitchen area to make them both a coffee, wishing their home was bigger, wishing there was somewhere to curl up and hide. Putting the capsules in the machine, she concentrated hard on the glug of the water, spinning round in surprise when she felt a hand on her shoulder.

Her husband was just inches away, his good looks catching her off guard even though they were so familiar to her it was like staring at her own reflection.

'What's wrong?' he asked softly.

Jem was unable to hold her tears in any longer. Even though she was still so angry with him, she took a step closer and allowed herself to be enveloped in his arms.

'What's happened?'

She shook her head miserably. She wanted to unload it all; she didn't want to keep anything from him.

'I met Angela today.'

'Well that's good, isn't it?' said Nat with an encouraging smile. 'Where did you go?'

'We went for a drink. At the W.'

'Nice. So why the tears?'

She hesitated. She could see he was pleased; he'd been hinting that Jem should make more of an effort with the other housemates, particularly den-mother Angela.

'Paul and Joel came too.'

'So?'

'They're not happy. About Michael. About the work he's doing . . .'

Nat didn't say anything for a moment.

'And you're surprised?' he said, stepping back.

'Not surprised, no. But they didn't have to ambush me.'

'Ambush?'

'I turned up thinking it was just a drink, but they'd brought me there to threaten me.'

'They threatened you?'

Jem nodded.

Nat went to the fridge to get a can of beer.

'Alice was their friend,' she said softly. 'I would have thought they'd want to know what happened to her, but they don't. They want to stop me.'

Nat snapped the ring pull on his drink and took a thirsty sip.

'Do you blame them?' he said, looking at her seriously. 'Alice slipped in the pool and drowned, Jem. End of story. You can hardly criticise them for wanting to leave her in peace. You've gone around digging up unwanted history. Things – people – have moved on. Why drag up the past when it won't change anything?'

Jem felt piqued. Of course it was in Nat's interests to let go of the past, to let time bury his indiscretions.

He cradled his can and looked out of the window, spotted with sparkling raindrops.

'Why was Joel there?'

Jem winced. She knew he wasn't going to like what she was going to say next.

'I found a clip of Joel on Alice's phone.'

'So you think Joel was having an affair with her too?' he said incredulously. 'What is this? *The Love Boat*?'

'Joel was involved in insider trading,' replied Jem, not liking his tone. 'Alice had filmed him getting a tip-off on a merger. That's how he could afford the house in Montauk.'

She watched Nat's conflicted expression. She knew he

hated the idea of rocking the boat or upsetting his new friends, but she could see that he liked the prospect of Joel getting into money trouble. Joel had always been the most boastful of the housemates, forever dropping into conversation how he'd bought a new car or boat or how he'd flown by private jet to some meeting or other, and to a naturally competitive man like Nat, it was a constant thorn in the side. She knew that a part of him was relishing the prospect of Joel getting taken down a peg or two.

'Have you told anyone about it?' he asked.

'No. Not yet.'

'Are you going to?'

'I don't know. Joel's panicking that we will.'

The look of disapproval was obvious on Nat's face.

'It's criminal activity, Nat,' said Jem, her eyes wide. 'It's not free money. He effectively stole it from someone, that's why it's illegal. I can't stand by and—'

'Stop!' shouted Nat, throwing his hands in the air. 'Seriously, Jem, you have to stop this. Stop working for bloody Michael Kearney, stop interfering in things that don't concern you. You and that pampered millionaire author playing Scooby-Doo is impacting on people's lives, on *our* lives . . .'

Jem could barely believe what she was hearing.

'Don't you want to find out what happened to Alice?'

'We *know* what happened to Alice,' Nat snapped. 'You're beginning to sound like one of those mad conspiracy theorists on the internet. I know you've been feeling bored and lonely, I know you want to occupy your time feeling *useful*, but now you're sounding hysterical.'

She gaped at him. It was as if a wall had been built between them and they were standing on opposite sides. She could feel the tears beginning again.

'I can't believe you're not supporting me here.'

'Of course I'm bloody supporting you,' he said. 'You're my wife. But honestly, I can see why Angela and Paul and Joel are pissed off with you. I mean, what's it going to be like this weekend at the house with all this going on?'

'They don't want us at the house. Not unless I stop.'

Nat looked at her in complete shock.

'They told you that?'

She nodded. 'As good as.'

Nat turned away, running a hand through his hair.

'Jesus, Jem.'

Suddenly Jem had the feeling that she was floating, weightless. Everything she thought she had known was falling apart. Everything she thought she had known about her husband was wrong. He was a cheat, a liar, and he would never put her first. Never.

'Is the beach house all that matters to you?'

'Not the bloody house!' he cried. 'Them! They're our friends, Jem.'

'Friends. Is that what you think?'

'Of course.'

'They're not our friends, Nat. Not really. Right now you're useful to them. Your connections, your British charm, the advertising money. You add something to the group. Do you honestly think they'd let us into the house share if you were some out-of-work nobody like me? Would they be our friends then?'

'Don't be so rude. They like you.'

'They like the fact that I can cook and that I do the washing-up.'

Nat shook his head. 'You've got to stop this right now. Call Angela, tell her you've given up working for Kearney.'

'But I haven't.'

'Yes you have!' he spat.

She blinked at him. He'd never shouted at her before, not

like that. Not with a face so twisted with anger and disgust and disappointment. She turned and headed for the bedroom. The apartment suddenly felt too small for both of them. She grabbed a bag and stuffed some things inside. A voice in her head told her that she was being overdramatic. But she couldn't stay.

'Where are you going?' said Nat as she walked out into the corridor.

'I don't know,' she said, picking up her keys, turning her back, every part of her willing him to run over, to hold her, to kiss her and beg for forgiveness, to pledge to support her whatever happened. But he didn't.

'I wouldn't try going to the beach house,' he called behind her, venom in his voice. 'They've probably changed the locks.'

Jem stepped onto the landing, closing the door behind her. In a daze, she walked down the stairs, out onto the street and away into the dark. She didn't even feel the rain.

Chapter 40

In her dream, Jem was trapped. She lay immobile on a bed, inside a featureless room. She wanted to get up, but she couldn't; it was as if the sheets themselves were holding her down. She could hear sounds outside: the pulsing roar of the waves, the sound of distant voices and laughter. The thud, thud of rhythmic drumming. It sounded good out there, light and open, and yet she was stuck, unable to rise, unable to speak, to call for help. And then there came a knocking. Someone was at the door. She turned, frightened, staring at the door she hadn't noticed before. It began to open, and a face appeared. Jem screamed.

She sat up, heart pounding. *Only a dream*. She looked around her at the unfamiliar room. Not the room from the dream, far from it; it was a luxurious room, with expensive-looking furniture, a desk and a widescreen TV. She looked at the bed she was sitting in, the crisp sheets. This was definitely her T-shirt, the one she'd worn yesterday. But she had no idea how she had got here, or why her head was thumping.

'Jem?' A muffled voice from behind the door. And the knock, knock from the dream. The door opened a crack and Michael looked in. 'You awake?'

'Yes,' she said, her voice gravelly. 'Yes, just about.'

Michael stepped inside holding up an iPad and a key card. 'The receptionist gave me two keys when we checked you in. I hope you don't mind.'

She shook her head, the memory jangling at the back of her head. The Four Seasons. She was at the Four Seasons.

'You booked me into a room?'

Michael sat on the corner of the bed.

'I had a hunch that you wouldn't remember much.'

She glanced around the room. She could see her jeans draped over the back of a chair, her shoes kicked off by the desk.

'Give me a minute, will you. Let me throw on a robe.'

'I can come back,' said Michael apologetically.

'Just chuck me that,' she said, pointing to a towelling robe on the back of the door.

Michael put it on the bed and went into the bathroom. He shut the door discreetly as Jem slid out of bed and put the robe on, tying the belt firmly around her waist.

'You can come out now,' she said awkwardly, knocking on the bathroom door.

'How are you feeling?' asked Michael, handing her a glass of water.

'Shocking. What was I drinking, meths?'

'Almost. You went through the entire contents of the minibar.'

'Oh God,' groaned Jem, covering her face in embarrassment. 'You must take it out of my wages. That and the room, too.'

'This is the Four Seasons, Jem. I'm not sure your wages will cover it.'

She had to look twice to make sure he was kidding.

'It's fine,' he laughed. 'I was glad to help out. You don't remember getting here?'

Fragments of memory started coming back to her. A text

message to Michael, a taxi ride into Manhattan. She remembered getting out on Park Avenue and pushing her way through the heavy revolving door of the hotel, and he was there, waiting for her. A solid embrace, the smell of aftershave, smoky and woody, on his jacket, the feeling of being safe.

She frowned. 'You were . . . wearing black tie?'

He laughed. 'Now you remember. Yes, I was at a publishing awards thing, where they drag old has-beens like myself to parade about.'

'Was it here? At the Four Seasons?'

'No, across town, but you sent me a message that you were on your way in.'

'I ruined your night,' she said, feeling mortified.

Michael smiled and shook his head. 'It gave me a decent excuse to slope off early.'

Jem looked doubtful.

'Seriously, you were good company. Until you got into the Scotch, anyway. I don't know anyone who isn't made maudlin by whisky.'

She smiled weakly. She could barely remember anything beyond the hotel lobby, and the thought that she had been drinking in a fancy suite, with her boss, the famous author, made her shudder. Not entirely with embarrassment; there was something else in there too: excitement, a sense of the forbidden. She glanced at her jeans and didn't dare think what time she took those off, although she was fairly sure that the evening had been chaste – certainly Michael's casual behaviour didn't suggest anything to the contrary, though you never could be too sure once alcohol was thrown into the mix.

She squeezed her eyes shut in horror, then shook her head and opened them again.

'I'm sorry to drag you into all this.'

'I dragged *you* into it, remember?'

For a second, he looked awkward.

'I've got something to show you,' he said, picking up the iPad.

Jem frowned. She wasn't in the mood for any more photos of the beach house, videos of Joel or Paul, Angela, Rebecca, any of them. Whatever he had on that iPad, if it was to do with the Hamptons, with Alice, she didn't want to see it.

He typed something into the virtual keyboard and a web page appeared on the screen. He handed her the device.

At first she could just see bright colours and photographs. She squinted at it, trying to work out what it was. Eventually she realised.

'"The Beach Kitchen",' she said quietly.

'You've been talking about this blog for weeks, all the cooking you've done for it. But you haven't even got a website.'

'How did you do this?' she said, looking at him and then back to the site. It was perfect: vibrant and fresh-looking. Dummy pictures had been slotted into a rolling carousel of photos. It looked like just the sort of blog she would want to follow.

'A good question, seeing as I can barely work out how to use Twitter . . .'

He paused.

'I threw some money at the problem. I spoke to a web designer on Monday. Told him we needed something quickly. It's probably nothing like you want, but at least it'll get you started. He'll make any design changes you need.'

'You did this for me?' she said, feeling emotional.

'It's the least I could do after everything you've done for me.'

She leant over and kissed him on the cheek. Feeling colour rush to her face, she recoiled quickly.

'Thank you,' she said.

'I should go.' He picked up the iPad. 'I've got an appointment with a video reconstruction artist at eleven. He enhances photographs, works with the police to clean up evidence; I sent him Alex's beach photo yesterday and he said he should have something to show us this morning. You're welcome to come. If not, there's no rush to check out here.'

They both turned when they heard a knock at the door.

'I'll get that,' Jem said, leaving Michael near the window.

When she opened the door, she was shocked to see Nat standing there.

'I thought you'd be here.'

Disappointment. Contempt. She heard it all in just a few words.

'Are you going to invite me in?'

Jem hesitated. She was embarrassed that Michael was in the room, knew how it looked, even though it was entirely innocent.

Nat didn't miss her reticence and pushed past her. He stopped when he saw Michael.

'I was just leaving,' said the older man.

'I bet you were.'

Michael turned to Jem.

'Or I can stay.'

'I'll see you in a few minutes,' she said sheepishly. 'And I will come to the meeting.'

She watched her husband's eyes dart around the room. She knew what he was looking for: a couple of champagne flutes, a pair of discarded boxer shorts or a tie; a condom wrapper perhaps.

'I know what you're thinking, and you insult me,' she said, folding her arms across her chest.

'I don't think it's unreasonable, do you?' he retorted. 'You leave the house. Don't come home all night. Don't answer my calls.'

Jem didn't want to admit she'd switched her mobile phone off. She'd meant to turn it back on, of course, but that was before she'd consumed the contents of the mini-bar.

'You haven't got any friends in the city, so I thought, "Where would she go?" And then I remembered. Michael was at the Four Seasons.'

She didn't miss the insult, and the way he said Michael's name with such distaste angered her even more.

'I've been worried sick about you. I didn't know if you were dead in a ditch, kidnapped, run off. I was thinking everything. But here you are with him.'

'I'm not *with* him, Nat. He sprung me a room. He's been a good friend.'

He snorted unkindly.

'What is your problem?'

'*He's* the problem, Jem. If there's any problem in our marriage it's Michael Kearney. Everything was great until he came along.'

She examined his face. Was he serious? Did he really think that?

'I've spoken to Angela,' he continued. 'I said you'd apologise and drop this nonsense.'

'What?'

But Nat didn't appear to be listening and ploughed on.

'Rebecca's gallery is having a party tonight. Our names are on the door; we should go. It's not too late to patch this up.'

Jem shook her head. 'You haven't been listening to a

word I've said, have you? I don't care what they think of me, I don't want to patch it up. They're not my friends and that is not my world.'

The look of confusion on Nat's face told Jem all she needed to know, and she was overcome with a real sadness. He genuinely didn't understand what she was saying. Why wouldn't she want to be friends with Angela and Joel and the rest of them? They were rich, successful, connected, all the things Nat felt a person should aspire to be. The fact that Jem didn't yearn to be just like them simply didn't compute.

'What happened to us, Nat?' she said softly.

'What do you mean?'

'We've been living separate lives since we got to New York. You work, you go to parties; when you come home, you're tired or you're working, building your brand.'

'What's wrong with that?'

'Perhaps if you weren't so distracted by your job, you'd notice that we need to work on our relationship. We used to go to the pictures, restaurants, or we'd just talk and laugh and be together. When was the last time we talked about anything?'

Nat frowned. 'So what do you want to talk about?'

Jem gave a soft laugh. 'Nothing, Nat.' She gestured to the door. 'Look, you'd better go. I need to get dressed. I've got an appointment.'

'With Michael?' His face twisted into a childish leer.

'Yes, with Michael.'

She moved towards the door. Nat was still standing in the middle of the room, his expression sour.

'You've got daddy issues.'

She looked at him disbelievingly.

'That's what this is; he's a father substitute. But you're not a child. You're a groupie.'

Jem raised her hand and slapped him across the cheek, recoiling in horror when she realised what she'd done.

Nat brought his palm up to his face.

'Truth hurts,' he said quietly, then he opened the door and left the room.

Chapter 41

A driver picked Michael and Jem up at the hotel and drove them north of the park towards Harlem – surprisingly shiny and vibrant compared to its reputation, thought Jem, as she took in the unfamiliar surroundings – then swung back across to Broadway, the north lane creeping beneath the criss-crossed green struts of the L train, the scene of countless New York action movies. She'd only been in the city for six months, but the narrow streets of Kensal Rise felt a world away, as if she had been here for years. She certainly felt as if she were a different person to the wide-eyed girl who had landed at JFK, but whether that was a good thing or not, only time would tell.

She glanced over at Michael, who had been quiet for the entire journey, as if he were lost in his thoughts.

'David wanted to meet me today,' she said to puncture the silence.

'Why?' asked Michael, turning and looking at her intently.

Jem shifted on the warm black leather seat of the town car.

'He wants an update on what's happening.'

'Did you make any arrangements?' Michael said after a pause, a deep crease appearing between his heavy brows.

Jem shook her head, feeling guilty. So much seemed to have happened over the past twenty-four hours that she hadn't thought to call him back, as she'd said she would. Even if she had, she was conscious that she was Michael's assistant – a rank amateur at this sort of work – and that it was her boss's job to relay their thoughts, theories and discoveries about the night Alice died.

'What are you thinking?' she asked when Michael didn't immediately respond.

'You know, we've only ever had David Holliday's word that he went to the beach house at nine thirty and found Alice in the pool,' he said, his voice low.

Jem had worked out that he knew the driver of the town car, the chit-chat and backslapping as they'd got into the vehicle suggesting that this was Michael's regular driver, but this was obviously going to be a sensitive conversation.

'So far we've taken it as a given that his is the correct version of events. But we have a photo of someone going into the beach house at ten past nine, and until we know who that person was, we have to keep an open mind.'

'You're suggesting it could be David?' said Jem, in shock.

Michael shrugged.

It was Jem's turn to frown. 'If he was lying, if he had something to hide, why would he encourage us to investigate the night Alice died?'

'I'm just saying we have to keep an open mind. And I don't want you meeting him alone,' said Michael.

'Thanks for being protective, but really—'

Michael cut her off with a glance.

'Please . . .' he said firmly, before settling back into a silence that suggested he didn't want to be disturbed.

Eventually the car turned into a long side street sloping down to the river, with tall red-brick buildings on either side that reminded Jem of warehouses. She peered up at the one on the right dubiously. It was grimy and intimidating, a lonely, isolated sort of spot, despite being within a stone's throw of a main road.

'What is this place?' she said, watching the car pull away. 'I thought we were going to meet some image expert.'

Michael raised his eyebrows and stepped over to a steel door. It was battered and rusty with a fading stencilled sign reading 'No Entry'. It looked like a loading bay. He pressed the button of an intercom.

'Where better to look for an expert,' he said as the door buzzed and swung open, 'than at one of the world's greatest universities?'

Open-mouthed, Jem followed him into a dark hallway. It certainly smelt municipal: dust and floor cleaner. Michael turned into a stairwell and took the steps down towards what could only be a basement.

'What kind of university is this?'

He pressed another buzzer, opening a double door and holding it for Jem.

'Columbia University, School of Technology.'

Stepping inside, Jem found herself in a large fluorescent-lit room alive with noise and activity. Ahead of them were two lines of desks, equipped with shiny silver computer screens and banks of unnamed machinery, with young people sitting in front of them tapping at keyboards or gazing at images swirling on the screens.

Before Jem could comment, a door to their left opened and a tall black man emerged. Fortyish and good-looking, he was wearing a basketball jersey, spectacles balanced on top of his shaved head.

'Jem Chapman, this is Professor Emmett Taylor, head of information technology.'

'Pleased to meet you, Jem,' said the man in a deep bass,

shaking her hand warmly. 'Not what you were expecting, huh? I think the Dean hides us away in the basement because he's scared we might be watching him. We *are*, by the way.'

The room the professor ushered them into was clearly his office and workspace: shelves of books and papers, pictures of family and, presumably, his favourite basketball team in action. And then there was his desk: two giant flat screens side by side, each featuring a series of images that made Jem stop. Pictures of Joel, Paul and Alice, all pulled from Alice's phone. But they weren't the grainy pixelated shots she had seen on the little three-by-four screen; these were sharp and punchy, like the pictures you'd see in a cinema.

'Quite the rogues' gallery, huh?' smiled Emmett, sitting in his ergonomic chair. 'Michael sent them over yesterday and I've been having a little play.'

He looked up at Jem. 'Mike and I have been working together on and off for years, so I'll spare him the speech, but suffice to say the beauty of digital images is that, unlike images on film, they are just a bunch of data.'

He swivelled the chair back towards the screen and, using a pen on a tablet rather than a mouse, pulled up an image of Alice. In the shot, she was standing in front of a fountain, grinning into the lens, happy and carefree, her arm around Rebecca, who was raising her glass to the camera.

'So we can clean this up,' said Emmett, clicking a button. Before Jem's eyes, the image became brighter, warmer, the colours more vivid. It felt as if she could reach out and touch Alice.

'Or we can add some filters,' he said, rapidly duplicating the image and changing the mood. One was black and white, which made Alice look regal and frosty; another had a kind of oversaturated sixties feel, like it had been shot at Woodstock.

'And then we can do stuff like this.'

414

On the screen to the right, Emmett opened another window. It was the same image, but Rebecca had gone. Standing in her place, still holding the glass in silent toast, was Marilyn Monroe. It was astonishing. If you hadn't known it was a trick, you'd have sworn Alice and Marilyn were old buddies posing for a snap.

'That's incredible.'

Emmett turned back to Jem, smiling modestly. 'My party trick. That's the one I show to students on the first day to demonstrate to them what's possible – and what's not.'

He zoomed in on the faces and tapped the screen with a finger.

'You see the shadows under Alice's chin here? Now look at Marilyn.'

Jem squinted. It was wrong somehow, but she couldn't say why. 'It looks . . . flat?'

The professor looked pleased. 'At a distance, it all looks fine, but when you look closer, it's out of balance. God is in the details, as they say. The point is, we can manipulate these images, but there are certain things we can't do.'

With a wave of his pen he opened a desktop file and spread half a dozen pictures across the two screens – Alex's photos of the back of the beach house.

'Take this picture as an example,' he said, enlarging one of the earlier shots. 'I think you both saw this figure in the window, yes? It's fuzzy, though, indistinct. Now watch.'

Slowly he clicked on a variety of filters and tools, bringing the window more and more into focus until Jem could see for certain that the hazy shadow was Alice. She could see her face, the hollows of her cheekbones, even the colour of her hair. It was amazing.

'Now we can see who it is, but the problem is, this is as far as we go.' Emmett peered up at them both. 'Look at the eyes.'

He zoomed in even further and the image became sharper, more rounded, but something had changed: it didn't look so much like Alice any more.

'The software works on complex algorithms, adding or taking away elements of the image according to probability; when it's not sure, it gives you what's most likely. So here it's given Alice green eyes when she had blue. It's given her angular features because her face is in shadow, which suggests high contrast, but from the reference shots on her phone she had a more rounded face. It's good, but it's not perfect.'

Michael raised an eyebrow. 'Why do I get the feeling you're trying to prepare us for something?' he said.

Jem looked back and forth between the two men, a sinking sense of disappointment in her chest. 'Couldn't you get anything from Alex's photos?'

'Quite the opposite,' said Emmett, the smile fallen from his face. 'I got plenty. What I was preparing you for, Michael, was the argument the opposing counsel will wheel out when you show the court these.'

Jem held her breath as he pulled up the photo of the beach house, the one with the open gateway at the back, the hazy, indistinct figure standing there.

She thought of Paul Ellis, angry and vengeful that they had discovered his affair with Alice. She thought of Joel, desperate and pleading after they had worked out that Alice knew about his illegal trades. And she thought of what Michael had said back in the car: *We've only ever had David Holliday's word that he went to the beach house at nine thirty.*

What had he been suggesting? Not that David had got his timing wrong. But that he had deliberately lied. Perhaps he hadn't found Alice dead in the pool at all. Perhaps she had been alive when he'd gone back to make amends after their argument at the Doberman party.

She felt sick with anticipation as Emmett concentrated on the screen, clicking slowly on his tablet, advancing the image, making it sharper and brighter. Now they could make out the outline more clearly, they could see that the figure was half turned, as if glancing over their shoulder.

'Now,' said Emmett quietly, enlarging the face, adding contrast and colour.

'I don't believe it,' whispered Jem as the image froze.

The figure in the doorway the night of Alice's death was a woman; the same woman standing next to Alice on that sunny afternoon by the fountain.

'It's Rebecca.'

Last summer

Chapter 42

There was no denying that the house still looked magical, strings of lights swaying over the deck and two glowing upstairs windows making the weathered clapboard building look like a particularly benevolent pumpkin.

How could anything in such a fairy-tale castle be wrong? she thought for a split second, before the nausea collecting at the base of her throat reminded her how very wrong things were.

Shifting her shoes to one hand, she let herself in through the French windows. The doors were unlocked, as they often left them, lazy days at the beach blurring their sense of caution, but still, there was the possibility that someone was home.

'Hello?' she called, listening, her voice echoing around the room. No, nothing but the soft hum of the air con. There was no one here. David would still be at the party; they all would, drinking champagne, laughing at each other's jokes, smiling politely at boasts about schools and business deals, gasping at the latest gossip.

She went to the fridge and took out a bottle of vodka. Alice was in the mood for spirits, not the weak fizz they had served at the party. Champagne made her giddy, giggly, but right now she wanted to lose herself completely.

She dropped ice into a glass and poured a large measure, hissing through her teeth as it burnt down her throat. Maybe she had been too harsh on David. He was a good husband; not perfect and not what she needed, but a decent man. He'd never hit her or lied to her or even asked very much of her as a wife. As for herself, Alice had responded in kind, giving him as little of the real her as she could manage.

She picked up the tumbler, pressed it against her forehead, taking comfort from the cold, trying to still the noise in her head.

What had people seen back at the party? she wondered. What had they heard? Was she the one they were all talking about back there, the whispers going from one person to the next, the shame spreading outward like ripples.

Yeah? Well let them talk.

She stepped outside; it was too hot in the house, despite the climate-controlled fans, and far too claustrophobic. She wanted to feel the breeze on her skin and look out over the endless sea. She still had that, at least. Maybe she could just jump in a boat and sail away.

Like you'd ever get in a boat. She could barely stand to be around the pool, never even dangled her feet into the water, not even on the hottest days.

The noise from the beach was getting louder and a crowd had gathered on the sand beyond the perimeter of the grounds.

Alice shook her head. She didn't need that, not tonight; the sights and sounds of young people having fun. Instead she walked to the right-hand side of the house, taking slow, steady sips of her vodka as she went.

She didn't come to this side of the property much; it made her shiver. She had successfully avoided the pool all summer, made her excuses when everyone else went swimming, and no one had ever asked why.

It was enclosed in a walled garden, with tall hedges that shielded it from the rest of the property. She pushed the white picket gate and went inside, shuddering as she stared at the sheet of turquoise water shimmering in front of her. She forced herself to look at it; she wasn't sure she could feel any more pain tonight, even if the sight of the pool dislodged unwelcome memories. She carefully skirted around the edge of the water, sipping the vodka as she went. It would be so easy just to end it right now, she thought, her eyes focusing on the intense blue. Just one step and a non-swimmer who'd had too much to drink would be gone. That would teach him, she thought bitterly.

The hedges had muffled the sounds from the beach but she could still pick out the rhythmic beat of drums from the bonfire party, the tempo steadily quickening to a frantic climax that reminded Alice of that day, that crazy afternoon in the rain, the wet cotton sticking to her skin, his hands on her . . . She tipped back the rest of her vodka, closed her eyes and let her hips sway.

If only all days could be like that, if only she could have the life she had imagined. If only . . .

Her eyes snapped open when she heard the scrape of the latch, the creak as the gate swung open behind her. Her heart jumped as she turned to face the figure, dark against the inky sky.

'Hello, Alice. I knew I'd find you here. I think it's time we had a talk.'

She recognised Rebecca's voice even before she stepped out of the shadows.

The thought of Paul, post-coital and naked in the Upper East Side apartment where they used to go for sex, evaporated instantly. Sobering up almost as quickly, Alice felt a hot, guilty flush creep up her neck. She hated feeling cornered, feeling caught out, and Rebecca could be a cold and intimidating creature at the best of times, let alone when she was challenging her husband's mistress.

She took a breath and pressed her front teeth into her bottom lip until she felt a sting of pain, telling herself that she could deal with this. She had had worse things thrown at her than a lover's angry wife, far worse. In the scheme of things, Rebecca Ellis was just an irritant that had to be dealt with in the same way that Alice treated all obstacles; with the same tough, street-smart guile that had dragged her from small-town Indiana to the most prestigious beachfront in the world.

There was a small wrought-iron table at the side of the pool. Alice put down her glass and drew herself up to her full height.

'What do you want to talk about?' she said, forcing her voice to remain light.

Rebecca didn't flinch. Alice had to appreciate how formidable the woman was, for a second imagining her at the gallery, a shrewd, ruthless negotiator who knew how to acquire and how to sell.

'I think you know,' she said, not moving her flinty gaze from Alice.

Alice didn't look away. She knew that the other woman was trying to make her admit the affair, and she felt a spike of defiance. Rebecca had picked the wrong person to shame and embarrass, and if she wanted to know the truth, hear the words from Alice's mouth, then she was going to give it to her all guns blazing.

Alice shifted her position so that she squared up to Rebecca. They were just a few feet apart.

'You want to talk about my relationship with Paul,' she said finally.

'Relationship? Is that what you think it is? I heard it was a few throwaway fucks.'

Alice felt her skin turn cold. She'd known that Rebecca wouldn't be a pushover, that she would try and hurt Alice with her words, but still, there was a shiver of truth to what she was saying, the shift of a deep-rooted insecurity that Alice had long tried to ignore.

'It's more than that,' she said steadily. 'Perhaps it started off like that, and perhaps that's what you want to think it is. But Paul and I – we love each other.'

'Really?' Rebecca scoffed.

Alice felt her cheeks grow warmer.

'I guess you don't know about our night in the Catskills,' she said defiantly. 'It was Paul's suggestion, by the way. The most romantic little place in the woods. His choice. He'd pre-ordered steaks and champagne so we wouldn't even have to leave. Some people might say we fucked on every square inch of that luxury cabin, but the truth is, we made love. And I don't just mean the sex. I mean the way Paul read to me in the bath, told me how beautiful I was, how he had never felt more turned on than when he was with me.'

She studied Rebecca's face for a chink of weakness, the admission of defeat, but there was none. She looked as cold and unimpressed as ever, and Alice knew she had to turn up the dial.

'Paul loves me,' she said.

'Did he tell you that?' Rebecca spoke with undisguised superiority.

'Yes,' said Alice. It was a lie, of course. They were the words she had been longing to hear from her lover, words that had never come – not yet. But she knew in her heart how much Paul cared for her.

I love you was a commitment. A line in the sand, a promise, and Paul wasn't ready for it quite yet. He was scared, Alice could tell that. Fearful of everything he would have to give up. But all he needed was a little push.

'I don't believe you,' said Rebecca cuttingly. 'Paul admitted he was screwing you, you know. I wondered where he was, on that little night away of yours, and I confronted him. It took a while to get the truth out of him, but when I did, he wasn't terribly flattering about your "relationship".'

The casual yet scornful way Rebecca had dismissed her had achieved its aim. Alice felt as if she had been kicked hard, and even though there had been no physical contact, she could feel her hands trembling in anger. After all, it made sense. Paul had called off their affair not long after the Catskills trip. He hadn't told her that he'd confessed all to Rebecca, but something had shifted and now it was beginning to make sense.

Perhaps Rebecca had threatened him with divorce. Or more likely some sort of professional ramifications. Rebecca was connected; Paul had mentioned that she had got him his current job, and Alice was in no doubt that she could just as easily make life difficult for him.

Well, two could play at that game, she thought with fury. The gloves were off. Rebecca needed to be hurt as she had tried to wound Alice and Paul.

'Admit it, Rebecca,' she growled. 'Your husband came looking for me and found what he wanted. Something that has been lacking from your relationship for a long time, I don't doubt. Fun, laughter, sex.'

'I hate to disappoint you, Alice, but we have a very happy, very passionate marriage.'

'Then why, when you were throwing your cash around on his fancy anniversary present, when you were *buying* his affection, was he was putting his cock in my mouth in the most romantic hotel in the whole of New York state?'

A lifetime of trying to better herself had almost rubbed

away Alice's sharp edges. But not quite. Sometimes you had to be crude, blunt; sometimes you had to lance the boil with a rusty blade.

Rebecca's cool blue eyes flashed. 'You tramp,' she hissed.

Alice felt a momentary spike of triumph that the other woman had been ruffled. More than that, she was glad that her relationship with Paul, what had happened between them, was out in the open. It needed to be. Paul needed to realise that the consequences of leaving his wife were not so bad. That he could have a happier life without her.

Rebecca stepped forward and jabbed a thin finger towards her.

It caught Alice off guard, and as she moved back, she could feel the edge of the pool fall away under her heel. She grabbed onto Rebecca's finger, not only to try and deflect it away from her face, but to steady herself. Rebecca sliced her hand through the air as if to swat her away, and Alice felt herself falling . . .

She felt the cold water slap against her back. She felt her head submerge beneath the surface. She opened her eyes, but her vision was blurred, an angry swirl of bubbles, white and blue, pressing down on her eyeballs. She opened her mouth and water rushed down her throat.

For a second she saw her sister Rosie. Imagined her struggling under the ice, her face almost unrecognisable, long and melted like that painting *The Scream*.

Rosie had fought. She was telling Alice to fight now. Kick, kick, kick. Alice didn't know how to swim, but she knew how to survive. Images flashed in her head. Paul, Nick Vlautin, David. Dear, dear David.

Another kick and her head was back above the surface of the pool. She gulped at the air with desperate hunger, fixing her gaze on the tiled side of the pool, just inches away.

'Help, Rebec—'

But her words were lost under the water again.

She flailed around wildly. She still had some breath in her lungs, some fight in her belly, but she was getting weaker. She needed more air, and one frantic kick took her back to the surface.

She could see her housemate, her shoes, her legs. Rebecca would save her. Ironic, but still . . .

And then she couldn't see her. She was back under the water. Her chest was burning and her head felt light and soft. Was it the drugs? she wondered with one final thought.

She couldn't move any more. She was tired. So tired. She just needed to sleep.

This summer

Chapter 43

The car was waiting for them when they'd finished with Emmett, and Michael instructed the driver to take them back to the hotel.

'So what are we going to do?' Jem knew it was an obvious question.

'I don't know yet,' replied Michael, looking out of the window.

His thoughtfulness annoyed her. They'd worked so hard to get to this point. Michael always seemed in control, knew what to do, and now more than ever she wanted him to fix this.

'You need to tell the police officer in charge of the original investigation,' she said, her mind a whirl of thoughts. 'Or what about the NYPD? Do they have jurisdiction? Surely with your contacts you can get in touch with the commissioner and he can have a word with the Hamptons police.'

He turned and looked at her.

'Are you ready for this?' he said simply.

'For what?'

'When we report Rebecca to the authorities, there will be repercussions.'

'Michael, there have already been repercussions.'

'Yes, but right now you can stop and back-pedal. The second we report Rebecca, it's permanent. Truth doesn't have to mean consequence, but when I call that photo in, it will do.'

Jem looked straight ahead. 'Rebecca, Joel . . . they can't be allowed to do bad things and get away with them.'

'Regardless of the cost to innocent people? Paul? Erica?'

'Paul wasn't innocent,' she replied crisply.

Michael was silent for a moment.

'Are you ready?' he said again.

'What if I said no?' she whispered.

'Then we'll find another way.'

They were already skirting the western side of the park. Jem puffed out her cheeks and rolled down the window.

Michael leant forward and touched the driver on the shoulder.

'We'll get out here,' he said.

They snaked into the garden, past the tourists and the city workers taking their lunch. Jem was hungry, but not so much that she wanted to do something about it. She just wanted to walk and work out what to do next.

She could see Belvedere Castle now, a gothic building that towered over the treeline, and she was reminded of a fairy tale: valiant innocent children and wicked queens. As she considered her own position, she wasn't sure which character she would be in such a storyline.

They walked down a path into a lush garden.

'The Shakespeare Garden,' she said, reading a sign. 'I've never been here.'

'I spent four years living in New York, and I only ever felt I scratched the surface of the park,' Michael said.

Jem looked at the tulips, foxgloves and hollyhocks and smiled. 'This place is great. It's like an English country garden. We have some fantastic ones in Cornwall,' she said, a sudden pang of homesickness almost knocking her over.

The garden was tiered; they walked down through the fragrant layers to a bench next to a bronze plaque inscribed with a quote from *Twelfth Night*. For a minute neither of them said anything; they just sat like two old companions content to be in each other's company.

'Are you going back to Amagansett?' Jem asked finally.

'I don't think so. I'm flying to Boston on Friday morning from La Guardia. Hardly seems much point.'

'What are you going to Boston for?'

He turned and smiled. 'My daughter's wedding. It's on Saturday. I have to take my position.'

'Well, you do have your DJ with you,' she said, snapping back into assistant mode.

She looked up as she heard a deep voice nearby: a Shakespearean actor rehearsing his lines. The public theatre was yards away and there was a play on that evening. Jem had always found Shakespeare dense and difficult, never having studied it in any significant way at school, but she felt soothed by the melodic lines and the rounded vowels of this English accent, the sound of her past.

'What do you think happened that night?' she asked.

'We'll never know for sure,' said Michael.

'Do you have enough for the police?'

'I don't know. I need to speak to them.'

'You have to do this, Michael.'

'What about Nat?' he said. 'Is he happy about all this? Have you talked to him about how it might impact on your relationship with your housemates?'

Jem gave a soft snort and felt tears well in her eyes. Michael looked immediately concerned.

'What is it?' he said, putting his hand on her arm. 'I

know you argued with Nat, but is it serious?'

She thought about her heart-to-heart with Michael at the beach; it seemed a lifetime ago. She hadn't revealed the true source of her conflict with Nat, and even in her drunken state last night she still hadn't told him what was really upsetting her. Now she shook her head.

'Nat was unfaithful,' she said simply. 'He was unfaithful with Alice.'

'What?' She wasn't sure if Michael looked more incredulous or angry. 'Tell me.'

She took a deep breath. She didn't dare look over at him, knowing how disappointed he'd be that she had disobeyed him.

'I spoke to Paul last weekend about Alice. I told him that I knew they'd had an affair, and he hit back. Told me that something had gone on between Alice and Nat too.'

She felt her shoulders lock.

'Look, I know I was wrong to have any sort of conversation with Paul, and I'm sorry. But I was so angry.'

'I don't blame you,' said Michael finally. 'I can imagine it wasn't easy being in the same house all weekend and not letting it slip.'

'That's the real reason why I took Alice's phone on Monday. I wanted to see if there was any evidence of them together, messages, photos . . . Nat swears it was a one-off. That he didn't sleep with Alice. That it was just a snog.'

'Snog?' said Michael, raising a brow.

'Kiss, make-out,' she said, feeling embarrassed talking about such personal details.

'Bastard,' he muttered under his breath.

She turned round and touched him on the arm.

'Look, I am so sorry I didn't tell you any of this before, but I didn't want you to think Nat had anything to do with Alice's death. He flew home the night of the Doberman

434

party, caught the red-eye – there was no way he could have been at the party or had any involvement with what happened, but I didn't want you to think he might have.'

She paused, wondering why she was trying to exonerate Nat, wondering if he deserved it. 'I'm not sure Nat is the man I thought he was,' she said, feeling the words catch in her throat. 'But he wouldn't hurt anyone.'

'He hurt you,' said Michael with a flash of quiet fury.

They didn't speak for another moment. Jem was glad she had got it all off her chest but she was still embarrassed.

'So are you going to go home?' asked Michael finally.

Jem shook her head. 'I don't feel ready.'

'Then I'll extend the hotel.'

'No, don't. It's so expensive. I'll find somewhere cheaper.'

'If it buys you some time to think, it's worth every cent.'

Jem felt soothed by his words and his protective presence. 'Are you sure?'

'I'm sure.'

'In which case, I'll go back to the apartment, collect some things. I know the service at the Four Seasons is so good they can telepathically provide me with a toothbrush and a phone charger, but I still like my own stuff.'

As she got up to leave, Michael put a hand on her arm.

'If you want me to stop this right now, just say.'

'This is bigger than me,' she whispered, pulling away from him.

'I don't want you to hate me because of it,' he insisted, not taking his eyes from hers.

'I'll see you back at the hotel,' she said, and walked away from him as quickly as she could without breaking into a run.

The apartment was hot and quiet. A plate sticky with breadcrumbs and egg yolk had begun to smell by the sink.

Coffee cups and beer cans were scattered in a trail around the living space, clues to how Nat had spent the past twenty-four hours.

Jem had never liked this apartment, but as she balanced on the edge of the sofa, looking around, wondering if she had already taken her final shower in the tiny bathroom, slept for the last time in the bed, she felt a wave of sadness that almost knocked her over.

She had never given much thought to how a marriage ended. Her only experience had been her parents' marriage, when her father's heart attack has irrevocably altered the status quo. She had a friend back in London, Karen, who was divorced. Jem had asked her once what had happened, and Karen had told her that an argument in the car over directions had spiralled out of control to the point that she had got out of the vehicle and never come home.

Back then, Jem had found it hard to believe, but perhaps it was the small things that made everything unravel, the tiny vents that made it all bubble to the surface, like a fault in the earth's crust. Thinking about it now, it wasn't Nat's unfaithfulness that had upset her so much; it was the lies afterwards. She remembered the morning he'd returned from the States, how she'd gone to Heathrow at 8.30 in the morning to meet him.

She'd held up a little Welcome Home sign and had his favourite chocolate bar in her pocket; and when he'd kissed her and told her how much he'd missed her, she had actually believed him. It hadn't occurred to her, not for one second, that he'd been intimately involved with another woman, however briefly, in New York. He'd lied to her, he'd betrayed what they had, and he'd carried on lying.

Going into the bedroom, she pulled her suitcase from under the bed and laid it on the duvet. She popped the lock and the lid flew open. She'd used a new leather holdall that Nat had been given to take to the Hamptons, so the last time she had used her old case was on a break to Westport at Easter. The weather had still been cold but she'd loved taking walks along Compo Beach, watching the sunset and feeling the wind on her cheeks. Grains of sand had collected in the corners of the case, like fragments of happy memories.

She began to pack: trousers, a pair of ballet flats, trainers, T-shirts, a sundress, jumpers in case it got cold. Underwear, laptop, make-up; they were all layered on top of one another until she realised there were more things in her suitcase than remained in the drawers.

Just a few things were left, and Jem couldn't help but recognise what they had in common: a garish designer handbag, a scarf by the latest hip name, the beauty products that had appeared on every must-buy list in the media but which Jem had found too scary and chemical-sounding to even try; all gifts from Nat that had never really chimed with what she wanted.

Opening the drawer of the tiny bedside cabinet, she saw a purse of English currency and her passport. She hesitated for a moment and then scooped them up in her tote bag.

A tear trickled down her cheek, but she knew that if she stopped now to consider her mixed-up emotions, she would never be brave enough to leave.

Her mobile buzzed. An incoming text from Nat.

Are you coming tonight?

She gave a soft, sad snort; it was typical of Nat not to understand the seriousness of what was happening. Putting the phone in her pocket, she strengthened her resolve and left the apartment, not wanting to admit to herself that she had just walked out on her marriage.

* * *

It was past six o'clock by the time she got back to the Four Seasons. She deposited her case in her room and went to knock on the door of Michael's suite. When there was no reply, she considered calling him to find out where he was, but realising that he could be with the police, or even Rebecca herself, she decided to wait until he came to find her.

She made a coffee, sat at her desk and turned on her laptop, putting Rebecca's gallery into the search engine. According to the home page, there was a major exhibition of an artist she had never heard of starting the next day, which no doubt meant the party that evening was its launch.

She imagined Nat turning up to the glamorous soirée, hobnobbing with the collectors and the celebrities who fancied themselves as art buffs; imagined the group holding court in a corner, basking in Rebecca's reflected glory.

Under normal circumstances she doubted that the likes of Angela and Joel would even notice that she wasn't there. But tonight would be different. She could picture it now, Angela sidling up to Nat, whispering in his ear. *How could Jem do such a thing? How could she work with Michael Kearney to pick over our business? How could she betray us in such a calculated fashion?*

A flash of cold anger rose inside her.

She knew what the housemates thought of her, but she wasn't going to be the bad guy any more. Not when it was Rebecca who had followed Alice along the beach before David had returned to the house, before anyone had returned to the house, then lied about it.

She grabbed her cardigan and bag and went down to the lobby.

'Taxi?' asked the doorman, but Jem shook her head. There wasn't much money in her bank account, just the month's wages that she'd earned from Michael, and some savings she'd kept tucked away. She suspected that the rainy day she'd budgeted for was looming on the horizon, so she knew she had to be careful.

Instead she caught the E train to 23rd Street. She came out of the subway, exchanging one hot, suffocating environment for another as a voice in her head told her it was not too late to turn back. To return to the hotel, watch a movie, wait for Michael.

There was a throng of people outside the gallery. Jem felt underdressed in her sundress, one of her favourites, navy with yellow daisies printed on the rim of the skirt. She used to call it her happy dress, but now she felt anything but.

Taking a breath, she decided to be fatalistic about it: if her name was on the door, she would go in and talk to Nat, Angela, Paul, Joel; do her best to clear the air and try and make them see that she was only trying to help David, who had also said he was going to the party and who deserved to know what she had discovered. She would tell them all about Rebecca. Perhaps get Rebecca herself to explain why she had gone back to the beach house at 9.10 when the official story, the one that David and the police believed, was that the housemates only arrived after David had found his wife in the pool.

She didn't know exactly how she would say all this to them; she tried to run some dialogue in her head, but it sounded garbled and unconvincing.

'Can I help you?'

She hadn't even noticed she was at the front of the queue. The cool blonde with a clipboard asked for her name, and Jem was surprised to find herself on the list. Not even Chapman plus one. Her own name, there in black and white, as if they wanted her to come.

She stepped inside and almost gasped. The gallery space

was cold but impressive, with vaulted skylights and double-height walls punctuated by a series of blood-red paintings, like giant scarlet windows.

Whoever the artist was, he'd attracted a lot of attention; the place was packed and the waiters, stern, handsome men in black, were struggling to keep up with the thrusting hands demanding champagne.

She searched the sea of faces looking for Nat. She knew she had overestimated her resolve coming here alone, and her chest started to tighten with panic. People blended into one another, the chatter crystallising into one loud, over-powering noise. She asked a waiter for water. He would find her some, he promised, but she knew it would be too late.

She glanced back towards the entrance, but as she debated making a run for the street, she saw Todd, Angela and Paul announcing themselves to the door girl. Nat was with them. Angela had her arm around his waist and they were laughing as if they didn't have a care in the world. Jem felt as if she had been punched in the throat. She wasn't sure what she had been expecting – she hadn't imagined that her husband would be waiting forlornly in a corner for her – but this felt like a betrayal, a deliberate taking of sides that made her feel sick.

She pulled out her phone to text David. Suddenly she wanted the reassurance of Alice's husband by her side. *Are you coming to the party?* she typed, then put her phone into the pocket of her sundress.

Glancing back at the door, she pushed her way through the crowds, away from Nat. She knew that the bathroom would be her only sanctuary in a place like this. Perhaps she could even find a back exit to slip out of into the alleyways of Chelsea.

There was a door at the far end of the gallery; it was so

discreet – just a fine rectangular outline – she wasn't sure if it was an artistic installation. She opened it and found herself in a corridor. It was cold and sterile back here, all white walls and concrete floors, and for a moment she felt as though she was in *One Flew Over the Cuckoo's Nest*. She was glad that she was wearing flat shoes that made very little sound. She expected to hear the bathroom chatter of model-grade collectors clamouring in front of a mirror. But the place was quiet; just the sound of a single voice from an office only feet away. She turned to return to the party, but stopped as she picked out a name.

'But Erica's here,' snapped a voice in crisp staccato. 'She's just arrived. I don't see why you can't just hop in a cab and stay half an hour.'

Jem took a step closer. Rebecca's voice was unmistakable now; she was obviously on the phone to Joel, persuading him to come to the gallery.

Ever since Jem had discovered that Rebecca had gone back to the beach house the night of Alice's death, she hadn't stopped wondering why. Suddenly it was the only thing she wanted to know, and when the office fell silent, she found herself being pulled towards it, unable to stop herself.

She hovered outside the door for a moment, thrusting her hands in her pockets and grasping her phone, the metal pressing into her fingers. She forced herself to think. What should she do? What would Alice do? she wondered, thinking of someone with more guile than herself.

The phone was hot in her hand now. Think, Jem. Think.

She took a step into the sparse white room and saw Rebecca standing behind a glass desk.

'Jem?' she said, looking genuinely puzzled to see her.

'Hello,' Jem said simply.

'What are you doing back here?' Rebecca said more

warmly, tucking her platinum blonde bob behind one ear.

Jem took a breath to steady herself.

'I couldn't see anyone I knew. I was meeting Nat here, but he hasn't arrived yet,' she lied.

Rebecca rolled her eyes. 'Neither has Joel. He's just been fobbing me off with ridiculous excuses. I'm quite cross with him. This is a big night for me. He's supposed to be my best friend. The least he could do is support me.'

Her expression had a trace of affection for him, like a head teacher discussing the insubordination of a favourite pupil with another member of staff, and at that moment, Jem realised she didn't know. Didn't know about Jem's confrontations with Paul and Joel. Didn't know about Michael and the threats Angela had made if she continued working with him.

Her heart was thudding hard and every instinct in her body was telling her to run away. If she jumped in a taxi, she could be back at the Four Seasons within fifteen minutes, but she knew she hadn't come this far to turn back now.

'I know what you did last summer,' she said finally.

Rebecca drew herself up to her full height and frowned. 'What are you talking about?'

'The night Alice died. You went back to the beach house when she was still alive.'

Rebecca gave a hard little laugh that echoed around the half-empty room.

'You really are going to have to explain what you mean, Jem. I was at the Dobermans' party all evening. Certainly until David phoned and told us the tragic news.'

'We have a photograph of you, Rebecca. Going into the beach house at ten past nine, when Alice was still alive. Why did you lie to the police?'

'What photo?' The tempo of her voice was quickening.

Only slightly, but Jem didn't miss it; didn't miss the fear in her tone.

'You might remember a drum circle on the sand when you went back to the house. There was a photographer there. He took dozens of photos that night. There's one of Alice silhouetted in the window at five past nine. There's one of you following her, arriving at the house a few minutes later.'

'This is ridiculous. The police weren't aware of any photographer on the beach.'

'They didn't speak to him. But I did.'

'Jem, what's going on?'

Jem gripped her phone in her pocket.

'Alice didn't slip into the water that night, did she? She fell backwards. She was pushed. By you.'

There was a tumbler of water, or perhaps something stronger, on the desk. Rebecca picked it up and knocked it back.

'Rubbish,' she said flashing Jem a look.

'It's not.'

There was a long silence.

'Where is this photo?' she said coolly.

'I don't have it with me. But I could get it, within twenty minutes. It's been cleaned up, by the way, by one of the country's top photographic-recognition artists. I think you'd appreciate his work, although perhaps not in this case. You really are quite unmistakable in the picture.'

Rebecca's pale face grew whiter. A tiny tic appeared under her right eye, pumping away like a shrunken heart. Then she shook her head in a clean snap, left to right, as if she were clearing her mind of clutter.

'Perhaps I did go back to the house,' she said slowly, as if she were trying to recall the evening. 'I can't remember too much about that night. As you can imagine, it was very traumatic for everyone.'

'Police statements were taken on the day. You said you were at the Dobermans' party until David rang Angela to tell her what had happened, and Paul and Joel both backed you up.'

Jem found her speech almost cathartic, so much so that she couldn't stop.

'You knew about Paul's affair with Alice, didn't you? He thought you didn't, but nothing gets past you, does it?'

She saw a gulp in the long, swan-like neck.

'Just tell me what happened,' she said more quietly.

Rebecca didn't speak for at least twenty seconds.

'Alice was a cuckoo in the nest,' she said eventually, her voice so low and quiet that Jem could hardly hear it. 'I knew what sort of woman she was the moment I met her. I knew to be on guard.'

Jem watched her bite her lip, a bubble of blood rising to the surface of her pink lips.

'Paul was careful, of course he was. But I heard them once, in the garage. Not fucking, but whispering, laughing, and I knew then what was going on.'

She blinked hard before she spoke again.

'I followed him one lunchtime. I felt completely demeaned, but I knew it had to be done. I saw them go to an apartment block on Park Avenue, one of Paul's renovation projects. Let's just say I knew they weren't going there to discuss wallpaper. And then Joel told me what Alice had done to him too. Was blackmail any worse than what he got up to in his financial affairs?'

Her gaze was cool and unflinching.

'Alice Holliday was a tramp,' she growled. 'She fucked my husband, and probably yours. They were all over each other at the polo last summer. I tried to warn you what he was like . . .'

A memory surfaced. Todd's gallery party. Rebecca had

444

commented on Nat's flirting prowess, and yet Jem had had no idea it was connected to Alice.

'She was trouble,' Rebecca said simply. 'And someone needed to stop her. I saw her at the Dobermans'; she was high, reckless. I didn't dare think what she might do. So when I saw her go back to the house, I followed her. Only to talk to her, you understand.'

Her composure began to crack, as if a thousand unwelcome memories were thawing from cold storage, and a tear slid slowly down her ivory cheek.

'I saw her go into the pool garden and I followed her. We argued. She fell in the water.'

'She couldn't swim, Rebecca. Did you leave her?'

'I didn't know she couldn't swim. I'd said what I wanted to say and left. I went back to the party. I didn't think she'd drown. Not for a second.'

Jem searched her face for sadness, regret, and for a moment she was almost taken in.

But she thought of Chase Alexander and the rest of his photos. Not one picture showed Rebecca leaving the beach house.

A thought began to brew.

'You didn't leave the way you came in,' she said slowly. 'If you'd thought Alice was okay, you would have gone the quickest way back to the Dobermans'. That would have been along the beach, not by the road. That way is twice as long. But that's the way you went. You knew something had happened to Alice and you didn't want to be seen.'

'Just go,' hissed Rebecca, sinking into her chair.

'How can you live with yourself?' asked Jem. 'How can you go back to the house every weekend knowing what you did? Does Paul know? Joel? Did they cover for you?'

She remembered her meeting with Angela at the W hotel. They'd tried to scare her off, to drop what she knew about

Paul and Alice, but was that because they knew more about the night of Alice's death than they'd let on?

'They know nothing.' Rebecca spoke fiercely.

'Really? You gave Paul his alibi when the police asked where you'd all been. What happened? Did he return the favour?'

'No. Joel did. He'd noticed my absence at the party but I explained it away and he believed me. He's a true friend.'

She stopped abruptly. Jem heard a noise behind her and turned. She was taken aback to see Michael and David, accompanied by a man she had never seen before; tall, grey-haired, with a look of authority. A tiny frown between Michael's brows suggested that he was as surprised to see her there as she was to see him, but he didn't register any further disapproval.

'This is a private office,' said Rebecca, regaining her composure. 'I'll have to ask you to go back to the gallery.'

'We've not officially met,' said Michael, keeping his distance. 'My name is Michael Kearney. This is Ted Harris, from Suffolk County Police at Riverhead. Obviously you know David.'

'What's going on?' Rebecca asked, her voice cracking. Two spots of pink appeared on her cheeks, reminding Jem of a Victorian porcelain doll: brittle, wide-eyed and haunted-looking.

'I think we need to talk,' said Harris, pulling out the chair in front of the desk as Rebecca stood up.

'Can we schedule an appointment for tomorrow? This is not convenient for me right now.'

'No, Mrs Ellis. We need to talk now.'

Jem put her hand in her pocket and pulled out her phone. The red button on the voice activation app was still flashing.

'You might want this,' she said, handing the device to Michael. 'I recorded our conversation.'

Michael nodded and touched her shoulder.

Jem glanced at David, whose eyes were glistening with tears.

'Thank you,' he said, mouthing the words so they were barely a whisper.

Jem nodded and headed back towards the gallery. It was time to put all this behind her.

Chapter 44

Jem's finger hovered over the booking button. The one-way flight to London, leaving in two days' time, was a great price, the tenants in their Kensal Rise cottage were moving out in a week, and she had found an Airbnb rental two streets away that she could stay in for a hundred pounds a night until she could move back in. But as she looked out of the window onto the expansive view of the city, she held back for a moment, just to take in its magnificence. The soaring skyscrapers, the gaping green hole that was Central Park, the pulse of energy from the streets that she could almost feel in her hotel room high above the sidewalk. New York was an incredible city, that much was inarguable. It was a city built on hopes and dreams, but over the past few months she had found out that they just weren't *her* dreams.

She clicked the mouse and a flight confirmation email pinged in her inbox almost immediately. She shivered in the cool of the air con. It was done, her decision had been made. She was going home.

She went to the minibar to look for chocolate, not caring about the cost, or that it was only ten o'clock in the morning; she was desperate for a sugar fix to take the edge off the sadness.

There was a knock at the door and she went to answer it with a mouth full of Kit Kat. It was Michael.

'Can I come in?'

She nodded, opening the door wide for him to enter, and went back to the desk.

'Heard from Ted Harris?' she asked, swallowing the chocolate.

She hadn't hung around at the gallery after Michael, David and the police officer had arrived to speak to Rebecca. She'd felt superfluous and exposed; an understudy who had stepped into the limelight but who knew it was time to retreat into the wings.

Back in her hotel room, she had felt relieved that the night had been less dramatic than it might have been in a film or cop drama. There were no flashing police cars, no handcuffs to lead Rebecca away.

The last thing she clearly remembered was Paul's arrival, his face pale with shock and fear; the knowledge that the events of the previous summer were about to catch up with him. She hadn't looked him in the eye. Instead she had left the party, weaving her way through the crowds, aware of the shiver of gossip that was already rustling through the gallery.

The phone calls from Nat had started almost as soon as she stepped into the Four Seasons lobby. She had spoken to him – she owed him that – but there wasn't much to say.

Rebecca had admitted pushing Alice into the pool and then leaving the house. Her housemates hadn't exactly covered up for her, but they had protected their own and hadn't dug very hard for the truth, content to believe that Alice's death had been an accident.

Michael put his hands in his pockets, and Jem found it hard to ignore how good he looked, despite the dark circles under his eyes from lack of sleep.

'Rebecca's still maintaining she didn't know Alice couldn't swim,' he said, shaking his head.

'And where does the law stand on that?' frowned Jem, thinking about the expensive lawyers that Rebecca had no doubt employed to defend her.

'Assuming it's turned over to the District Attorney's office, it depends what charge they pursue,' replied Michael. 'I suspect they'll argue that it's manslaughter. If they can show that Rebecca knew Alice couldn't swim, if she pushed her in intentionally, it could be murder, but I think that would be very difficult to prove.'

Jem turned to look at the window and drew her arms tightly across her chest, the Kit Kat suddenly making her feel sick.

'Flowers?' said Michael.

She turned around to see him motioning towards a huge arrangement by the television.

She gave a soft snort. 'From Nat,' she shrugged. 'We're meeting tonight.'

'To talk?'

Jem nodded. 'I've just booked my flight home.'

'I think a break will probably do you good,' said Michael encouragingly.

Jem looked at the floor.

'It's not a holiday. I'm moving back home.'

'Don't do anything too hasty,' he said, standing up straighter.

'I miss it,' she replied, searching his face for emotion, for a clue to what he thought about her decision to go back to London. 'I miss my old life.'

She saw a flicker of disappointment pass across his face.

'What does Nat say about it?' he asked finally.

She walked towards the window.

'He doesn't know yet, but I'm not sure he'll be surprised.'

Michael came towards her and put his arms around her. For a second she resisted, and then let herself relax into him, blotting her nose, damp with emotional sniffles, on the soft cotton of his shirt as she laid her head on his shoulder, inhaling the faint scent of soap and sea.

She stayed like that for a few more seconds and then pulled away, not wanting to complicate matters further.

'I have an idea,' he said, holding her shoulders. 'I'm going to Boston tomorrow morning and I think you should come. There's a rehearsal dinner tomorrow night and I can bring a guest. I don't know when you're heading back to London, but I'm sure it would do you good to get out of New York for the weekend.'

Jem's smile fell. 'I'm sure it would be fun, and part of me thinks I should be there to make sure you don't wrestle Tony to the ground as he's walking your daughter down the aisle. But . . .'

'Why not?' he said simply.

There was a shimmer of something, something Jem didn't want to think about, something that made her nervous but excited and hopeful about the future.

She extinguished the thought as quickly as it had come. She simply couldn't contemplate having any feelings for Michael Kearney beyond the strictly platonic. Desire, feeling flattered by attention from the opposite sex, had caused so much destruction around her this summer that she had to shut it down immediately. She was better than Nat, Paul and Alice, who had been so casual about the bond of marriage, and the last thing she wanted was the possibility, however remote, of something romantic happening between her and Michael when she was still married.

'I leave on Sunday,' she said finally. 'There won't be time to get to Boston and back.'

'Oh.'

He looked as sad as she felt, and she wondered why. Was it the premature loss of a good and loyal assistant who had put everything on the line to help him? Was it the genuine sadness that a friend's marriage had failed, and a reminder of his own imploded family life? Or was it something else?

Certainly the thought that she would soon be back in England, that she would probably never see him again, made her heart feel heavy. It was Nat's belief that Michael had ruined everything, but he was wrong. He had *changed* everything. He had opened her eyes and made her see in sharp focus who she was and what she wanted. She was going to miss him, so much.

'I know I should have discussed it with you,' she said, trying to fill the silence. 'But I can still do all your fan mail stuff from London, certainly until Celine is back from maternity leave.'

Michael puffed out his cheeks.

'I think the word they'd use in England is *bugger*.'

Jem giggled. 'Come on now, you're not Hugh Grant.'

Neither of them spoke for a few seconds.

'Let me show you something,' she said quickly, turning around and flipping open her laptop. 'My blog. I've downloaded some photos and recipes this morning. I needed to take my mind off everything that's been going on, and look, don't you think it looks fantastic?'

She could see him out of the corner of her eye, watching her click on her debut blog posts with a sense of pride, and she wondered if she had made a terrible mistake in booking her flight home.

'It's a good feeling, isn't it?' he said after a moment.

'What?'

'Knowing you've done something worthwhile.'

Jem waved a modest hand. 'It's just a bit of fun.'

'It's how I started in the shed on the beach. I asked myself every day, is this any good, and every day it was easier to believe that it was garbage, that I was wasting my time. But a voice in my head told me to keep writing, that it wasn't just good, it was great. Your blog is like my Jack Garcia novel. I can see it already as a cookbook. I can see you with your range of pots and pans, the new Martha Stewart, and I'll be able to say I knew you when.'

'You can be the voice in my head,' she smiled.

They stood in awkward silence.

'I should go,' he said finally. 'I'm sure you've got things to do. I'll still be in Boston on Sunday, but I can get my driver to take you to the airport.'

Jem waved a hand. 'I don't need a driver. London girls prefer the subway.'

He walked towards the door then paused.

'I'm going to miss you,' he said, his eyes creasing with his smile.

'Me too,' she said, feeling emotional. 'Now you behave at the wedding, Kearney. No chasing the bridesmaids, okay? Not unless they like burritos.'

'I won't,' he said, and deep down Jem knew he wouldn't.

Epilogue

'Do you have any more coffee, and some of those miniature cream puffs we had for afternoon tea?' asked the organiser of Loxton Insurance's annual away-day, poking her head into the tiny gallery kitchen where Jem and her assistant Meg Doyle were still trying to clear away the detritus from the three-course lunch.

'I thought you'd finished for the day,' said Jem, glancing at her watch and noting that the conference was running at least an hour longer than scheduled.

'Just having one final recap,' smiled the organiser thinly, unable to disguise her impatience for the refreshments.

'We'll bring some fresh pots out in a mo,' said Jem, trying to keep her cool. They were all out of cream puffs, but she had brought some emergency chocolate cake and she wondered whether, if she cut it into squares, she could pass them off as brownie bites and keep everyone quiet until she could slope off home.

'What are you doing tonight?' said Meg, drying the dinner plates and stacking them into the long plastic crates they'd brought with them.

'A friend, my old boss actually, is having a party,' Jem said as casually as she could. 'I'm just debating whether I should go.'

'You should,' said Meg playfully. 'Might be some nice single men there. It's about time you got back in the bloody saddle.'

Jem deflected the banter with a good-natured scoff. It had been a stretch putting the young cook on the payroll, but Meg hadn't just made business easier, she had made it more fun, and for that it had been worth scrimping and saving, cutting down on her nights out, instead spending her evenings catching up with old friends over a bottle of wine and home-made suppers at the cottage.

The conference finally wound to a close and Jem and Meg lugged the crates out to Jem's Ford Ka. It was a squeeze getting everything into the boot – hiring Meg has meant she hadn't been able to buy the van she knew she needed – but for now it would do, and having spent the previous weekend stencilling the words 'Sparkling Jems' onto the doors, it might even drum up some more business.

'Can't believe they've nicked eleven teaspoons,' muttered Meg as she slammed the boot shut. 'We came with fifty; we've only got thirty-nine. I bet it's revenge for the lack of cream puffs.'

Jem nodded distractedly. Usually she got mad when stuff went missing – just the week before, a client had taken her favourite orange Le Creuset dish – but today she had other things on her mind.

'Do you still want all this crap to come back to my flat?' continued Meg without pausing for breath.

Jem looked at her friend and grinned.

'Crap? It's our livelihood.'

'You know what I mean.'

'Would you? I've got the estate agent coming round to the cottage this evening and I won't have time to wash it all and clear everything away before he arrives.'

'How are the viewings coming along?' asked Meg as

they got into the car.

'Only needs one to make a sale,' smiled Jem, her cheery disposition betraying the mixed emotions she had about getting rid of the cottage.

Jem glanced at her watch as she stopped at the lights on Harrow Road on their way back from the venue in Kensington to Meg's flat in Harlesden. It was almost six o'clock and dusk was creeping across London. It was only mid-September, but already the days were getting shorter, the leaves crisper and more golden by the day. Jem had been so busy with her catering business over the past few months that she had barely noticed summer come and go, but already winter was in the air; not much, not yet, but people had started wearing coats, and the number of bare legs on show had definitely started to shrink.

Staring down at her own feet, at the comfortable trainers she'd worn for the day's full-on catering job, she wished she'd opted for something a little prettier. She hadn't planned this well at all. She'd hoped to finish at the away-day well before five o'clock and have time to get back to Kensal Rise to quickly change. But she hadn't planned on things running so late, and now it was impossible to get home before the estate agent arrived for the evening viewings.

The agent had been quite adamant that Jem stay out of the house whilst she was showing people round. Jem didn't ask why, but when the agent had heard that the house sale was part of a divorce settlement, she had muttered something about it being helpful for the occupants to keep away from the viewings.

Jem could see where that school of thought came from. Moving house was about new beginnings. She imagined the people who would come to view their two-bedroom cottage: hard-working newlyweds, spending their life savings on a deposit. She imagined them admiring her freshly vacuumed carpet as they inhaled the smell of the sweet peas she'd arranged in a vase on the coffee table. They didn't want the ghost of a failed marriage in their potential new home, and Jem knew she'd have to stay out of the cottage until the evening's final viewing was over.

Meg's boyfriend helped them unload the car, and Jem watched the two of them laughing and joking as they balanced the crates of plates like a crockery Jenga. She found herself smiling. She didn't want to think about her own easy days of cohabiting with Nat, but it was good to see two people so happy together.

The car smelt of Thai green curry and she was in desperate need of a shower, but it was now almost 6.45, and the event, being held at Waterstones on the King's Road, was due to start at seven.

She weaved through the streets of Kensington, parking in one of Chelsea's grand squares lined with stuccoed terraces, dodging commuters as she ran towards the venue, grateful now that she was in her trainers.

The bookshop was full. A blackboard announced the evening's special guest: Michael Kearney. A glamorous fifty-something brunette, presumably Michael's British editor, was holding a microphone and telling everyone how excited she was to be publishing his new book. Jem found herself only half listening, her thoughts drifting to whether this attractive, creative creature liked burritos.

The brunette encouraged a round of applause and looked towards the back of the shop. For a second Jem almost didn't recognise her former boss as he approached a chair in the centre of the room. He was a little leaner and more muscular than she remembered; smarter too, in a sharp navy suit and blue shirt that showed off his Hamptons tan and a faint sweep of stubble that suggested he had more important things to do than shave. She felt a shift in the atmosphere; an excitable frisson among the female guests, who nudged their friends and whispered appreciatively. Jem felt herself blush, and was glad she had not chosen to sit closer to the front – not that she had a choice. The room was packed, and a table stacked with copies of Michael's latest book indicated how much interest there was in the signing.

There was a short Q and A; a male journalist sitting on a plastic chair opposite Michael ran through some questions about the writing process of *Let Me Live*, the Jack Garcia prequel that was a shoo-in to reach number one on the *Sunday Times* bestseller list the following week. Michael made a few jokes about being unable to resurrect Garcia from the grave, so final had his send-off been in his previous novel, deciding instead to cover his hero's early years, much to the delight of his fans in the audience.

At no point did he mention the next book he was going to write. The book about Alice and the beach house.

Jem had been in sporadic touch with her old boss in the months after her departure from New York and he'd kept her updated about the SEC investigation into Joel and Ed Dunston. Apparently the authorities had already been on to the two men, someone somewhere having picked up on a share trading irregularity, and although the video of Alice eavesdropping on her housemate had been deemed useful, they would have been brought to justice anyway, a thought that gave Jem some comfort at night when she thought of Erica and her baby boy.

He had also told her the reason why Alice was blackmailing Joel in the first place. When the investigation into her death had been re-opened, the police had discovered that Alice herself was being blackmailed. A manager at the

Manhattan gym where she had worked had disclosed that a Nick Vlautin had been leaving messages for Alice in the days preceding her death, and when the police followed this up, they'd found out that Vlautin had been a low-rent soft-porn director and Alice one of his 'stars'. When threatened with arrest, it had taken very little pressure on Vlautin to admit that he'd asked for 'financial support' from Alice in return for keeping her cinematic exploits underwraps.

But with the case against Rebecca Ellis dragging on without any conviction, Michael had also told her he had shelved the book about Alice for now, although *Vanity Fair* had been in contact and were keen for him to write a flagship story about the case for them.

With no more Alice Holliday related news to report, contact between Jem and Michael had eventually petered out, and now her old life in New York seemed so remote that she sometimes wondered if she had ever lived it; whether the drama of Alice and the beach house was a movie she had seen and only half remembered.

She certainly hadn't known what Michael had been working on, and she knew him well enough to get the message that that was probably the way he wanted things to be. She felt sad that he was no longer part of her life, and had spent many hours wondering why their friendship hadn't continued. She'd believed him when he'd said he'd miss her, and she missed him enough to know that it was possibly a bad idea coming here this evening.

She reminded herself that he had invited her, albeit via a press release sent by his publishers. He'd followed it up with a text and she'd said she would come. But now, watching him so poised and confident on the makeshift stage, flanked by his striking editor, she had a sense that she should have stayed away.

A grumble of applause indicated that the interview had

finished and a surge of people made their way to the desk where Michael was going to be signing.

Jem stood up, smoothed out the wrinkles in her skirt and went to get a book. She paid for it at the counter and waited in the queue, conscious of the fact that she smelt of Thai curry, but aware that their meeting would be so fleeting that Michael wouldn't notice the smell.

She felt nervous as the queue edged closer to the desk. Perhaps she would invite him for a coffee the next day; she had no idea where the Four Seasons was in London, but she imagined Michael staying there, imagined meeting him in the grand lobby as she had done back in New York.

She was near the front of the queue now, and up close she could see that his hair was flecked with silver at the temples and there were a few more lines around his eyes. She felt a surge of something in her heart, a flutter of excitement as the number of people in front of her became fewer and fewer, until . . .

'Hello.'

Michael looked dumbstruck to see her.

'What on earth are you doing in the queue?' he asked, putting down his pen and fixing her with his cool blue gaze.

'I've not driven all the way here tonight not to get this signed,' she grinned, thrusting the book towards him.

He flicked the book open and scribbled his name.

'How long are you staying?'

The chatter and laughter behind her seemed to tune out so she could just hear his deep and soothing baritone.

'Not long,' she replied quickly. 'I've had a busy day.'

'You can't go,' he pressed, his eyes not leaving hers. 'I'll be done here soon. Just a few more minutes.'

The brunette leant over disapprovingly.

'The queue's still very long; we should hurry things up.'

'Then I'll skulk around,' said Jem, taking her book and falling back into the crowds.

She accepted a glass of Prosecco from one of the staff and hung around on the fringes of the party. She noticed that Michael kept glancing up, checking to see where she was, and she giggled as she watched him get mobbed by a particularly enthusiastic fan.

For a second, she found herself comparing him to Paul and Nat. Michael's brand of attractiveness was less obvious than that of the two younger men, whose classic good looks commanded your instant attention. In contrast, Michael's appeal grew on you; his face more striking the more you looked at it. It was a face that spoke of experience and wisdom and confidence, the faint lines reminding you of a life well lived, and Jem wondered why she had never truly noticed it before.

Shaking herself out of her thoughts, she noticed that the event was starting to wind down. She hung around the door, and as she kept one eye on Michael saying goodbye to the team from his publishers, she flicked through the book to find the acknowledgements, cursing her ego when she realised that she hoped to find herself there. The page was not particularly expansive; more a shopping list of publishing personnel than the effusive Oscar-winner's speech that could sometimes be found at the back of a book. She couldn't help feeling disappointed that her name wasn't there, until the book fell open on the dedication page.

She almost stopped breathing when she read the few words of type.

For J. The voice in my head.

She read it again and again, wondering, hoping that she was J and the secret message was Michael's way of telling her . . . what?

She felt a hand on her shoulder and turned.

'Where does a thirsty Yank get a drink around here?' he asked, touching the small of her back and leading her towards the door.

The temperature had dipped since she had arrived and her cardigan was insubstantial to keep out the chill. She put the book in her tote bag and started walking. Michael increased his stride to catch up with her.

'Where are we going?'

'I don't know,' she said, feeling on edge. 'I don't know this part of town very well.'

'What about Bluebird?'

Jem nodded, grateful that he was making decisions.

'It's good to see you,' he said, trying to slow the pace down.

'I thought I'd pop in. A Jack Garcia prequel, hey? You kept that quiet.'

She thought he'd make a joke of it, but he looked serious.

'I had to write something quickly to meet my deadline. It seemed the logical thing to do.'

'I thought you had writer's block with Garcia. That's why you wanted a change in direction.'

'It was easier than I thought,' he said with a shrug. 'I took myself to AA, got a clearer head. Turns out it was the whisky that was the problem, not my writing.'

Jem grinned back at him in approval.

'So what about you?' he asked.

The conversation was a little forced, but she supposed it was only natural after a year.

'My catering business is doing pretty well and my blog has decent traffic,' she said modestly, not wanted to admit that publishers had already started contacting her. 'Although I might have to change the name now. I'm not sure how authentic "The Beach Kitchen" is when I'm working out of a terraced house in Kensal Rise.'

It was his turn to look impressed.

'Well, let me know when you need an agent. I've got everyone lined up as soon as you give the word.'

There was a gust of wind and Jem shivered. It would be typically chivalrous of Michael to notice and give her his jacket, but that thought made her feel even more unsettled.

'Do you mind if I go and get my coat from the car? It's a bit cold,' she said, turning off the King's Road onto a leafy square. She felt her pulse quicken as they stepped away from the bright lights and the roar of the mid-evening traffic into the quieter residential street.

They stopped at the Ford Ka and Michael grinned when he saw the logo painted on the door.

'Nice,' he said, touching the paintwork.

'Cheap marketing,' she said, retrieving her jacket.

He leant against the car and put his hands in his pockets. In the soft light of the street lamp he looked cool and handsome, like a lost member of *Ocean's Eleven*.

'How are you, Jem?' he asked, watching her put on her coat.

'I made the right decision,' she said without looking at him.

'And how's Nat?'

'He's fine.' She paused. 'I hear he's fine anyway. You know he's editor-in-chief of the magazine now. We're obviously in touch to finalise the divorce, but these days I hear more about his life from the media. Apparently he has a new girlfriend. I found that out from *People* magazine. She's an it girl from the Upper East Side. In some reality TV show,' she added as casually as she could, trying hard not to remember how painful it was seeing Nat in the society pages, just where he always wanted to be.

'So the divorce. It's almost through.'

She nodded quickly and changed the subject.

'How long are you in London?'

'That depends,' he said in a quieter voice. She felt the mood shift between them.

'Depends on what?'

'On you,' he said, not taking his eyes off her.

She gave a nervous laugh. She could really smell the Thai curry now, and she stepped away from the car, looking down at the pavement. She felt him move closer, then he took her hand.

She couldn't believe he was being so forward. Then again, she knew the tremor of attraction had always been there. Mutual respect had kept a lid on it, but these months apart had helped her be more honest about her feelings towards him.

'I've missed you,' he said finally.

His frankness put her on edge.

'You've a funny way of showing it,' she said as lightly as she could. 'You stopped emailing me.'

Michael took another step forward so they were almost breathing the same air.

'I stopped because you were still married,' he said simply. 'I didn't want to be the man who broke up your relationship. I had to be sure it was over before I told you how I feel.'

'Which is what?' she whispered, feeling her heart banging so hard she thought it would burst out of her chest.

'That you're the voice in my head. The person I want to speak to when I wake up in the morning, the person I want to speak to when I'm sad or down or thrilled or proud. You're the person I want to share it all with.'

'Me?' she whispered, her voice barely audible.

Michael smiled and glanced away.

'I think you had me from the moment you broke into my office and told me I was a self-pitying drunk.'

'I never said that,' she protested, eyes wide.

'I've missed you so much,' he said, looking at her as if she was the most beautiful girl in the world.

'I've missed you too. I've never stopped thinking about you. About last summer,' she said, finally admitting all the feelings she had tried to keep locked in her heart, finally realising why she had never deleted any of his emails or text messages, why she turned on her computer every day hoping for some overnight missive from the States that had never come.

He held her close and she pressed her head against his chest. Her jacket was thin, but she felt warm and secure, safe in the knowledge she was exactly where she wanted to be.

'Let's go to Bluebird,' he murmured into her hair.

She took his hand and smiled. 'Only if they sell burritos.'

Acknowledgements

Thanks to the wonderful team at Headline; Sherise Hobbs, Fran Gough, Mari Evans, Jo Liddiard, Yeti Lambregts, Vicky Palmer, Emily Gowers, copy-editor Jane Selley and all the sales teams at home and overseas.

Thank you to my fantastic agent Eugenie Furniss and Liane-Louise Smith. Also to Alan Gasmer, Stephen Brown at the Rose Theatre and Hebe Neate Clegg. Fellow writers and friends are a great source of fun and support; thank you Belinda, Alison, Polly, Claire, Adele. A special shout out goes to Bella Andre for our writers' boot camp in Martha's Vineyard. (We must get that Tiny and Amy script written one day!) Thanks also to Sarra M, Kerry P, Jo B, Suzanne and Henry.

To the fun and fabulous Andy, Brad and Larry in Sag Harbor; thanks for your wonderful hospitality. A car (with beach permits!), not to mention your kindness showing us the sights and sounds of the Hamptons, meant I got a real insider's flavour of this gorgeous part of the world and had a whole lot of fun with new friends in the process.

Thank you to my mum, dad (for the titles!) Digs, Dan and Far. And of course John and Fin. The best soundboards and travelling companions ever.

The House on Sunset Lake

No one forgets a summer at Casa D'Or . . .

Casa D'Or, the mysterious plantation house on Sunset Lake, has been in the Wyatt family for over fifty years. Jennifer Wyatt returns there from university full of hope, as summer by the lake stretches ahead of her. Yet by the time it is over her heart will be broken, her family in tatters, her dreams long gone.

Twenty years later, Casa D'Or stands neglected, a victim of tragic events. Jennifer has closed the door on her past. Then Jim, the man she met and fell in love with that magical summer, comes back into her life, with a plan to return Casa D'Or to its former glory. Their reunion will stir up old ghosts for both of them, and reveal the dark secrets the house still holds close . . .

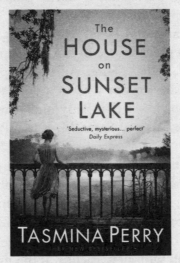

Available now from

REVIEW

The Last Kiss Goodbye

Everyone remembers their first kiss. But what about the last?

1961. Journalist Rosamund Bailey is ready to change the world. When she meets explorer and man about town Dominic Blake, she realises she has found the love of her life. Just as happiness is in their grasp, the worst happens, and their future is snatched away.

2014. Deep in the vaults of a museum, archivist Abby Gordon stumbles upon a breathtaking find. A faded photograph of a man saying goodbye to the woman he loves. Looking for a way to escape her own heartache, Abby becomes obsessed with the story, little realising that behind the image frozen in time lies a secret altogether more extraordinary.

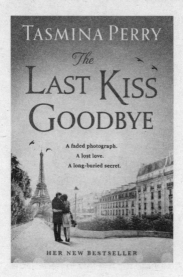

Available now from

The Proposal

1958. At eighteen, Georgia Hamilton is sent to London for the Debutante Season. Independent, and with secret dreams to be a writer, she has no wish to join the other debs competing for a husband. But when tragedy strikes, her fate appears to have been sealed.

2012. Hurrying to meet her lover, Amy Carrell hopes tonight will change her destiny. And it does – but not in the way she imagined. Desolate and desperate to get out of London, she accepts a position as companion to a mysterious stranger, bound for Manhattan – little knowing she is about to unlock a love story that has waited fifty years to be told. And a heart waiting to come back to life . . .

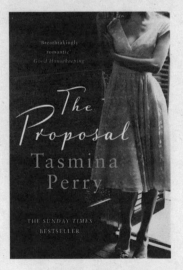

Available now from

Deep Blue Sea

Beneath the shimmering surface lies a dark secret . . .

Diana and Julian Denver have the world at their feet.
With a blissful marriage, a darling son and beautiful homes in
London and the country, Diana's life, to the outside world,
is perfect. But nothing is as it seems . . .

When Julian dies suddenly and tragically, Diana is convinced
there is more to it than meets the eye. She calls on the one person
she had never wanted to see again – her sister, Rachel.

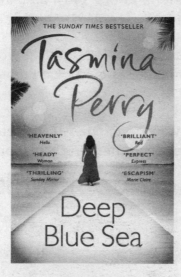

Available now from